# LOVES

## of

# SHADOW

## and

# POWER

*The Immortal Beings series is set in alternate fantasy world where magic is based on color. The main characters are all immortals; some are gods with mortal worshippers.*

*This is the second book and should be read after the first.*

by Edith Pawlicki

*Minerva*

The Immortal Beings Series
*Vows of Gold and Laughter*

*Loves of Shadow and Power*

*Trials of Fire and Rebirth*

*edithpawlicki.com*

# Loves of Shadow and Power

## Edith Pawlicki

*For Helen because she supported my decision to split this story into two parts and then waited impatiently for the second.*

# Contents

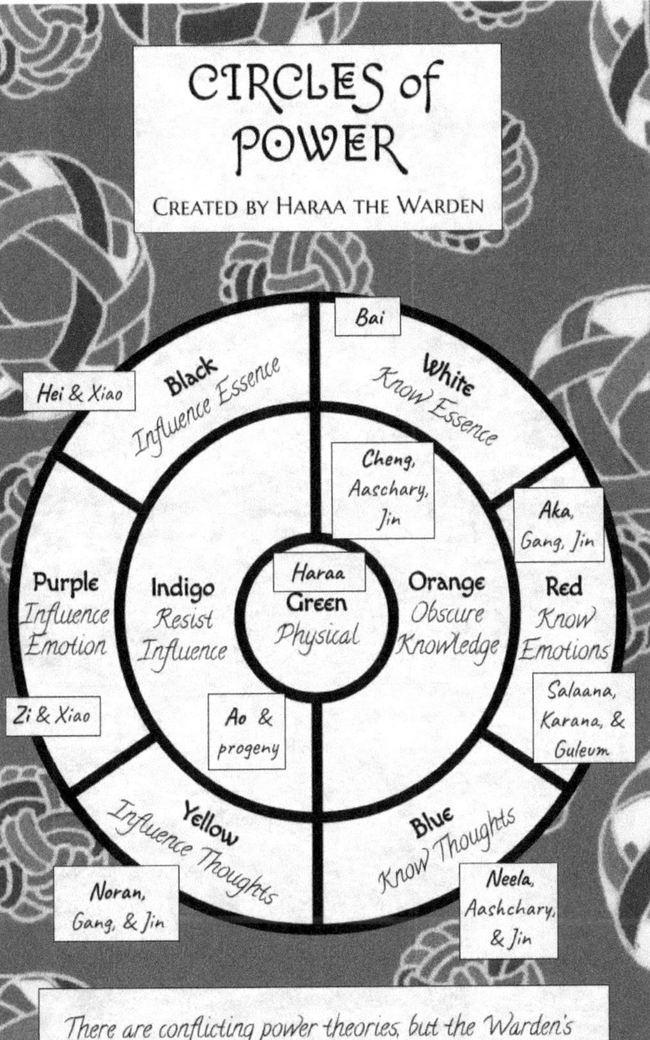


There are conflicting power theories, but the Warden's Circles of Power is the most popular, and even the First agrees it is the easiest to understand. The Nine Colors and their progeny have such a large amount of power that their knowledge and influence is truly remarkable. As for the rest of us, unless our power is increased by a few million worshippers, these powers tend to come across as a sixth sense or unusually glib tongue.

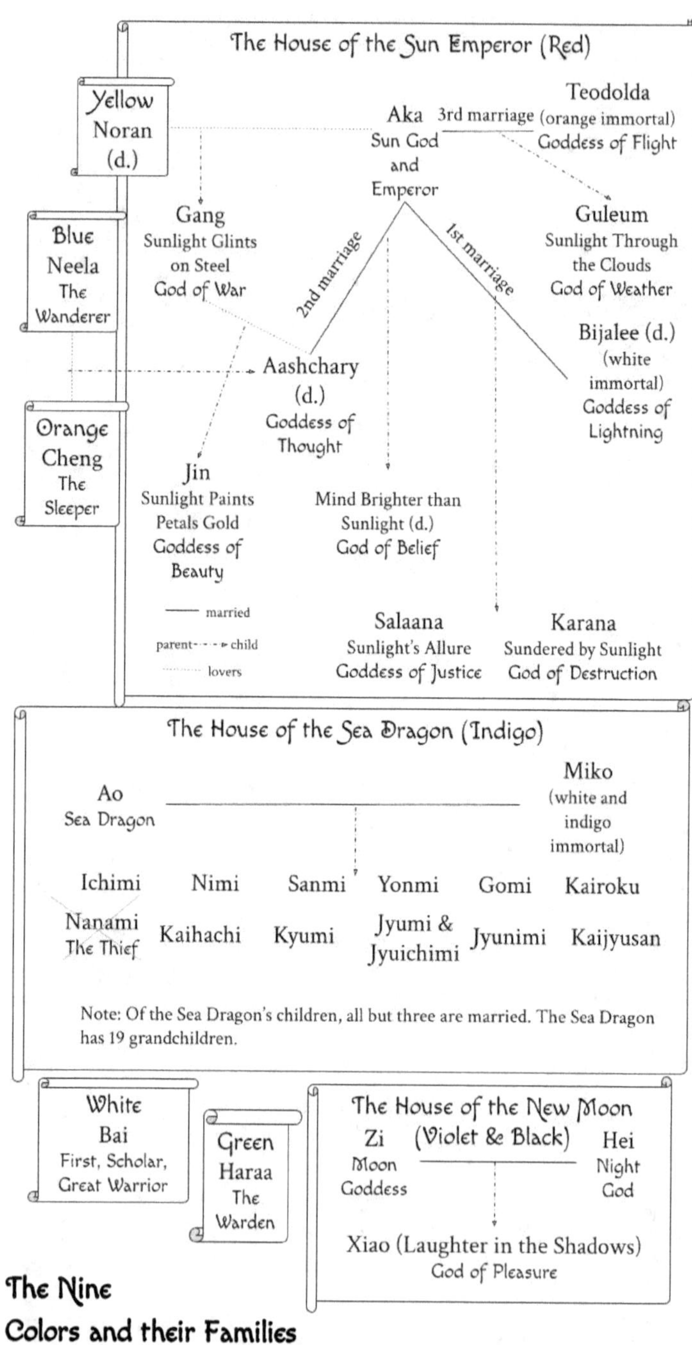


# The Nine
# Colors and their Families

# Of Yearning

54,000 *years ago*

THE sun was just setting when Bai arrived at the newly created New Moon Manor. The sky that surrounded it was a riot of color—full, rosy clouds that would never obey Bai, a brilliant stripe of sun edging them before softening to a delicate lavender and then a pale blue.

New Moon Manor itself floated in Heaven, on stone of twilight and shadow. Bai had teleported, as requested, to the "entrance" of the manor. He was standing on darkest basalt and a few feet in front of him was an amethyst arch of two crescent moons bent inward. The arch was purely decorative—there were no walls—and the basalt wove an unbroken path through the rock garden that stretched on the other side of the arch. Everything was purple and black; Bai struggled not to hate it on sight.

He did like colors besides white, but this was oppressive. And there was something else strange about this place...

He was still standing at the arch when a hand settled on his shoulder.

He turned and was greeted by a shock of orange hair and ember eyes. Cheng was grinning, making his broad nose and big jaw seem even wider than usual. "Ready to go to a wedding?"

Bai shook his head. "I was surprised they invited me," he confessed. "They never have before—not even when they were celebrating becoming gods. If you hadn't begged—"

Cheng snorted. "It's good for you to socialize. They didn't invite you to their deification because you spent Aka's celebration telling him what a stupid choice he had made. But aren't you glad to be invited? You must be curious about what it will be."

Bai shrugged. "They said it's about two people becoming one. I just hope they don't intend to have sex in front of us. Surely they know others have figured that out too?"

Cheng barked a laugh. "Fate, that might be it! Well, we can always teleport away if we want."

"Can we though?" Bai frowned at the garden, once again trying to decode the magic embedded in its pillars of obsidian and amethyst.

"What do you mean?"

"It's something I've never seen before—some magic Zi and Hei have done past the gate. I don't think we can teleport inside there. Maybe you can," Bai conceded, "since others' magic doesn't affect you."

"It does sometimes," Cheng objected. "You think they

blocked teleporting?" He scratched his jaw. "Well, so what? It's their home. I wouldn't mind learning such a trick myself. Then Meili couldn't pop in on me whenever he wants. Last time I was in the middle of a bath."

"You should just sleep with him," Bai said as he continued to study the essence of the rock garden. "Either you'll like it, and you can finally get over Neela, or you won't, and you can say no with more confidence."

Cheng elbowed him. "I really, really hope I'm there when you fall in love. And I hope it's full-on, idiot-making infatuation."

Bai ignored him—Cheng had been saying Bai would fall in love eventually for millennia now. Bai enjoyed the occasional physical release with other immortals, but he didn't think he was made to love. He just didn't connect to others as fully as they seemed to do with each other, perhaps because he had been alone when he first formed.

Cheng tugged Bai's elbow impatiently. "Let's go in. I doubt Zi and Hei would want us to live with them. And if they do try to trap us, there's no way they could overpower all seven other Colors. Even Aka would work with you in such circumstances."

Bai scoffed, then focused on Cheng. "Are all the Colors going to be here? Good, I still haven't met Yellow or Indigo."

As they walked through the arch, he thought he heard Cheng mumble, "That's because you're so cursed antisocial."

The basalt path led them to the steps of a large circular hall. Tall ebony pillars marched its circumference, and violet silks hung between them. Music and laughter echoed inside, and the scents of pepper and roast duck wafted out to greet them. Cheng rubbed his hands together in anticipation.

"Come on, Bai, I'm starving!"

Bai rolled his eyes. "You can't starve. You're molten rock."

"But I do like to eat!"

And then they were inside the hideously full hall. Bai had to stop himself from backing out again. There must be a hundred people here!

Zi, wearing more shades of purple than Bai knew existed, and Hei, in unrelieved black, stood just inside. They bowed in greeting, and Bai belatedly remembered to bow back when Cheng bumped his foot. Despite Bai's sincere effort, Zi's eyes narrowed ominously.

Using a massive silver fan set with amethysts, Zi waved toward a long table near the head of the hall. "You may both sit there, if you please."

"How lovely. Thank you, Zi, Hei," Cheng put in hurriedly before pulling Bai along behind him.

The table had nine wide stools along one side, four currently empty. The other five held Neela, Aka, Haraa, and two unfamiliar immortals.

The first was a small man—he was seated, but Bai thought he would be even shorter than Cheng—with a very long indigo beard, which proclaimed his identity. And the other...

The other was a woman. Her hair was the lightest Bai had ever seen besides his own, the color of freshly cut blond wood. Her eyes were gold, so gold that they seemed to glow from within, and her eyelids seemed heavy, as if her shiny long lashes truly were made of metal and pulling them down. She saw Bai staring at her, and her pale pink lips curved in a shy smile. With one graceful movement she raised a slim-fingered hand and indicated the empty seat next to her.

Bai barely remembered moving, but he was suddenly there, seated and facing her. Her smile had grown, revealing one dimple in her white cheek.

"You must be Bai," she murmured, and her voice was the soft wash of waves on a sandy beach. That perfect, fragile hand settled on his arm, surprisingly warm. "I am Noran."

Bai knew he said something in reply, but he wasn't sure what.

Soon afterward Zi and Hei conducted a ceremony full of flash and power, with shadows that became birds and flower petals that exploded into miniature fireworks, but Bai wouldn't have noticed even if they had had sex in front of them all, for he had eyes only for Noran.

She blushed under his intent gaze, and her lashes fluttered with emotion.

When dinner ended, disciples of Zi and Hei led the guests to their rooms, for the wedding celebration was to last two weeks. Bai started to follow Noran, but Cheng grabbed his arm and pulled him away. In the relative privacy of a black and purple room, Cheng asked, "What are you doing?"

"I'm getting ready to rest. What are you doing?"

Cheng scoffed. "Noran. What are you doing with Noran?"

Bai shrugged. "Maybe I'm falling in love. Shouldn't you be delighted?"

Cheng slapped his forehead. "Don't you even know how she became an immortal? When Aka slept on her beach, she changed herself from sand to a being that could attract his attention."

"So?"

"So! Aka spent all dinner thinking about boiling your

blood!"

"You don't know that," Bai said as he climbed into the bed and made himself a pillow from a bit of his robe—he didn't like the one that had been provided.

"Some of us don't need magic to know what others are thinking," Cheng said dryly. "You should stay away from her. I'm telling you, she's trouble."

"She's beauty and power," Bai corrected.

Cheng groaned. "That's what she wants you to think. Her magic influences your thoughts!"

Bai closed his eyes and smiled. "If she's influencing me, that just shows how powerful she is."

Cheng continued to ramble at him, but Bai fell asleep picturing the way Noran had peered at him through her lashes.

BAI woke early the next morning and decided to sketch New Moon Manor. Even though he abhorred its aesthetic, its achievement was worth recording.

Hei found him by the arches and watched Bai paint in silence for some time. "Zi would like that," he finally said. "What would you take for it?"

Bai almost said he could have it for nothing, but he impulsively answered, "A story. I heard that you became an immortal for Zi. Tell me about it, and I'll give you the painting."

Hei nodded. "A fair exchange." The basalt path he stood on morphed into an armchair, and Hei sat.

"It was off the frozen sea of Ehkoron. She had made special shoes from some violet ice at dawn and was using them to glide over the water. At first, I was long and strong as I followed her, reveling in her grace and athleticism. But I grew smaller and smaller, and I realized I would disappear when the sun reached its zenith. I couldn't bear to leave her side, so I became a man."

Bai's brush stopped, and he had to whisk it away quickly as a black blob formed beneath its bristles. "The way you tell it—do you mean to say that you were Zi's shadow? Not just a shadow on the ice, but hers specifically?"

"Of course. Just as Aka was once your blood."

Bai snorted. "Yes, but Aka was thrilled to be free of me whereas you—well, you are still following Zi around like a shadow."

"She is my reason for existing," Hei said, his expression placid. "I love her. That is why we promised to be with each other for all of eternity in front of witnesses. So that you would all know of our unbreakable bond."

Bai felt disconcerted. He wasn't sure that he could be so confident when it came to another being's feelings. But he also felt relieved. Even if Noran became an immortal when she saw Aka, it wasn't as if she'd been his shadow. She had been a grain of sand, a distinct being. And Bai knew better than anyone that being present at another immortal's inception did not dictate a lasting bond.

He was further reassured when Noran sought him out. Oh, now that Cheng had pointed it out, he did see Aka eying them sulkily, but it didn't bother Bai. In fact, a petty part of him was glad that her flirting forced Aka to acknowledge him. *See, someone likes me*, he wanted to say.

For the two weeks that the wedding lasted, Noran strolled with him through the abominable garden, rested her silky hair against his shoulder, and fed him the tastiest morsels from her own chopsticks at meals.

On the last night, Bai braided a bracelet from his own hair and gathered starlight to create a pendant. He presented it to her with a flourish, intending to share his feelings as well.

Her white fingers pressed against her pink lips, and she said, "How beautiful!"

She extended her hand, and he fastened it about her wrist.

"With this, you can find me anywhere on Earth," he told her. "And if you call for me, I'll come."

"What a kind present! I would be sad to lose touch with you, when you've become such a dear friend."

"Yes—well. Where do you go next? Have you ever seen—?"

She smiled at him. "I will help Aka build a palace in the Heavens, even greater than this one," she told Bai. "I'll let you know when I finish it, shall I?"

Her delicate fingers seized his own. "Thank you again, Bai. You have given me a great gift these past two weeks."

Bai was confused—she didn't seem to be speaking of the bracelet.

A few hours later, she left the wedding with Aka.

"I'm sorry," Cheng told him later, while the two of them shared a meal on Earth.

"What are you sorry for?"

"I shouldn't have wished..."

Bai shrugged and smiled slightly. "This is just the beginning."

If anything, the pity in Cheng's eyes grew more pronounced.

Bai patted him on the back. "Hey, don't act as if it's all decided. You're my friend; you're supposed to cheer me on."

Cheng shrugged. "I don't want to give you false hope."

Bai sighed.

*20,000 years ago*

NANAMI lay stomach-down on the stone bench, one hand scratching lines in the fine pebbles with a silver stick while the other pillowed her chin. The day was warm and pleasant, a light breeze balancing the sunshine, but Nanami's mood was more suited to thunderclouds.

Her mother had entered labor nearly a week ago—her tenth labor—and it had not progressed easily. Although Miko had birthed nine healthy children, this was her first time carrying twins, and something had not been right. Ao had sent for Haraa, and he had sent the "children" away to his father-in-law's at Tsuku.

Nanami resented being called a child. After all, she was six thousand years old—her adulthood ceremony had been held a thousand years ago, and even that was rather late. She knew too, that if anyone deserved to feel bitter over the decision, it was Ichimi who had also been sent with them. Ichimi was eighteen thousand years old, had already been married, and had experienced pregnancy loss. Nanami had heard her mother say that Ichimi should be sent with the others because the birth might remind her of those sorrows. The fact her parents wouldn't just ask Ichimi and let her decide for herself offended Nanami on her sister's behalf.

But Ichimi had put a good face on things by playing shuttlecock with their cousins. Even now, Nanami could hear them at the other end of the garden, laughter punctuated by the thwack of the paddles against the shuttle. So Nanami felt guilty for sulking, but not guilty enough to stop.

The crunch of pebbles nearby made Nanami look up, and she saw Kairoku approaching. He was an inch or two taller than her but far more solidly built, and right now he loomed threateningly over her.

"Yeah?" she said. "What do you want?"

His light grey eyes flashed, and he tugged on his scraggly copy of their father's dense beard twice before snatching the hair stick out of her hand.

"Where did you get this?" he demanded.

"I found it on the floor," Nanami said irritably. That floor had been in her cousin's room, which she was sharing until they were allowed to go home, but Kairoku didn't need to know that.

"This is Eiko's hair stick!" he shouted. "She's been looking all over for it! And you're just digging in the dirt with it? What's wrong with you? You must have realized it belonged to somebody."

Nanami sat up and hunched her shoulders. "The rocks aren't that dirty, and it's metal. It'll wash off easily enough."

Kairoku grabbed her arm and hauled her to her feet. "You're coming with me."

"To where?" asked Nanami.

"To apologize!"

And so he dragged her across the garden to the shuttlecock game. Nanami stumbled behind him, creating messy furrows in the carefully raked pebbles of the garden.

At their approach, the six women holding paddles all stopped playing shuttlecock, and Ichimi neatly caught the shuttle in her hand. Ichimi was beautiful, the same height as Nanami but with generous curves and an elegant oval face instead of Nanami's too round one.

"Kairoku?" she asked. "Why are you pulling your sister around so roughly?"

Kairoku ignored his older sister, instead focusing on their cousin as he held up the silver hair stick. "Cousin Eiko, is this not yours?"

"My hair stick!" She hurried over to take it from him. "Thank you, thank you. But where did you find it?"

Kairoku smirked, then pushed Nanami in front of him. "Make your apologies," he ordered her.

Nanami grit her teeth then squeezed out, "I found it and was playing with it. I'm sorry."

Eiko was examining the stem closely and her gaze jerked up. "Playing with it? You bent it! What were you doing, pushing rocks?"

Nanami frowned—the hair stick had been bent when she found it. "I didn't—"

Kairoku interrupted. "Yes, she was digging in the pebbles with it." He bowed. "I'm sorry that we are such poor guests. Nanami, wash the hair stick for Eiko."

Nanami pressed her lips together and bowed herself, holding out a hand for the hair stick. There was no point in arguing it had already been bent. She had no proof, anyway.

But Eiko clutched the stick to her chest. "If I let you wash it, who knows what will happen!"

That was a bit much, and Nanami looked at her sisters for support. But Ichimi, Sanmi, Yonmi, and Gomi were shaking their heads in disgust. Kairoku practically hummed with gloating next to her. Nanami's fists balled up, and her nails dug into her palms.

"I'm sorry," she said again.

Eiko sniffed. She turned back to the game, and Kairoku at last let go of Nanami's arm. Nanami strode away, but she didn't go back to the other side of the garden. She strode right out the front gate and teleported to Po.

When Nanami reappeared, she was in a flower-laden bower; red petals dripped toward the sand underfoot like drops of blood; lush purple flowers slashed with chartreuse beckoned all that passed them. Thick green surged around and underneath her. It was hot and damp, and the air was so sweet that it was like being immersed in honey.

Nanami gulped in the honey-thick air in big gasps, swallowing her tears. She had mostly recovered when the foliage shifted, revealing the Koch-ssi.

*What is wrong, Nanami?*

The Koch-ssi was about seven feet tall, making Nanami look like a child, but she always treated Nanami with respect. Nanami had first met her when she was around two thousand, when Ao brought the entire family to Po. She looked like a sculpture of a woman made from plants. Flowers rioted over her head, her cheeks were peony petals and her eyes unshelled macadamia nuts. The Koch-ssi's berry mouth made no sound, so the creature spoke mind-to-mind. Her siblings found the large creature unnerving and had avoided her for the whole year they stayed on Po, but Nanami loved the Koch-ssi.

Nanami threw herself into those strong cattail arms and laid her head on a bosom of hydrangeas. The sweet smell that filled the air grew even stronger, and Nanami let go of her tears.

"They don't even try to understand—I know I shouldn't have—but couldn't they..."

*Hush, flower. All will be well.*

Nanami cried into the Koch-ssi's arms for a short time, and then she related the past few days.

"Why am I so upset about this?" she asked the Koch-ssi. "It's such a stupid little incident."

The Koch-ssi's cattail fingers combed Nanami's hair.

*It's more upsetting to be caught doing something we know is wrong than to be wrongly accused because you can't just brush it off. And because your siblings failed you. You wanted them to take your side just because you are their sister.*

Nanami sighed. "That doesn't make me feel any better. It makes me feel... Weak. Needy."

*It may be needy, but that isn't always bad. I need sunlight and water and earth. Is there something wrong with me because of it? Should I be training myself not to need those things?*

Nanami laughed.

*You need love and support,* the Koch-ssi told her. *That is nothing to be ashamed of.*

*3,000 years ago*

XIAO wove his way through the crowd of silks and perfumes, sure that Jin was here because he had heard Neela's distinctive cackle. It would be easier if he weren't so short—and, actually, he was rather tall for two thousand years old, but well below eye level of his parents' adult guests. He caught a glimpse of a shiny cerulean sari to his right, and Xiao threaded his way toward it. A rather large rear-end collided with his shoulder at one point, and Xiao almost pointed out to the lady that it was his birthday and she really ought to be a little more mindful, but he caught the words and replaced them with an apology before moving on.

Ah, there was Jin. She was dressed in robin's egg blue, but there were little pink knots, like flowers, all over her robes. She must have sewn those herself—Neela didn't sew and she definitely wouldn't have magicked up anything pink. Jin's hands were clasped behind her back and her head was bowed modestly when Neela laughed again at something the God of Festivals said.

Xiao rolled his eyes. *She'd stay there all night, bored out of her mind, if I didn't rescue her.* Jin was a mere month younger than he was—maybe he'd get to go with them to the caravan when the party ended so that he could celebrate her birthday with her. His parents liked it when he stayed with Jin because he and she were going to get married someday.

Xiao grabbed Jin's clasped hands and squeezed her plump fingers. Jin's head jerked up, and she looked over her shoulder at him.

Xiao winked, and Jin grinned. By unspoken agreement, they wove back through the crowd, their hands latched. When they made it out of the crowded courtyard and into the empty hall, Jin asked, "Did you find something good?"

His parents' guests might not be interested in him, but it was his birthday after all, so all of them brought a present. Most of them were pretty lame, meant for his mother rather than him, but Jin's brother had pulled through.

"Karana brought firecrackers!" Xiao told her. "Big ones,

shaped like dragons. Help me carry them to the back garden!"

Jin clapped her hands in delight, and the two of them ran to the main hall, where the presents were piled. Xiao directed her to a pile of large bamboo tubes, which were painted with red and white swirls and had carved wooden heads.

Jin picked up the top one with two hands. "Oh, wow, he made these himself! They're going to be amazing!"

As God of Destruction, Karana had a strong affinity with fire, and his firecrackers were famous in the Heavens. He wouldn't sell them, but sometimes he gave them away.

"I know! Come on, let's go!"

He loaded Jin up with three of the crackers and took the remaining four himself. They didn't run now, out of respect for their precious cargo. When they reached the back garden, where his parents' disciples grew vegetables and such, Xiao directed Jin in setting up the firecrackers on long wooden poles that were supposed to support fragile plants. When all seven were arranged to his satisfaction, Xiao produced some flint from his pocket and knelt behind the first firecracker. Jin leaned over his shoulder, her hand on his back, and she was practically bouncing in excitement.

Xiao liked that about Jin—she'd probably seen Karana's fireworks many times before, but she was always as excited as the first time. A good spark hit the tail of the firecracker and began burning the thin wick. Xiao clapped his hands over his ears—he assumed Jin did the same, as her hand left his back.

The little tube launched itself upward—it just cleared the roof of the New Moon Manor when BOOM!

It exploded in glorious red and white sparks. Jin and Xiao both laughed as he set to lighting two more.

They exploded in quick succession, their radiant flowers merging overhead, but Xiao never got to light a fourth.

Instead, a hand reached out and snagged his ear.

Xiao cried out in pain and tried to pull away from his father's tight grip, but that just hurt more.

"Jin, go find your grandmother," Hei ordered as he led Xiao away. Xiao caught a glimpse of Jin's white face before she was gone.

*Coward*, he thought, but without heat.

Hei pulled Xiao along by his ear, and Xiao hurried to keep pace with his much taller father. It wasn't until they reached Xiao's room that Hei released him.

"What were you thinking?" Hei demanded, crossing his arms.

"I—they were a present for me. I thought it'd be alright—"

Hei shook his head. "I don't care about the firecrackers. Your mother was in the middle of giving a speech."

"Oh—oh, I'm sorry," Xiao stuttered. "When I left the party, everyone was just chatting. I didn't realize..."

Hei shook his head. "Your mother is upset. You embarrassed her. Don't come out of your room until I come get you."

Hei gave the order like Xiao had a choice, but his father locked the room when he left.

Xiao flopped on the bed, bored and frustrated. He supposed he wouldn't get to go with Jin and Neela when they left—his parents would be too mad.

How long did they plan to leave him in here anyway? Maybe they'd make him miss dinner, but surely they'd still let him attend the toast. He was the guest of honor, after all.

The hours ticked by, and Xiao eventually fetched a scroll

from his shelf to read. But he was too upset to concentrate on the words, and he ended up tossing it aside. His stomach rumbled its displeasure—he hadn't bothered eating lunch so that he'd have more room for treats at the party. Not that he needed to eat, but the thought of all those honey-soaked almonds and chicken skewers and fruit crepes filled him with longing.

He eventually fell asleep, wondering if Jin asked to say good-bye and was denied or if she had been too bashful.

When he woke the next morning, he waited a long time for someone to come to the door—if not one of his parents, then a disciple. He tracked the sun's movement on his floor and by the time it disappeared completely, no one had come. He didn't cry that night, nor the next, or even the one after that, but on the fifth night, the tears came hot and fast and sobs racked his whole body.

Still no one came, even when he hollered for help or screamed his rage or smashed the beautiful pottery that decorated his shelves.

*Just let me die,* he begged of no one. *I'd rather die than live here alone for the rest of my life.*

1,000 *years ago*

"YOU'RE going out?" Jin asked Neela in surprise. Jin had just returned to the blue caravan with a basket of mangoes and found Neela tying her sandals. She was dressed in a brilliant blue sari and her long silver hair was braided over one shoulder. She looked like any Jeevanti grandmother, except for her eyes, which were the color of the sky.

"Yes, there's a famous sitar player coming to Shahar today. I want to hear him play and dance in the square." She wasn't even looking at Jin. Instead, she had her head tilted back, her eyes half closed, just absorbing the sun. Jin sometimes got annoyed when her grandmother did this, but Neela would always reply that flowers needed sunshine.

"But I'm leaving tomorrow morning for the Sun Court. I have to pack." Jin sat the mangoes down on the small table sandwiched between two plush benches.

"Well, it's not like you need me to help, do you?" Neela finished with her sandals and stood. "You're an adult now."

Jin flushed and nodded. "Of course, I can do it by myself. Enjoy the music."

"Oh, I will," Neela smiled.

Neela was a handsome woman, elegant and refined in her maturity, but when she smiled, her eyes took on a mischievous glint and young men flirted with her. Jin loved that smile, but sometimes she wished it would be prompted by her rather than, well, random musicians in Shahar. Half the reason Jin tried to master every craft they encountered was because she hoped her grandmother would praise her as she did the original artisans, but whenever Jin mastered something, Neela would say, "Well, of course you can do it—you have as many years as you need, after all."

Jin followed Neela to the caravan door and shaded her eyes against the bright sun as she watched Neela begin the two-mile walk to Shahar. Neela preferred to travel like a mortal most of the time—as Jin watched, Neela knelt and plucked a wild anemone. She admired it before tucking it into her braid.

Impulsively, Jin called out to her when Neela reached the edge of the clearing, "You'll be back before I go? To say good-bye?"

Neela stopped and waved once.

Jin clasped her hands together and chewed on her lower lip before shaking off her melancholy.

"Well," she said brightly to no one, "there's a lot to do! I don't want to make Karana wait on me tomorrow."

She went back into the caravan and began going through the cupboard for all the treasures she had accumulated over the years. Neela frequently insisted she purge her collection because the caravan was too crowded, but it was still quite large.

When she finished, the bed was piled high with silks and pottery, while the cupboards were almost empty.

*I guess NeeNee is finally getting her wish.* Jin blinked rapidly. *Will she miss me?*

Neela had insisted on raising Jin with her after Jin's mother was murdered by a concubine, but she had never seemed to exactly enjoy it. Xiao was always telling Jin how jealous he was of her, that she got to drift around the world with no obligations, and it was often wonderful, except when it wasn't, and Jin wondered what it would be like to have her own room in an estate belonging to her mother and father.

Well, she would soon find out, wouldn't she? Except for the mother part.

Jin had everything packed by dark, and she prepared a meal for both her and Neela over the firepit outside. When Neela didn't come by the time the food had grown cold, Jin put the rice and curry in bowls and covered them with beeswax cloths.

They both had enough spice that they'd last through tomorrow.

Jin slept alone in the big bed that she and Neela shared—when Neela slept at home—but for once it didn't feel comfortable. It felt hot and close in the caravan, so she took a blanket into the field to sleep under the stars. The mosquitoes were plentiful, but Jin could spell herself to be unappealing to them. She drifted off wondering if Karana would be as early as he claimed.

Jin had just finished dressing after her morning wash when Karana appeared in the clearing. He was dressed simply, in a long, deep red tunic and loose black trousers, and his hair was tied in a loose ponytail. Despite his casual attire, he had taken the time to paint his face, wearing his usual black cat eyes and lips.

He smiled. "Hello, little sister. Where's the Wanderer?"

"Wandering," Jin said as she gave him a hug.

"Should we wait for her?"

Jin shook her head. "She hates good-byes."

Karana nodded, and helped her gather her bundles. "Well, are you ready to see your new home? Father finished it yesterday."

"Oh, yes, I'm very excited!"

They reappeared in Karana's residence in the Sun Palace, as it was the only place the two of them could teleport within the palace walls. Two of Salaana's Light Hands—Karana didn't have any disciples of his own—relieved them of their bundles and Karana led all four of them out of his gate and along the red gravel path that curved around the north wall of Aka's residence.

"You probably don't remember all this, do you, Jin? That is

Gang's residence."

Jin would have realized that without Karana pointing it out. Huge gold disks were set every few feet along the red wall, each with a raised character for battle on it. She nodded. "And those buildings over there?"

"Gang's and Salaana's disciples live there. I haven't any disciples, so I don't have to bother with that."

He stopped in front of a wooden gate set in another curved red wall. "This is you. Father already keyed it to your blood." He showed her that it was locked for him and stepped aside. "So only you can open it."

Jin shivered. Since she was moving back home, shouldn't her family be able to come in to see her whenever they wanted?

Jin touched the doors and they swung inward. Jin saw a large single-story house of vermillion painted wood, a large pond, and a great deal of dirt.

Karana scratched his chin. "I know it isn't beautiful, but Father said you would want to design and cultivate everything yourself."

Jin nodded. "Of course, how thoughtful."

It would have been nice if it was a little more finished though, even if she had decided to change things.

They carried her bundles into the empty house, which turned out to be one large room.

"Can I help you unpack?" Karana asked.

"Oh, no, I'll want to fuss with everything myself," she said brightly.

Karana nodded and tousled her hair. Jin walked him and the disciples to the gate, determinedly projecting cheer.

But when the gate swung closed behind them, Jin let the

tears out.

Since Karana had shown her how the door locked, she was shocked when a hand clapped on her shoulder. Jin sat up, dashing the tears from cheeks. She was mortified that someone had witnessed her wallowing in self-pity.

Slowly, she turned her head to see who it was.

Her father sat next to her on the bed, his red eyes solemn.

"Are you so sad to live here?"

Jin shook her head quickly. "Oh, no, I'm happy to come home, I just... I'm sorry, it's not quite what I expected."

His eyes were distant, as if he were focusing on something intensely. At last, "I can feel your disappointment. What's disappointing?"

Jin twisted her fingers together. "I don't want to complain."

Aka lightly tapped her nose with his finger. "You, my girl, are one of five beings whose complaints I care about. Don't waste that privilege."

Jin blushed and her lips quirked up—she rather liked that. "I had pictured this—my room, living with my family many times. I hadn't expected each of my siblings to live in their own residence, and it to be so—unfinished. I know," she hurried to add, "that you left it so I could finish it to my tastes—"

He collected her hand with his own. "I did, but that doesn't mean it was right." He leaned close, conspiratorially. "Don't tell anybody, but very occasionally, I make a mistake." Then he winked.

Jin snorted.

"Come, walk me around and let's figure out what we'll do with your garden. At least there's plenty of sunshine for you here, so that's one need met."

Jin giggled. "Isn't there sunshine everywhere in this world?"

Aka smiled. " Except for some caves and the Underworld."

"Well, I don't suppose I'll ever go there."

"No, I certainly hope not!" And Aka pulled her into a one-sided hug.

Jin smiled. She had a father at last. It would be too greedy to ask for a mother, too.

# EARTH

## 100,000 YEARS AFTER CREATION

This map shows the regions immortals use rather than the mortal nations of Earth. The only mortal creations drawn are their largest cities; other points of interest are immortal residences and magical sites made by immortal beings.

# How Blood Flowed



*Present Day*

BAI balanced atop the vermillion torii gate that led to the Underworld when Kunjee unlocked it. The wind plucked at his loose white robes, asking him to apologize for the abrupt slaughter of two justice disciples. Those women sagged on the white pikes he had driven through their hearts, their blood steaming as it stained their white saris.

Bai crushed the remorse he felt—he knew that later he would have to address it, but he couldn't falter now. If Salaana succeeded in destroying the gate, Bai might never see Jin again. That was unacceptable. For now, he scanned the remaining disciples—nearly a hundred women. All of them held either a sword or a glaive, but they were afraid and looked toward their lady for guidance.

Salaana was dressed for war, with a red leather armor breastplate and arm guards. Her reddish-brown hair was bound in a tower by an elaborate silver hairpiece, making her patrician features even harsher. Her eyes—the color of dried blood—were locked on Bai. Calmly, she reached behind her and drew a wickedly curved sword. Holding it with the easy confidence of a seasoned fighter, Salaana stepped forward, and signaled her disciples to remain where they were.

*Will Jin forgive me if I kill her aunt?*

"Why are you doing this?" Bai asked. "You are the Goddess of Justice. How do you justify this?"

A few paces away, her sword held ready, Salaana paused and nodded slightly, signaling her willingness to talk. "Jin is an abomination, just like the immortal creatures. The Underworld is where she belongs."

Bai was surprised to hear her assert so casually that the creatures belonged in the Underworld, but he focused on the more pressing issue. "She's your family, but you call her an abomination?"

"You are the one who wrote how power corrupted Chao the Conqueror. You must be aware of how much power she has. How could she possibly not be corrupted?"

Bai crossed his arms, still balanced on the top beam of the gate. "She's the kindest, most sincere being I've ever met. Chao was always corrupt—his power just revealed that corruption."

Salaana smiled tightly. "That's not what you wrote twenty millennia ago. My brother said you were infatuated with Jin, but I didn't believe that you would so easily change your views."

Bai forced himself to think rather than immediately

respond. "My views changed after years of reflection. But am I right about Jin?"

"She is kind. So kind that she can't bear to let anyone die. She's trying to save my father, even though he's a murderous, selfish bastard."

"Selfish, I'll grant you, but do you know he's a murderer? Where's your proof?"

Salaana's very red lips curved upward, though Bai didn't see what had amused her. "Three mothers of his children are dead—as is the son who could have overpowered him."

Bai shook his head. "That's circumstance, not proof. Besides, Gang could have overpowered him, and Aka never tried to eliminate him."

"I suppose you are allied with Gang."

"I haven't seen Gang since before you watched me beat your father at Jieqi."

Salaana nodded. It seemed this was what she wanted to confirm because she said, "We've talked enough." Salaana surged forward, sword ready.

Bai drove a shaft at her from the snow—not a pike to pierce her heart, but a rod to knock her down. That was irrelevant though, for she destroyed it with a burst of lightning. She leapt into the air, her sword aimed at Bai. With a sweep of his arms, he directed the wind to knock her aside.

"You don't get to judge who is worthy of the world they are born into," he declared, wanting his words to carry to all her disciples. "Both the immortal creatures and Jin—locking them in the Underworld just for existing is wrong. If you were truly just, you would be searching for a way to free them, not trap them forever."

Salaana landed on her feet. "But I do get to make that judgement. I am the ultimate arbiter of what is just in this world. Creatures that cause death and mayhem are not just. A being who can raise the dead is not just."

"Capability is different from deed."

Salaana didn't bother to answer. She rapidly swung her sword, this time aiming her attack at the gate rather than Bai. He was forced to leap down and create snow shields to block the razor-like slices of air. Salaana's attack was fierce and shattered the hastily constructed shields to leave cuts on Bai's arms.

He reached into his belt for the Starlight Sword, shrunken for travel, but he hesitated. He remembered Jin's look of betrayal when she learned he could ride a cloud. She trusted him too much. It was burdensome being so well thought of— and yet, he wasn't willing to give it up.

He withdrew the Water Shield instead. Salaana took advantage of his distraction to charge—he expanded the shield just in time to catch her blow. The Water Shield reflected the force of her blow, and Salaana tumbled back, flipping through the air to land elegantly on the snow.

Five disciples had approached the gate, and Bai whipped the snow into the air to blast them—they covered their eyes and retreated.

Fifteen more entered the fray even as Salaana resumed her attack. Bai's existence became limited to this moment. The snow became an extension of himself as he whirled and blocked, sending the disciples flying even as he countered Salaana's blows.

He could kill her. She was a skilled fighter and a powerful

immortal, but Bai could kill her. She was a threat to Jin, and her arrogance and judgement alarmed him.

But he couldn't bear the idea of telling Jin that he had done so.

Jin, who couldn't even stand by as Aka died without a proper hearing for his sins, wouldn't accept the death of Salaana just because she tried to trap Jin in the Underworld. His remorse for those first two disciples that he had killed so quickly wasn't only because of his own guilt—he wasn't sure if Jin understood who he was. That he had killed more people than she had met.

But if he didn't kill Salaana, he wasn't sure she wouldn't kill him.

JIN'S dress of flame lit her path, though there wasn't much for her to see. Rough gray stone, empty caverns, small enough that Jin could reach the ceiling and walls if she stretched her arms. She hadn't seen another creature since the Xuezei had fled from her, and given the monotony of the tunnels, she feared she was walking in circles.

Bai had said the Underworld was unmappable. *What if my path is shifting so I can never leave here?*

Bai had spoken wistfully of the Underworld, remembering a place of wonder and beauty. These rough stone caves and endless gloom could not be all there was, and Jin stoked her faith. *I just need to keep walking and eventually I will find another place. I will mark the wall so I know if I come back on my own path.*

She stretched out her hand and encouraged the fire to spread over her fingers. It scorched the wall, leaving a dark smudge on the stone. Jin resumed her stride, leaving a line of her progress behind her.

With the unchanging light, it was hard to tell time here, but Jin had grown weary and the bottoms of her feet were feeling tender when the tunnel widened abruptly. She had reached an intersection, and the second tunnel was much larger with an underground river.

With a cry of relief, for finally something had gone her way in this forsaken place, she dropped to her knees by the fast-flowing water and cupped her hands to capture the water. As part flower, she had more needs than immortals like Bai and Xiao. She brought it to her lips, but its strong metallic tang made her hesitant to drink. Could this water be poisoned by metal?

She tried to swallow as she thought, but her mouth was so dry that she could not. Tentatively, Jin touched her tongue to the liquid and promptly gagged.

It was blood. That was why the Xuezei must live here, to subsist on this river of blood. Jin tried to shake the blood from her fingers, but it clung stubbornly.

She gritted her teeth and thought, *At least I can use it.*

She changed the blood on her fingers to cotton and used it to clean her hands. She pulled more blood from the river and made herself a new set of clothes.

The weight of the cloth was familiar and soothing. She was glad not to be clothed in flame any longer, though she collected a ball of fire on her hand and raised it to examine her options moving forward.

The tunnel she had been following continued on the other side of the blood river, but Jin was disinclined to take that path.

She looked up the river and shivered, a little afraid to discover the source of all this blood.

Downriver then.

Remembering how Bai had made a riverboat to carry them down the Kuanbai, and Jin began shaping the blood itself into a vessel that would carry her onward.

She hadn't even finished the bow before a faint sound came from across the river. Emerging from a tunnel were a dozen or so Xuezei.

Their white faces seemed to float in the gloom, the rest of their bodies obscured by their black fur. The Xuezei froze, as surprised to see Jin as she was to see them. She shouldn't have been of course—she had already realized that the river must be their source of food, but she was so focused on the next step that she hadn't considered meeting more Xuezei.

"Hot, fresh blood," whispered one. The others made a strange sound, a sort of high-pitched whiffling laugh, before plunging into the river. They swam with fast, sure strokes, and Jin wasted no time turning herself into a torch.

But this group was bolder—or stupider—than the others she had encountered. Despite the flames that engulfed her, two launched themselves from the riverbank, their narrow fangs leading the way. Both Xuezei latched on to her shoulders, biting through the flame and her skin.

Jin screamed in pain, even as the two Xuezei dropped to the ground.

They howled, rolling on the rough rock and clutching their mouths.

"It's real fire," hissed one of their more cautious packmates. "She must have magic—kill her first."

They launched themselves at her, claws aiming for her throat, but they were all covered in blood. Without conscious decision, Jin changed the blood into needles, and pierced their skin. Some still managed to slash her but all were soon immobilized by agony. Jin methodically set each one on fire.

She collapsed to the ground, panting. Once she caught her breath, she realized she could hear the dying cries of Xuezei as they burned. The flame was hot enough that they died quickly, but Jin's dry retching continued for some time after.

*Is it the same as killing an immortal being?* She wondered. *Did I just murder a dozen sentient creatures? Or are they more like animals?*

She shuddered. In the moment, she had feared her own death and had responded with the greatest possible force. Now she wondered if she could have killed one and driven the others off.

She pulled her knees up, naked once more, and rested her cheek on them. Her eyes drifted shut, but she snapped them back open. There must be more Xuezei here—she couldn't sleep. She should make the riverboat quickly.

She was thirsty and hungry as well as tired, but she hadn't been here long—surely less than three days. Yes, she needed water and nourishment, but just like a dayflower, she could last a week or more without them. And she didn't have to sleep. So why was she feeling so weak?

It must be in her head.

Jin dragged herself to her feet and summoned more of the blood from the river. A small amount became a long tunic, which seemed simpler than robes, and the rest she began shaping into a boat.

BAI caught Salaana's strike with the Water Shield on his arm, and as she leaned in, hungry for the victory, he kicked her legs out from under her. He twisted her sword from her grip, then immobilized her with rapid blows to three pressure points. It was risky, because it required his focus, and even as he dragged her upright, her own sword at her throat, one of her disciples succeeded in striking the gate with her glaive.

But Bai had underestimated Aka's protections. The gate, despite looking like wood, sparked like hot steel being struck with a hammer. The bold disciple flew backwards, and Bai shouted, "Anyone else tries that, and she's dead."

Salaana might have called Bai's bluff, but at least for a few more minutes she wouldn't even be able to speak. Before that happened, he had to decide if he would kill her or not. And if her disciples threw their lives after hers, would he take those as well?

The justice disciples pressed close together, and Bai noticed two lying on the ground who had been knocked backward by his swings. Unconscious or dead?

Bai's hand tightened convulsively on Salaana's sword as he imagined lovers and children mourning the fallen women. He wanted to soothe himself by focusing only on their callousness in trying to trap Jin, but he had decided not to do that anymore. He had vowed to own the deaths he caused and not just excuse them.

Two of the disciples, whose white saris were shot with silver, were talking in low voices, occasionally gesturing at the unconscious Salaana in his arms.

At this rate, Salaana would wake up and force his hand. "If

you leave now, you may take the dead and wounded with you," he offered.

It was the wrong thing to say—it was too soft.

The two leading disciples drew their weapons and gestured the others into formation.

"Drop her now, and we'll let you live," said one. "You can't stop us all."

Bai sighed. He really had been out of the world too long—his legends had been forgotten or dismissed as invention. At the height of his fame, a group like this would be too terrified to try him.

But he had to choose wisely. Dealing with a hundred of them at once would certainly leave him too drained for another mass attack.

Breaking their legs was messy and might cripple them, but if he strangled them with those white saris, they would just wake up in a few minutes. And if he misjudged the timing, they would die.

Broken bones it was. He gently set Salaana on the ground before resuming a fighting stance. The head disciple laughed coldly, believing he had conceded to their demands. Bai merged with the snow, letting it amplify his power.

"The Great Warrior isn't so scary after all—"

Bai leapt and kicked with both feet at once, aiming at the shins of an imaginary opponent. The effect was not imagined, and the shattering of two hundred bones rent the air. That was nothing compared to the screams that followed.

THE blood river's current carried the boat smoothly, and Jin sagged beneath the canopy in the middle. She hadn't bothered with any lanterns, hoping that she would attract less attention that way, and she really didn't want to see any more of the river. She knew it would be foolish to fall asleep, but she had to at least sit down. Her legs tangled in front of her, and her head lolled to one side. She was panting. It felt like someone was squeezing her chest so that she could never get enough air. Maybe she had lost too much blood?

Her cheek and hand had scabbed over, but her shoulders hadn't quite. She ought to make bandages—there was ample source material, given the river, but she was too tired.

Her hunger pangs had been replaced by nausea, but she was desperately thirsty.

*You can go a week without water*, she reminded herself. *Longer without food.*

But she was tired, even so.

Jin's eyelids fell closed. She jerked them open again. She didn't need to sleep. She had once stayed awake for two hundred years just to win a bet with Xiao.

She blinked again. She had to stay awake. She hadn't seen or heard anything in the past few hours, but there must be more Xuezei still out there.

She'd stay awake until she escaped these awful caverns, and she would find the Lonely Island. Maybe this river even led to it. Now that would be lucky.

The boat would carry her to the island, and she'd pick a black peony. It probably looked like a normal peony, but with black petals. She wished she had clarified that with Bai, when he told her they grew on the Lonely Island.

The boat rocked suddenly, and Jin leapt to her feet in alarm.

She ran out from under the canopy, fire in her hands, but it wasn't the Xuezei after all.

Bai smiled at her and pulled her into her arms.

"Bai," she whispered, and she went limp in relief. He nuzzled her temple before his lips skimmed down the side of her face to her neck. Jin leaned back on the bed as clouds closed around them, soft and warm. Suddenly Bai bit her neck, and Jin struggled to escape his arms, but it was too difficult.

"Please—please stop! It hurts!" she cried.

"You thought I would let you escape your vow because you aren't my daughter?" Aka seized her upper arm and squeezed it painfully. "You will bear Xiao's child and give it to me!"

"Please, no! I love Bai!"

"You don't know Bai." Gang pressed a knife against her ribs. "I'm sorry, Jin, but it's for your own good. This will let you sleep until everything is settled."

The wicked slice he made on her ribs didn't feel like it was for her own good.

Jin bucked against him, unable to move her arms.

"Please, spare me," she cried, though her mouth felt like it was filled with dust.

And then Gang became a monstrous creature of light and fire. Its flame was so hot that Jin thought she might burn. She struggled, trying to flee. When that failed, she opened her mouth to scream, but no sound escaped, no matter how hard she tried.

"Your family trapped me here, and now you shall pay for it," the Golden Phoenix told her.

Suddenly Neela pushed the Phoenix aside. Her hands clamped on Jin's shoulders, and Jin trembled. Was Neela going to lock her in stone, for her own good?

But she scooped Jin up instead, and Jin was swathed in rose petals, softer than silk and sweeter than summer.

*Hush, flower.*

It wasn't Neela at all—it was Aashchary. Had Jin died then?

Jin rested her head against her mother's bosom.

"Mama—I'm sorry..." The tears leaked freely, but the words became tangled.

A sweet lullaby filled her ears, and Jin couldn't bring herself to care if she were dying or already dead.

ALL of Salaana's disciples collapsed. Some grabbed their shins; others studiously didn't touch them. Some grit their teeth in silence against the pain but were overwhelmed by the majority that vocalized their agony.

Bai himself was trembling from sheer exertion of power. He managed to remain on his feet, but he doubted that he could manage even a single teleport within the next few hours. He forced himself to focus on Salaana. She would regain consciousness soon.

She wouldn't give up her goals easily. Finding her hundred disciples in pain, possibly crippled, would she resume her attack? Fetch another army?

What if she forced Bai to teleport along with her? Bai wouldn't recover any power while between, and if she dragged him to the Sun Palace—

No, he couldn't allow that to happen.

He could still fight her physically, and if she left to fetch another army, he could meditate to partially recover his power before they returned. Salaana might be able to teleport in less than half an hour, but her disciples would be skilled if they could manage an hour—if she used the same conceit again, making them all arrive simultaneously, it would be enough time for Bai to wrangle something. So he had to make sure she didn't touch him.

He dragged her away from the gate and searched her for weapons. A few of her disciples watched, but most were consumed by their own misfortune. He relieved her of two daggers and a whip. He still preferred her sword to any of those. Burning them wasn't a worthwhile expenditure of his energy and they all contained so much red that Bai had no intention of keeping them on his body, so he buried them in the snow.

As he did so, a single disciple crawled toward him, dragging herself as her legs trailed behind.

"Do you crave death that badly?" Bai asked her.

She did not reply but removed a whip like the one Salaana had borne and slashed at him. Bai dodged it and cut off her hand. Salaana's sword was perfectly sharp—it barely made a noise as it dismembered the disciple.

There was a cry of horror behind him—Salaana had awoken. Bai turned to find lightning dancing on her fingers. He dodged with impossible speed, and the bolt struck the snow where he had been.

Salaana froze. "What was that? Why didn't you reflect it back?"

She came to her feet and surveyed her wailing army.

Her lips curved up as her eyes turned harder than ever. "You expended a great deal of power, didn't you, First? Do you like dancing?"

The lightning was fast and incessant, melting the snow it touched and scorching the stone beneath. Bai couldn't remember the last time he had demanded so much of his body, becoming a whirlwind of continuous movement.

At this rate, she would leave him as exhausted physically as he was magically. He had to go on the offensive. He couldn't avoid killing her any longer.

And so he danced—for that was as apt a term as any—ever closer to her. Salaana didn't seem concerned. Instead she prepared more lightning, ready to welcome him into her embrace.

Only a few feet away, he sent her sword on without him, straight through her belly. Salaana's lips parted, and she fell to the ground.

Bai pulled the Starlight Sword out immediately and found enough power to grow it to full size. He loomed over Salaana, wondering if he should finish it now or show mercy. The belly cut would prove fatal if untreated, but if she went now to Haraa, she might survive.

Salaana clasped her hands around her sword, and it turned white hot. She pulled it from her abdomen, and the wound closed, cauterized. She fainted.

Bai looked at it—no matter how drained he was, he could still see the essence of things. He now saw that while Salaana had saved herself from bleeding out, she had not repaired the internal damage. Her time was still limited.

A throat cleared behind him, and Bai whirled impatiently. That handless disciple was tenacious, he'd give her that.

But it was not she who had cleared her throat but an old

man, standing beneath the gate, and watching him warily.

Bai's brows snapped together, and then he noticed the man's luminous golden eyes. The very eyes that had recalled him to the world.

Bai quivered in relief and fear. "Jin," he murmured and took a step toward her.

Then another man appeared a few feet behind the first. He wore red leather plates emblazoned with a golden sun and his hand rested on the broad sword at his waist.

Bai's eyes snapped back to the first man. This time Bai noticed the gold epaulets on his shoulders and recognized the Sun Sword in his hands. It was purely coincidence that he had teleported exactly under the gate, looking as if he had emerged from the Underworld. And Bai must be more tired than he had admitted to himself if he mistook Gang for Jin, even a magically altered Jin.

He hoped Gang hadn't heard his whisper of her name.

Gang moved the Sun Sword slowly, its golden blade gleaming in the sunlight, and Bai belatedly realized he had more pressing concerns.

# NEW MOON MANOR

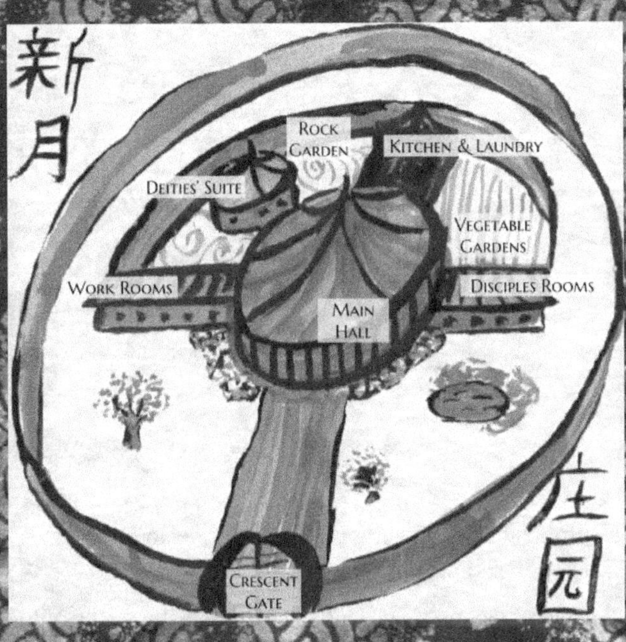



New Moon Manor is the home of the Moon and Night Deities. Made of twilight and shadow 45,000 years after creation, it is suspended in the Heavens by their will. In addition to the deities, it houses about fifty disciples and, of course, their son, the God of Pleasure.

# How Power Was Stolen

THE tumblers of Xiao's door shifted, and Xiao opened his eyes in time to see Hei enter.

Hei was tall and lightly muscled, much like Xiao himself. Where his son's face was full and mischievous though, Hei's was long and serious. His hair was so impossibly dark, it was hard to identify single strands. His winged brows were dark smudges of coal and the iris and pupil of his eyes matched in color. Hei had the same brown skin as his son, even though he avoided sunshine.

He was dressed, as he always was, in simple black robes. No trailing sleeves or skirt for Hei; no embroidery or ribbons. Even his belt was plain black cotton.

Hei closed the door silently behind him, holding Xiao's eyes as he did so. He glided forward and sat facing Xiao on the rug, like a warped mirror.

"And what brings the Night God to see little old me?"

Hei was about as emotive as a boulder, but those eyes of pitch narrowed slightly. "Since when do you address me as 'Night God'?"

"Is there a better way to address you?" Xiao blinked his eyes for effect.

"'Father,' 'Dad,' or even 'Papa,' if you must."

"Didn't you hear me yesterday? I no longer associate that title with you."

"It was three days ago that you spewed your nonsense."

Xiao stiffened. He had slept for three days? He, who didn't need sleep? Xiao forced himself to smile. "Yesterday or three days ago, either way, my point stands."

"You can't choose your parents," Hei said, slowly and a little too loud, as if he thought Xiao was stupid or hard of hearing or both. "Your mother and I lay together, and she bore you as a result. That makes me your father."

"I understand how reproduction works. I also happen to understand adoption, fostering, abandonment, and neglect. You regularly isolated and starved me, so I reject you as a father."

"You can't starve," Hei pointed out.

"Not to death, but I can feel so hungry that I want to throw up. I feel all the pain and discomfort and eventually apathy of starvation, I just keep living."

Hei blinked twice, and Xiao wondered if that was a revelation to him. Had Hei and Zi thought Xiao's cries and begging when they locked him away were simply because of his willful nature? Xiao found his hands fisting on his thighs.

"I am sorry."

Those fists balled tighter. "Too little, too late. I've always wondered, why did you even have a child?"

Hei looked at his hands for a long time. Then, instead of answering, he withdrew a black bottle from his belt and offered it to Xiao. "A present," he said.

Xiao almost ignored the offering, but he was curious. He took the bottle and uncorked it.

One sniff revealed its contents to be a strong rice wine, much more potent than the liquor dispensed by the Infinite Jug. Xiao's hand trembled—that's how badly he wanted to drain it— but instead he flung it with all his strength against the wall. The bottle didn't shatter, but the wine began pouring out. And pouring and pouring.

"It won't run out," Hei promised him. He stood, but Xiao stood with him and tried to land a punch. Hei neatly sidestepped, and Xiao ended up meeting the floor. He stayed down, furious and mortified, until he heard the door click shut again.

After a moment, Xiao got up to retrieve the Infinite Flask. He recorked it and stuffed it under the mattress of his bed. He didn't want it. And if he was going to find a way out of here, he needed all his faculties.

The room reeked of wine.

NANAMI lit a stick of incense at the black iron brazier, releasing the scent of lavender, distilled and concentrated until it seared her nostrils. She took a few steps across the dark wood floor of Dalbam Temple to the Moon Goddess statue and stabbed the unlit end of the incense into the sand-filled pot at its feet. Incense secured, Nanami raised her eyes to the silver face. The features were Zi's, but the expression was tender—nothing like Zi's as she glared at Xiao in the grand hall of New Moon Manor. Nanami kept her thoughts clear of anything that could be perceived as a request or a wish as the thick smoke attempted to carry her prayers to Zi.

After Nanami had fled New Moon Manor, she had visited the Sanctuary Caves, where all magic was nullified, and she was restored to her full-size. From there she had gone to Daedo, the capital of Bando and home of Dalbam Temple.

This was Nanami's first time inside a temple of the Moon and Night deities, though of course she had seen dozens from the outside. Zi and Hei were second only to Aka in popularity, and every major mortal city had at least one temple to them. This was the largest of all.

All immortals knew different regions of the Earth by certain names, but only Bando exactly corresponded to a mortal nation. The royal family of Bando traced its line back twenty-five thousand years, the first significant power on the Bandoan peninsula, and they claimed to have been chosen by the Sun Emperor. It wasn't far from the truth—they had been selected by the Golden Phoenix itself when the oldest son of that family saved and raised a nest of orphaned golden eagle chicks. The royal family owed much of its stability to its famously successful marriages, and they built the first temple to the Moon and Night deities shortly after establishing their dynasty.

Of course, the temple Nanami visited now was not the same structure. Mortal constructions did not last as immortal ones did, even when they were brilliant examples of engineering. Dalbam Temple was only five hundred years old and an attempt at recreating the grand hall of New Moon Manor. Instead of silver, the walls were gleaming blonde wood, and rather than inlaid obsidian, the constellations were burned onto them. The room was large, if not as large as what it imitated, and violet prayer mats covered the dark wood floor. Nanami knelt at the head of the temple, where altars had been placed before roughly life-size statues of amethyst and obsidian. There were several other niches along the walls where more incense burned as offerings.

The space was almost empty now—the temple was open from dusk to dawn every night, but it saw its largest crowds in the early evening. Now, when dawn had not quite arrived, there was no one but Nanami and the monks who appeared to be sleeping at the entrance.

Nanami looked up at the twelve-foot ceiling, where dozens of carved stone ornaments dangled. The ornaments were hollowed eggs of obsidian and amethyst and collected prayers as the smoke passed through them. It was these that she intended to steal—the incense itself was too easily replaced, but these collectors were magic, made by Zi and Hei—or perhaps their disciples.

Thick beams supported the roof and held the collectors—Nanami could scale the walls and use the beams themselves to reach the collectors. They would all fit in a large sack—she could even do it now and be done by dawn.

But what then? Dalbam might be the largest temple of the Moon and Night deities, but taking only its collectors would hardly have a significant impact on Zi and Hei's power. There were several hundred temples of varying size around the world, and fervent worshippers would even have prayer collectors in their own homes.

Nanami needed to know roughly how long she had to steal most of those in order to make a plan—so she needed to know how long it would take to replace the collectors. She went up on the balls of her feet and ran at the wall. With a leap and one perfectly timed kick, she was able to catch a beam and pull herself up. She lay on the beam and waited a few moments, to see if either of the monks would stir. When they continued to sleep, she began to walk along the beams, looking for collectors hanging from particularly frayed ropes. She found one and reached out to it, only to find her stump extended rather than her hand. With a grimace of impatience, she switched sides, and helped the rope along its natural course by spinning the collector until the rope gave out and caught it in her hand.

Nanami didn't want to create a mystery, she just wanted to see the procedure for replacing the collector. She wrapped it in cloth and crushed it beneath her heel. Then, after reversing her ascent, she dropped the broken collector on the prayer mat over which it had hung. Eager to speed things on their way now, she shook the monk awake.

"An ornament fell and broke," she told the monk, pointing at the prayer mat.

With a groan and yawn, the monk shuffled over to the prayer mat. "Curse it," she mumbled. "Don't touch this," she warned Nanami before leaving the room.

Nanami waited for her return, but she faded back into a niche, hoping the woman might forget about her.

The monk returned shortly after to sweep up the broken

shards, threw them out, and went back to sleep.

For the next few days, Nanami returned just before dawn to check on the missing prayer collector and on the fifth morning, it had been replaced.

Nanami's heart sank.

It would of course take longer to replace all thirty if she stole them simultaneously, but the first replacements would be hung in five days—maybe less, since there would be a sense of urgency. How could she possibly steal thousands of prayer collectors from hundreds of temples within that timeline?

AFTER Xiao sopped up the spilled wine with a cloth, he put the soaked fabric in one of those black ceramic pots and lit it with flint.

It was easier to pretend the flask didn't exist when rice wine wasn't tickling his nostrils, and he sat on the bed to survey the room.

Like the rest of New Moon Manor, it had a black basalt floor, and violet chiffon billowed from the ceiling like storm clouds. The door, locked and bolted from the outside, was of black iron. There were five large windows, a full moon in the center and waxing and waning crescents to either side. They looked out on the expansive gardens, but they were barred with more black iron. This room was made by his parents, but Bai had told him surrounding himself in his essential colors would help him restore his powers, so it would suit him well enough for now.

Slipping off the bed, he walked to the middle of the floor and rooted himself on the stone with his right foot. The other leg slid up to press against the opposite thigh, and his hands stretched up and up until his fingers brushed the violet chiffon above. Time held no meaning as Xiao stood, treelike, in his room. Hunger, sleep, and other earthly pulls disappeared, just as they had when he had practiced in Bai's white cave.

When Xiao opened his eyes, hours—or maybe days—later, his fear had receded, and his power once again flowed through him. So what if he couldn't face his parents in a direct challenge yet? That didn't mean his only option was to remain here as their prisoner. He strolled around the dark room, the door locked and the windows barred. He stopped at the window and pushed on that iron.

It was strong, and not just physically. Hei had made these bars himself, and Xiao might drain himself again trying to break them. He traced the sides of the bars gently—the gap between them was too narrow for even Xiao's fist to pass through, but it was also a gap in the barrier of Hei's power. An ant, a little black ant, could easily fit through.

No sooner thought than done, Xiao the ant crept through the gap in the bars and down the black stone of the manor's outer wall.

Just like his previous transformations, being an ant felt natural to Xiao, as if he'd been one all his life. Part of Xiao realized that the world looked different than it always had— even more so than when he had transformed before—but tracking the scents of the garden with his antennae also seemed perfectly instinctive.

Xiao moved very quickly for his size—it should only take him two or three hours to reach the front gate if he was able to keep this up.

The sun was blotted out, and Xiao ran every which way before accepting that he was trapped.

Everything flipped—ah, it was a cup—and light returned. A blurry face loomed over him for what felt like a long time, and Xiao wondered if he should shapeshift again or keep pretending to be an ant. Would whoever had caught him crush him?

A hand closed over the cup gently, and Xiao could feel himself swinging through the air inside the cup. He decided to wait and see what would happen.

Soon—less than ten minutes later—the cup was set down on its side and Xiao scurried out of it.

They were past the gate! He was free! Free of New Moon Manor! And it had been so easy.

Bands of violet power wrapped around his tiny ant body before he could transform or leap off the edge of the manor.

His power was being drained again.

THE inn where Nanami was staying had two stories, with small narrow rooms upstairs for sleeping and a large central hall below for dining. Nanami sat in the hall now, at a long table with several mortals who had left her just enough elbow room to eat her meal without bumping them. She amused herself by mentally snagging their purses while she ate, but the game lost its appeal after she realized she had just used two hands. She set her chopsticks across her bowl and wrapped her hand around her stump.

It didn't hurt. Not physically, though she occasionally woke up feeling like her hand was on fire, and it always took her a little time to convince herself she was fine. Right now, it was just one more thing that felt overwhelming. She took a slow breath.

It wasn't as if having another hand would have allowed her to steal all the prayer collectors, but she couldn't help but wish that she had asked Jin and Bai to try to rebuild it before they left the Yanou.

Fate laughs, that felt like years ago.

She closed her eyes briefly, remembering how it had felt to be encompassed in Jin's fire, a vast ocean that had welcomed Nanami at that moment, but so easily could have destroyed her.

Every magical color had its own unique power, and Nanami had always felt that indigo was the best, for it made it impossible for other immortals to influence her. Except that Xiao had managed to do just that—briefly—in the Wood Pavilions. In that moment, Nanami had known that Jin could overwhelm her too, but thankfully Jin was a knowing immortal, not an influencing one...

Wait, was that right?

Nanami massaged her stump, and her eyes closed as she tried to work through Jin's convoluted heritage. The Wanderer and the Sleeper were one set of grandparents—blue was knowing thoughts and orange was being unknowable. A power that Nanami would love to have for herself. The Sun Emperor was Jin's other grandfather—red knew emotion—and her grandmother was Noran, the lost Color. Nanami didn't know much about her, beside the fact that she was the God of War's mother, but she abruptly remembered that it was Noran who made the cursed Sowon Gold which had caused a falling out between Nanami and He Who Walked in Shadow.

*The Sowon Gold!*

If the Sowon Gold were the payment, He Who Walked in Shadow would do anything Nanami asked, even though he despised her.

Oh, but she couldn't bring the Sowon Gold back into the world. It should stay buried, unable to influence anyone.

That brought Nanami's thoughts full circle, as she realized Jin could influence thoughts, but she shoved those ruminations aside, in favor of her possible plan.

Unlike Nanami, He Who Walked in Shadow had disciples, dozens of lesser thieves who would do whatever he asked.

If she could hire even ten other thieves, her task would be doable. There was no way she could move him with a plea—he was selfish, greedy, and lacking in respect for other sentient beings. That was why he'd wanted the Sowon Gold in the first place. And he'd do anything for it. But could she really pay him with it?

She thought of Xiao. Xiao, who had strolled into her family's home and demanded they respect her. Apologize to her. He had risked his life for her—what were her scruples next to that? And surely, once he was free, they could find a way to deal with He Who Walks in Shadow. Xiao was the Night Dragon, as fate smiles!

Even though Nanami made up her mind quickly, she couldn't exactly go knock on He Who Walks in Shadow's door. Like anyone who was hunted, he had the habit of changing his hideout every few decades.

Nanami slurped up the rest of her noodles, and pushed away from the long table so forcefully that her neighbors both looked up at her. Nanami didn't pay them any mind—she needed to find a thief.

The next several evenings, she strolled the streets of Daedo just after dark, when the city was still teeming with the businesses of night—the smells of hot oil and sour pickles slipped out the uncovered windows of restaurants, tipsy men and women clogging the streets agreed to find more private venues, and thieves stole. During this time, she felt increasingly desperate and nervous, to the point that one evening she thought she heard Xiao's voice. He whispered, right in her ear, "Are you well? I'm still here."

She whirled, startling some mortals, but no one stood near her. Yet she heard his voice again. "I tried to escape but it failed, and I can't think of another idea."

"Escape? I'm working on it... I'll steal power from your parents, so you can face them—"

"I'm scared, a bit, I admit. Do you have any suggestions?"

"Yes, you just need to wait. Xiao, where are you? In New Moon Manor? How are you speaking to me?"

There was no reply. Nanami stood in the street a long time, until even the mortals began to eye her curiously. She called it an early night and returned to her inn where she lay awake a long time, sometimes whispering Xiao's name to no avail. She soon doubted her own memory, but the next night she resumed her task with even more determination.

Not just any thief would do, and those sworn to He Who Walked in Shadow didn't exactly wear placards identifying themselves, but a little after a week, Nanami spotted a promising young man.

He wasn't a particularly good thief, for he swaggered down the street and chose too many marks too close together. Of average height but of exceptional build, he had defined features, the smooth skin of youth, and he dressed in embroidered silks. A memorable man, he shouldn't have been able to pass through the crowd the way that he did—none of the mortals whose purses he lifted seemed to notice him at all.

Nanami tried not to get her hopes up, but she followed him through the crowd, and soon he left the wide cobbled avenue for a narrow dirt alley. He was easy to follow, not even bothering to look behind him, so confident he was in whatever magic cloaked him. Luckily, Nanami was immune to such influences because of the essential power inherited from her father.

The handsome thief climbed some rough stone steps at the end of the alley, and then wound through two more alleys so narrow that Nanami had to turn sideways to fit through. He stopped at a dead end, where a small black shrine had been fixed to the wall.

This was no altar to the Night God, but a way point for He Who Walks in Shadow. It was only by coming here, and having a sufficient offering, that one could teleport to the Cave of Shadows—wherever it was now.

Nanami stopped her sneaking and seized the man's arm.

He froze, but as soon as he saw how slight and small she was, his face relaxed in a charming grin.

"What's this then? Looking for some fun?"

He tugged her side bangs with his free hand.

*Idiot. He hasn't even thought about the fact I saw through his magic.*

"Directions, actually."

"Lost?" He stepped closer to her and in the narrow alley, it meant he practically pushed her against the wall.

"No, I've got you. Take me to the Cave."

"The Cave?" His smile faltered before he found it again. "You want to be a thief? You have some potential, following me like you did."

Nanami bit back a snarky retort. "Yes, will you bring me?"

"All right, sweetheart, all right." And they moved in between.

XIAO abandoned the ant form, and the violet bands of power stretched with him.

He was momentarily disoriented, for his vision had changed so drastically, but he soon found his mother's face, rigid with fury. She was not looking at him however, and he followed her gaze to the supplicating disciple who must have carried him in the cup.

Xiao was surprised to recognize the man as Dawa, Zi's third disciple. He was a soft-spoken man with graying hair that he always braided around the crown of his head. Xiao wasn't sure how long Dawa had been a disciple—longer than Xiao had been alive—but he had always looked old, with deep folds in his tanned face. He was kneeling now, his head bowed to the basalt rock and his hands stretched before him.

"I do not tolerate traitors in my domain." Zi's words cracked like a whip.

"Please, divinity, it was a misunderstanding—I sought to rid the garden of a pest—"

Zi barked her scorn. "You're not a fool—you know there are no insects here. Why didn't you immediately bring him to me?"

Though Dawa pressed his palms hard against the stone, Xiao could see tremors in his fingers. Had he known who Xiao was then and tried to help him escape?

Dawa had always been the disciple to let Xiao out of his room after he'd been in isolation as a child, whether it had been a matter of days or weeks. He'd always bowed his head and offered Xiao water and a steamed pork bun.

Xiao had always assumed that he was following Zi's orders but now he wondered when and how he would have been released if Dawa hadn't been there.

"Leave," ordered Zi.

"Divinity, I cannot teleport—"

"Not within the manor grounds. So leave them." She pointed into the open air, past the stone edge of the manor. Dawa stood slowly, his shaking growing more pronounced, and he shuffled in his wood clogs to the edge. There he stood hesitating several moments before he finally jumped.

But he did not fall—instead, bands of violet power wrapped around him, much as they did around Xiao. In mere moments, the man sagged, all of his power drained. And then the bands released him, and he plummeted.

"No," cried Xiao, "He'll die."

"Indeed," replied the being that had birthed him.

Xiao flung his power out, not to bind but to transform. He imagined Dawa becoming a crow just as Xiao had on the Yanou. He didn't see a bird rise though, nor any other indication it had worked. Xiao closed his eyes to try to hold in tears.

He could feel the weight of Zi's gaze on him, so he looked up, meeting her lavender eyes with his own.

"I didn't expect you to restore yourself so quickly. You've been studying." She smiled. "That's fine—it just means more power for us to harvest. Will you walk to your room or be dragged?"

A thousand pointless questions boiled in Xiao's mouth, from *Do you hate me?* to *Why don't you kill me?* He slumped against the stone. "Drag me then."

Zi shrugged. "Suit yourself."

Two disciples appeared, summoned no doubt by some tie to Zi, and each seized one of Xiao's arms. They dragged him through the large amethyst arch set in the black wall that encircled the entire compound.

Xiao stared at his feet as they scraped and bumped along the basalt path. It was better than seeing the disciples who gaped at his passing. When he was in his room, Zi dismissed the servants. "Your father is occupied at present." She walked around the room, examining possible escape routes. "If you choose to become an ant again, you will be caught more quickly with the same result. I suggest you wait here, unless you like being dragged around the manor for everyone to see."

"Moon Goddess, you do realize that I'm not an extension of you, don't you? I'm not a child but an adult with my own thoughts and desires."

"All the world knows of your desires. As for being an adult..." she sniffed. "I'll consider you worthy of conversation when you reach twenty millennia, and not before."

Xiao was so angry that he didn't realize immediately the import of her original words. *Your father is occupied...*

Xiao lay flat on the floor, his arms and legs gently spread. Eyes closed, he found the source of his power was only half-drained. Well, a little more than that because he had transformed himself and maybe another.

But Zi hadn't been able to touch his power that came from Hei. He should act now, before his father came. But how and to what purpose? He had no desire to see another servant plummet off the edge of New Moon Manor, even supposing he made it that far.

Xiao touched the braided ring of Nanami's hair on his pinky with his thumb. He didn't want to summon her, but he wished so badly to speak with her, to hear her voice. To not be alone.

Focusing on Nanami, he imagined the way her lips quirked when she was amused, the way her eyes changed from shy to bold, the way her body had felt in his arms when they had lain together.

*Nanami, can you hear me? Are you well? I'm still here. I tried to escape but it failed, and I can't think of another idea... I'm scared, a bit, I admit. Do you have any suggestions?*

He waited a long time before admitting to himself that it was useless. He knew his parents had some way to communicate with each other over long distances, but whatever they did, it wasn't this.

He moved his thumb off the ring at the base of his pinky and slowly slid it up to the pad. He paused there, finding the faint scar that remained from when he and Jin had exchanged their blood.

Jin wouldn't be in danger if she came here—she might not be able to help him, but his parents would hardly punish her. Would she leave Kunjee behind to teleport though?

At least she would know he was in trouble—maybe she would send Bai...

Xiao tried to focus on Jin, to send out the tendril of power that would summon her, but suddenly his power gushed forth, a broken dam over which he had no control. Usually a summons took less power than a teleport, but it was as if his power couldn't find Jin, and he couldn't stop it from searching for her.

At length, the summons ended, leaving him drained. *At least there's nothing for Hei to take,* he told himself.

Xiao fell asleep on the stone floor, darkness and blood haunting his dreams.

NANAMI and the flirtatious thief reappeared in a dark stone cave, lit by flickering torches mounted on the walls. The air smelled both smoky and damp, and Nanami wondered, not for the first time, why He Who Walks in Shadow felt his Cave of Shadows had to be a literal cave. Not too far away, she could hear the sounds of revelry—boisterous singing, the clink of cups, and roar of laughter.

The thief was smirking at her and holding a raggedy red curtain open. "This is my room."

"How wonderful for you," said Nanami and strode toward the party.

"Hey, hey—I can help you out here, tell you who's who..."

"In exchange for what? Sex?"

His cheeks turned ruddy. He sputtered. "Well, it could be fun—"

"It could be, but I'm not interested, thanks." She didn't break her stride.

He settled his hand on her arm, his face genuinely

concerned. "Forget the sex, then. But—are you sure you want to walk in there alone? It could be bad for you."

Three months ago, Nanami would have silently shrugged off his hand. Even now, she was suspicions of his wish to help.

But she found herself thinking that if Xiao were here, he'd listen and smile at this fool. That wasn't her, but she brought herself to say, "It will be bad for me, but worse for you if you come with me. Silly boy, I'm Nanami the Thief, He Who Walks in Shadow's first and most hated disciple."

His mouth dropped open.

"So if anyone asks you, I suggest denying any knowledge of me."

This time he let her go as she strode into the thieves' den.

No one paid Nanami any attention when she entered the room. It was crowded, forty or so beings, varying from an elderly woman in raggedy Jeevantian silks to a group of young men dressed in Bandoan scholar's linens. And yet there was a commonality in the group, from their quick, shifting eyes to their deft, smooth movements, even under the influence of alcohol. These were the Shadow Thieves, the disciples collected by He Who Walks in Shadow after his falling out with Nanami.

Looking at the group, Nanami wondered if she had erred coming here. If she was able to persuade a dozen of these thieves to aid her, she needn't involve He Who Walks in Shadow at all—

Nanami felt the whisper of air against her neck, and she just caught a hand before its dagger pressed against her artery. She met her former master's coal black eyes.

His lips curled angrily, stretching the pock marks of his otherwise unremarkable face. Despite the bitterness of his expression, he looked like a youth, younger even than Xiao, though Nanami had long believed him to be about the same age as her grandfather, the Moon Deer. He was shockingly slight, though Nanami knew him to be far stronger than he looked, and he only reached her own nose in height. As Nanami took this in, he used his other hand to fling poison needles at her.

# The God of War and
# the Golden Phoenix

JIN paced around Xiao's room, eyeing the black iron bars uneasily. The whole place was like a prison. She glanced back at Xiao, slumped on the hard basalt floor by the foot of his bed, tears coursing down his cheeks and horrible tension contorting his usually handsome features. His left hand was strangely posed, his thumb and his pinky pressing so hard into each other that the pads were white, while his other three fingers strained outward, as if in great pain.

She returned to his side and tried to touch him, as she had a few minutes earlier, but her hands simply passed through him again. She huddled next to him, trying to hug him, an odd business when she could not feel him at all.

"Xiao," she murmured over and over, "what's wrong? What has happened?" If he heard her at all though, he gave no sign of it. Suddenly his hand relaxed, and the world became a dark golden haze. Jin slowly realized she was seeing bright light through closed lids.

She opened her eyes and found herself cradled by the softest down feathers and bathed with the rich gold of late summer. She still wore the simple red tunic that she had made from the blood river, but someone had applied moss compacts to her wounds from the Xuezei. Above her grew an araliya tree, with shiny green leaves and spiraled white flowers. Those sweet, citrusy blooms seduced her into breathing more deeply, and her confused worry about Xiao faded somewhat under their influence.

Had she been dreaming then? And yet it had not felt like any dream she knew. When she fell asleep—when she fell asleep—

She didn't remember falling asleep at all. She remembered the blood river, and making a boat, and then...

Now that she was awake and rested, she realized that seeing Aka and Gang and Neela must have been a dream. She shuddered and tried to convince herself all the cruelty was simply from her deepest fears—not a true reflection of those immortals. The cuts—she must have been attacked by the Xuezei again... But then, why was she here? Where was here?

She tried to sit up but sank deeper into the soft down bed. She blinked at the feathers and lifted one to examine more closely. The golden light that bathed her came from the feathers themselves, as if they were tiny suns.

She remembered the Golden Phoenix attacking in her

dream—could that have been real? Had it saved her from the Xuezei and taken her to its nest? She struggled to escape the down.

A strong hand wrapped around her arm and hauled her to her feet. Jin looked up and up to find the face of her helper, only to utter a soft cry of alarm when she found it.

The creature seemed to be made of plants. There were shiny nutshells in place of eyes, and red berries formed a parody of lips. Its skin was pink petals, and small wildflowers from fawnlilies to violets grew like a mane down its back.

*Don't be afraid, flower. I mean you no harm.*

"Ah, thank you, I'm sorry, I'm just a little confused at present."

*That's understandable. I haven't seen any of your kind in almost twenty millennia.* The creature's berry lips shifted—Jin realized it was smiling at her. *I have many questions for you, but first you must eat.*

The creature released her arm, and Jin took a step, only to find herself a bit dizzy. It noticed her distress immediately, and its strong arm wrapped around her waist in support. Jin let her hand rest on its cattail fingers. Despite its strangeness, this creature set her at ease. She reminded herself that it was Aka who trapped it here, rightly or wrongly, and it might view her as an enemy when it learned that.

"How do I call you?" she asked it as they crossed a flower-speckled field that could have been from Earth.

*I am the Koch-ssi. I lived on Po until I was trapped here. And you are a child of Neela.*

Jin's eyes widened in surprise. "She is my grandmother—how did you know?"

*I take care of all plants, and I can feel that you are one, if only in part.*

A little nervous, Jin tried to make her tone merely curious as she asked, "Can you read my whole nature?"

The Koch-ssi's lips parted in a silent laugh. *My essence is not white. I know only plants.* Its face shifted, somehow conveying solemnity. *The Underworld is not a good place for plants,* it scolded her, *for there is no sunlight here, and we need it to survive. You are lucky that we found you, else you would have wilted and died, even if the bloodsuckers hadn't targeted you.*

"Oh—sunlight!" Jin felt like an idiot, and adrenaline rushed through her, far too late to matter. She rarely thought about her need for sunlight, for it was ubiquitous on Earth and in the Heavens. "That's why I felt so sick. I could have died!" Jin realized.

The Koch-ssi nodded placidly beside her. *The Underworld is not meant for such as us. I too would die without the Phoenix.*

"The Phoenix?" Jin echoed. "Was it with you? I dreamed…"

*Indeed. My survival here depends on it, for its feathers make sunlight.*

Those bright gold feathers. "So I was sleeping on its down then?"

*Yes.*

"Thank you, and my gratitude to the Phoenix."

The Koch-ssi gestured ahead of them. *Thank it yourself.*

It was a sign of Jin's hunger that the first thing she registered was a peony-laden table, punctuated by heaping dishes. Her stomach rumbled its approval.

Then she looked past the table and saw the Golden Phoenix.

GANG had been Bai's student for ten millennia and the closest thing he'd ever had to family. He had looked the same age as Bai ever since his beard had come in, but he now looked decidedly older, that full beard more grey than anything else. Gang had always been a big man, but he was broader and thicker now, a bull rather than a stallion. His face had escaped Bai's recognition—besides those luminous eyes, it was dominated by deep crow's feet and a permanently furrowed brow.

Another Sun Guard appeared to the side and then another. Comparing it with the way Salaana's disciples had appeared simultaneously, Bai wondered if it were urgency or a disregard for theater that had Gang's arriving one by one.

Gang held the Sun Sword, a broadsword of gleaming gold with red tracery, before him, so Bai kept the Starlight Sword out as well. Gang did not seem inclined to speak yet, running his eyes over the fallen justice disciples and then his half-sister, who still lay in a faint by Bai's foot.

Bai tried to match Gang's patience, but, by the time twenty Sun Guards had appeared, fear drove him to ask, "And do you also come to destroy the gate you stand beneath, Gang?"

Gang's brows lifted upward, much as Bai's did when he was surprised. He stepped out from under the gate, and at last sheathed the Sun Sword. He clasped his right fist in his left hand and bowed to Bai.

Bai sheathed the Starlight Sword as well, even though it left him feeling painfully vulnerable as he had drained his magic. But to hold it ready, when Gang was bowing, would expose how weak he felt.

When Gang straightened, he said, "Bai-shifu. When I learned

my sister had come here, I followed to stop any such destruction. I apologize for my silence. I had not expected to see you here, and although it is obvious you are not on my sister's side, I didn't assume that meant you were on mine."

Salaana whimpered. Bai glanced at her and saw she had regained consciousness. "She is dying. She needs to see Haraa soon, if she is to have a chance."

She gritted her teeth. "You don't scare me."

She hadn't noticed Gang yet, it seemed. She attempted yet another lightning bolt, but it barely sparked as it left her fingertips.

"Salaana!" barked Gang and hurried to her side. Bai wasn't sure if the bark was out of concern for her health or in reprimand for the lightning.

She looked at her brother at last and grimaced. "You are lucky he was here, brother. Otherwise the gate would be gone already."

"Salaana, you need to go to Haraa, let one of my guards—"

She snorted. "You think to get rid of me so lightly? I won't go unless you drag me yourself."

Gang's lips compressed so that they were hidden under his bushy beard and his eyes closed briefly. "And what exactly do you think we're trying to do here that you must be privy to?"

"An alliance—plotting—" she snarled. Bai suspected that pain was largely responsible for the contortion of her face.

"Do you really want to discuss this in front of so many witnesses?" Gang muttered. At that, Bai glanced around the peak once more. There were now at least hundred Sun Guards; they seemed to be debating whether or not they should give aid to the justice disciples.

"It's not just the Goddess of Justice who needs aid," Bai pointed out. "Perhaps the Sun Guards..."

Gang looked around. He turned back to Salaana. "Well, can you agree to that much? My disciples will help the Light Hands return to the Sun Palace and seek care."

Salaana's anger was palpable, but she cared deeply about her disciples. "Fine. Lift me so I can address my Hands."

Gang scooped her in his arms and created a chair with his arms. Bai respected the strength she summoned to project her voice across the peak.

"You all have served me well. You will return with the Sun Guards to the Sun Palace and have your wounds tended. This is now a private matter between my brother and myself."

Despite her efforts, Bai wasn't sure that all her disciples—the Light Hands—processed her words. Too many of them were still living in their pain. But no one resisted as Gang directed the Sun Guards to escort the Light Hands, and soon there were only a few Sun Guards remaining—Gang must have brought more disciples than Salaana. He sent all but one of them away, the first to have appeared, and asked Salaana once again to go to Haraa's.

"Send him for my Right Hand, and I will go with her when she comes," Salaana decided.

"That will be an hour, at least," Gang objected.

"My death isn't that imminent."

Gang looked at Bai for confirmation. Bai hesitated—he wouldn't mind Gang dragging Salaana off now. But if he lied, and Haraa corrected it, Gang might be harder to deal with. "She isn't bleeding and there's no infection, so yes, she could probably live for a few days as she is, in great pain."

Salaana snorted.

"Fetch the Hand," Gang told his man, who teleported away.

With that, Gang set Salaana on the ground and began pulling things out of a small pouch. They were all miniaturized, just as Bai had taught him to travel, and he grew them quickly. Soon a beautifully carved yellow wood table was set with a gold tea set. Gang began stuffing the pot with snow.

"The Goddess can't drink anything," Bai warned, "Her intestines are cut and cauterized."

Salaana grinned at him, a rabid expression. "Lucky me— now I have an excuse to avoid the nasty liquid grass Gang always drinks."

Bai seated himself across from her. He didn't like her, but he respected her grit.

He looked at Gang, who was now heating the pot with magical fire.

*Are we enemies or friends?* Bai wondered. *The last time I saw Gang, he persuaded me to go to Cheolmun Pass. To die.*

Gang didn't seem upset to see him now, but Bai knew there were layers to his student that he hadn't seen.

Gang added a fine green powder to the tea and sat silently as it steeped. Salaana, despite her pain, waited patiently as well, and it was Bai who shifted restlessly on the snow. It seemed the past few months of being with youths like Jin and Xiao had given him a sense of urgency.

Eventually Gang poured the tea and handed Bai a cup. As Bai sipped, Gang finally broached the topic that hung over them.

"So Jin entered the Underworld?"

"Presumably. She passed through the gate a few hours ago,

wearing Kunjee. The key your father made."

"Rumor said you were travelling with her?"

Bai nodded, glancing at Salaana to see her reaction as well. "Yes, and I had intended to accompany her into the Underworld. But I somehow misjudged the key—only Jin disappeared through the gate, though we walked together."

"And Salaana? You came with the intention of trapping Jin in the Underworld? I realize you do not answer to me, but perhaps you would tell me why...?"

Salaana deliberately drew the moment out. "What do you already know?"

"Very little," Gang admitted. "I was informed by my captain that you and your first hundred disciples had teleported to the Gate to the Underworld. Rumor said you intended to destroy it. I decided I wanted to know more."

Salaana covered the ghastly scar that peeked through her torn robes almost absently. "Bai could probably explain better than I, since I only heard what happened from Karana." She turned dried-blood eyes to Bai and quirked crimson lips. "Why don't you tell Gang what happened with Cheng?"

Bai squeezed his own cup tighter, trying to decide which secrets to keep and which to share. He looked at the vermillion gate at Gang's back; these decisions were Jin's to make. And what he said might very well determine if that gate remained for her to return through.

So he only revealed what Karana already knew. "I found Cheng enclosed in turquoise, buried on the slopes of Taitou. I brought him—still enclosed in the rock—to Tsuku, where Jin and Karana were, as well as the Moon Deer's household. Jin melted away the rock, and we found Cheng in a desiccated, comatose state. Jin restored his physical health, but he did not regain consciousness. Karana vowed to protect Cheng and brought him to Haraa. A few days later, Jin and I flew here, with the intention of entering the Underworld. And I already told you what happened then."

Salaana didn't seem quite pleased with his recounting; he supposed she had been hoping he'd reveal new information.

"That doesn't tell me why you wish to destroy the gate," Gang told his sister.

"The kind of power that Jin showed reviving Cheng is excessive—just like her brother, the God of Belief, she has more power than any one being should. She should remain in the Underworld with the immortal creatures."

"So you would imprison her just for existing?" Gang said, his voice dangerously quiet.

Bai was reminded of a youthful Gang, when he first came to Bai for training. He had only been three thousand years old, and a different immortal had shown up each week with the intention of killing him. Some mistakenly thought they could somehow steal his raw power for themselves; others feared his tyranny when he finished maturing. And of course, his title as God of War was hardly suited to set their minds at ease.

Bai had easily dealt with all would be assassins, but one night he had heard Gang crying beneath his blanket.

"It's not my fault," he had told Bai. "I didn't choose to be like this, or to be born."

Bai had held Gang in his arms and rubbed the boy's back. "When people act in fear, it brings forth the worst of them. Act from hope," he had advised the boy.

And he thought, perhaps that was why he had been so drawn

to Jin. Because she refused to be fearful and cowardly, even when she had reason to be so.

Salaana bristled at Gang's question. "She chose to enter the Underworld—"

"She didn't choose to stay there," Gang growled. "Surely it's not unjust to save a man from a prison of rock and to heal him?" His beard quivered.

Salaana pressed her hand more firmly against her abdomen. "You've never bothered with Jin before. Why now?"

Gang's brows arched. "Did you try to imprison her before?"

Salaana shook her head impatiently. "Someone recently told me that you seduced our stepmother. Is Jin your daughter?"

Gang scoffed. "Where on Earth did you hear such a thing?"

Salaana shrugged. "My sister-in-law. You aren't denying it. Does Father know?"

Gang stared her down, but Salaana's gaze didn't falter.

Bai was surprised that Gang didn't simply lie. Belatedly, he realized it was because Gang didn't trust him and didn't want to offer any confirmation. Bai laughed out loud at the ridiculousness of it all, and both siblings turned their glares to him.

"Does it matter?" he asked. "Whether he's her father or not, he's protecting her route of return. Isn't that all you need to know?"

Salaana's red lips twisted, and she looked back at Gang. "You know, dear brother, daughters don't always love their fathers. I would know."

"One can only choose the love one gives, Salaana, not the love one receives. I'm surprised you haven't figured that out by now."

She bared her teeth at him.

"So now what?" she demanded. "You two are allies?" To Bai, "You're going to support him as the next Sun Emperor?"

"I had not intended on involving myself in your power struggle at all," Bai admitted.

Her eyes narrowed, and Bai thought she didn't believe him. "Then what brought you off your mountain? Why now?"

"You already know. I wished to accompany Jin into the Underworld."

"If you wanted to go to the Underworld, you could have any time in the last eighteen millennia," objected Salaana. "There's no better place to protect the key, after all."

Bai shrugged.

"Deny it all you want; you are siding with Gang and are thus my enemy," she declared.

Bai arched a brow. "If you had already decided that, why ask?"

A short woman in an indigo kimono appeared a few feet from them. Bai startled. "Ichimi?" he asked.

Ichimi's pretty face froze with indecision. She glanced at Salaana, then gave Bai the barest nod. "First. My love, are you well?" she touched Salaana's arm.

Salaana's face wholly transformed, softening. Even her eyes changed from dried-blood to the warm-rust of a deer's coat. "I will be fine, love. I will transport us to Haraa's."

Ichimi nodded, casting one last uncertain look at Bai and Gang.

When the women were gone, Gang sighed heavily.

"Bai-shifu, you don't need to remain here. I will make sure the gate is protected."

Bai spread his hands before him on the table, sorting through his thoughts. "Daughters don't always love their fathers, and fathers don't always protect their daughters. You poisoned Jin with godsbane."

Gang's gaze jerked up, and he met Bai's eyes. After a moment he smirked. "I forgot you did that—state even vague suspicions in hopes you'll trigger something that you can read for truth. I vowed to do whatever was in my power to protect Jin. But..."

Gang stood and drew the massive broadsword tied at his waist. Gripping it in both hands, he faced Bai head on.

GLOWING rich gold, the Phoenix seemed to be a creature of fire and light rather than feathers and bone, though its down had felt solid enough. It lifted its head at their approach, its long neck arching higher than Jin was tall. Its face was sharp and triangular, with the sharp beak of a chicken and a flaring crest. Its tail at least doubled its length with long, elaborate feathers that reminded Jin of a peacock's tail, yet were far more flexible and almost cat-like in the way they moved.

"Are you well, little one?" Its voice was burning wood, filled with a deep crackling and, despite its pleasant warmth, potential danger.

Jin swallowed. "Thanks to you both. Just a bit hungry."

The Koch-ssi urged her to sit and waved its cattail hands over the table, urging her to help herself. Jin surveyed the table, feeling overwhelmed. There were wooden plates of pickled fiddlehead ferns, loose green leaves, little seed cakes piled in a pyramid, and unfamiliar roots, washed and chopped. Then there were carved bowls of insects, pupae, and larva, all thankfully dead but wholly ungarnished and mainly raw. Lifting a set of wooden chopsticks, Jin started with the ferns, which had the benefit of being passingly familiar. Her mortal painting teacher of the Crescent Moon had been exceedingly fond of fiddleheads. When they proved shockingly delicious, with tender leaves and crunchy stalks, she took some of the leaves and roots. These too she found flavorful and fresh, and the seed cakes, while a little dry, were filling and had a pleasant nutty aftertaste.

"Eat some of these, little one," and the Phoenix, using its beak, buried her small plate beneath shiny brown pupae. "You need meat after losing all that blood."

Jin forced a smile. She had eaten insects before, both roasted and deep fried, but she had always despised the way their little shells got caught in her teeth. And never had anyone served her with their mouth. She picked up one medium-sized pupa between her chopsticks and popped it between her lips. She chewed determinedly, telling herself that the squishy innards were a pleasant contradiction to the crunchy outer shell. The taste was fine—vaguely spicy.

The Phoenix clucked approvingly, and the Koch-ssi ducked its head—silently laughing, Jin suspected.

Suddenly one of the peonies decorating the table stood up and said, "If you don't like them, leave them for us."

It was a tiny person with dark green skin, leaf-like hands, and large fuchsia petals on its head. It smiled at her, its tiny black eyes sparkling, and it stuffed a pupa much larger than the one Jin had chosen into its suddenly gaping mouth. Jin swallowed the pupa so that she could speak.

"Hello. What are you?"

Another peony-person jumped in front of her. "Well, that's just rude. What are *you*?"

"I'm an immortal—the Goddess of Beauty. My name is Jin." The offended creature sniffed, but the other one laughed, a funny sound like rustling leaves.

"We're Mudanren," said the first, waving at the table. Sure enough, now that Jin knew to look, all the peonies were in fact Mudanren. It was a little hard for Jin to read their expressions, but the way dozens of black eyes watched her, she supposed they were curious.

"I don't know anything about you," Jin confessed. "All of you were locked here long before I was born."

The friendly Mudanren plopped down next to Jin's plate and ate another pupa. Jin selected another seed cake for herself, though the Phoenix clicked its beak in reprimand.

"We eat insects. A long time ago, we lived in gardens, and gardeners left us sweets to thank us for keeping pests away from their plants."

"And because we look beautiful," added the prudish one, fluffing its petals.

"You're very lovely," agreed Jin.

"Yes—so you'd better remember us now, if you're going to go around calling yourself the Goddess of Beauty."

"Absolutely," said Jin.

*Now the Mudanren live in my garden,* the Koch-ssi explained. *We consider the Gray Realm ours—the Phoenix's, mine, and the Mudanren's.*

"The Gray Realm?" asked Jin.

The Phoenix unfolded one wing, unleashing sparks, and

gestured upward.

Jin looked up and found a gray—well, it wasn't like any sky she knew, but that seemed more apt than ceiling.

"The Underworld is divided into many realms. Ours is the most suitable for us, though it resembles a perpetually overcast day. You came from the Blood River, the Xuezei's territory, as you know.

"I have been wanting to ask you, since it's come up, how you came to be there at all?"

"Well—that was where I emerged when I passed through the gate."

All the Mudanren began to chatter quickly, clearly excited.

*You came through the red torii gate made by the Sun God?* asked the Koch-ssi.

"Yes," Jin admitted.

"But why?" asked the Golden Phoenix. "Why would you come here?"

"I'm seeking a black peony," Jin said.

*A black peony—you seek to save a life already condemned.*

"Yes—do you grow them in your garden?"

The Koch-ssi shook her head. *The black peonies cannot be cultivated. There is only one place they grow—on the Lonely Island in the Sea of Souls.*

"Where—"

"That's not the question that needs to be answered first," interrupted the Phoenix. "Before we tell you how to find the peonies, you must tell us whose life you seek to save."

"I WASN'T sure how." Gang turned the sword down, pointed

it into the Earth and knelt behind it. "I—I have made many mistakes, shifu. I'm sorry."

Bai pressed his hands together behind his back. This was a familiar scene in some ways. How many times had a youthful Gang knelt before him, frustrated by a lack of progress or repeated failure?

And yet Bai found himself unsure how to respond. Was Gang his student or the father of the woman he was courting? How could he be both above and below Bai in the social hierarchy? Bai wished he could summon his lost obliviousness to such considerations, but he cared too much. Why did he care so much?

His eyes went to the tall red gate which separated him from Jin. He looked back at Gang, kneeling in the snow, petitioning as if Bai had answers for him.

Bai offered his hand. "Please, stand up."

Gang took his hand and rose. They used to be the same height, but Gang was slightly shorter now, his experiences weighing him down.

Even though Bai felt overwhelmed by this moment, he had imagined this conversation many times on White Mountain. He had initially felt betrayed that Gang had sent him to Cheolmun Pass, that he hadn't told Bai of Aka's battle with the Golden Phoenix. If he had seen Gang at Aka's court when he had come to fetch Kunjee, he might have lashed at him in anger.

But he had let go of that long ago. Aka was Gang's father. Bai had been his mentor. Gang had felt loyalty to both of them and had sometimes been pulled in different directions. And those years before Cheolmun Pass, Bai had been spinning out of control, eagerly seeking the next battle, the next threat to his life, his next chance to rest in peace for eternity. When their wishes had been in conflict, why wouldn't Gang have supported Aka's?

When Bai had finally realized the only thing stopping him from finding that peace while living was himself, he had forgiven Gang. There was nothing Gang could have said or done—it was something Bai had to work out for himself. And yet he realized the words he had chosen in his garden, soothed by the scent of jasmine and the chirrup of the mountain spring, weren't the right ones. To claim sole responsibility would demean Gang's sincerity and his own heartache.

So he said, "You were right that I was seeking death—I was glad to go to Cheolmun Pass. It was only when I survived the onslaught there that I realized if I wanted my life to change, I had to change.

"I did feel angry and hurt that you did not tell me of Aka's plans, but after millennia of reflection, I think I understand why, and why you don't apologize for it now.

"As for any other sins you feel you have committed, they aren't my business and I have no absolution to offer. But, I will confess that I have no right to judge anyone for poor choices when it comes to falling in love and acting upon those feelings.

"What I wish for now is to converse openly and bluntly about the state of the world and to see if we cannot be allies going forward."

Gang nodded slowly. "I will tell you my story then, from that day at Cheolmun Pass. It must be abbreviated of course, but I will try not to leave out anything important."

"I—" JIN hesitated. She didn't want to tell these creatures that she was trying to save Aka. Though they seemed far more benevolent than the Xuezei, Jin didn't fool herself that they were harmless, and how could they bear Aka anything but enmity?

She wished she knew what powers they had. Could any of them tell if she lied? Perhaps she could tell the truth and mislead them at the same time, the way Bai always did. "I seek to save my grandfather."

"And his name?"

Jin's hand bunched in her tunic where it lay on her thigh.

*Don't lie to it, flower. You don't want it to burn you.*

Jin's eyes darted to the Koch-ssi and read the tension in its reed arms and the arch of its root neck.

"Aka."

"The First God." Smoke, dark and acrid, seeped from the Phoenix's mouth and Jin wondered if her truth would have the same consequence as a lie.

The Phoenix rose to its feet and spread its wings. Might she be as immune to its fire as her own? It was obviously a yellow creature, and so their natures were not inimical to each other...

The Mudanren leapt off the table to huddle at the Koch-ssi's feet, trembling.

*Shh, little flowers. The Golden Phoenix will not hurt you.* It looked at Jin. *Or you. It is simply angry.*

Indeed, the Phoenix paced away from the table before launching itself into the air and soaring up to the monotonous gray overhead. It left a path of fire in its wake, a blaze of gold against the cool sky that was both beautiful and threatening.

Jin turned to the Koch-ssi. "I'm sorry—I know—" She

swallowed and tried again. "Perhaps you think he deserves to die, for his unfair imprisonment of you."

The Koch-ssi cocked its head. *Deserves to die?* It shook its large head slowly, sending a waft of sweet wildflowers toward Jin. *You were born, but immortals like myself and your grandfather gained our immortality through our sheer will to persist. I rose up in a garden just before the first frost because death terrified me. It still does—I want so passionately to see the next day, the next sunrise, the next bloom.*

*So I would never say someone deserves to die. But this place...*

*It is indeed a prison. So we hate him for putting us here.*

The Koch-ssi resumed eating, seemingly oblivious to the fiery display in the air.

"So what will happen now?" asked Jin. "I suppose you are no longer willing to help me..."

The Koch-ssi shrugged. *I never had much help to offer. As long as you stay here in the Gray Realm, I am willing to care for you, but I will not leave here for the Lonely Isle. As for the Golden Phoenix, it is a volatile creature. It may yet offer you aid.*

Without much else to do, Jin also resumed eating. If she was to leave here, she might as well eat while she could.

The Phoenix stayed in the sky, burning golden paths, and eventually the Mudanren stopped huddling around the Koch-ssi to eat as well.

It was the Mudanren who led her back to the down nest beneath the araliya tree. The friendly one and its testy friend stayed, playing with Jin's hair and asking her about the Sun Court. Even though they were only half a foot tall, they weren't wholly unlike Yeppeun and Luye, even down to their personalities, and she felt at ease.

"Do you have names?" she asked.

"Names? Of course, we have a name, did you forget already? We're Mudanren!"

The other's little green face squished up in amusement. "We are all Mudanren. We don't have names beyond that. But gardeners used names to distinguish between us. If you'd like, you may call me Wu Zhe."

The first crossed its arms, like folding two leaves together. "Then call me Tiao Xian. Why are names so important to things like you anyway?"

"I suppose because our own names are so integral to our sense of self, it's hard for us to understand that others might not feel the same way," Jin said.

Wu Zhe and Tiao Xian resumed playing with her hair and she fell asleep still mumbling answers to their questions.

She was awakened by heat and fire, flames licking her face. She sat up in alarm, but soon realized that although her tunic would not survive, she herself was not burning. The yellow flames did her no more harm than the dress of flame that she had made.

The Golden Phoenix watched her through the flames until they had faded. Only its golden down, her tessen, and Jin herself, clad in naught but her gold chain with its two pendants—Kunjee and the peacock from Aka—survived the flames. The Phoenix said, "You are a child of Noran, are you not?"

Jin nodded. "My father was the son of Noran and Aka."

The Phoenix sighed. "She loved him fiercely, though I never understood why. Your father is Sunlight Glints on Steel?"

"Yes," Jin said.

The Phoenix mulled this over, rustling its wings and preening its tail. Jin grew impatient and wrapped her hands in the Phoenix's soft down. When she withdrew them, she was holding gilt robes, patterned like feathers and with swirling flames along the hems. The Phoenix stopped its preening to watch her dress.

"Your creation is beautiful. You are perhaps deserving of your title." It shook its head, and its crest danced.

"I cannot harm you because I loved Noran. The Koch-ssi will not harm you because you are a flower. The Mudanren like you.

"So if you still wish to travel to the Lonely Isle on some foolish quest to save the most selfish immortal I ever met, then I won't stop you. If you wear that dress, the sunlight in it will nourish you.

"And if you forsake your quest, then you will be welcome here in the Gray Realm."

Impulsively, Jin leapt forward and wrapped her arms around the base of the Phoenix's neck. "Thank you. I shall repay you someday."

It clucked unhappily. "A foolish promise to make. Ask the Mudanren to guide you. They can find any plant, be it in the Heavens, Earth, or here."

"Thank you, I will."

The Phoenix let her hug it a minute more before it pulled back and flew up into the endless gray again.

Wu Zhe leapt out of the araliya tree where it had been hiding. It latched onto Jin's golden skirt and climbed to her belt where it tucked itself. "I will go with you," it told her.

"Oh, fate, I had better go too then," announced Tiao Xian,

who jumped from the tree onto Jin's shoulder. "Otherwise who will keep you two dirt brains from wandering into the Sea of Souls and becoming mud?"

Jin smiled. "Thank you both."

"We aren't ready to leave yet," Tiao Xian said. "Or were you planning on heading out without supplies from the Koch-ssi?"

Jin didn't bother defending her intentions but instead followed the Mudanren's instructions.

They directed her to the Koch-ssi's garden bower. It was a little difficult to walk through, for gourd-bearing vines rioted underfoot amidst clustered ferns and shoots. Rather than a fence, the garden was contained by fruit trees that supported the largest, roundest, deepest indigo grapes that Jin had ever seen. This improbable symbiosis was clearly magic, and Jin surveyed the garden in a daze, so overwhelmed by textures and colors that she initially missed the Koch-ssi itself. Jin jerked in surprise when it stepped directly in front of her.

It threaded its cattail fingers through Jin's long hair and gave her a sad smile. *You are leaving us then?*

Jin nodded.

*I can't claim to understand the bonds of family, as I have none and can have none, but I have some familiarity with them. So I shall not be disappointed in your decision, though it makes little sense to me.*

It looked at the two Mudanren, still tucked in Jin's belt.

*And you will go with her?*

They chirped their agreement.

The Koch-ssi led them through its garden and swept back a curtain of honeysuckle to reveal the boat Jin made from the Blood River, docked in a river of cloudy gray water. *I have packed your boat with supplies. You can follow the rivers to the Sea of Souls, and there—well, the Mudanren will tell you.*

Jin nodded and thanked the creature again.

The three of them boarded the boat, and soon a fast current was carrying them down the river.

Without the sun to mark the days, Jin soon lost track of time, but the Mudanren helped her adopt a meal and sleeping schedule as they navigated the strange rivers of the Underworld. They explained to her how these rivers connected most—but not all—the realms of the Underworld. Unfamiliar and curious shores slipped by them—there were crystals of impossible height, trees of stone, and music that made Jin shiver. They never stopped, instead relying on the bounty that the Koch-ssi had packed them.

It was at least a week, possibly three, before their boat was set spinning in an impossibly blue sea with rainbows dancing on its surface. The sky became smooth white and the air shifted from the sweet scent of the Gray Realm to a salty tang that Jin had last smelled aboard the Yanou.

"We're here, we're here!" cheered her Mudanren guides.

Jin laughed, for it was truly gorgeous and because she was starting to feel the Underworld was not such a fearsome place after all. She stood and scanned the sea.

A few hundred feet away, something glinted and moved in the water. Jin shaded her eyes and leaned against the side of the boat, trying to identify it.

It was slicing through the waves at a shockingly rapid pace, and when it was perhaps a hundred feet from them, Jin abruptly recognized it as a silver fin, taller than Jin herself.

"Wu Zhe? Tiao Xian? There's a very large fin coming toward

us..."

The Mudanren both stopped their dance to look.

"That," said Tiao Xian unhappily, "is the Sea Serpent."

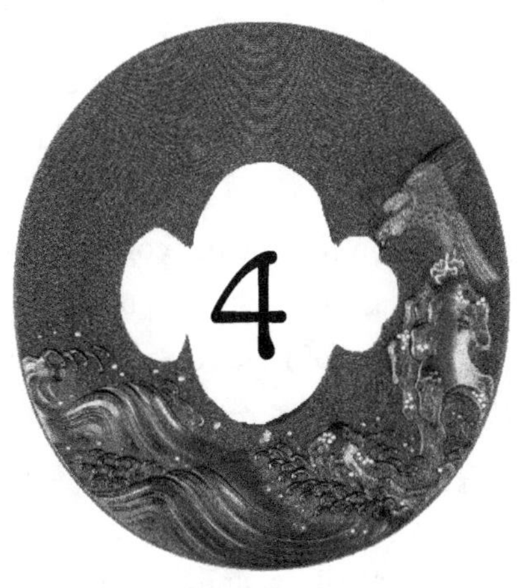

# Of Steel and Wonder

"IT will destroy our boat," warned Wu Zhe. "The Sea Serpent always destroys any boats it finds."

Tiao Xian squeaked in alarm and dove into Jin's belt. "I can't swim!"

Jin had heard only one story about the Sea Serpent. "Then we will ride it," she declared, with far more confidence than she felt.

Wu Zhe turned to face her with wide eyes. "Only the First ever rode the Sea Serpent," it told her.

Jin hadn't known that, and Wu Zhe's awe of Bai secretly intimidated her. But she forged ahead. "He did it by controlling the foaming water around it until it bowed to his wishes. This sea is cerulean, so it will obey me."

*Maybe. If I can figure it out. After all, I still haven't changed into a bird.*

Jin thought about that a moment. Could she change into a bird—an eagle perhaps, so that she could still carry the Mudanren?

But she felt more confident about controlling the water than she did about becoming a bird. She stepped close to the rail and parted the water in front of the Sea Serpent. It was shockingly easy—the crystalline blue water seemed to call to her, begging for her guidance. The parting created a high spray and revealed the pointed face of the Sea Serpent.

Its skin was lightest silver, and its mouth gaped. Its fangs were like steel spikes each the length of Jin's legs—which were quavering. She squeezed the side of the boat to keep herself steady, oddly aware of the rough grain against her palms.

"Why did you do that?" squawked Tiao Xian, practically tearing her belt in its anxiety.

Wu Zhe's grip was as fierce as its partner's, but it said calmly, "Hush, let her work."

"And why did *you* want to guide her?" Tiao Xian demanded. Wu Zhe tsked.

Jin was inclined to agree with Tiao Xian—why had she parted the waves? She had felt the instinctive need to see her opponent's face, but it was horrifying and if anything, parting the water let the serpent move even faster toward them.

As if she were a puppeteer and the water her puppet, Jin swung her hands together and lifted the serpent up so that it was many feet above the rest of the sea. The Sea Serpent was far bigger than the Golden Phoenix. Jin guessed that it was nearly a hundred feet long. It screamed in fury, thrashing wildly, and Jin looked past its gigantic teeth to its mad eyes.

Silver and blue, they rolled in its head like those of a horse whose been startled and seeks to crush the threat beneath its hooves.

"Why, it's afraid of the boat," Jin said in surprise.

"Who cares? I like the boat!"

"No, we need to let it destroy it so it can calm down."

"I understand you want to calm it," said Wu Zhe carefully, "but what about us while it's smashing our ride to little pieces?"

In answer, Jin put Wu Zhe in her belt next to Tiao Xian. "Hold on tight," she said, before climbing onto the rail of her boat and jumping off.

Both Mudanren screamed, but a swell rose to meet them before they even reached the sea. The tang of salt was overpowering as spray hit Jin's face—but the wave felt solid beneath her feet. She rode it a safe distance away before she released the Sea Serpent. It barreled into the small river boat, and the splintering of wood uncomfortably loud as it broke in half. The serpent began beating the wreckage with its tail, making Jin suspect its pretty silver scales were akin to armor.

"The food!" yelled Tiao Xian, and Jin quickly began pulling the crates packed by the Koch-ssi out of harm's way.

Once they had the three remaining crates, Wu Zhe asked, "Why are we sticking around? Can't you just bring us to the isle like this, floating on the surface of the water?"

Jin flushed. She probably could—it didn't take much power to control the waves. It seemed like the easier route but...

She imagined telling Bai that she had also rode the Sea Serpent. Only the First and the Goddess of Beauty could tame the fierce creature... Then when people commented that she was too young for him, when he assumed that look of infinite patience because he realized the depth of her ignorance, there would still be this. The fact she had accomplished one of his famous feats.

It was so immature that Jin couldn't admit her ambition to the Mudanren, but she couldn't give it up either. "I'd like to try to ride the Sea Serpent," she said blandly.

Tiao Xian groaned. "You shouldn't have taunted her," it said to Wu Zhe. "These things are all about pride. Now she has to prove that she can ride it."

Jin's flush deepened. She hadn't realized it would be so obvious.

Wu Zhe patted its friend's petals. "She's young. Let us be tolerant of her idiosyncrasies."

That was almost enough to send Jin on without addressing the Sea Serpent, but the last bits of her boat drifted away then, no bigger than the Mudanren, and she wanted to at least speak to the serpent.

The violent thrashing of the Sea Serpent calmed, and its eyes stopped rolling in its head. "Hello," Jin called to it. The serpent swam leisurely over to where Jin waited, a wholly different creature than the one they had seen earlier, and soon they were encircled by its argent coils.

*I dislike boats*, came the serpent's silent voice, in a massive understatement, and Jin marveled at the change in the creature.

"Well, we all have something that sets us off, don't we?" said Jin, and she could feel the Mudanren shaking their heads.

*You are a being of great power, to control the Sea of Souls*, it observed.

Jin blinked in surprise and realized that it wasn't just the color of the sea that made it so responsive to her. The water itself was a swirl of faint emotion and thought—her heritage from Neela and Aka meant that she had an affinity to the souls that filled it.

"What souls are they?" she asked the serpent.

*Why, the souls of the dead.*

"Even mortals'?"

*Yes, of course.*

"But is there enough room?" she looked around. "There are ever more mortals dying..."

*So the sea grows. It is at least five times larger than when I first came here.*

Jin remembered Bai's claim that the Underworld was unmappable. An ever-growing sea would indeed be difficult to map.

*How did you come here?* the Sea Serpent asked.

"I came through the gate."

The serpent reared up backward and leveled an eye at her, causing the Mudanren at her belt to whimper.

*You have the key then? The key that used to steal our power?*

"Yes," said Jin, and impulsively, she withdrew Kunjee from her golden robes so that the serpent could see it.

*It can no longer steal our power after all,* said the serpent. *I felt the change a few months ago, but I had not fully believed it until this moment. How did this come to pass?*

"I fixed it," Jin said.

The Sea Serpent's coils writhed and shook, but Jin could feel its amusement and so wasn't frightened. *I am glad that you "fixed" the key. You're charming. Why have you come to my sea?*

"I need to travel to the Lonely Isle," she told it.

*Then let us keep company. I shall give you a ride.*

Jin was shocked. "Just like that? You're not what I expected, based on the stories I heard from the First."

*Let's not ruin this lovely chat by bringing up that rudesby,* the Serpent chided her.

Once Jin was situated just behind its triangular head, the serpent set off, so fast that the sea sprayed in Jin's face. It was exhilarating though—she couldn't wait to tell Bai.

"Why did you trust my answers?" she asked the serpent. "I might have been lying about fixing Kunjee."

Once again she felt its amusement. *I can see through any lies.*

"Like the Phoenix?" asked Jin. "Can all immortal creatures hear lies, then?"

*Like the Phoenix? Indeed not—that bird brain will believe any fib you tell it.*

"Oh," said Jin, realizing the Koch-ssi had tricked her.

*It is only white creatures that can sort truth from deceit and some blue ones. I am both, so I can never be fooled.*

"Ah," said Jin. "I had thought my orange nature interfered with that."

The Mudanren tittered, and the Sea Serpent made no reply. Whu Ze leaned close after a moment.

"It does," it whispered. "So the Serpent wouldn't have known if you were lying either."

Jin shifted self-consciously on the serpent's scales—they were indeed as hard as metal. However, the serpent soon began to chat again and its eagerness for conversation set Jin at ease. Jin thought it must have been lonely here in the Sea of Souls, for she saw nothing else living.

*Of course not,* said the serpent. *Most creatures are wise enough to avoid me.*

Jin caught its mockery of herself, but she let it go.

*I am not alone though. I like the souls here; they are interesting. A rather unique one is next to us.*

Jin glanced around but saw nothing unusual about the blue water. "What do you mean?"

*It is a double soul—a mother that died with her unborn child. It is following you.*

Jin stiffened. Could it possibly be?

She closed her eyes and let her awareness drift through the water, feeling the souls all around them, nothing but emotion and confused thought.

But there, by her foot, was one that was different. A little bigger than the others, it did not seem confused at all.

"Mother," whispered Jin in awe.

BAI sat next to Gang on the edge of the caldera, a precarious and cold perch, but Gang was oblivious to discomfort. Instead, his luminous gold eyes were lit by long ago memories. He had ceased to exist in this moment, his voice growing deeper and softer as emotions held him surely in the past. Bai knew his presence had been almost forgotten, so he listened patiently, silent and still.

"I returned to the palace shortly after you left with Kunjee. Father was in a fury—he had retreated to the top floor of his pagoda, and it was on fire. Not that it was in any danger of burning from his own flames, but the disciples and courtesans were terrified. I forced my way in and found him engulfed in fire.

"I don't remember what I said, but he calmed down and

convinced himself that he wouldn't miss Kunjee after all. He announced that he had put the key in your safe keeping, a lie accepted by the court because he believed it.

"But his original purpose in creating Kunjee had not disappeared. He had been seeking an advantage over Zi and Hei, for though he was called emperor, he knew that together their power was greater than his. I sometimes wondered, if you had left Kunjee, if the empress would still be alive and if he would have left Aashchary alone."

Gang shook his head. Bai's own gut clenched at the idea, but he had no time to dwell on it as Gang kept trudging through the past.

"At any rate, he became obsessed with the idea of having a partner as powerful as himself, and he was constantly nitpicking Bijalee over her lack. Bijalee was never a very happy being. She was worshipped by mortals almost as soon as she spawned, for lightning has always fascinated them and several mortals happened to witness the moment she became an immortal.

"Father had been thrilled by that, and he liked the image of Lightning and Sun together, but he was disappointed to realize that despite her deification, she was nowhere near as powerful as him or me. And he was disappointed that Salaana and Karana were weaker than me. He picked at her constantly, amplifying her natural insecurities, and she spent many of her days secluded. Only Salaana and Karana saw her with any regularity. When she appeared for formal occasions, she was a mouse, furtive and quiet. In danger of being crushed by her own silk robes.

"I know Father approached Haraa while Bijalee was still

alive, but she rejected him unreservedly. He wasn't so foolish to try Neela, even after Cheng disappeared. Or—if Neela imprisoned Cheng, perhaps Father knew that and was wary of her.

"I don't know when he met Aashchary, but I believe it was a few thousand years before Bijalee's death. I wish...

"I wish I had met her first. Then things might have been different.

"But maybe that is just wishful thinking, for he was truly determined. She was powerful, as powerful as me, a self-made goddess, and a popular one at that."

Gang smiled suddenly. "And she was beautiful. Long limbs and delicate features, with large eyes like dark pools from the deepest jungle and just as mysterious. She had taken the peacock as her symbol, and she dressed in its colors, long flowing skirts of royal blue and tangerine scarves... Her hair was deepest brown, and she wore it long and loose. She seemed to know everything about everyone, and no one knew anything about her."

Bai wondered if Gang knew Aashchary was Cheng's daughter—Neela had seemed to think it was a secret. But his next words confirmed that he did.

"Truly a child of Neela and Cheng, though Father didn't realize it. He just saw her power and her beauty and wanted it for himself. He didn't understand that he would never own her, even if they wed.

"The first time I met her, she was with child, at least halfway into her pregnancy. Bijalee was less than a thousand years dead, by her own hand, for her depression and anxiety had become more than she could bear.

"Aashchary strode into the reception hall like the empress she would become, the thunder to Bijalee's lightning. I think— I think I was a little in love with her from that moment.

"She announced that she accepted Father's proposal, and he was overjoyed. He even seemed content and happy until the wedding celebration. But—at the wedding, they both made a display of power, and people wondered if Aashchary was more powerful than Father. She might have been. She had many worshippers.

"And she treated him with contempt. She never accepted him again as a lover and she often criticized him before others.

"When the baby was born, she softened somewhat. She was enthralled with him. But she named him the God of Belief, and even Father was perturbed by that, never mind all the other deities of his court."

*It was an apt title though*, Bai mused to himself. Jin could have been the Goddess of Belief herself, having the ability to understand thought and emotion.

"I made Karana leave the Sun Court when I realized the role he had played." Gang swiped at his face.

"Aashchary was devastated. I was afraid that she might kill herself as Bijalee had done. So when Father kept his distance from her, I—well, I befriended her. And my initial admiration deepened to something more.

"Father never said a thing to me about it, but he must have known that we were lovers for he was unsurprised by Aashchary's pregnancy, and when Jin was born, he declared her his second daughter.

"I think he must have known she was mine, for he would not have accepted someone else's progeny. He was absolutely delighted by Jin—how powerful she could be, and how Aashchary had effectively hid that power by declaring her the Goddess of Beauty. He still kept his distance from Aashchary, but he would take Jin for walks around the palace. The easiest way to please him those days was to compliment her—he granted several immortals places in the court because they realized this.

"It was... a wonderful time for me. I deluded myself into thinking it would last forever. Even though I could not openly claim Jin as my daughter, I was happy. I thought Aashchary was happy as well.

"She became pregnant again though, and she suddenly was no longer willing to live as the Sun Empress. She wanted to leave the Sun Court and to live openly as a family with me and our children.

"I agreed. I knew I could manipulate the court perception—make them forget us even—and change Father's mind if I had to. I reached out to Karana and Salaana, thinking that their support might make that easier.

"But the night before I spoke with them, one of Father's courtesans murdered Aashchary."

GO *on, pick it up,* the Sea Serpent told Jin.

"Pick it up? But I don't want to hurt it."

Amusement thrummed through the serpent again. *Souls like to be touched—and they are stronger than you think. Pick it up.*

Wu Zhe uncovered its eyes long enough to whisper, "Don't worry. He's right."

So Jin gingerly gathered the extra-large soul into her two

hands.

As she brought it close to her face, she felt feathers tickle her cheeks and then a swirl of blue and orange engulfed her.

TEARS streaked down Aashchary's face as Atsuko handed the baby to her, and Aashchary cradled her against her chest.

The little face was squashed and red, but she already had a thick hatch of hair, albeit wet and plastered to her head.

"Gang," Aashchary murmured, and his large, muscular hand was immediately beneath her own, supporting the baby's head. "What should we call her?"

She felt Gang's fingers flex ever so slightly. "She needs to be called Sunlight in some way."

Aashchary compressed her lips. "But Gold too—we can put both in her name."

Gang's fingers relaxed, and she knew he had feared her arguing. But she was both too tired and too happy to argue today.

"She's so beautiful," Gang said, and his lips brushed Aashchary's own temple.

"Yes—" Though she tried not too, Aashchary remembered her son. Clarity, she had named him. Gang understood how she felt—in fact, it often seemed like he could read her emotions even though he claimed he could not—and slid his arms around her shoulders.

"I will keep her safe, I promise. No one will hurt her."

"Yes..." said Aashchary again, before helping the baby latch. She winced as the milk began to flow—it was just a little painful, but she knew from experience that it would be easier soon.

"She will be the Goddess of Beauty," Aashchary decided. She looked up at Gang to see his reaction. His thick orange brows had pulled together and there was a question in his gold eyes.

"Because others won't see her that way," Aashchary explained. "They will see her power and be afraid. So we need to make her as beautiful to them as she is to us."

His eyebrows settled back, and his generous lips turned down. He nodded. "You are wise, my love."

With one finger, he gently stroked the tiny hand that was compulsively pushing against Aashchary's chest.

After a moment, Gang said, "How about 'Sunlight turns Petals Gold'?"

"Petals?" echoed Aashchary, and then she smiled. "My mother will like that. Very well, I like it too. And we will call her Jin."

"Jin? Not Pankhadee?"

"No, Jin," Aashchary insisted.

"Alright."

Atsuko had been bustling around the room cleaning, and she now stopped before them. "I will give you all some privacy," she said. "Is there anything else you need?"

"No, thank you," Aashchary told her. "Please let the Moon Deer know that I'll see him in the morning."

Atsuko smiled. "He'll be happy to hear that—but please don't push yourself."

Aashchary smiled. "I never have to push myself to visit the Moon Deer."

Atsuko tsked. "Make sure she doesn't overexert herself, won't you, Gang?"

Gang smiled. "I'll do my best, Atsuko, but when Aashchary makes a decision, there isn't much I, or anyone, can do about it."

That he understood her so well made Aashchary smile, and she turned her attention to Jin, who was ready to nurse on the other side. She switched her, and the two of them fell asleep on the futon mattress that Atsuko had prepared, Gang watching over them.

AASHCHARY sat back on the pile of colorful cushions, but no matter how she shifted, she just couldn't get comfortable. She was nearly seven hundred years along and felt as big as an ox and four times as clumsy. She didn't know why this pregnancy was so much harder than her first two, unless it was because she had a toddler who always wanted to sleep next to her and still hadn't fully weaned. They had also been stuck at the Sun Court for over a year now, which meant Aashchary barely got to see Gang.

But all three of them were at Tsuku now, so she shouldn't waste the minutes worrying about what couldn't be changed.

If only she could get comfortable!

Gang was pouring milk for Jin in a beautiful red and gold china cup that Atsuko had just given them.

"She'll spill it," Aashchary warned.

"Then I'll clean it," he said indulgently. "It's about time she drank from a cup anyway. You can't keep nursing her."

Aashchary sighed. "I know, it's just so hard to refuse when that bottom lip starts to tremble." And Aashchary liked the closeness, the communion it brought.

Jin did better than Aashchary had expected with the cup. Maybe Gang was right, and she coddled her too much. But it was hard not to, for Aashchary was so afraid that Jin might die, struck down by jealous gods. She kept waking in the night lately, partly because the baby was pressing on her bladder, but mostly because she had nightmares about Jin dying. Every time she woke, she couldn't sleep again until she verified that Jin was breathing. She tried to hide from Gang how worried she was, but she thought he knew anyway.

"How hard would it be to leave the Sun Court forever? To have your father set aside our marriage?"

Gang's head jerked up, and Jin looked back and forth between the two of them. "Ooo?" she said.

Aashchary smiled at Jin. "It's okay, flower, Mama and Papa are just talking."

Gang ruffled Jin's loose hair and she went back to drinking her milk.

"Hard. But possible."

"I need to," Aashchary said, and wiped some tears off her face. "It's not just the pregnancy talking," she told Gang, picking it up from his thoughts. "I can't live like this anymore. I want—I want to marry you. For everyone to know we are partners and to raise our children together. I don't want them to only see you when we come here or to call you brother."

The tears came harder and faster now, and Gang stood and strode to her side. He pulled her into his lap—she must have weighed a ton with the baby, but he always said she weighed less than his Sun Armor. She doubted the truth of that, but she liked that he said it. She liked him. She—

"I love you, Gang. I know I made a mistake marrying Aka.

If only—if only—"

He rubbed her back. "I know," he said. "I love you, and I think those if onlys every day we are apart."

He took a deep breath, and Aashchary stroked his beloved face, tugging on his beard gently, just to reassure herself.

"I will find a way," he told her. "I will find a way for us to live as a family." And he kissed her.

Jin toddled over then, puckering her lips. Aashchary laughed and kissed their daughter's nose.

AASHCHARY held her massive abdomen with one hand and the handrail with the other as she climbed the second flight of stairs inside the Sun Pagoda. She wasn't sure if it was the exertion or the pressure of the baby on her internal organs or the infernal redness of everything in sight, but she felt nauseous.

*Just a month now,* she reminded herself. *Just a month and I can forget the Sun Court forever.*

Gang had promised to take her and Jin and their future baby away from here, even if it meant losing his godhood. Aashchary didn't think it would come to that. Aka loved his eldest son more than he loved anyone besides himself.

She finished the second flight and sighed as she faced the third. Couldn't even an unbearable narcissist like Aka understand that a heavily pregnant being shouldn't be made to climb five flights of stairs? What could he possibly want from her right now anyway? Perhaps she should have summoned Gang to accompany her.

Fifteen minutes later, she stood outside Aka's personal

sanctuary, panting. She would catch her breath before going in.

When she slid open the door though, Aka was nowhere in sight. Instead his favorite courtesan, an immortal born in the Land of Winter stood waiting.

"Eriko? What are you doing here?" Aashchary stepped in and slid the door shut behind her. "Did you use the Sun Emperor's stamp to summon me?" She tsked. "I don't mind speaking with you, but this is ridiculous. Do you und—"

Eriko leapt forward, long dagger pulled.

Aashchary had never trained much in fighting. She had enough power at her fingertips that she needn't waste time with weapons.

But she moved too slow. Maybe because she was pregnant, maybe because she was exhausted from the stairs.

Before she even began to react, the dagger slashed her jugular.

The door slid open then. "What's—" came Aka's voice.

Aashchary watched Eriko fall, burned beyond recognition between breaths. And then Aka was her side, using magic to stop the bleeding. "I will bring you to Haraa," he assured her.

But Aashchary died before they even came out of between.

SLOWLY the light faded, and Jin was once again in the Underworld, adrift in the Sea of Souls on the back of the Sea Serpent.

*Are you with us, colorful one?*

"Yes," said Jin, still a little dazed. "Is that all true? Did that really happen?"

*The souls can't lie, if that's what you are asking. I don't know if it's possible for them to remember wrongly.*

Jin took a few steadying breaths of the salty air, the strong taste helping her to gather her wits.

She wished she had some way to bring peace to her mother's soul. Its yearning for life was palpable, but Jin had no way to grant such a wish.

Finally, reluctantly, she said goodbye and released it back into the Sea of Souls.

"AND then?" Bai asked, when it became clear that Gang would not continue without prompting.

"Then?" he echoed, as if confused. "Well, Neela fetched Jin from the Sun Court to raise her, and I went on as I always had, still pretending she was Father's daughter and that I was his loyal subject."

"But you weren't?"

Gang shrugged. "If you keep a pretense up long enough, it becomes real." He cleared his throat. "I wasn't the one who cursed Father, but I don't want Jin to save him. I know she loves him—she only ever saw the indulgent side of him. I cannot forgive him for the death of Aashchary and our unborn child."

"You know he manipulated the courtesan, then?"

Gang shook his head. "No, but I still blame him." He swiped away tears. "Still, Jin is the being I care about the most now. I will protect this gate with my life—and I have more resources to do so than you." He leaned forward conspiratorially. "You exhausted your power fighting Salaana just now, didn't you?"

Bai barked a short laugh. "I tried to hide that from you."

Gang shrugged. "You prepared to dodge Salaana's lightning. Otherwise I would have asked you to melt the snow for our tea."

Bai nodded. "You've become more tactful."

"It has been eighteen millennia. Unlike you, we can't all remain unchanged."

Bai grew serious. "I have changed, just not in ways you can see." He squeezed his hands, wondering if now was the moment to broach his feelings for Jin. But the words stuck in his throat. Bai had heard many stories about fathers despising their daughters' admirers...

"You're free to leave—will you go to Cheng?"

Bai hesitated. He might be free to leave—certainly Gang was sincere in his intent to protect the gate—but he didn't want to. He was afraid for Jin, he wanted to find a way into the Underworld, he wanted to be here the moment she emerged—

"I don't see why I should leave, even if you are staying here. Unless my company is so reprehensible to you..."

"Not at all," said Gang, "but I would have thought you'd be eager to make sure Cheng is well. He is your oldest friend, after all."

Still Bai hesitated.

Gang looked down at his hands, his manner too casual. "What exactly is your relationship with Jin? I supposed you wanted to teach her, as you did me..."

"Of course I was teaching her. And I wouldn't have abandoned you either, when you were my student."

Gang snorted and stood. "You are truly skilled at misleading others while being truthful. But Neela came to see me over a month ago."

Bai came to his feet as well, balancing on the caldera's edge.

Gang leaned closer to him, using his greater size to crowd Bai. "I know that you see Jin as some sort of second chance. She looks like my mother—I always expected people to notice that and accuse me of fathering her, but Eomma died so long ago that almost no one remembers her. But you do, don't you, Bai?

"Let me be very clear about this—Jin is not some consolation prize. Stop pursuing her, or you won't need fate to curse you—I'll take care of it myself."

Bai flushed. So all his careful speech had been for nothing. He would have been better off confessing his feelings openly. "I do not think of Jin as Noran—"

Gang's bushy brows snapped together, and his golden eyes sparked. "You try to lie to me because I cannot hear your thoughts? Neela has already told me the truth!"

"When I saw Neela, I wasn't sure—"

Gang snorted. "And in three weeks, you became sure?" He shook his head. "I was trying to let you go gracefully, for old times' sake, but if you won't leave of your own free will, I will force you."

Gang drew the Sun Sword once again, and this time he meant to use it. Bai drew the Starlight Sword as well—Gang had never bested him in a fight before he retreated from the world, but he had been close.

Gang wasn't interested in a test of skill though. He sliced the air with the Sun Sword and each stroke sent a blast of fire.

He was faster than Salaaana—or perhaps Bai was slower than before—and Bai was hit twice in less than a minute. He gasped from the pain and saw hideous burns slashing his right arm and his left leg.

"Go."

"No, please let me—"

And again came the flaming cuts, this time crossing Bai's back from shoulder to waist and another across his cheek.

And then Bai's blood literally boiled in a way he had only heard about. He knew it wouldn't kill him, but the physical pain was the worst he had ever known.

When it stopped, he was on his hands and knees.

"Go," Gang said again, and this time Bai went.

He had no magic to teleport, not even enough to summon a cloud, so he half-ran, half-stumbled down the Korikami's Tomb, sliding on the ice and snow.

One bad fall sent him tumbling over a hundred feet to stop in a patch of gravel. If he hadn't been a stone, he would surely have broken all his bones; as it was, he hurt everywhere.

He breathed deeply, centering himself. There was no longer any snow, for the air had warmed considerably, but there also weren't any plants yet, just reddish gray stones. Gang hadn't specified how far Bai had to go, and truly Bai needed to rest soon, but he felt that he had better leave the alpine zone or face Gang again.

He pulled himself to his feet and trudged on. After half an hour, he reached the first short mountain plants, a ground cover with many small, light green leaves.

Ahead, he could see scrubby little kousa trees, with shiny dark leaves and white flowers consisting of four tear-drop petals. Although he had no power to shape anything at present, it would be good to be near the kousa trees when he did. Bai found a clear patch of stone to sit and folded himself into asana.

Closing his eyes, he let pain flow out and power flow in.

# How the Shadows Darkened

NANAMI bent backward to dodge the needles, more amused than threatened. If He Who Walks in Shadow had thrown the needles at her torso, she would have been in more danger, but he had always preferred drama over efficiency.

Willing to oblige since she was, after all, a petitioner, Nanami executed a high kick in his direction. He spun out of the way—this was easier than it would have been minutes earlier for his Shadow Thieves had moved away from them, leaving about six feet in all directions empty. A stage.

He Who Walks in Shadow leapt up onto a table so Nanami followed suit.

Punches and kicks flew. Finally, when he had his arms locked around Nanami's neck, their heads bent close together, she tickled his ribs with a dagger, letting the folds of his tunic hide the weapon.

He paused.

"Aren't you curious as to why I came?" Nanami whispered.

He snorted. "My only interest is sending you to the Goddess of Justice so you can be properly punished."

Nanami smiled and pushed her stump right under his nose. "Been there, done that. Besides, do you want to spend the next hour packing? Or do you want the Sowon Gold?"

Greed and pride warred on his face.

Nanami returned the dagger to her belt and lifted a wine gourd tied at her waist. "Daedo's best soju."

He burst into laughter and released her. "Very well, let's drink and negotiate."

He jumped off the table. Gradually and silently, his thieves moved back into the stage—the show was over.

Nanami and He Who Walks in Shadow made their way through the crowd. He Who Walks in Shadow moved like a ghost, not even brushing one of his thieves despite the narrow spaces between tables and many limbs flung with drunken exuberance. Nanami found his exaggerated care absurd, but she was even more ridiculous, for she imitated him just to prove she could.

In some ways this man was another family that she had lost, but by her choice.

At last they reached the darkest corner of the room, where an unoccupied table waited for them. It was already set with several bottles and a stack of gold cups. He sat first, then stared at her. Nanami took a seat across from him, noting that the zabuton cushions he had chosen were of fine Liushi silk with golden threads. They would probably be ruined soon, given the rough stone floor and the general state of filth in the cave, but that wouldn't bother He Who Walks in Shadow. He would simply steal more—or, more likely, have more stolen.

Nanami untied the gourd she'd brought and pulled its stopper. She poured a cup for He Who Walks in Shadow and offered it to him with an inclination of her head.

He smiled at last, greed lighting his eyes. "So you come as a petitioner." He accepted the cup and gulped the wine, with no pretense at manners. He held the cup out to her, and she refilled it. Truthfully, Nanami was just as happy to not drink. She was aware that she was in enemy territory, and after committing to Xiao, she doubted she could ever enjoy drinking again.

To He Who Walks in Shadow, Nanami said, "I wish to steal all the prayer collectors from the Night and Moon deities' largest temples on the same night. I want to hire your thieves."

He tossed back more liquor. "There was a rumor that you had been spending time with the God of Pleasure. Some sort of family rift? If he wants to hire thieves, I'll speak to him directly."

"I'm not here at anyone's request," she said. "This is personal—for me."

He wiped his lips with the back of his hand. "You have a grudge against the Night and Moon Deities?"

She refilled the cup again. "My reasons aren't important."

He shrugged. He drained the cup a third time. "So why would I help you, after you stole the Sowon Gold from me?"

"Because your besetting sin is greed, not wrath. Wouldn't you like that gold back?"

He leaned forward eagerly, even licking his lips. "You'll give me the Sowon Gold in exchange?"

The power to have whatever he wanted, without the need to steal or bully or connive. The gold made by Noran that bought other's minds.

Nanami curled her hand into a fist. "Yes, I'll pay you in Sowon Gold if your thieves succeed in their task."

He Who Walks in Shadow stroked his chin. "Swear it. Stake your immortality on it."

"I vow to pay you in Sowon Gold in exchange for the successful theft of all the prayer collectors from the hundred largest temples of the Moon and Night deities."

"*One hundred* pieces of Sowon Gold."

She amended the vow.

He stared at her, those black eyes fathomless as he thought. "Swear you won't ever steal it back."

Nanami grit her teeth. Then, "I vow never to steal the Sowon Gold from you again."

He smiled. "Then I accept the job."

THREE days after Xiao tried to summon Jin, his power was almost fully restored, and Zi and Hei came once again to Xiao's room.

They were followed by three disciples who arranged many dishes on a table under Zi's watchful eye. Not one of the disciples met Xiao's eyes, and he wondered if they knew what had happened to Dawa because he dared carry an ant out of the manor.

The disciples shuffled out as soon as their task was finished. Zi withdrew three smooth amethyst stones and made each into a cushioned seat. She and Hei each took one and Zi looked pointedly at the third.

Xiao sighed, then heaved himself off the bed to join them.

He scanned the table curiously and was half-irritated, half-surprised to see that his favorite dishes had been prepared. He refused to be moved. There were spicy pickled cucumbers and rice steamed in bamboo leaves; cubed salmon with perilla leaves and shaved daikon; battered fried chicken and wheat noodles with black bean sauce; scallion pancakes with black vinegar on the side; even a green curry with shrimp that smelled of coconut and lime. He wanted to be aloof, but his stomach growled without his consent.

Zi smirked, and Xiao almost swept all the dishes onto the floor where they would undoubtedly shatter.

Instead he sat patiently while she served him and Hei. At her silent urging he tried the salmon. It practically melted in his mouth and it took an embarrassing amount of effort to eat a triangle of scallion pancake at a moderate pace rather than stuffing everything into his mouth at once.

*You don't require food,* he reminded himself.

After every dish had been sampled, Hei said, "We have realized that perhaps we went about this the wrong way. We are a family after all."

"I beg to differ on that last point, but I'll admit to some curiosity. What exactly did you do wrong?"

"You are old enough now that we should discuss our plans with you," said Zi, and Xiao remembered her comment that he wouldn't be worth her time until he reached twenty millennia. He didn't miss that she hadn't really answered his question.

"Things are shifting in the Heavens. Now that Aka has fallen, Gang and Salaana have begun a power struggle. It would be good to consolidate more power within our family. Your marriage to Jin would do that, and it would bind Neela to us."

Xiao stuffed some of the fried chicken into his mouth. It was delightfully crunchy, and almost too salty—just how he liked it. He looked for a drink and realized there was only sweet wine. He hesitated, then ate a cucumber instead.

"So that is why you must marry Jin," Hei finished.

Xiao grabbed some noodles and made a show of chewing them thoroughly. "While it's true that the betrothal made me realize that I could cut ties with you, it's not the main reason I did so. It's because you don't treat me like a sentient being but rather a tool for your use."

Zi scoffed and Hei laid a placating hand over hers. To Xiao, he said, "We've explained why we arranged this marriage."

"How about why you drained away my power?"

"Because you tried to escape," said Zi.

"When I first arrived at the hall—"

"You were belligerent. You could hardly expect us to treat with you then."

"I wasn't—" Xiao caught himself, realizing that his voice was raising. In a more moderate tone, he continued, "How did you expect me to respond when you threatened me with confinement?"

"We suggested the punishment only because—"

"Because I said you are no longer my parents. You were angry at losing your tool. Not because you loved me. If you were mourning the loss of a son, you would have responded emotionally, not with calculation. You were all too ready to steal my power. I wonder—have you done it before? I know you steal and sell my worshippers' dreams, and perhaps their prayers."

"You are our son, so everything that is yours belongs to us."

"No! That's not how it works!" Xiao stood up. "I can't do this. It's like talking to a wall. I want to leave here. Will you let me?"

"Of course not," said Zi.

Xiao grabbed Hei's shoulder with one hand. Hei was surprised enough that he held still, trying to understand what Xiao wanted.

Which was Hei's sword. Xiao pulled it from its scabbard and swept it over the table. Both Zi and Hei took a step back, Hei pushing Zi behind himself.

*That's why their callousness hurts so much,* Xiao realized. *Because their care for each other is so great. Like they've used up all their love on each other and there's none left for me.* "Let me go or—"

Xiao was ready for the power whip when it came—that was why he had grabbed the sword. He used it to deflect the whip just as he would a physical one, and it worked.

His triumph was short-lived though, for Hei seized one of the black ceramic pots that lined the shelves and made a twin to the sword Xiao held.

He stepped forward and soon they were dancing, the swords meeting angrily and often. It was all Xiao could do to keep pace with his father, and while he was distracted, Zi's whip wrapped around his waist. Xiao didn't give up, but he realized now that Hei had been purposely meeting him at his level to keep him distracted. Now that Zi was draining his power, Hei locked swords with Xiao once more and struck his wrist with his other hand. Xiao dropped the sword.

Hei's whip wrapped around him, too.

"This—this is wrong. Even if I were a stranger to you, stealing my power in this way..."

Zi sighed. "If you would cooperate, we wouldn't have to do this."

"So you're saying I can't act unless it's according to your will?"

"We won't allow you to be foolish and bring shame upon our family," said Hei.

Xiao closed his eyes, once again bested. For now.

THE early morning sunlight painted the Frozen Desert of Ehkoron blue and gold. The tundra stretched out before Nanami in low rolling hills, swathes of snow and ice, and some hardy bushes that persevered with the tenacity of a mother saving her child. Nanami had dressed warmly of course, wrapped in woolen robes and a fur cap, but she still rubbed her nose, exposed above her scarf. She cursed that she chosen Ehkoron to hide the Sowon Gold—it was such a barren place that only a handful of mortals lived in the northern region. Of course, that was exactly why she had chosen it.

The Sowon Gold was a frightening thing. After Nanami had stolen it back from He Who Walks in Shadow, she had determined that while it only influenced mortals, it did work in anyone's hands. The more gold, the stronger the influence.

Truth be told, she had tried to destroy it, but it had not melted no matter how hot she had heated it. Moreover, though it looked like pure gold, it was harder than steel—nothing Nanami tried scratched or dented that gilt surface.

In the end, she had decided to bury each piece separately so that if it was found, it was in a lesser amount. The Frozen Desert, where every night saw the ground hard with ice, had been an excellent choice. Six thousand years ago, she hadn't been able to imagine a day when she would seek the gold again and hadn't bothered with any map—just rough pacings based on landmarks that had been altered by millennia of wind and snow.

But she had promised all one hundred pieces of the Sowon Gold to He Who Walks in Shadow, so she had spent the past month painstakingly crossing the tundra retracing her steps as best she was able and excavating the half-frozen ground.

And in her thief's pouch, she had seventy pieces of the most vibrant yellow metal she had ever seen, one side bearing a many-petalled chrysanthemum and the other the divine character for gold. As for the remaining thirty pieces...

Nanami knelt again next to one of the bear totems she had found where the gold had been buried. There had been thirty in all, each about a foot tall and carved from brownstone. There were sigils on the bear's chest that might have been attempts to replicate the symbols on the gold itself—it was hard to tell because these totems were not new. Still, Nanami was confident that they were less than a hundred years old—probably less than fifty. Find the carvers of the totems, and she would probably find the gold. She was fairly sure the carvers were mortal, given the roughness of the totems, so she wouldn't find it too hard to steal the gold back—and she wouldn't feel guilty about taking such a terrible power away from them.

Only trouble was, she didn't know where any people were in this cursed land. If only she could turn into a bird like Xiao had...

Nanami bit her lip beneath her wool scarf. Both her parents could turn into dragons—it was simply a manifestation of one's own power.

Nanami closed her eyes, remembering her father's change, then Xiao's, then her mother's. She felt her power ripple through her body, and when she opened her eyes, she was covered in indigo scales. Her claws were silver. In the barren desert, it was hard to judge, but she thought she was probably half the size of the Sea Dragon. For a moment, Nanami wondered if it would be possible to find a mirror, then mocked herself. Just as Xiao had described, she somehow found this body as familiar as her own, and it was a matter of instinct to stretch out and ascend into the air. She didn't have wings, but her serpentine body navigated the air currents with the same ease of an oarfish in the sea.

It took some days but Nanami found a mortal encampment on the edge of the Frozen Desert. It was larger than she expected, at least a hundred people. Dark red flags with the snarling face of a brown bear were snapping in the wind. Nanami flew closer, looking for some sign of the gold.

Her impatience and overconfidence were punished; an arrow punctured her side, and then another and another. Nanami plummeted to the hard ground.

She was met by young men with wickedly curved daggers.

"What is it?" one asked.

"No idea, but this'll be enough meat for a week," crowed a second.

Nanami was shaking in terror and pain. She had never felt like this before, as if her very essence had been razed. Panicked, she tried to teleport.

Perhaps she had used too much magic already, or perhaps there were rules about her transformation that she didn't understand, but instead of teleporting, she reverted to her natural form.

"Fate!" cried the first, raising his dagger in alarm.

"No! Don't touch her! She is a goddess! If you kill her, our whole tribe will be fate-cursed."

The crowd of youths parted as if by magic to reveal an elderly mortal woman with long gray dreadlocks.

And it was by magic, for around the woman's neck, at least twenty pieces of brilliant Sowon Gold were bound in a necklace.

XIAO took a sip from the flask, swishing the alcohol around his mouth so that its slight burn touched everywhere before he swallowed. He sat splay-legged on the ground, with several days sweat dried on him, and took another swig.

There was no point in transforming into anything. Zi and Hei always caught him just outside his room, drained him, and locked him in again.

There was no point in summoning anyone. Either they couldn't feel it, or they couldn't break the teleportation ban or...

Or they just didn't care that much about him.

There was no point in trying to make a key that worked in all locks or an indestructible sword or anything useful. After hundreds of failed attempts, the crockery was smashed and the hangings torn. The destruction hadn't been part of the process but had been done out of frustration.

And so he was drinking. He didn't need to drink, but he was so bored, and nothing else had been brought for him to consume since that debacle a few weeks ago. Was it just a few weeks? Maybe it was a few months. Or a few years. He should scratch a count in the floor to keep track. But when should he do it? When he woke? How would he know if he had slept a few hours or a few days?

It was a long time anyway, and he was thirsty. Those were the only reasons he was drinking—thirst and boredom.

He spilled some of the liquor on his robes. He tried to wipe at it, but he used the hand holding the flask and ended up spilling more.

*Curse it, I'm drunk.* He started to laugh, but he cried at the same time. "You are a liar," he accused himself. "A pathetic liar." The words ran circles in his mind. *Pathetic. Liar.*

He swiped a hand in front of him, as if he could wave them away. When that didn't work, he took another swig.

"You know Nanami is coming for you, and you have to be ready when she shows up." He laughed again. "Nope, that's a lie too. She's not coming. She can't. Besides, you already gave her sex, which was all she wanted in the first place."

Was that true?

She had lusted after him. Xiao knew that; hadn't she once suggested that whatever he could offer was enough? Why would she want to be with a weakling like him anyway?

He couldn't even go a month without turning to alcohol, exactly as Zi and Hei wanted. He chucked the flask against the wall.

He hated himself—no, he hated Zi and Hei.

He wasn't going to play into their hands. "You cursed

manip—manipulators!" he yelled. "I hope you can hear me! You should be ashamed of yourselves."

If they wanted him to drink, then he wouldn't. He struggled to his feet, using the bed to pull himself up. "I'll show you," he muttered. "I'll show you that I can do it. That I'm worthy of respect."

He tried to take the fighter's stance, but somehow spreading his legs ended up with his falling on the ground. He lay there for a few moments, his cheek pressed against the rough basalt.

"Why aren't I better?" he asked. "Why can't I be the person I want to be?"

*I know what I want. I want to be strong, relentless. I want to be clever and innovative.*

Instead, he was weak and fragile. Easily dissuaded; easily forgotten.

He thought of Bai, and their first meeting when he had disarmed Xiao in a matter of moments. The way he was always focused and controlled.

How everyone immediately remembered him. *The First.*

Bai spent eighteen millennia alone on a mountain, and the whole time he had been training, reflecting, and improving himself.

To the floor, Xiao mumbled, "Eighteen millennia while I can't last a cursed month." *Or whatever it's been.*

He crawled across the floor and picked up the flask, which had made a sizable puddle.

"Maybe I can just fill the room with rice wine, and they'll have to let me out for fear that I'll drown." That made him laugh for real.

He cuddled the bottle against himself. If he were a mortal,

he would have passed out by now, possibly drowning in his own vomit.

Alcohol, despite its preservative and antiseptic properties, was poison. It poisoned the body and the brain, and, if used the way Xiao used it, eventually the soul. And soon it became the only option, the only thing that made him feel better and forget how lost he was.

Xiao took another long pull.

"If I can't do anything worthwhile anyway, I might as well drink."

*Liar.*

NANAMI must have passed out from the pain of the arrows when they moved her, for she awoke in a dark room—no, it was a tent, cylindrical with many thick red poles supporting a domed roof. Nanami was surprisingly comfortable on a bed of furs. A small fire in the middle of the space made the air smoky and warm, despite a vent in the center of the roof.

Aching, Nanami gingerly touched her side. There were no arrows, but a thick bandage beneath an unfamiliar tunic. Nanami wondered if she should teleport to the Wood Pavilions, but decided she didn't feel like she was dying, so it was more important to try to recover the gold.

Her movement was noticed—a moment later a girl's face bent over her hers, dark eyes wide and round, nose snub and freckled. Her delicate face seemed even smaller because it was half-swallowed by a fur-lined hood. The girl blinked once and then a smile split her face.

"Divinity, you have awoken! I'm sorry that Batu and

Ganbold shot you. They think with their bodies, not with their heads. A bad way to be but common in young men, so Great-mother says."

Nanami didn't say anything, trying to figure out who exactly she was to this mortal.

The girl went on. "My name is Ankhbayar. Great-mother told me to get you whatever you needed when you woke and then to fetch her. Are you hungry? Thirsty? Do you need to piss?"

Nanami almost shook her head, impatient, but realized her mouth was uncomfortably dry. "Water."

The girl supported her head and tipped an animal hide flask against her lips.

It wasn't water. Nanami thought it was fermented milk, and she didn't like it, but she drank a little anyway. She pushed herself up more fully and away from the girl's supporting arm.

"Tell me about your tribe," she commanded. Nanami had decided social niceties were not in keeping with being a goddess and was doing her best impression of Salaana.

"We are the Bear People, divinity. We have recently moved inland for wild storms come off the North Sea at the end of summer. We live off the animals we hunt, which is why the boys tried to fell you. We are all hungry."

*She's scared that I might punish them for shooting me.* Perhaps if they were still by the fierce North Sea, they'd be right to fear her, but there was little Nanami could do to them here.

She swept her gaze over the girl and spotted a knotted necklace tucked under the girl's coat. She pulled it free and sure enough, it had a Sowon Gold pendant. Ankhbayar leaned forward obligingly, letting Nanami twist it in her fingers. "Tell me about this," she ordered.

"My shaman's mark? It means I'm an apprentice of the great-mother."

"And she has ten apprentices?"

"Yes, at present. How did you know?"

Nanami glanced down at her hip to find her thief's pouch with its seventy gold pieces. Since it was keyed to Nanami's essence, these mortals wouldn't be able to open it, but she worried about it all the same.

"What does the mark allow you to do?"

"I—what do you mean, divinity? What are my duties as an apprentice?"

Nanami shook her head. She wondered if the girl really didn't understand the power of the gold. Even if she was ignorant, surely the same couldn't be true for this "great-mother."

"Fetch your great-mother now," she told the girl. The girl nodded and genuflected before rising and running out of the tent, leaving the door flapping behind her.

Nanami took the time to examine her surroundings. Ropes were suspended from the red poles of the ceiling, and these were filled with dried herbs. They smelled sweet and grassy—aster was there for sure, but Nanami would have been hard-pressed to identify the others. Given that the girl had implied the tribe was nomadic, Nanami was surprised by the amount of furniture. In addition to the brazier, there were five beds lining the walls—the girl must have been sitting on one of these when Nanami awoke. They were made of sticks and ropes—perhaps they could be disassembled when the tribe moved? Nanami shuddered—being a mortal just seemed like so much work. She touched the soft furs that filled the bed. Despite the low light, Nanami could tell that many of these had been brightly dyed, and colorful thread had been used to sew them together. The pop and hiss of the fire in the center of the room brought Nanami's eyes to the brazier. She noted a short iron poke hanging there—it was the only obvious weapon in the tent.

Nanami pressed her side again. It hurt, but the binding seemed to have been done well. Being immortal, it was unlikely Nanami would contract an infection, though she would be mindful anyway. Just as she was weighing inspecting her wounds against not wasting a good bandage, the girl returned, leading the old mortal who had, perhaps, saved Nanami's life.

Placing Nanami's status above her own age, the great-mother went down on her knees just inside the tent and intoned, "Forgive us, divinity."

Nanami surveyed her coolly. "My forgiveness may be forthcoming, depending on your worthiness. I have come to observe you and see if you are using your gifts well and wisely."

The woman raised her hands to the gold and nodded. "Ankhbayar, join the other girls in their candle making. I wish to speak to her divinity privately."

When the girl left—there was no fear she'd stay and eavesdrop when she couldn't help but follow her teacher's wishes—the great-mother came closer and placed a stool next to Nanami's bed.

"Have you come to teach us about the shaman marks? My teacher found the first of them in the Frozen Desert over fifty years ago now, when she was banished from her tribe as a youth. She brought them to the Bear People in hopes of joining us, but the chief fell in love with her and bade her to keep them. She travelled back into the desert with her apprentices, and we found several more. She gave one to each of her apprentices, and upon her death, when I was chosen as a successor, they came to me."

"Indeed, I was the one who buried them in the desert."

The old woman seized Nanami's hand and pressed her forehead to it. "Oh, thank you, thank you, generous one. This bounty saved our tribe."

Nanami felt a little guilty being praised for something that had nothing to do with her, especially when her intention was to take the "bounty" away again. So she wasn't sure of her own motivation when she said, "I would hear your story. Tell me how things changed."

The old woman nodded, and the creases of her face deepened as her dark eyes went far away. "When I was a girl, our tribe was much smaller, and there was always fighting among the hunters. It was common for young men to kill each other or be exiled for their acts. But the marks brought peace to our tribe. The old chief, a great warrior, was a cunning man with little kindness in him. My teacher was not a beautiful woman, but she was patient and wise. The chief saw the blessing that had been granted her, and he sought her advice. Her wisdom won his heart and gentled his temper. For most of my life, our tribe has prospered and grown larger than both the Eagle and Whale tribes. Even our most hot-blooded warriors respect the shamans and listen when we speak."

*And of course, you women have easier lives for it.*

She had to admit though, it seemed like they were using the Sowon Gold for good. It didn't matter—both her immortality and Xiao's freedom depended on Nanami bringing all the gold to He Who Walks in Shadow—but she was curious about it.

*I need a little time to recover and locate all the pieces,* Nanami decided. *I will watch—even though this woman saved me, doesn't mean she isn't abusing her power in other ways. A little extra food for herself, the best goods for her tent...*

BATU and Ganbold were brought before Nanami to apologize and beg for their lives. Nanami tried to make her eyes cold and her mouth hard as they rubbed their palms at her feet, but she mostly felt wonder at how young they were. When they had loomed over her, arrows embedded in her side, Nanami had been afraid of them. But now she realized they were boys—a little thin, a little dirty, and very terrified of her.

Either she wasn't as callous as she imagined herself or Xiao had already changed her, for she found forgiving them easier than maintaining a pretense of anger.

She accepted the offerings they made, a large carved canine tooth from Batu and a braided necklace from Ganbold.

She turned the canine tooth over between her fingers. "When you first saw me, I was a dragon," she told them. "Never shoot one again—it will always be a god, a sin to kill and a greater one to eat."

Both boys nodded—Nanami thought she saw tears at the corners of Ganbold's eyes. "Go," she said. "I don't wish to look on you."

The great-mother then asked Nanami if she might bring in all her apprentices for blessing. Seeing an opportunity to locate all thirty gold pieces, Nanami readily agreed.

When they were all lined up, Nanami could indeed count thirty marks about their necks, and, as she said a blessing, she envisioned running around the tent grabbing them all, then teleporting out of there.

But she didn't know how they'd react. Were the hunters of the tribe waiting just outside, ready to pepper her with arrows? Would the girls tackle her or stab her with the knives at their belts?

She had better wait a little longer.

No sooner was her blessing finished than a young boy burst into the tent. Cheeks damp and snot running from his nose, he seized the great-mother's hand. "Please come quickly."

The great-mother bowed once to Nanami, waved to her apprentices, and then the lot of them scurried from the tent. Nanami pressed her hand against her ribs and followed.

A restless crowd was gathered by an outdoor grill. Two men, one drunk, both belligerent, were trying to fight each other. Trying because about four others were doing their utmost to keep the two separated at great risk to their own persons. A woman with flushed cheeks and clasped hands was looking on—from the yelling and cursing, Nanami gathered that she had taken both combatants as lovers and they were fighting over her.

The apprentices ran into the fray, grabbing all the principals. Nanami nearly cried out in alarm, to see such slight, young girls next to men who had bloodshed on their minds.

But the Sowon Gold worked its magic. The tension in the men's shoulders was released, and the two instigators stopped straining toward each other. Their snarls relaxed into apologetic expressions. The violence dissipated so quickly that

Nanami wasn't sure if she felt disturbed or relieved.

Unlike Nanami, the crowd seemed to be accustomed to such rapid shifts, and it began dispersing.

That night, Nanami lay in the warm bed of the shaman's tent. She stroked the soft furs absently, replaying the scene in her mind. It reminded her of something...

Jin. Or rather, Bai's reaction to Jin. Nanami had seen the First remain wholly detached from numerous suitors, but he had been instantly infatuated with Jin. Nanami had been surprised at the time, and now she thought it unnatural, just as the fight's cessation had been unnatural. Jin was beautiful, yes, very earnest and kind, but the First hadn't been interested in *anyone* for oh, forty millennia? And before that, the only being to attract his attention had been Noran... Who of course had the same power, having made the Sowon Gold.

Nanami felt deeply uneasy and a little frightened that Jin might be able to influence the First in such a manner. The way she changed water into flesh...

Nanami had never seen anything like it, and she wasn't sure one being should have so much power.

The more she thought about it, the more she wondered if the way Xiao always bowed to Jin's wishes was love or influence. Nanami was resistant to influence, but she remembered how Xiao had fooled her with an illusion because he was so powerful and because Nanami had prayed to him. And so she wondered, had Jin even influenced her?

Wanting to understand this odd magic better, Nanami delayed stealing the gold.

Over the next few days, Nanami observed the tribe with great interest.

She could best see the power dynamics at the mid-day meal when the whole tribe gathered outside around grills to enjoy the sunniest part of the day and visit with each other. Nanami noted that the shamans of the Bear People got the best bits of meat and their cups were never empty.

In the afternoons, Nanami watched women—except for the shamans—working with the animal hides, curing new ones and mending old ones. The shamans had the finest clothes in the tribe though they never had to fix their own.

Most of the shamans didn't seem to realize it was because of the gold though. Instead, they accepted the gifts from others as signs of respect.

They weren't totally wrong—it was a little hard for Nanami herself to determine what was offered because the giver wanted to and what was offered because the receiver wanted it. Under the great-mother's watchful eye, the apprentices did not accept excessive offerings—after all, there is a difference between wanting something and taking it.

And they did guide the community to a more peaceful way of life. A mother was turned from beating her child to consoling it in the presence of the shamans; a dispute over some fermented milk was settled equitably and quickly.

Nanami didn't like seeing a child hit and she thought pulling out someone's hair over fermented milk was ridiculous, but...

But she would have let both happen rather than cancel another being's ability to choose for themselves. After all, were those difficulties truly overcome this way? Were any lessons learned? Was there any growth?

By the third night, Nanami had seen enough. Near midnight, when the fires had guttered out, Nanami slipped from her bed and crept through the camp. The young women slept well and deeply, for their lives were comfortable, and so they didn't stir as Nanami tugged the "shaman's marks" out of their tunics and cut their cords.

And then only the great-mother and her twenty pieces remained. Unlike her apprentices, she woke when Nanami lifted her heavy necklace. Her eyes glittered in the dark tent, and her hand clamped on Nanami's like a vise.

"Why?" she asked, her voice low and urgent.

"You know the secret of the gold," Nanami accused. "You know that it controls others."

"But that is why I only accept girls as apprentices," protested the great-mother. "Women are naturally kind—they do not take advantage of others."

Nanami snorted her disbelief. "If you believe that, you are a fool."

"Please," begged the great-mother. "We need this gold. It makes our tribe safer and more orderly."

"It makes it less free."

"What's the difference between a golden tongue and this gold?" argued the mortal.

Nanami snorted. "Magic."

She tugged her hand free, and the great-mother screamed. She wrapped her hands around Nanami's neck. It hurt and Nanami could barely breathe, but killing an old mortal was beneath her, so she focused on the gold.

As apprentices poured into the tent, Nanami was distantly aware of the great-mother ordering her death, but Nanami had already finished cutting the necklace.

She teleported to the Cave of Shadows.

✿  ✿  ✿

A LOUD pounding awoke Xiao. At first, he wasn't certain if the sound came from his own head or not—he had drunk until he slept and his body was protesting the abuse, even if he couldn't die from alcohol poisoning.

But the clamor was definitely external. At New Moon Manor, where control and intentionality ruled, that was strange.

Xiao took a few gulps from the Infinite Flask and coughed when some went down wrong, before dragging himself to his feet and lurching to the nearest window.

The window looked out on the vegetable garden where Xiao had once set off fireworks. It looked bright and green, but the section he was at was empty of beings. He could hear voices though, so he pressed his face into the cursed iron bars, trying to see the speakers. It was useless. Frustrated, Xiao seized the bars, and they crumbled into black sand. Stunned, he pushed the fine grains with his finger. Just how drunk was he?

After a moment, he brushed the sand off the sill and leaned over it.

About twenty paces to his right, Moon and Night disciples huddled together. They were whispering, or trying to, but several of them gasped loudly and one exclaimed, "No!" before the others hushed her.

His mother and father's first disciples came running into the garden soon after. Their robes were hitched up around their knees and flapping ridiculously—Xiao didn't think he'd seen either of them running before. The disciples dispersed under their angry gazes, but they were all so preoccupied that they didn't even notice him as they walked by his window.

Impulsively, he swung himself over the sill and ended up flopping in a heap at the base of the wall. *This is a good time to escape,* he thought gleefully, then, *Maybe I shouldn't have drunk so much.* He glanced back at the barless window and decided maybe it was alright that he had.

He took a swig of the rice liquor, trying to decide what to do next.

"Xiao."

Xiao banged his head looking for the speaker, and while he was rubbing it, he found Bai with a large black crow on his shoulder. He was at the window that Xiao had just exited, leaning over the sill.

"Bai!" Xiao stood again, cursing when it took him two tries. "Are you responsible for all this then?" He tried to clap Bai on the shoulder but almost hit the bird. It squawked indignantly, and Bai caught his wrist.

Xiao stared at that hand wrapped around his wrist—he could feel the calluses on Bai's palm. "I'm not dreaming, am I?"

Bai looked at Xiao's other hand. "I don't think you'll need that."

Xiao followed his gaze but saw only the Infinite Flask. He took a sip. "Don't need what?"

Bai shook his head and pulled Xiao between.

# WOOD PAVILIONS

The Wood Pavilions, home to Haraa the Warden, are in central Zhongtu on the Lake of Reflection. All are welcome, and there is only one rule: do not damage the plants.

# How Jin Plucked the Peony

THE Lonely Isle was bursting with life. The rocky gray shore where Jin stood had deep blue tidal pools boasting barnacles and scuttling crabs, and several unfamiliar striped birds chased after them. At her back, the Sea of Souls lapped the shore softly, punctuated by the occasional splash of rainbow jumping fish. About a dozen yards inland was a thick jungle wall, all deep green leaves and ropey vines as thick as Jin's wrist. Large black flowers with matte petals were everywhere, looking like nothing so much as oversized flies.

None of those flowers resembled a peony though.

She turned to the peony-like people perched on her left shoulder.

"I thought a place called the Lonely Isle would be more," she waved her hand as she searched for the right word, "barren."

"Oh, the 'Lonely' refers to the fact that it's the only island in the Sea of Souls. There's plenty of life here."

Jin nodded. "Why doesn't the Koch-ssi live here? It's so sunny—"

"No, no, it only looks like sunlight. There isn't any real sunlight in the whole Underworld, as the Phoenix told you. The plants here aren't like the ones the Koch-ssi grows. You mustn't eat any of them," Wu Zhe said earnestly. "The black flowers are all of life and death and can be dangerous to living things, even immortals like us."

"I see."

From the depths of the jungle, a loud baying came. It sounded like a pack of dogs after prey—fierce, deep barks, accompanied by a mournful keening. "What's that?" Jin asked.

"Bulgae," said Tiao Xian. "Nasty beasts. They'll eat anything they can get their jaws on. Whatever they're chasing is probably trying for the water—they won't go in it."

Jin blinked in surprise. "But then why would they—"

Tiao Xian scoffed. "Because this is where they landed, obviously. The Gate never opens to the same place. The Bulgae arrived on this island twenty millennia ago, and they've been trapped here ever since. Now why anything would choose to share the isle with them, I'm sure I don't know."

Jin took a step toward the baying noise.

"What are you doing?" asked Tiao Xian. "We should avoid the Bulgae."

"She wants to help," Wu Zhe put in.

Jin flushed. She did, but she would be a fool to ignore the advice of her guides. While she stood frozen with indecision, a beautiful child burst out of the woods. Her long orange hair was tumbled and messy, and a tattered orange shirt revealed bloody legs. She was trying valiantly to run, but one leg was dragging. Two dogs made of fire emerged moments after her, flame falling from their mouths like spittle.

Jin charged forward; the Mudanren would have fallen if they hadn't both grabbed her hair. Jin caught the girl and swung her behind her. Wasting no time to check on the child, she faced down the Bulgae.

She hadn't been quick enough—jaws clamped on her arm before she could draw her tessen.

Its sharp fangs tore into Jin's skin, but its flames didn't hurt her. Jin changed her blood that was pouring freely from her arm into armor. Plates of the same iridescent rainbow metal as the key she had created slid over her golden robes to her wrist and up her shoulder to form a breastplate. In mere moments, she was ready for battle. She bashed the Bulgae with her free arm, and it released her. Suspecting that fire would have no effect on them, Jin drew her tessen and spread it. The two Bulgae leapt for her. Jin sliced left and then right, and the Bulgae fell to either side of her. Their bodies burst into geysers of blue flame. Within minutes, they burnt out, leaving nothing behind.

Three more Bulgae burst from the trees, teeth bared as they growled.

Jin had committed herself to protecting the girl from these creatures, but watching their abrupt and dramatic deaths made her reluctant to kill more. Inspired by the flaming geysers, she reached for the cerulean sea at her back, and it responded. Two funnels of water washed over the rocky beach and stopped at Jin's sides, columns of potential destruction.

"Leave," she ordered the Bulgae, letting power fill her voice, the same power she had used to change the purpose of Bai's golem.

Their curled tails tucked between their legs, and they fled to the trees so quickly that their feet skittered on the rocks.

Jin turned to the girl and realized her blurred first impression had been quite wrong. It was another immortal creature, though it certainly bore a resemblance to a human female around twelve years of age. The "tattered" orange skirt was in fact several tails curling about its legs. They were hard to count, but Jin had a sudden suspicion that there were nine of them. It wore a white robe of sorts that wrapped around its torso and hung long in the front but was cropped short in back so as to not inhibit the tails. The creature had long pointed ears that protruded from its orange hair and its wide orange eyes were watching Jin curiously.

"Thank you," it said earnestly. "My name is Hyeon-ju."

"And I am Jin, the Goddess of Beauty," she paused a moment. "You are the first immortal creature I've met with a name. Or perhaps you only offer one because you know it makes beings like me more comfortable?"

Tiao Xian laughed, a chirrupy, slightly mocking sound. "No, Huli Jing name themselves because they are always breeding and there's too many of them to keep track of otherwise."

Jin was surprised. Did that mean Hyeon-ju was indeed young and perhaps female?

Hyeon-ju bristled. "I'm not a Huli Jing; I'm a Gumiho!"

Tiao Xian shrugged. "Same difference."

"Is not!"

Jin reached out a hand and rested it on Hyeon-ju's shoulder. "Please don't mind Tiao Xian. It likes to rile people. What's the difference between a Gumiho and a Huli Jing?"

"Well—Huli Jing live in Zhongtu and Gumiho live in Bando and—and—"

"And I suppose you've been to both?" asked Tiao Xian cynically. "You don't look more than two thousand to me."

"I was born here, on the Lonely Isle—"

"So doesn't that mean you aren't either?"

"Oh, stop teasing her!" Wu Zhe scolded. To Jin, it explained, "The nine-tailed foxes spread all over the world and adopted many names before they were trapped here with the rest of us. From a physical and magical perspective, they are the same creatures, but the Gumiho have distinct traditions and family rules from the other fox tribes, which has nothing to do with where they live. It matters a great deal to them how you call them."

"And not at all to the rest of us," Tiao Xian muttered.

Jin cleared her throat, hoping Hyeon-ju's ears weren't keen enough to pick up Tiao Xian's comment, though from the way she narrowed her eyes, it seemed they were. "Hyeon-ju, it looks like your leg needs some attention. Will you let me look at it?"

Hyeon-ju hesitated, then nodded.

Once she was arrayed on the shore, Jin washed the wound with sea water. The delicate skin had been shredded by the Bulgae's teeth and Jin had to suppress a wince of sympathy. To distract the girl, whose luminous orange eyes were watering, Jin began to chatter about the Underworld and her adventures so far. She knew she had succeeded when Hyeon-ju asked, "Do you mean to say that you are from Earth? That you came through the gate? But why ever would you come here?"

"I need a black peony," Jin said.

"Oh! I know where some are," Hyeon-ju answered. "I can show you the way, but it'll take two days to walk there. Maybe longer." She looked doubtfully at her leg.

Jin cast about for another story to tell when Hyeon-ju asked her a question. "When you said you're a goddess, do you mean you are worshipped by mortals on Earth?"

"Yes," said Jin. "My parents were both worshipped, so I was named a goddess at birth. But I've only had worshippers for the past thousand years or so."

"I should like to be worshipped," said Hyeon-ju. "That's what Halmeoni says she misses the most about Earth."

"Were the Gumiho worshipped?"

"Oh, yes," said Hyeon-ju. "Mortals regularly asked us for help when they were being threatened or hurt by those in power."

"Yes, and then you'd rip out the hearts of the bullies," said Tiao Xian.

Hyeon-ju looked wounded. "It was justice. We never ate innocent deaths."

"I didn't see you refuse the deaths of the Bulgae just now," mused Wu Zhe.

"Well, Eomma says that is because of necessity. Besides, the Bulgae die and are then reborn, so eating their deaths is better than eating yours," Hyeon-ju smiled at Wu Zhe, showing her sharp teeth.

"Ah, yes, indeed," said the Mudanren, pressing against Jin's neck. "Much better."

Jin reknit Hyeon-ju's skin over her cuts, much the way that she had revived Cheng. Hyeon-ju was shocked and then excited.

Partially to stop her gushing, Jin asked, "What do you mean by eating death?"

"That's what nourishes them," said Tiao Xian, "just like sunlight nourishes us."

"But here in the Underworld, we are deprived of our natural food source," said Hyeon-ju.

"Mortals," said Jin.

"Yes, mortals," she agreed.

Jin hesitated. "Why not restrict yourself to natural mortal deaths rather than vengeful ones?"

Hyeon-ju shrugged. "I hear the vengeful ones are tastier. Would you only eat the peach that has already fallen from the tree rather than picking the perfectly ripe one still on the branch?"

"Are there peaches here?" Jin asked.

"No, but that was how Halmeoni explained it to me," and Hyeon-ju smiled again.

"And what did you mean about the Bulgae being reborn?"

"Oh, they are just like the Golden Phoenix," Wu Zhe said. "They burn when they die and then their bodies reform in flame and their souls return."

"That's another way you know the Gumiho aren't native to Bando," sniffed Tiao Xian. "Bandoan creatures are always reborn in fire."

Hyeon-ju hissed at Tiao Xian. "That's speculation! You don't know that."

"She's right," put in Wu Zhe, ending the argument, "No one knows where the foxes originate from. And rebirth might be tied to their fiery nature rather than their homeland."

Once Hyeon-ju's leg was healed, Jin suggested that rather than going for the peony, perhaps they had better find Hyonju's family.

Hyeon-ju waved a careless hand. "I often go off by myself for days at a time. They won't miss me."

And so they set out for the peonies.

WHEN Bai opened his eyes, dawn was reaching over the horizon, a splash of pink and orange that reminded him of Jin. She would have enjoyed this view of the mountain, long shadows of violet and indigo fleeing before the rising sun. If she were here, she would have a hundred and one observations and comments to share—the soft whistle of the breeze was an inadequate substitute for her voice.

He hoped she was safe, then chided himself for having any doubt. *Fate smiles upon her,* he insisted silently.

He wanted, of course, to return to the peak and test Gang's determination now that his pool of power was refilled.

But Gang had been more powerful than Bai even before millions of mortals had offered up their belief to him. Now, if Xiao were here with him...

Bai stood up, pleased. Xiao and Nanami must still be at the Sea Palace since they hadn't come to the Korikami's Tomb. He would go there to meet them—perhaps they needed help—and then form a plan together. If nothing else, as Jin's friend, Xiao at least had a valid reason to inquire after her.

Bai strode over to the nearest kousa tree and plucked a petal to shape.

He didn't bother with bandages—the burns from Gang's flaming cuts had been agonizing, but they had already turned to scars on his skin, like veins of jasper in quartz.

Instead, Bai made new robes to replace the ones Gang had burned. He wasn't sure what he would find at the Sea Palace, but Ao put enough stock in appearances that he wasn't going to make the same mistake he had at New Moon Manor and show up half-dressed.

When he was satisfied, he took one last lingering look up the mountain. Then he moved between.

Bai reappeared on the ceremonial dock of the Sea Palace, the only place visitors could come and go freely.

The last time he had come, there had been a large gong for guests to ring, but this time he was greeted by two guards dressed in indigo armor made of sharkskin. Past them the building was a little larger than he remembered, but more importantly, the central hall lay in ruins. Bai felt a frisson of unease.

"Welcome to the Sea Palace," said the shorter of the two, a young woman. "What is your name and business?"

"I am Bai."

There was no flicker of recognition in the guards' eyes, but Bai wasn't surprised by that. He thought they were both less than four thousand millennia. "I am an old friend of the Sea Dragon. I had hoped to speak with him." He hesitated. "Might I know what happened to the hall?"

The guards shook their heads. "The Sea Dragon will tell you, if he's so inclined," said the woman. She turned to the boy next to her. "Tell her ladyship that Bai is here and that he wishes to speak with our lord."

The boy hurried off, and within five minutes, Bai saw Miko coming toward him, the boy following in her wake.

She looked tired and worried and a little older than Bai remembered—edging into grandmotherly rather than matronly—but he recognized her easily enough. She bowed to Bai, and he bowed his head in acknowledgement.

"Welcome to our home, First," she said. "Please won't you come in and have some refreshments?"

Acting on instinct, Bai accepted her invitation. He fell in step next to Miko as she walked to a large tea house. They were served by Nimi who smiled at Bai when she bowed to him.

"Is all well here, Lady Miko?" he asked her.

Miko waved her daughter away before replying. "You mean the hall, I assume? A young thug with too much raw power did that." She sighed. "Perhaps four thousand years after you disappeared from the world, my husband had a falling out with Nanami. She returned a few days ago with her lover—my husband and he fought, destroying the hall."

Bai arched his brows. "Is Ao all right? I suppose he taught the thug a lesson?"

Miko shook her head. "He was greatly shamed by the encounter, and has not fully healed, but he will be all right in time."

Bai rubbed his lower lip, and then broached a delicate subject. "When I was last in the world, I feared no other power. But all these mortals have shifted things. Immortals who become deities have an advantage over the rest of us. Unless you too...?"

"Me, a goddess?" Miko laughed. "No, I am too much like my parents. I prefer life to be simple. Though Ao is worshipped by several thousand mortals for he," she caught herself and looked sheepish. "Well, you know Ao."

Bai nodded. "So sailors and fishermen pray to him? He's built temples?"

"You don't need a temple. Things collect power too. Mortals pray directly to the sea, and Ao pulls the power of their beliefs through it."

"Fascinating," said Bai, remembering how the White Willow had felt altered by years of mortal worship. Would it be possible...?

Miko laughed. "Yes, you always found magical theory more interesting than I do. But is that the only reason you came? How long since you returned to the world?"

"Not long. It is much changed."

She nodded. "We've heard that Sun Emperor is dying, so the God of War and the Goddess of Justice are both preparing to take his throne." She hesitated. "I do not wish to offend you, but we intend on supporting the goddess."

Ichimi must have been too busy caring for her lover to have told her family about the confrontation on the Korikami's Tomb. He widened his eyes in surprise, content with seeming as ignorant as possible and said, "She was barely an adult last I saw her. Has Gang upset Ao in some way?"

Miko shook her head. "No, but my eldest daughter will marry the goddess."

"Congratulations," said Bai, "I hope she will be happy." Ichimi had been quietly miserable in her first marriage, and she deserved happiness. Truthfully, Bai did not want Salaana to suffer unduly either, even though she was obviously misguided.

"How are Zi and Hei?" he asked.

Miko pulled a face and looked to the hall. "Perhaps as stressed as we are. Nanami's lover is their son. I believe they went there after they left us."

Bai froze. Xiao had gone to confront his parents? And he still hadn't come looking for Jin?

"They told you that was where they were going?"

"No," Miko admitted, "Just my intuition. They were very openly declaring their love for each other, but Zi and Hei have already arranged a betrothal for him. I suspected that they would go there next, to end it."

"I'm surprised you aren't happier about the match. Xiao is more powerful than the Goddess of Justice."

"Yes, but it doesn't benefit us. Nanami is no longer a member of the family." Miko's brows suddenly pulled together. "How did you know his name?"

"Sorry?"

"You said Xiao just now. How did you know his name?"

Bai tried to think of a reason, and decided a partial truth was best. "It was the Goddess of Beauty who disturbed my solitude. She told me his name, for they are betrothed."

Miko looked surprised but accepted the explanation. Bai spent several hours with her, hearing more news, before she invited him to sleep at the Sea Palace for the evening. Bai wondered if he should hurry on, to look for Xiao at New Moon Manor, but he was loath to confront Zi and Hei again. He already knew they could overpower him magically.

"Thank you," he said to Miko. "I would be glad to stay a while. Perhaps I can help you rebuild." He gestured at the hall.

Miko smiled. "We would be honored."

XIAO lay on the floor, his shirt drenched with distilled rice wine, its smell so strong that it stung Jin's nostrils. Xiao's eyes were open, though his awareness seemed questionable. As Jin watched, he took another sip from a small black flask. A strange sound, half whimper and half laugh, tore from him and hit Jin right in the heart. She knelt and fruitlessly tried to shake Xiao's shoulder.

"Xiao? What's going on? What's wrong? Where's Nanami?"

Jin had been in Xiao's bedroom occasionally, but she had never seen it like this. The black vases were shattered and scattered about the floor. She paced back and forth, trying to touch or move anything, but it was as if she had no substance. She was quite frustrated by the time the large double doors of the room swung open. Xiao's mother entered, followed by his father.

"Leave me alone," Xiao hissed at them, and Jin jumped to hear him speak.

Zi clucked her tongue impatiently and knelt by Xiao. Tendrils of twilight unfurled from her fingertips, and for a moment Jin thought she was going to help Xiao, but the light curled around his wrist and he howled as if burned. Hei knelt at the other side, and coils of shadow wrapped Xiao's other wrist. Xiao writhed between them, his face contorted in pain.

Jin screamed and tried to hit both of them. When that had no effect, she summoned fire. It licked her arms, but neither Zi nor Hei seemed to feel it at all.

Something bit Jin's earlobe.

She jerked upright to find herself in a world on fire, with flames burning along her arms. They had spread from her to the thick foliage on which she slept. Hyeon-ju was doing her best to beat out the flames, while Wu Zhe shrieked in fear. Tiao Xian had bitten her earlobe.

"Put it out," it shrieked.

She extinguished the flames instantly, pitching them into darkness.

"I'm so sorry," Jin said. "I was having a dream—it was both terrible and so real—but it was like I wasn't truly there..."

"Maybe someone summoned you," suggested Hyeon-ju, who seemed more excited than scared by the recent destruction. "Mortals used to summon Halmeoni regularly and when she couldn't answer their summons, she would have visions of them in her sleep. Did you have no substance, and no one seemed to see you?"

Jin stiffened. "Yes. But—does that mean it is really happening? Xiao—his parents—"

"Probably," said Hyeon-ju with a yawn. No longer concerned, she lay down and curled up, her tails enfolding her like a cocoon. She was soon asleep, but Jin was far too upset to follow suit.

"What did you dream of?" Wu Zhe asked her quietly.

"My best friend. He—he was being tortured by his parents. I think—I think they were draining his power."

Wu Zhe shuddered. "I know what that's like. When we first came here, our power was stolen. It burns worse than fire and leaves you hollow."

Jin stiffened. Her fingers found her gold chain and drifted down, over the peacock pendant, to Kunjee. It was through this that Wu Zhe's power—and Tiao Xian's and presumably all the other creatures' power—had been stolen. She suddenly remembered Bai's reaction when she told him that she'd fixed the pendant. But it hadn't been a flaw—it had been intentional. Someone—Aka—had deliberately stolen the power from these creatures. That was why Bai had taken it.

Jin found her fingers were trembling. Could Xiao's parents truly be stealing power from Xiao like that? But he was their son! How could anyone—

She thought of Cheng, trapped in stone for longer than Jin had been alive. A few weeks ago, she wouldn't have believed anyone could do that. The truth was, power in no way tempered spite or malice, and it could amplify them to the point of horror.

Bai had been right to warn her that as her power grew any corruption within her would be revealed in catastrophic ways. She wished that he were here now—not because she needed his help but because she wanted him. Her yearning for his voice was a physical ache.

Something snapped in the dark, pulling Jin back to the present. A white light flickered through the half-burnt foliage.

"Did you see that?" she asked Wu Zhe.

"Yes," it whispered in her ear. "Let us be quiet; perhaps it might pass us by."

But more lights joined the first and soon a dozen of them emerged from the foliage to surround Jin and her companions. The light revealed nine-tailed foxes whose faces ranged from suspicious to hungry. Jin had the sinking feeling it was her death for which they hungered.

She rose slowly, and she rested her hand on her tessen. "And what are you seeking?"

The oldest one, a woman with white hair and deep folds about her yellow eyes, pointed at Hyeon-ju, still sleeping. "My granddaughter."

Hyeon-ju twitched in her sleep, as if feeling the weight of that finger, and opened her eyes. She blinked sleepily then clumsily leapt to her feet. "Halmeoni! What are you doing here?"

"We saw the flames and feared the Bulgae had caught you." The old Gumiho's suspicious gaze did not shift from Jin. "And what might you be?"

"She is the Goddess of Beauty," Hyeon-ju said excitedly. "Her name is Jin."

With florid descriptions and some exaggeration, Hyeon-ju described Jin's "triumphant, glorious" rescue and declared her intention to lead Jin to the black peony.

"Forget that," said a voice, young and male. "Let's rip out her heart and eat her death."

"How dare you!" snapped Hyeon-ju's grandmother, who Jin had decided was the leader of the tribe. "She defended my granddaughter—by our own code, we must never eat her death."

The male fox stepped forward, his deep red hair a wild mess and his nose snarling. "She's an immortal. They trapped us here to starve! How can any of them be protected by the code?"

A shouting match began, those who felt Jin must be protected and those who felt her death should be eaten. Jin wrapped her hand around the base of her tessen and called fire to her veins.

But when the male fox lunged at her, Hyeon-ju's

grandmother thrust her hand into his back and ripped out his heart, blood spraying horrifically. Jin's gorge rose, and she fought the urge to vomit.

"It goes against the code, and I am the keeper of the code!" howled Hyeon-ju's grandmother, sounding more wolf than fox. The others all knelt and bowed their heads. Jin let the fire fade and released her tessen.

The rest of the night saw Jin tucked between Hyeon-ju and her grandmother. Given the turmoil of the evening, she hadn't thought to sleep more, but the great heat from the Gumiho was soothing. Jin gradually drifted off, and dreamed that she was a child again, cuddled by Xiao and Neela in the blue caravan.

In the morning, all the foxes but Hyeon-ju were gone.

"Halmeoni said it would be better for them to see as little of you as possible. Everyone was terribly upset over Bong-jun's death."

"I'm sorry."

Hyeon-ju shook her head fiercely. "You don't have anything to apologize for. Now come, let's get the black peony quickly."

WHEN a roof once again flared its eaves over the main hall of the Sea Palace—and twice as high as it used to—Bai moved on to the Wood Pavilions. There had been no evidence to support Miko's intuition that Xiao and Nanami had gone to New Moon Manor, and it wasn't as if he would be welcomed there. Was it worth observing without any surety that Xiao was trapped there?

Besides, the Wood Pavilions had two benefits as a destination: he might hear news of either Xiao or Nanami and he could check on Cheng.

Unlike most of the Colors, Haraa didn't bother with gates and walls and immortals could enter from any side. Having been advised by Kairoku that the Wood Pavilions had expanded threefold since Bai had been there last, Bai chose to teleport to the only approach that had not changed—the algae-coated docks off the Lake of Reflection.

He paused for a moment to look over the vast lake—it was so wide that Bai could not see the land on the other side. As usual, there was little wind here, so the lake lay smooth and placid, reflecting the sun like a mirror—hence its name.

Bai then turned to the Wood Pavilions, and despite Kairoku's warning, he blinked at the sheer number of green copper roofs peeking above the trees like marmots surveying the land around their burrows.

A pebble path stretched from the dock into the woods, meandering among large trees and boulders, insisting its followers enjoy the nature that surrounded them. And the wise followed the path's suggestion, for Haraa would attack anyone who damaged her plants. Summer was hot and humid here, painting the woods deep green and filling the air with the chirps of cicadas.

Even the crunch of the gravel path was drowned out by the insects, and it seemed any visitors were escaping the heat inside the pavilions. So Bai stretched his magic to seek the essences of either Haraa or Cheng. After about an hour, he found both together, in a three-story pavilion.

In front of the pavilion, several guards wilted in the heat, their red trousers and white tunics damp with sweat. Bai paused a dozen yards away, remembering how he killed two Light

Hands a week ago, and broke the legs of a hundred others. He couldn't imagine Salaana's disciples giving him a ready welcome.

Bai approached slowly, ready to teleport or defend himself if need be. One straggled to his feet when he noticed Bai. "I'm sorry, but if you are looking for Haraa, you must wait here. She should be out in a half hour."

Bai nodded. "Is your lady here?"

The guard blinked. "No, the goddess assigned us to help her brother."

"Karana?" asked Bai.

The man's mouth worked soundlessly, and Bai corrected himself. "The God of Destruction."

"Yes," managed the Light Hand.

"I would speak to him, please."

It seemed addressing Karana by name had deeply impressed the guards, for one ran to fetch him.

Karana came quickly enough, his black lips quirked in curiosity. "I thought you'd be in the Underworld by now."

"Trapped there, you mean?"

Karana blinked, and Bai knew he was genuinely surprised. "Trapped?"

"So you didn't know that Salaana intended to destroy the gate to trap Jin?"

Karana stiffened. "I did tell her what happened at Tsuku, but I didn't expect... I'm sorry. I will try to talk her around." After a moment, "Is Jin alright?"

Bai nodded. "And the gate is well-guarded against future attempts."

Karana grabbed Bai's upper arm, and Bai resisted the urge

to shake him off. "But you aren't saying that Jin is in the Underworld by herself?"

"Of course not. There's hundreds of immortal creatures there too."

Karana shook his head. "I thought you were going to accompany her."

Bai didn't want to admit that he had made a mistake. "I was needed to protect the gate."

Karana dropped Bai's arm to gesture at his face. "Is that how you picked that up?"

Bai knew he was referring to the scar from Gang's flames.

"Salaaana didn't manage to land a blow on me," Bai said.

Karana cocked his head, then pressed a hand to his belly. "I have a scar that looks like that. I thought Gang was going to kill me." Bai couldn't wholly suppress his emotional response, and Karana smirked knowingly. "So it was Gang then." Karana frowned. "But why?

"That isn't your business."

"He thinks you're too old for Jin," Karana guessed, "Though I wouldn't have expected Gang to care."

Bai crossed his arms. He needed to change subjects. "How is Cheng?"

Karana sighed. "There's been no change. Here, come with me."

The inside of the pavilion was as green as the outside, with mossy walls and plants crowding the windows. The rickety staircase's banister was growing leaves.

The second floor was filled with cots rather than plants. Only one was occupied at present though—Cheng lay motionless on it.

Standing beside him was Haraa, her long emerald hair twisted about her. Her tan face was solemn, her mossy eyes trained on Cheng's face while her long, elegant fingers rubbed his temples.

She finished her task before pulling her hands back and looking at Bai.

"Bai. Karana said you'd returned, and that you found Cheng, but I did not fully believe it until this moment."

Bai bowed to her and took a seat. "Do you think he will ever wake up?"

Haraa shrugged. "Perhaps if I knew more of what happened to him..."

Bai shot a glance at Karana who spread his hands, almost in challenge.

"He was encased in turquoise and buried. I presume for several millennia."

Like the leaf she had been, Haraa simply accepted whatever the wind blew her way, but at Bai's words, she actually blinked a few times. A little hesitantly, "I have never seen anything like that. I suppose I don't know then. Why won't Karana let me tell Neela?"

Bai tapped his fingers together. "Haraa, who do you think could encase a being—particularly a Color—in turquoise?"

Haraa's eyelashes lowered. "Neela wouldn't do that." Then she shrugged. "I suppose there's no reason to tell her anything though."

Bai could read the doubt in Haraa, but he supposed this was the biggest concession he could expect from her. Neela was her oldest friend after all. "Thank you."

BAI stayed a month at the Wood Pavilions. He helped with Cheng's care, talking or reading to him a few times a day, and exercising his limbs according to Haraa's specifications. He would spar with Karana, both verbally and physically, and he developed a grudging rapport with the younger being, even though he could not quite forget that Karana had once caused the death of an infant. He resisted the impulse to return to the Korikami's Tomb—he knew that Gang would simply force him away again. He had perhaps made a mistake avoiding worship all these years—if only there was a way to rectify it quickly!

In the meantime, he meditated each day to look for Xiao's essence on Earth. So far, he'd had no luck. He wondered if Xiao and Nanami had perhaps returned to Jin's residence at the Sun Palace, for Jin's wardings would keep them safe.

One day, while he was massaging Cheng's fingers, he heard a familiar querulous voice raised outside the pavilion. And for the first time in sixty millennia, that voice caused the hair on the back of his neck to stand up.

"Do you not know who I am? I wish to see Haraa now. What are you doing here anyway? Is Karana ill? I don't care if he—"

Bai hurried to the window to see Neela jabbing her finger at a Light Hand.

Neela's head whipped up and she looked straight at him. Her lips parted in surprise, then she launched herself at the window, displaying a martial prowess that Bai had never known she had.

Bai leapt from the window and caught her hand; they spun together before landing on the ground.

"Why are you here?" she demanded, tugging her hand from

Bai's. "Did something happen to my granddaughter?"

"Jin is not here," Bai said calmly, trying to keep his thoughts on Neela and the present moment. "I would think you'd be glad that I'm keeping my distance from her."

Neela scowled. "Why are you here?"

"I've been getting to know Karana better. Jin introduced us."

"So Karana is sick?"

"He's been staying here for some time—"

"He's not sick." Her sky-blue eyes narrowed dangerously.

"There's lots of people who visit the Wood Pavilions without being sick," Bai pointed out.

"Yes, but they don't stay at Haraa's personal pavilion. Who's inside? Who are you and Karana looking after?"

Haraa came out then. "This is ridiculous," she drawled. "Neela, Karana and Bai brought Cheng here. They are hiding it from you because they think *you* trapped him in stone several millennia ago."

Neela froze. "Cheng? He's alive? How lucky."

She meant the last, but Bai suspected she meant lucky for Cheng—not her. "May I speak with him?"

Haraa's brows arched smugly; she obviously considered her best friend excused of any wrongdoing. "He is comatose, I'm afraid."

"I see." She turned to Karana. "You should make sure those Light Hands know who I am. I hope they won't bar my way in the future."

Karana inclined his head. "I will make sure they all recognize you."

Neela nodded. "I came to go walking, Haraa. Have you no time?"

"I'm not needed urgently. Let's walk." And the two women moved off, Haraa talking so much that she probably didn't notice Neela's unusual reserve.

Bai turned to Karana, but Karana held up a hand. "No need to tell me. I felt her feelings when she heard you found Cheng. She definitely had something to do with his imprisonment."

"Thank you," said Bai. He hesitated, then said, "I'm going to eavesdrop on them. Probably I will learn nothing."

Karana shrugged, and went back into the Pavilion.

Bai changed into a small white butterfly and chased after Haraa and Neela.

"But why are you so quiet?" Haraa was asking. "Don't you have any news for me?"

Bai could see the tension in Neela's fingers as she squeezed her silvered braid. "Indeed I do. I told you I was worried about Jin and Xiao's betrothal, didn't I? Well, he went to his parents' hall, turned into a *dragon*, and demanded they end it."

"No," gasped Haraa. "But what did Zi do?"

"What does any mother do when her child is mouthy? Spank him and send him to his room."

Bai almost forgot to flap his wings. So Xiao really was at New Moon Manor? And trapped?

Haraa shook her head. "But imagine spanking a dragon! Are you sure this won't be the end of the betrothal?"

Neela nodded. "I'm sure. Zi promised me that she will see it through."

"Do you honestly think their child could bring back Aashchary?"

Bai was confused. Their child? Xiao?

"I have to believe it, else I'd lose my reason for existing."

Haraa patted Neela's hand. "For your sake then, I hope they do get married."

Bai understood—and remembered his comment to Neela. *It's almost as if someone is trying to combine all the colors.*

Could a child of Jin and Xiao resurrect a soul? Bai thought of Nanami's hand and Cheng's restoration and wondered if Jin could resurrect a soul.

They went on to speak of meaningless things, and when she left, Bai returned to the pavilion.

He found Karana in his room and changed back into a man.

"Can you teach me how to do that?" Karana asked.

"What?"

"Shapeshift."

"Of course," said Bai.

Karana's eyes lit. "Now?"

Bai shook his head. "I'm afraid I must leave now."

"Why, what did you hear?"

Bai hesitated. "I believe Xiao needs help."

"Xiao?" Karana echoed in surprise. "But he's betrothed to Jin. Shouldn't you and he be, I don't know, enemies?"

Bai shrugged. "I would try to help anyone Jin loved—even you, I suppose."

Karana rolled his eyes and snorted.

"But actually—Xiao is not as bad as I first thought. And I would help almost anyone in the same situation."

Karana's brows pulled together. "It must be untenable then. What happened to Xiao?"

Bai shook his head. "I haven't confirmed anything yet. I am just going to check. But I don't know when I will return. You will look after Cheng?"

"Yes, yes," Karana waved a hand. "You already have my vow. What more is there?"

Bai smiled. "Thank you."

WHEN Hyeon-ju grew tired during their hike, Jin carried her on her back and was shocked by how little she weighed. Perhaps the Gumiho were naturally slight, but Jin worried that the deaths of the Bulgae weren't enough to sustain them properly. That night, Jin dreamed again of Xiao, but this time she watched his suffering silently without starting any fires. The next day they encountered Bulgae once more, and Jin slayed them quickly, now that she knew they would return to life and that Hyeon-ju needed their deaths. After that, Hyeon-ju was able to walk on her own—still Jin felt bad for the Gumiho.

Just as the light was fading from the forest, stretching the shadows longer and coloring them darker, a rich floral scent seemed to fill the air. Jin blinked and found herself walking faster. Hyeon-ju laughed. "Yes, that is the peonies. They have a reviving effect, which is why they can help those who are dying." Hyeon-ju broke into a run, and Jin followed, Tiao Xian screeching its displeasure while Wu Zhe laughed.

They burst into a glade so thick with peony bushes that it was like running in water. The peonies resembled their earthly counterparts—large, full blooms with many petals on tall stalks with large green leaves—but the petals were the same matte black of all the other flowers on the island. Jin touched one flower gingerly and was alarmed by its delicacy.

"How will I carry this home?" she wondered aloud.

Tiao Xian sighed. "Wu Zhe and I will care for it until we reach the gate. Don't worry—it won't fade under our watch."

"Pick two," suggested Wu Zhe. "We will each take one."

They slept that night among the peonies, and no visions of Xiao disturbed Jin, though she did dream of Bai. It was not a vision though, and when she woke, she remembered only a feeling of longing.

Jin insisted on escorting Hyeon-ju to her family before returning to the Sea of Souls, and then had an escort herself when Hyeon-ju and her grandmother insisted on walking her to the shore.

Hyeon-ju started crying when Jin bid her farewell. "Can I come with you? To Earth?"

Jin hesitated. She wanted to bring Hyeon-ju. But how could she take her away from her family? And could she bring all of the Gumiho with her?

"I think," said Jin, "that is not a good idea this time, as I expect a hostile welcome. But—I won't forget you. I will find a way for you to return to Earth."

The words were as surprising to her as they were to the Gumiho listening—yellow eyes widened and pointed ears perked up—but as soon as she said them, Jin felt a sense of rightness. The creatures could be dangerous, but they didn't belong here. It wasn't right to imprison them for their very nature. By that logic, she herself might be imprisoned for being too powerful.

"Trapping you here was wrong. I will free you. All of you."

Hyeon-ju's grandmother's eyes narrowed in a predatory way. "Will you swear to it?"

Jin stiffened in surprise, but impulsively nodded. "Yes. I vow to find a way for you to return home."

Hyeon-ju's grandmother snorted, but she also blinked, and Jin thought she was holding back tears. "Fate smile on you."

And Jin waded into the cerulean sea.

# Sacrifice and Worry

BAI was wary of attracting Zi and Hei's attention, so he changed into an egret before he teleported. He didn't dare enter the building itself—Zi and Hei would certainly notice a new bird in their gardens and be suspicious of it. The two of them were meticulous in every detail and trusted only each other.

However, he couldn't fly around the manor indefinitely, so he landed on a cloud. He was there some minutes, trying to figure out what he should be looking for, when a large black crow attempted to land next to him. Of course, the cloud was solid only for Bai, so the crow passed through it.

There was something odd about the crow though, in addition to the fact it was so high in the Heavens, so Bai lifted it back up with the cloud.

"Why, you are a man," he said in surprise.

The crow cawed back. That was understandable. It had taken Bai about four thousand years before he had figured out how to preserve his ability to speak while transformed, and he couldn't do it in every form. And this man hadn't even transformed himself—Xiao's power signature was all over him. Did he somehow know that Bai was here?

"Did Xiao send you?" he asked the crow.

The crow hopped back and forth on its two feet for a moment, then it managed, in the way crows mimic speech, "No! No!" He cawed again.

Had Xiao punished this man then? Bai wouldn't have thought it of him, but... "Did Xiao force you to become a crow?"

The crow went off on a long tirade that had nothing coherent in it. Ultimately, "Xiao save! Xiao! Save!"

"He saved you then. Here, why don't you hop for no and bob your head for yes. Is Xiao in New Moon Manor?"

Yes.

"Is he trapped or imprisoned?"

Yes.

"Do you know a way to help him?"

No.

"Is Nanami with him?"

The crow neither hopped nor bobbed, and Bai assumed it didn't know the answer. He tried a different question. "Do you know where he is in the manor?"

Yes.

"Well, it's lucky I met you. But I'm not powerful enough to face Zi and Hei alone. We'll have to wait and see if an opportunity arises... Perhaps they will leave for a while."

The crow bobbed and hopped. Bai took that to mean that

he didn't like Bai's proposal, but he didn't have a better one.

Bai rubbed his chin, chafing at his lack of power. Even his creations like the Great Willow had grown with mortal belief, while he had stagnated!

Glad no one but this strange crow was here to witness this exercise in humility, Bai settled in for a long wait.

ALMOST as soon as Jin entered the Sea of Souls and attempted to control the water, the Sea Serpent's large silver fin appeared. It raised its big head and said, very nonchalantly, *I thought I might as well give you a ride to shore.*

Jin smiled and thanked it. Despite its claim to the contrary, the big creature must have been even lonelier than she had realized. Once she was settled in behind its triangular head, sluicing through the bright blue water, the Mudanren brought up the hasty vow that she had made to Gumiho.

"When you said all of you, did you mean us too?" asked Wu Zhe.

"Yes," said Jin. "All the immortal creatures should be allowed to return to their homes if they wish. Even the Xuezei."

*Fine talk, but do you know how to accomplish such a feat?*

"Well, no," Jin admitted, "But Bai might, or my father might... or I will find a way."

The Sea Serpent blew bubbles in skepticism.

Eager to change the subject, Jin said, "First I need to find the gate to Earth anyway."

"It will be on the Mirror Mount. The better question is, how do we find the Mirror Mount?" replied Tiao Xian.

*The Mirror Mount is far from here. Its land is not connected to my sea.*

"The surest way of getting there is through the Spirit Jungle," Wu Zhe said, "but it's also the most dangerous."

"Why?" asked Jin.

"Both the Achamba and the Giant Tiger have tried to claim it. They will happily consume anyone who comes into their territory."

*I can bring you to the Spirit Jungle,* and Jin could feel the Sea Serpent's amusement at their expense, *if that's what you want.*

"Are they so much more dangerous than the creatures I have met so far?"

The Sea Serpent's amusement increased. *Perhaps not more dangerous, but certainly less reasonable.*

Tiao Xian scowled fiercely, its little pink face wrinkling like dried fruit. "Unfortunately, Wu Zhe is right. It's the only reliable way to reach the Mirror Mount."

"Then we will have to try it," Jin decided.

Jin had intended to converse with the Sea Serpent, to show her gratitude for its kindness, but she was lost in thought instead. The sea reminded her of her mother, yearning to return to her lover in the upper realms. It wasn't fair that she couldn't return to a body like the Bulgae. After all, Aashchary was almost a being of fire, of blue and orange flame.

Couldn't Jin build a body from flame, a vessel for her mother's soul? Bai had been speculating that he might make the bones for Nanami's hand before the Sea Dragon had interrupted their experiment...

"Wait!" Jin suddenly cried out, and the Sea Serpent paused in the water. "I—I need to check something."

Jin lifted the Mudanren off her shoulders, shaking her head

to their many questions, and slid down the side of the Sea Serpent, into the cerulean water.

*Mother!* She cried, reaching her hands out through the water. As if they had been waiting for her, Jin's mother and unborn brother came promptly to her hands. Jin sifted through her feelings and asked a question.

It was hard to explain how the souls answered, but Jin gripped the peacock pendant made of carnelian and sapphire and molded it into a lacy ornament, like the prayer collectors used in temples. She poured the souls inside, and let the ornament settle next to Kunjee.

"You're taking the souls with you?" asked Wu Zhe in surprise.

"Yes."

"But why?" asked Tiao Xian.

*She thinks she can resurrect them,* said the Sea Serpent, and the two Mudanren flinched. Perhaps they had forgotten their mode of transport.

"I—yes, perhaps," Jin admitted again.

*No one has ever resurrected a being, you know, though your grandmother tried.*

"My grandmother—Neela?" Jin asked in surprise.

*Yes. It was before I was here, of course, but the souls told me about it. She loved a mortal man who did not even live out his limited years. So she came here to reclaim his soul. She thought that because the sea was the same color as her, she could make it obey, but she wasn't colorful enough.*

"What happened to the man—the soul she tried to resurrect?"

*He was destroyed. Forever. That's why it's remembered so well, of course. And although the souls like being touched, they cannot last long out of the water. Unless you wrap them in another soul. Your mother's soul will last no more than a few weeks in that pretty prison.*

Jin grabbed the pendant, horrified. Before she removed it though, she asked, "Wrap them in another? You mean sacrifice the second soul, don't you?"

Jin heard confirmation from Sea Serpent's thoughts.

Jin's hand trembled around the pendant. "No. No, I mustn't..."

But it was hard to release the soul back. And then another pressed against her side.

*Not even if you have a volunteer?*

Jin frowned. Who would possibly be willing to have their soul destroyed just so she could carry her mother with her?

Still, she was curious, so she picked it up.

It was smaller than her mother and brother's joint soul, but it shone brilliantly anyway, a yellow chrysanthemum painted gold by a setting sun.

Jin brought this soul to her face and laughter rang in her ears.

❋　❋　❋

NORAN looked at the polished silver, a present from Bai, and twisted her head back and forth.

That chin, those eyes, those lips. By fate, she was gorgeous.

Too bad that wasn't enough for Aka.

Noran floated from her dressing room, her flowing silk robes showcasing her slim figure and emphasizing her grace. She slid open the door across from hers and confirmed that her son was still asleep.

His lay on his stomach, his butt pushed into the air in way that seemed uncomfortable but was his usual way of sleeping. His face was turned toward her, the bed smooshing one plump cheek so that his lips were slightly puckered, and his yellow and red—okay, fine, his *orange*—hair formed half a mane around that sweet little face, a lion cub that was far less fierce than it believed itself.

Noran's heart lurched, and she reminded herself that she was doing what was best for Gang—getting him away from his father's influence.

She still loved Aka—she always would she supposed, without rhyme or reason—but his philandering and his constant denigration had become too much. It seemed like Gang was always watching them with wide eyes and a closed mouth, his stress and confusion obvious to her, even though Aka was oblivious.

Aka still refused to get married—he didn't understand that she was just as powerful as he was. He was convinced that age mattered because he could not shake his belief that Bai was more powerful than him.

Noran touched the white bracelet at her wrist, catching the star pendant between her thumb and forefinger. Bai would never have treated her like this. And yet, she didn't love him.

Sometimes she wondered what was wrong with her, that she craved the stingy affection of a selfish ass instead of the generous love of an earnest man.

Noran let the pendant fall and slid Gang's door shut again. If she wanted to finish fighting with Aka before Gang woke, she had to hurry.

She found him at the top of his pagoda in bed with a bird.

Aka had a thing for former birds—he romanticized them far more than sand, even though Noran was clearly prettier than the drab being next to him.

When they had first built the Sun Palace together, Aka had insisted they each needed their own building, so they had built a pagoda for him and a hall for her. She hadn't realized that he needed his own building so that he could have sex with other beings.

She wanted to slap him, pour cold water on his head, drive her foot into his balls.

She smiled. "I'm leaving with Gang."

He scratched his chest lazily. "Okay. When will you be back?"

Noran shook her head. "We're not coming back. I'm leaving you."

He sat up, and the covers slid to his waist, revealing that far too sexy torso which had deluded her for too long.

"Come again?"

Of course he couldn't understand it—his ego was too big to accept that someone would want to leave him.

"I'm leaving you, and I'm taking my son with me. We aren't going to live here anymore. Don't worry—I won't destroy all the things I built."

*I hope every time you see them, you remember me and regret.*

Of course, he probably would just gloat over all the magic he got out of her. But she could dream.

He leapt out of bed, and Noran averted her eyes. She wasn't going to look at him anymore.

He grabbed her wrist; she ripped it free.

"I'm not letting you leave."

"As if you could keep me here," she snorted.

He pulled himself up. "I'm a god."

"In your own mind," she muttered, and strode toward the stairs. He started to follow her but turned back to grab a robe. Though she had wanted to look graceful and in control in front of him, she started running now. She should have just taken Gang and gone—she hadn't expected him to be this upset.

Aka caught up with her in the pond pavilion—he must have run too.

Heat was pouring off of him, red flames flickering around his fingers.

Well, two could play that game, and everyone knew yellow flame was hotter than red. When he tried to grab her arm, he flinched back, blisters appearing on his fingers.

Noran smiled. "Just because you refuse to acknowledge my power doesn't mean it's not there!"

Aka stared at his hand. "Just because I don't want you to control every aspect of my life doesn't mean I don't acknowledge you!"

"Every aspect?" Noran knew she was shrieking, but she didn't care. "How is asking you to not sleep with other beings controlling every aspect? Zi and Hei—"

"We aren't Zi and Hei! We are Noran and Aka! What works for them doesn't work for us—or do you wish that I had no personality so I could follow you like a shadow?"

She tried to slap him, but he caught her hand. "I like you the way you are," she whispered, "but you aren't good enough for my son!"

"He's my son, too!"

This time when Noran tried to pull away from him, he held

fast.

"You're hurting me!" she cried, for his grip had grown punishing.

His face contorted, but still he didn't let go. She tried to teleport—he tried to stop her. Their wills pitted against each other, his blood-red eyes glaring accusation.

She broke through and reappeared in Gang's room. She gathered him into her arms, even though he was almost too big for her to carry. As it was, his legs dangled almost to her knees.

"Hmm?" His eyes fluttered open. "Eomma?"

"Shh, baby, Eomma has you." His head settled on her shoulder.

Aka appeared in the room. "Don't touch my son!" he roared.

Gang's head jerked up, his eyes yet again wide and fearful. His fear gave her strength, and Noran teleported them.

Half an hour later they appeared in a valley in the Cold Peaks. Noran had chosen it because Aka wouldn't expect it of her. She preferred warm places, like the southern beach in Bando where she had gained life.

"Eomma? Why Baba mad?" Noran sat down and settled Gang on her lap.

"Baba and Eomma need a little space from each other. Like sometimes you want to be alone in your room when you feel angry. So Eomma and you are going to have an adventure! We're going to explore these mountains!" As Noran spoke, she realized she wasn't as committed to leaving Aka as she had thought. Aka's emotion when she declared her intent had moved her. If he found them, begged them to come home...

Still, he needed to miss her for at least a year before she'd go back. Maybe then he'd appreciate her.

Noran set about making a comfortable camp, turning yellow flowers that she found into a golden tent, and yellow silk blankets. Gang, once he saw her occupied and calm, began to climb trees and make "traps" from sticks.

Noran used more magic to get them their meals and all the comforts of home. When it was time to sleep, Gang begged her for a light show story. She hesitated, knowing that breaking Aka's teleportation ban had already siphoned away most of her power, but she agreed because she couldn't resist his big eyes.

Storytime had just ended early because Noran couldn't draw any more power when a voice said, "That's a lot of gold."

Noran was on her feet in a flash. "Who are you? What do you want?" Her heart was in her throat, for stepping into the firelight were dozens of mortal men. They looked lean and hungry, dangerous like any desperate animal.

"Just the goods," the leader said. Noran didn't trust him, and she found the star pendant at her wrist. *Bai, Bai, I need you.*

It would take Bai five minutes to arrive of course, so in the meantime, she tried to cooperate. Without her magic, she didn't see what other choice she had.

But the goods weren't enough for some of them, and one man grabbed Noran and stuck his hand in her robes.

She went stiff, not wanting to scare Gang, but it was too late for that.

He suddenly attacked the men.

Noran wasn't sure if it was good that he was no ordinary child or unfortunate. If he'd been ordinary, he might have died, but maybe the men would only have laughed at his antics and left him alone.

As it was, his fireballs terrified them. At least three men died in his initial outburst.

But God of War or no, he was still just a child. Gang drew as much power as he could to make terrifying fiery pillars and then they were gone, while most of the bandits remained.

Noran ran to him, sheltering his body with her own.

She couldn't stop crying. If she hadn't been so stubborn, they'd still be safe at the Sun Palace. If she hadn't used all of her magic, she would have been able to influence these men and render them harmless. If Bai had come...

Gang was trying to tell her something, but hysteria made the words unrecognizable, his face contorted in a manner that broke Noran's heart. She wrapped her body around his small one, as if she could somehow shield him from the impending violence.

*I would do anything, anything for you, my love. Anything to make up for my mistakes. Please, let fate smile on him, don't let him die! Don't leave him alone!*

Something hit the side of her head.

JIN was breathing hard and clutching the side of her head when she returned to herself in the Sea of Souls. Tears were streaming down her face, though Wu Zhe and Tiao Xian were doing their best to wipe them away.

"I understand," she told the golden soul—her grandmother. Gang's mother.

She hesitated a moment, then spread Noran's soul out, like a kerchief. She poured her mother and brother's soul into it and wrapped them up.

"How long will they last this way?" she asked the Sea

Serpent, as she once again slipped them in the peacock ornament.

He considered. *That's a very determined soul you are using. A month, maybe two.*

Jin stroked the pendant gently.

BAI sat on the cloud for two weeks. He meditated and thought, and watched people go in and out of New Moon Manor. Of Xiao, there was no sign.

Then suddenly, for no reason that Bai could see, the teleportation ban on New Moon Manor suddenly disappeared. Bai perked up and a moment later, the crow did the same. It cocked its head this way and that, looking for whatever had interested Bai.

"This may be our chance," he told it. "Something happened to the teleportation ban."

There was soon chaos inside the manor, people running this way and that; and then Zi and Hei, for the first time in two weeks, both left the manor at once.

Resuming his crane form, he ordered the crow, "Lead me to Xiao."

They flew past several disciples, all of whom were too upset to pay them attention, into an open window. Bai's wingspan was too wide to comfortably navigate the hallway, so he resumed his natural form. The crow led him to a set of double doors with a large padlock. With the palm of his hand, Bai shattered one of the doors.

The smell of alcohol assaulted his nostrils. He lifted his sleeve to shield his nose and stepped into the room. It looked like wild animals had ravaged the place—broken pottery, torn silk, and splintered wood, all piled haphazardly. For this reason Bai wasted time shifting the debris to his search for Xiao, but he finally had to conclude he wasn't there. "Did they put him somewhere else?" he wondered, looking at the crow.

The creature landed on his shoulder, cawed loudly, and pointed its beak toward a window.

For the first time, Bai realized that all the other windows in the room were barred, but this one had only a pile of sand on the sill.

Bai hurried over to it and looked out into the garden. He didn't see Xiao. Then a loud burp drew his attention downward.

Xiao slumped against the wall, a magical artifact in his hand. Upon closer inspection, Bai saw that it was a flask that dispensed an unlimited supply of strong rice wine.

Bai sighed. "Xiao. Xiao!"

Slowly, Xiao tilted his head back and blinked at Bai. He slurred something with Bai's name.

"We need to leave quickly," Bai told him. "Why don't you leave the flask?"

There was no response—Xiao was too focused on standing up, which he eventually managed.

Xiao went to grab Bai's shoulder and almost smacked the crow. "I'm not dreaming?" Xiao asked.

"I don't think you'll need that," Bai said, pointing to the flask.

Xiao followed the direction of his finger, but just blinked. "What?"

"Never mind," Bai muttered. He grabbed Xiao's hand and

teleported the three of them to the White Mountain.

# Nightmares and True Dreams

NEVER had Nanami been so happy to breathe in the smoky, damp air of the Cave of Shadows. She was so close now—once she delivered the Sowon Gold to He Who Walks in Shadow, he and his disciples would steal the prayer collectors and then—

And then—

For the first time in almost two months, Nanami let herself remember Xiao as she had last seen him. In dragon form, whips of violet and black power entangling him.

He had saved her from her father, forced her family to acknowledge her, made love with her, and she had *abandoned* him when he was most vulnerable.

She didn't regret it precisely—she knew that there was nothing she could do against the might of the Moon and Night deities, but she had felt horrible. Had been suppressing guilt and fear since she'd left. Only now, when she was so close to helping him, could she confront the dark turmoil of her feelings.

*Soon, Xiao,* she thought. *Hold on, my love.*

The Sowon Gold lay heavily against her hip as she swaggered into the hall of the Cave of Shadows. She scanned the smoke-filled room, ignoring the raucous laughter and explicit invitations from the crowd, to look for her old master.

He Who Walks in Shadow saw her first, and a wide grin split his pockmarked face. He strode toward her, hand outstretched.

His hand met her shoulder as lightly as a mosquito landing on its victim, and he ushered her down an unfamiliar passageway. Nanami suspected that they were going to his private rooms, and she mused that anyone who saw his barely restrained excitement would assume he was hurrying his lover to their bed.

He Who Walks in Shadow led her through a wooden door frame—the first she had seen in the caverns—and swung a thick, hardwood door shut behind them, pitching the room into unrelieved dark. Nanami heard rather than saw him throw the bolt behind him, for even she found it hard to see. She knew He Who Walks in Shadow was not similarly disadvantaged, but she ignored a twinge of unease—she had extracted a vow from him to steal the prayer collectors. Any other mischief he threw at her she could handle.

"You found it? You have it?" His voice was eerie, disembodied in the black.

Nanami lifted her thief's pouch.

He said impatiently. "I know that pouch, and I know only you can open it."

Even though she couldn't see the drawstrings, Nanami deftly loosened them to reveal the hundred pieces of Sowon Gold.

He Who Walks in Shadow charged at her.

Nanami dropped her pouch, and she heard the gold hitting the stone floor with an improbably sweet chiming. Trusting her instincts, she managed to turn two blows of He Who Walks in Shadow.

"Aren't you forgetting something?" Nanami did her best to keep her voice even. "You don't want the Sowon Gold for a few measly decades. If you don't follow through with our deal—"

His foot connected to her belly, driving the air from her lungs. "I swore to steal the prayer collectors from the hundred largest temples of the Moon and Night deities—I didn't swear that you would be free when I did so."

Nanami cursed him violently, but it was simply to appease him. The betrayal didn't surprise her, and she knew she was dozens of times more powerful than He Who Walks in Shadow. She was the better fighter too, and while he was busy kicking the pouch away from her—foolishly, for she had to give it to him or lose her immortality—she managed to press her dagger against his throat.

He teleported away.

Nanami stood and tried to teleport too.

She couldn't.

Just as she had been unable to break the teleportation ban at New Moon Manor, she was held fast here. She tried twice more, just because she couldn't believe that He Who Walks in Shadow had the strength to hold her. It was only after her third failure that Nanami explored her surroundings.

She felt hard, cold iron bars, and much closer than she had expected.

She had walked into a cage.

And she didn't think He Who Walks in Shadow had built it.

WHEN they came out of between, Xiao promptly vomited. Bai was not fond of alcohol—or any drug—and had not anticipated such a consequence, so most of the vomit ended up on him. Bai released Xiao, who sat on the floor, and stripped down to his trousers. He put everything else in the fireplace and burned it.

Xiao laughed. "Seems excessive."

"I can make new clothes faster than I can clean these," Bai told him. Bai gestured to the crow, which had landed next to Xiao and was inspecting him. "What's with the crow?"

"I don't know," said Xiao. "Should I?"

"He's supposed to be a man. Aren't you the one who transformed him?"

Xiao frowned and bent his head to look more closely at the crow. Even though he seemed more sober for having teleported and vomited, he still misjudged the distance to the crow, and had to grab the floor to steady himself.

"Dawa?" asked Xiao. He smiled in relief. "So you lived."

"Then you do know him."

"Yes. He is—was—my mother's third disciple. He tried to help me escape, and as punishment, she made him jump off of the manor."

"Why didn't he just teleport?" asked Bai.

"She drained him first."

Bai sighed. "Then you did well, transforming him."

Xiao looked back at Bai. "Compliments from the First? This calls for a celebration." And he drank from that cursed flask that he had been unable to leave behind.

Bai rubbed one eyebrow. "I get why you got drunk when you were locked up. But why are you still drinking? We have a lot to do—unless you want to leave Dawa as a crow forever? And Jin needs you."

"Jin?" Xiao snorted. "Why didn't she come when I needed her?"

Bai raised a brow. "You summoned her? She couldn't come—she's in the Underworld."

Xiao paused at that and set down the flask. "Then why aren't you there too?"

Bai preferred to keep his mistakes to himself, but he felt Xiao deserved the truth. "I'm not sure. I should have examined Kunjee more closely. When we walked through the gate, Kunjee only unlocked it for Jin. However, being left behind meant I was able to stop Salaana from destroying the gate."

"Ah, yes, even your mistakes have a higher purpose."

Bai didn't appreciate Xiao's sarcasm and gave him a look, but the younger being simply stood up and said, "It seems we have a lot to catch up on. If you don't want me to drink this, how about some food?"

Xiao didn't drink for the rest of the evening, and Bai began to think his unease had been for nothing. They caught up on the past month, and Xiao tried to change Dawa back into a man.

"I'll have to think on it," he muttered after his first attempt failed. "It's not the same as changing myself."

The next morning, when Bai woke, Xiao was already out in the garden. And he was drunk again.

"What are you doing?" Bai demanded.

"Relax," said Xiao. "I was just feeling a little stressed."

Bai shook his head and sighed. "If you can't help me protect Jin, I need to find a way to do it myself." Bai paused to look at Dawa, who was watching Xiao from a few feet away. "Are you staying with him?"

The crow bobbed his head.

"I'll be at the Wood Pavilions for now," he told them both, and moved between.

IT felt like Nanami had only just fallen asleep in the cage when He Who Walks in Shadow's voice woke her.

"See, she's here, just like I promised."

There was a flare of purple light, and Nanami blinked to see Zi and Hei through the bars of her cage.

Zi looked at her husband; he nodded and a moment later Nanami was pulled between, along with the cage. They came out no more than twenty minutes later in the middle of the main hall of New Moon Manor. The place they had tortured their son and harvested his power.

She came to her feet, not wanting to seem submissive or fearful—even though she was the latter. But Zi and Hei ignored her for He Who Walks in Shadow.

"Divinities," he cried from his knees, his plain, pockmarked face twisted in fear, "I have given you what you wanted!"

"You just left out one important detail. The theft of our prayer collectors."

"But I have returned them—and not one broken! I had to steal them! She made me vow—I would have lost my powers otherwise."

"You will lose your powers anyway," said Zi, "for breaking our trust in you."

And just as he had with Xiao, Hei wrapped He Who Walks in Shadow in a whip of power, a black shadow that seemed to swallow all light.

He Who Walks in Shadow did not try to disguise his pain. He screamed and writhed, thrashing his limbs, and Nanami flinched, remembering Xiao's roars.

It lasted only a few moments, and then Hei pulled the power whip back. He Who Walks in Shadow lay in a pile on the basalt floor, and Nanami realized that He Who Walks in Shadow had indeed been drained dry—he just had far less power than Xiao had.

"We will speak in three days," Zi announced, but Nanami doubted that He Who Walks in Shadow could hear her.

Two disciples were summoned in a way invisible to Nanami's eyes, and they dragged He Who Walks in Shadow away. Their expressions were so bored that Nanami knew this must not be an unusual occurrence.

When Nanami remembered how often she whined about her father to Xiao, she felt horribly guilty. She had wanted more attention, but her parents had done the best they could for all their children. It hadn't been right for her, but they were nothing like Zi and Hei. Even Ao's threat to eat her had been from honest anger rather than cruelty.

"Welcome, Nanami the Thief," Zi said, as if Nanami had accepted their invitation. "We do not need to be enemies. In fact, we could be allies, if you are willing to persuade Xiao to follow through with the marriage we arranged."

Zi's small lips were curled in a polite smile, and Nanami looked for Xiao in her face. She found him too—Zi's large lavender eyes were the same color as her son's and surely his sharply defined chin had come from her. But she was so distant, so aloof from other beings, while Xiao felt things so deeply.

Nanami considered Zi's proposal. "I do not need to marry Xiao," Nanami told Zi, "but I need him to be happy and healthy. He says that marrying me is crucial to his happiness."

"He's young," Hei said, with a slight wave of his hand.

"I heard," said Nanami, "that you met the Moon Goddess at the moment of your creation—that you became a man for her. Did your feelings ever waver?"

Hei narrowed his eyes. "I was Zi's shadow. We are two parts of a whole."

Zi elaborated when Hei stopped speaking. "Whereas you and Xiao are very different people. Come, Nanami, you are nearly thirty millennia old. You've known Xiao for what, a few months? Will you sacrifice your freedom for him?"

"Is that what you are threatening me with—my freedom? You intend on locking me up if I won't support your goals?"

Zi smiled more broadly, a rather frightening sight.

But Nanami refused to be intimidated. "I don't understand why you aren't more sympathetic to his feelings. Could either of you have endured marriage to someone else?"

"He is our son," Zi insisted. "It is his duty to obey us. We should come first in his heart."

"That only happens when you put him first in yours," objected Nanami. "And even then, children grow up and start families of their own. How do you not understand this?"

"Is it pointless to negotiate with you then?" asked Zi. "You are determined to defy us?"

Nanami hesitated. "Is this a negotiation? I wasn't aware you offered me anything for my cooperation—only punishment if I proved intractable."

"Of course we are offering you something!" said Zi. "We will accept you into our house as Xiao's concubine."

"Lucky me," muttered Nanami. She braced herself and said, "I will be willing to negotiate if you let me see Xiao. Once I know that he is alright, I will consider your terms."

Hei nodded once, in approval or acceptance, Nanami supposed.

Her cage disintegrated, but before she could appreciate that, an iron manacle appeared around her wrist, the end of its chain in Hei's hand.

He and Zi led her through the manor, and this time Nanami took it in. The high ceilings, windows depicting the moon's phases, and rich wall hangings were even more impressive and beautiful than the Sea Palace, but it seemed to lack something. Friendliness? Life? It felt somehow austere and harsh.

They stopped suddenly, and both Zi and Hei's backs went stiff. They were both much taller than Nanami was, but she managed to peer around the side of them.

Ahead were a pair of doors, but one of them had been completely shattered.

Hei handed Zi the chain and stepped through the shattered door by himself.

Less than five minutes later he returned, shaking his head. Zi hissed.

Her efforts had not been in vain then. Nanami was light-headed with relief.

NANAMI woke abruptly in the early morning when twilight reigned. She had felt a summoning from Xiao, and she tried, before she remembered where she was, to teleport to him.

She slammed into Zi and Hei's teleportation ban and sagged back into the soft mattress that they had given her.

"I'm sorry," she told Xiao, though he could not hear her. "You know though, that I would come if I could, don't you?"

A single tear slid down her cheek.

Zi and Hei had made a comfortable prison for her, but it was still a prison.

"You did well," she said into the dark, "Escaping on your own. I will find you soon."

XIAO watched Bai teleport away, and despite the wine in his stomach, his anxiety spiked. Or maybe the wine was making it worse—it was a little hard to tell at present. He raised the flask in a salute to Dawa.

"Guess it's just us now," he said to the crow and tried to take a drink.

Dawa flew into his hand, knocking the flask onto the ground.

"Hey!"

"Change. Change. Change. Me!"

Xiao looked at Dawa for a moment. "Yes, I'm sorry, I should change you back, but I can't. I can't do anything or help anybody. I'm useless."

This morning he had woken up feeling hopeful. Jin hadn't abandoned him after all, Bai had come to help him, and he had managed to save Dawa.

Then he had tried to summon Nanami. When she hadn't come, Xiao had wondered if she somehow knew that he'd thrown himself into wine-soaked oblivion. He had thought about Jin alone in the Underworld, and Bai and Nanami's warnings about the immortal creatures had rung in his ears. He had looked at Dawa, hopping around on the ground, and realized he still had no idea how to change him back. Xiao belatedly recognized the look on Bai's face at New Moon Manor as one of disgust.

His hands had started shaking, and he had reached for the flask without even thinking about it and taken a large gulp in his mouth. It had burned slightly, for it didn't have the comfortable familiarity of Infinite Jug's cheap wine, instead tasting of shame and despair, but Xiao had swallowed anyway.

Life felt out of his control. Xiao lurched to his feet and over to the mountain spring where Bai liked to meditate. Xiao plunged into the cold water—it was unpleasant, but the cold didn't affect him—and then climbed up onto a rock. When he and Bai had left the Yanou to come here, Bai had stood on this rock, harmonizing with the world.

Xiao tried to stand on one now, but he kept slipping and falling into the water. He looked to shore and found Dawa watching him.

"See? I can't even manage this. How could I ever turn you

back? You need to be free—it's a mistake to follow me around. You'd be better off going to those—what are they called—the Safe Caves. No, that's not right. The Sanitary Caves. Ah, fate curse it. Point is, there's no reason to stick around me."

And to his shock, Dawa disappeared.

"I didn't think you'd really leave. I did save your life, after all."

Xiao closed his eyes to try and hold in the tears, but they leaked out anyway.

He was the only one standing in his own way now.

Where was the Night Dragon, who saved his lover from her family and even mocked them cheekily while doing it?

Where was the spy who only feigned drunkenness while collecting intelligence at the Sun Court?

Why was he the useless god again, only good for drinking and making other people glad they weren't him? Why couldn't he do this? Why couldn't he be his best self, without fear, without anxiety?

Alone in Bai's garden, Xiao drank until he fell asleep.

1,000 *years ago*

HEI settled a hand on Xiao's shoulder, and Xiao resisted the urge to shrug it off. "Yes, Father?"

It was late on the day of Xiao's adulthood ceremony, and most of the hundreds of guests had already left. The sun was setting, throwing long shadows across the formal front gardens of New Moon Manor.

"I have a present for you," Hei announced. "Come with me."

Xiao wasn't particularly excited. His parents usually gave him a gift on his centennial birthdays, but it was never something he liked. Black and purple robes were the most common present.

Hei brought Xiao before a massive jug, as big as Xiao's torso and made from black clay. Hei gestured to it proudly. "You're an adult now. I thought you and Jin might want to have another party with your friends."

Hei produced two cups and turned a spigot at the bottom of the jug. One he passed to Xiao, which he promptly clinked with his own cup.

Xiao took a sip while Hei tossed back his cup.

"This is wine?" Xiao asked. He'd had a sip once or twice before in his life, but he had never really drunken alcohol before. "Thanks."

He supposed it might be fun to drink with Jin, but this sure seemed like a lot of wine for just them. What friends did Hei imagine Xiao inviting? The God of Festivals, maybe?

"It will never run out," Hei boasted. "I call it the Infinite Jug."

Xiao blinked. Ah. So his father had made it. Xiao finished his drink and smiled.

"What are you waiting for?" Hei asked. "Neela and Jin are waiting for you."

Xiao looked at the imposing jug once more. It didn't look very portable. "Well. Thanks." He picked up the jug, and it was just heavy as it looked.

Neela laughed at the sight of him. "A generous gift, Hei," she told his father. To Xiao, "Maybe you'll let me borrow it sometimes?"

Jin flushed and hunched her shoulders. She could be overly sensitive about Neela's carefree manners.

Neela took all three of them together, so that they'd arrive at her caravan simultaneously. Jin's adulthood ceremony—and her return to the Sun Palace—was in one month, and Xiao planned on staying with her until then.

Zi had told him it would be a good time to solidify his place in her heart, before she lived among the Sun Court, and Xiao hadn't needed the advice. He'd noticed for himself that Jin was growing up, and he had been wondering what it would be like to kiss her for some time now.

Neela announced her intention to go out, and said she hoped they would behave themselves—with a lascivious wink that suggested the opposite.

Once she was gone, Xiao suddenly felt nervous.

"Want a cup of wine?" he blurted.

Jin smiled, her lips dark, plump, and perfect. "Okay."

Xiao started a fire while Jin went in the caravan to fetch some cups. Soon they were sitting arm to arm by the fire, both drinking slowly.

Jin's shoulder was a bit lower than his, and after they had both refilled their cups once, Xiao set his arm about her shoulders.

She turned to face him, her gold eyes catching the fire even in the dark, and her lips slightly parted. Xiao wondered if she could feel his heartbeat—it felt all-consuming to him.

He bent his head. She didn't lean in, but she didn't pull away either. Xiao closed his eyes and went the rest of the way.

Only, instead of soft lips, he kissed a hair-covered ear.

His eyes flew open, and Jin jerked out of his embrace. She

was on her feet and glaring at him before he even finished processing what happened. "Don't! Don't do that again!"

She ran into the caravan.

Xiao touched his lips with his thumb. Well, if this wasn't the most awkward moment of his life so far, he didn't know what was. Going into the caravan now was out of the question.

Sleep seemed even farther away.

He looked at the Infinite Jug. He had never been to the Wood Pavilions, but according to Neela, it was a never-ending party. If he brought the jug with him, surely he'd find some immortals who were willing to distract him in exchange for free, unlimited wine.

Xiao arrived at the docks of the Wood Pavilions an hour later. He set the jug down on the slippery green wood trying to get his bearings.

Luckily two immortals were tying a boat up, and they both looked at him with friendly interest. "What do you have there?" asked one. They might have been a woman or a man, with a slim, elegant build and short hair. Their voice was smooth and melodious, alluring in itself.

"Wine," Xiao said.

"Well," said their companion, a short, muscular man, "Are you looking for people to share it with? 'Cause Kulap and I know what to do with wine. I'm Mu Rong. You?"

"I'm Xiao. I'd be happy to share. Want to help me carry it? It's a beast."

"Absolutely!"

IT turned out that wine wasn't the only thing Kulap and Mu

Rong knew what to do with. Xiao awoke the next morning lying between them.

He had enjoyed everything they had done, but he was also mortified to be sandwiched naked between two near strangers. Remembering how everything had felt easy and comfortable last night, he got up and poured himself a cup of wine. By the time he saw the bottom of the cup, he was feeling better. So what if Jin didn't want to kiss him? They were plenty of beings who did.

And he was the God of Pleasure after all. Now that he was an adult, it was time to take up that mantle. He could do worse than learn about pleasure from Kulap and Mu Rong and the other beings who frequented the Wood Pavilions.

*200 years ago*

XIAO was late for the Sun Emperor's birthday celebration. He wasn't worried though—he doubted Aka cared too much about his attendance and besides, with those mushrooms he'd eaten, it was more or less impossible to worry about anything.

He probably should have gone to the South Gate, where guests would be greeted by courtiers, but he impulsively went straight to Jin's residence. She was practicing her dancing while her disciple—Yeppeun, yes, that was her name—played the flute in accompaniment.

Xiao started dancing too, and scooped Jin up in his arms. He misjudged how her weight would affect his balance though, and they came crashing down on the flagstone path.

Jin cried out. "You okay, Little Jin?" asked Xiao.

"No, you idiot!" She probed her ankle and tried to stand. "I won't be able to dance tonight!" she cried.

Xiao collected the tears from her cheeks. "Diamonds," he murmured and spread them on his own cheeks.

Jin moved her face close to his own. "Xiao? What's wrong with you?"

"Everything is right," Xiao sang, before making spectacles from his fingers and ringing Jin's eyes. "Diamonds from gold."

"He's intoxicated, my lady," said Yeppeun.

"He doesn't smell like wine," Jin said, pressing her hand to his forehead. Xiao pinned it there. "Maybe he's ill."

"There are drugs besides alcohol. I would guess he's on something psychedelic."

"Well, we've got to get him presentable for the celebration," said Jin. "I mean, what in the Heavens is he wearing?"

"Mud and flowers, I think."

Xiao had a great time in the bath, even though both Jin and Yeppeun refused to join him. But he wasn't feeling so good when they went into the hall. He pressed a fist to his mouth.

The Sun Emperor himself came over to greet Jin. "My darling girl! What happened?"

"I—I fell, Papa. I'm sorry, I won't be able to dance—"

That was as long as Xiao could hold it in. He moved his fist, and vomit spewed forth.

A moment later, there was nothing but heat in the world. The burning was inside of him. He would never eat mushrooms again if this was the result. He screamed and cried but the burning went on and on.

When it finally stopped, Xiao was sprawled on the white marble floor of the hall. Sober now, he realized it was not the mushrooms that had lit his blood on fire, but the Sun Emperor, looming over him and radiating fury.

"I'm sorry," he said, noticing his vomit dripping down the emperor's vermillion robes and onto his red-booted feet.

The Sun Emperor stormed away, probably to get changed, and Xiao looked at Jin. Her face was as red as the emperor's boots and she wouldn't meet Xiao's eyes.

# Old Friends and New Enemies

THE Spirit Jungle was gorgeous and lush, if alien. The densely packed trees and vines burst with leaves in a bright kaleidoscope of colors, and when dark fell, they glowed with soft neon light. The jungle was filled with creatures as colorful as the leaves. Their shades ran free and wild, yet were totally silent. In fact, even rustling leaves and bird calls were conspicuously absent, and when Jin bent to smell a flower, it was odorless. That was when she realized she didn't even smell dirt or mulch, as in any forest on Earth. It was as if the whole place were confined only to one sense, sight.

The jungle itself did not seem to pose any danger to them, and despite the Mudanren's warnings about the Great Tiger and the Achamba, nothing had bothered them yesterday or last night. In fact, the only thing worrying Jin at present was her failure to dream about Xiao.

Had the dreams stopped because he had been freed? Or had something even worse befallen him so that he could not summon Jin at all? It was another reason to choose the Spirit Jungle rather than risk a longer route, and she was eager to hurry. But Wu Zhe and Tiao Xian insisted on eating a full breakfast before they set out in the morning. Jin asked warily if they could truly eat the plants of the Spirit Jungle.

"Yes," Tiao Xian told her, "and they will nourish us, but they taste like dust."

Indeed, dust was an accurate description for the mango shaped blue and violet fruits Jin ate. She went to have another, just to fill her belly, but Wu Zhe told her to eat some black and red nuts instead. "Even though they taste the same," it explained, "they are just like fruits and nuts on Earth. Variety is good for you."

"How do you know this?" she asked.

"The Koch-ssi has studied all—or almost all—of the plants in the Underworld. That is how we know the Underworld so well. We gathered them for her."

"So how did you cross the Sea of Souls before?"

"We made a deal with some Nisei who flew us across."

They set off soon after, and Wu Zhe began to sing a song to fill the eerie silence of the jungle.

> *When raindrops hit leaves*
> *The leaves will bend and drip.*
> *When sunlight hits leaves*
> *The leaves will stretch and reach.*

The lyrics were simple and the tune light and cheerful, so Jin hummed along. Even Tiao Xian joined in.

Perhaps that is why they didn't hear footsteps behind them—or perhaps the tiger's padded paws were too quiet to be heard.

His roar, delivered mere inches from Jin's back, was not.

She whirled and stumbled back, confronted with teeth as long as her arm. It was amazing that a beast of such size could slip through the dense jungle undetected.

Wu Zhe held onto Jin's hair as if its life depended on her, and whispered urgently into her ear, "Don't scream, or cry, or show fear."

*A bit late for that*, mused Jin, but she calmed herself.

"You smell like Cheng," rumbled the Great Tiger and the force of its breath pushed Jin's hair back just as surely as a strong breeze. "Why is that?"

Wu Zhe's warning reminded Jin of the winter she had spent in northern Jeevanti, when a hungry tiger had acquired a taste for mortal flesh. Neela had stayed to see how the village hunters would catch the fearsome beast, and Jin remembered one of the older hunters warning that if cornered by a tiger, it was better to become the aggressor.

So Jin stood tall, tessen in hand and looked straight into those hot ember eyes. "Cheng is my grandfather."

The tiger sat back on its haunches, and its head was suddenly even with the treetops. Surveying Jin like a cat does a mouse, it twitched its tail back and forth.

"It has been quite some time since living prey came through my jungle. I thought to eat you, but when I smelled Cheng, I decided to talk to you before pouncing. Now I regret it, for I am not sure if I can in good conscience eat his granddaughter. Is he fond of you? Would your death bother him terribly?"

When Jin hesitated, Tiao Xian pinched her ear. "Yes, yes, of course!" it squeaked.

"Wouldn't any grandfather mourn his granddaughter?" she asked instead, feeling like a prime idiot. But a five-thousand-year-old habit of meticulous honesty was hard to break. Even this hedging felt like a lie to her, and Jin internally squirmed with discomfort.

The tiger cocked its head. "Is that a no? Cheng doesn't love you? Fate teases me, but now I am even more curious, for as you say, grandfatherly affection is quite the norm. Were you a naughty child? Did you flout his wishes?"

"Actually, I have never spoken with him," Jin admitted. "I didn't know he was my grandfather until a few months ago."

"A few months? And how old are you?"

"I will be five thousand millennia next year."

And so the questions continued, and Jin became so invested in forming clear answers that she could almost forget the threat of the tiger. If it hadn't been for the way Wu Zhe and Tiao Xian quivered on her shoulders (the first begging fate to smile on them and the other threatening to run off and leave Jin to her fate) and the way the Great Tiger periodically flexed his very large, very pointy claws, Jin probably would have.

Finally the tiger announced, "It's been ten thousand years since I have enjoyed a conversation so much. Truth be told, I'm not sure I've had a conversation since then. Yet how irritating, for now I cannot make up my mind whether I should eat you or not. I need more time to decide. You had better stay as my guest."

"But," objected Jin, "I'm in a bit of a rush—"

The tiger shrugged its mighty shoulders. "Then I shall attempt to eat you now. You clearly have some power, so perhaps you will kill me and escape?"

Jin wasn't sure if she could or not, and honestly, she didn't want to. She hated killing, and she was already beginning to think of the tiger as a friend. "How close is the Mirror Mount from your home?"

"Oh, just half a days' walk. Why?"

"That is my destination," Jin said. She touched the pendant that contained the souls of her family. The Sea Serpent had only given Aashchary one to two months. "I can stay one week, and then you will have to decide, or we will fight, for I cannot spare longer than that. Will you agree?"

The tiger grumbled, but he accepted. Wu Zhe and Tiao Xian sagged against the side of Jin's neck, heaving identical sighs of relief.

BAI entered Cheng's room and froze. A stranger was leaning over his friend, hands on either side of Cheng's face, lips pressed against his. They were tall and slim, dressed in loose green and orange shawls. Bai almost surged forward to defend the unconscious Cheng, but he saw Haraa looking on, her face solemn and calm.

He strode to Haraa first. "What's going on?"

"We are trying to awaken him through sexual arousal. I would have asked the God of Pleasure, but he is unavailable, so Kulap was the next best choice."

If anyone could figure out how to waken Cheng, Bai

believed it was Haraa. Nonetheless, he objected. "But Cheng could not consent to this."

"If you could ask him, don't you think he'd choose being pleasured by a stranger than being unconscious for the rest of his life?"

"No," said Bai, "I do not know what he'd pick. People have the right to choose for their own bodies." Already knowing the answer, "Would you rather be pleasured by a stranger?"

"That's different. Sexual arousal wouldn't affect me—but it might work on Cheng."

The being who was presently kissing Cheng stood up. "I think your concern is valid," they said to Bai, "But I did not feel just a kiss was excessive, which is what I agreed to. And I think it worked."

Bai looked past the stranger to Cheng, and saw his eyes were open. Bai surged forward and took Cheng's hand in his.

Cheng opened his mouth, and made a strange noise, as if he'd forgotten speech. Bai slipped an arm behind Cheng's back and brought him into a sitting position.

Cheng's eyes slowly focused on Bai's face, and then his arms swung up and around Bai's body.

Bai was surprised. They were old friends, but he could probably count the times they had embraced on one hand. Bai slid his arms around Cheng. Tremors shook Cheng's body. "It's okay," Bai murmured. "I'm here. You're not alone."

When Cheng pulled back, he had found his voice. "Neela ambushed me! But why? Did she free me from the stone?"

Haraa gasped. "It really was Neela? But she said—"

Cheng turned to look at her. "She sealed me in stone, without even telling me why."

"Haraa," said Bai, "would it be possible for Cheng and me to speak alone? There are things he needs to hear."

Haraa looked upset, but she gestured at the being who had kissed Cheng. The two of them shut the sliding door behind them.

"It wasn't Neela who freed you," said Bai, "It was your granddaughter."

Cheng blinked slowly, then laughed. "You finally found a sense of humor!"

"No," said Bai, "It was your granddaughter."

Cheng knocked Bai on the head. "I haven't even had a child, which last I heard was a prerequisite for grandchildren."

Bai nodded. "You did have a daughter—with Neela. This is conjecture, but I believe that is why she attacked you."

Cheng shook his head. "That's impossible—I..."

"She told me that you disguised yourself as a mortal."

"I never disguised myself! Are you certain that her daughter is mine?"

Bai nodded. "She must have been. She was unknowable and had an affinity with orange, besides being very powerful."

"Have been? Is she not alive?" Cheng grabbed Bai's upper arm in a bruising grip. "How long was I in that stone?"

Bai hesitated, and Cheng's fingers dug deeper into his bicep. "How long was it after Aka put the Phoenix in the Underworld that you were sealed away?"

Cheng's brow knit. "I suppose—a hundred years?"

Bai swallowed. "Then it is close to eighteen millennia that you were in there."

Cheng's grip went slack, and he fell back against the bed. Cheng shook his head in disbelief. "How could she hate me so much?" Then, "You are right. Her daughter must have been mine. What happened to her?"

"Neela?"

"No, my daughter."

Bai sighed. "It's a sad story."

"Tell me."

"We can wait—"

"Tell me." Cheng's broad jaw was clenched, and Bai relented.

"She married Aka." Cheng's eyes widened in surprise. "But after her marriage, she fell in love with Gang. They planned to flee the Sun Court, but shortly before they could, she was murdered."

Cheng leapt from the bed, only to collapse on the floor. "I will kill Aka!"

"No, wait," said Bai. "Although the timing is suspicious, there is no proof he had anything to do with her death. And— he's dying, anyway. Your granddaughter is on a quest to save him."

"Why would my granddaughter—wait, is Aka her father?" Cheng looked like he might have an apoplexy.

Bai ran a hand through his hair. "Her father is Gang. Aka is her grandfather."

"If it were anyone but you saying this, I wouldn't believe it," admitted Cheng. "She's the scion of *four* Colors?"

Bai nodded.

Cheng rubbed his eyes. "I have more questions."

"I'll try to answer them."

About three hours later, Cheng said, "It isn't fair that the world keeps moving forward when you've been standing still."

Bai nodded. "I know exactly what you mean." Bai cleared his throat. "Cheng, it isn't my business, but I really want to know how you had a child when you thought it was impossible."

Chang snorted. "There's only one possibility. It must have been at the River Festival on the northern Dataa. I went because I knew Neela would be there. And she was at the center of the crowd, quite intoxicated. I drank as well. She kissed me—but I don't remember anything beyond that. When I woke the next morning, I was alone on a raft floating down the river." Cheng shrugged.

Bai leaned against the cot at their backs. "You didn't set out to trick her then."

"Of course not!" Cheng's hand sliced through the air definitively. "I was in love with her."

Bai nodded. "I'm glad. Jin will be relieved."

"Why are you so interested in my granddaughter anyway?"

Bai flushed and coughed.

Cheng's eyes widened. "You are over Noran? But—Jin is too young for you. You said she's only five thousand years old."

"She's an adult," Bai said defensively.

"Barely," muttered Cheng.

Knowing he was a petitioner, Bai rose up on his knees and bowed once before meeting Cheng's ember eyes. "I truly care about Jin. It is she that made me realize how cowardly I was to hide away from the world and focus on my development in isolation. There are beings, both mortal and immortal, whose lives, whose sanctity of self, are not being respected by those with power. As someone who could have enough power to challenge those individuals, I think I have a duty to do so. Jin does that." And Bai recounted how she helped the Forever Child. "She is humble and is constantly striving to be better.

"I want to be more active in the world and help people like she does so that—" He hesitated. "So that I will be worthy of her."

Cheng groaned. "How can I complain about your infatuation when you say something like that? It would be strange of me to act as a grandfather rather than your friend anyway. I don't even know what a grandfather is supposed to be like." He scratched at his scraggly orange beard. "When the others deified themselves, I laughed behind my sleeve thinking them vain. Now I'm fearful. If either of us wants to be more active in the world, we'll have to court mortal worshippers."

"Actually, I've been thinking about that. It might be easier to tap into their beliefs than you are thinking."

Cheng raised both his brows.

"Want to go on a trip with me? To the Sanctuary Caves?"

WHEN the Great Tiger told Jin that its home was half a day from the Mirror Mount, it was referring to the edge of Spirit Jungle. That meant they still had to traverse the jungle itself.

Each day the tiger guided her deeper into the jungle, asking her a great many questions. At first Jin did her best to answer these questions as thoroughly as possible, but as the tiger grew more irascible, Jin began to realize that it preferred her to ask questions in return. It particularly liked it when they had long philosophical discussions with no clear resolution.

Orange was unknowable, and it seemed that the Great Tiger celebrated that state.

One thing that the tiger was particularly curious about was the soul pendant that Jin had hung next to Kunjee.

"This smells like Cheng, too," it told her. "What's in it?"

"Cheng's daughter; my mother."

"What happened to her?"

"A lover of her husband murdered her."

"Why?"

The relentless questioning was exhausting, but Jin also found it clarifying. In trying to appease the tiger's curiosity, she was gradually coming to accept and understand her own family.

The tiger asked, "What are you going to do with the soul though?"

"I want to resurrect it," said Jin, "Do you think that's possible?"

In response, the tiger expounded on whether or not it should even be attempted. "If you bring back that soul, won't every mortal who loses a loved one want you to do the same for them? And if everyone lives forever, what then? Should immortal creatures even be able to have children? Aren't beings like you, which can do both, burdens on the world?"

"But," protested Jin, "you speak as if the world can only hold a finite number of beings!"

"Can't it?"

Jin considered. "Surely the Heavens and the Underworld are not limited in such a way. And if we are nourished by the spirits of the plants and animals here, doesn't that make our supply unlimited?"

The tiger, which had been picking its way through the jungle, paused and swung its head toward Jin. "You don't understand, do you? Whenever we eat the shade of a plant or animal in this jungle, we are consuming its spirit. It is gone forever."

Jin froze as well. Suddenly the ash-like berries that she'd had for breakfast seemed like rocks in her belly. "Oh."

"Every day, every moment, we have to make choices, me or that." The tiger then embarked on a rant about the innate selfishness of all beings, and how pretending to be above it was the worst kind of lying.

Jin did her best to engage, for she hoped that if she was intriguing enough, it would let her go without a fight when they reached the edge of the jungle, but she was relieved when they stopped to sleep for the night. And she had to admit that she felt strangely comfortable with the massive beast. When worry kept her awake, she buried her face in the tiger's fur and drifted off peacefully.

After a few days of this, Jin woke and immediately felt something was wrong. She leapt to her feet.

The massive tiger was still sleeping, a soothing purr telling Jin that nothing was amiss with it. She found Wu Zhe and Tiao Xian curled up together, also sleeping peacefully. Nothing was different about their surroundings, other than the change of light. Eventually, she concluded she must have had bad dreams, even if none of them had been about Xiao. To comfort herself, she tried to wrap her hand around the soul pendant.

Both it and Kunjee were gone.

THE Sanctuary Caves were in the Byeong Mountains, the range that created the border between Zhongtu and Bando, only a few days' hike from the infamous Cheolmun Pass where Bai had once slaughtered hundreds of mortal men in just a few days.

The Byeong Mountains were volcanic, created as the tectonic plate beneath the Ge Man lifted upward into the Zhongtu landmass. It was here that Cheng had been born of magma by refusing to cool into rock and so became the third immortal being.

When Bai first met Cheng, they had eagerly shared with each other all the wonders of the world they had discovered, and the first place that Cheng brought Bai had been the Sanctuary Caves.

An underground stream had carved its path through the dusty orange stone of the caves. When Cheng had found it, he cut away large swathes of the rock until he had created nearly four miles of linked caverns. But when he showed them to Bai, they had been on the verge of collapse, to Cheng's sorrow.

It had been difficult, for Bai could not read the caves' structure any more than he could read Cheng himself, but with their combined understanding of geology, he had created white marble pillars to support key places in the caves. Their magic combined together, and the Sanctuary Caves distilled the essence of anything inside and nullified anything disrupting that essence. And not just magical disruptions; the caves also eased trauma and disease while inside of them.

After seeing how the Great Willow was worshipped, Bai had come to suspect that even more worshippers would surely gather at the Sanctuary Caves, for they had already been a refuge before Bai went into seclusion.

And indeed he was right.

When Bai and Cheng arrived outside the largest entrance to

the caves, a week after Cheng had first awoken, they found farms. Not large ones, mind, for the land here was rocky and steep, but generations of mortals had taken the time to carve rice paddies into the mountain side. There were small tool sheds near the paddies, but no houses. Several workers tending the fields looked at them and bowed.

"What's all this, then?" Cheng asked.

"I told you," said Bai, "There are millions of mortals now."

He pointed above the cave's entrance, where silk ribbons hung from a rope as thick as his own torso. "They hang those on things they worship. My willow tree has one, though it isn't as thick as this one."

"But they don't need to worship the caves," Cheng pointed out. "They'll work just fine, worship or no."

Bai shrugged. "That doesn't seem to stop them. And now, it may be to our benefit."

Remembering how Jin made a point of greeting her worshippers, Bai now waved to the mortals in the field and Cheng copied him after a moment.

Then they began their descent down the caves, an easier trip than it used to be, for steps had been chiseled in the stone, and decorative lanterns hung at even intervals along the walls. Citrus and jasmine incense thickened the air, almost masking the damp, musty smell of the caves themselves.

At the bottom of the stone staircase, they were greeted by merchants who wanted to sell them prayer mats, incense, and stone chips that they had removed from the cave. Cheng seized one of the chips, a dark orange triangle.

"Are you a fool?" he demanded of the mortal man who offered it. "If you chip away the sides, you're chipping away the magic of the cave." Cheng propelled all the orange chips toward the wall, where they melted and rehardened. The merchant and his fellows gasped and fell to the ground, genuflecting before them.

Cheng's brows crawled up his forehead and his large mouth twisted in bemusement. He looked at Bai, and his eyes bugged out.

Instinctively, Bai glanced down at himself and found his clothes had reverted to the wisps of clouds he had gathered on the White Mountain to make them.

*Fate laugh at me, how could I have forgotten?*

Luckily, he *had* remembered to revert the Starlight Sword and the Water Shield to full-size, both of which had been bound to his back with actual cloth at the Wood Pavilions.

No longer able to defy their nature, his former clothes were dissipating with every passing air current. Bai looked around the cave and found a cloth banner of white linen hanging over a merchant's booth. He pulled it through the air.

"Hey," the owner lifted his head from the ground to object, "that—"

"—was made by your grandmother and has been draped over this booth for the past twenty years." Bai couldn't control the fog as well as he could outside of the caves, but he encouraged it to creep along the floor of the cave, surrounding the merchants. "The embroidery of the pine is particularly fine; she pushed herself to make such small, close stitches that she damaged her eyes." He tied the banner like a sarong at his waist.

"However, when she entered these caves, her eyesight always sharpened. That is why she put this cloth on that booth, to thank the deities that made them. And so it is fitting that I collect it today, for I am one of them.

"I am the Knowing God, and my friend is the Steadfast God. We made these caves seventy millennia ago, and today we return to them to greet you and reward you for your faith."

The merchant who had objected gaped at Bai and pressed his head back into the ground.

Bai glanced at Cheng who nodded and gestured that Bai should keep going. Bai glared at him, but then decided Cheng deserved some slack, given the last several millennia. So Bai continued. Unable to affect his listeners in any substantial way, he settled for reading each of their essences, and reciting their own histories back to them. Then, with a few cuts of the Starlight Sword, he carved the divine characters for "Knowing God" into the wall. Cheng followed suit, melting the orange stone and re-cooling it to say "Steadfast God" as well.

"Remember our names," ordered Bai, "and let visitors know the importance of them."

Then he and Cheng passed deeper into the caves.

They climbed to an isolated ledge to meditate. Usually power slowly trickled back while mediating but not here.

Thousands of fervent prayers had accumulated over the centuries, so that the caves were filled to overflowing. That power poured into Bai like a waterfall, and the well inside of him grew to accommodate it. Bai could tell this power was a temporary increase rather than one that would replenish on its own, but he thought even Gang would find him a challenge now.

Cheng breathed out slowly. "That's better than wine," he said. He cleared his throat. "But this isn't sustainable. We've been here what, three hours? And we were only able to collect so much power because the caves had stored prayers for at least twenty millennia. If we came again tomorrow, there'd barely be anything to collect."

Bai nodded. "Jin explained this to me. We need to make prayer collectors and receptacles; then we could gather prayers here from our own homes."

"Convenient. How?'

Bai grimaced. "I've never seen a prayer collector, so I'm not sure."

"You mean Aka figured out something you couldn't?" Cheng waggled his brows.

"Of course I could," said Bai, "if I had a few hundred years to do so, like he did. But for today, I think we're out of luck."

Cheng snorted. "Alright. Where to next, Bai-shifu?"

Bai elbowed him for the mockery and said, "I want to go to the Great Willow. You don't have to accompany me."

Cheng shrugged. "Where else would I go? Come on, then." He leapt down from the ledge and Bai reflected that Jin certainly had done a wonderful job restoring him. It was hard to believe that he'd been imprisoned in stone until just two months ago and in a coma until recently.

Leaving the caves took an obnoxiously long time as every mortal they passed wanted to touch them, but they eventually made it out to the rice paddies.

It was evening in Liushi when they arrived at the Great Willow. Though the sun had set, the city was lit by colorful paper lanterns. The streets were crowded with dancers in fanciful costumes—Bai saw several "Great Warriors" with improbably large paper swords—and he was glad that he had chosen to teleport inside of the willow's fence. *It must be a festival,* Bai thought. Not caring about mortal festivals, he turned away from the crowd to approach the tree.

But Cheng grabbed his arm and growled. Bai turned back, thinking his friend must be overwhelmed by the noise and bustle of the mortal city, but his explanation died on his lips.

About three feet away, just on the other side of the fence, was Neela.

JIN scanned the leafy neon vines that surrounded her, opening her magical senses to seek out unfamiliar thoughts and feelings, but she found nothing besides her sleeping companions.

She woke the Mudanren first, who expressed shock and dismay, and then the tiger. It yawned once, its gaping maw threatening death for disturbing it, but Jin was not alarmed until it leapt suddenly to its feet and growled.

But it wasn't growling at her.

"I smell the Achamba!" The Achamba, Wu Zhe had told Jin, was a massive snake, and the Great Tiger's life-long enemy. First in the jungles of Jeevanti, and now here in the Spirit Jungle, they competed for territory and dominance over other jungle-dwelling immortals. "And that cursed monkey!" added the tiger. "What mischief are they up to now?" The tiger stuck its muzzle into the bushes, searching.

"They took the key to Earth," Jin put in quickly. *And my family's souls.* That scared her more—had she taken her mother, brother, and grandmother from the Sea of Souls just for them to be eaten by a giant snake? But it was Kunjee that would interest the tiger. "I must get it back, or I will never find a way to reopen the Underworld."

The tiger's nose wrinkled into a snarl, "That belly-crawler must be trying to sneak through on its own." It roared its fury. Then, "Get on my back! It's been hours since they were here—we must move faster than your tiny legs will go!"

As soon as Jin was mounted behind the Great Tiger's head, the tiger surged forward, the trees blurring and the air resistance threatening to topple her. Jin held onto its thick ruff fiercely, and let her body move with the tiger's, lest she be tossed off.

"What monkey was the Tiger talking about?" she asked Wu Zhe and Tiao Xian, half-hidden in the tiger's thick, long fur.

"The Only Monkey. It's the Achamba's lackey," Tiao Xian called over the wind.

Wu Zhe pressed closed to Jin. "Creatures are either large and singular or small and plural. The smaller we are, the more of us there are. The monkey is smaller than the Bulgae, but it's the only one. Some people say that mortals slaughtered its kin, and the Achamba saved it, so it's grateful."

Tiao Xian scoffed. "Or the Achamba ate all the other monkeys itself, and this one begged to be spared, promising to serve the Achamba for all eternity in exchange."

"How can I get my pendants back?" she asked.

The tiger, who had been listening even as it ran, laughed. "Not by talking. You'll have to fight for them."

"I don't understand," said Jin. "Other creatures want to leave the Underworld. Why has none tried to take the key before now?"

Wu Zhe shook its head. Tiao Xian said, "The locked gate isn't the only obstacle to leaving here. The Korikami, the ice wolf, stands guard over the Mirror Mount."

"And why doesn't the Achamba fear the Korikami?"

"The Achamba is of orange and yellow, so it will use an illusion to hide physically, and it naturally hides from magical detection. If the Korikami knew to look for it, it might be able to see through the illusion, for it is indigo, but the Achamba's magic is powerful. And unlike the tiger, the Korikami cannot smell."

"A wolf that cannot smell?" Jin asked in surprise.

"Legend says the Red Immortal burned his nose in their fight. He has smelled nothing in thirty millennia."

Jin pressed her lips together. The Golden Phoenix had not fought her for love of Noran, and the Great Tiger was humoring her for Cheng's sake—it sounded like she couldn't hope for the same from the Korikami. Even assuming they managed to catch the Achamba in time. She resisted the urge to tell the tiger to hurry, for its paws were already eating up the ground at an incredible rate, and she knew it shared her sense of urgency.

Suddenly they burst from the Spirit Jungle. Jin glanced backward and saw shades of birds taking to the sky. They should have been crying warnings, and Jin shivered at their silence. Facing forward, she saw the Mirror Mount rising before them. Its profile was indeed the same as the Korikami's Tomb—Mount Korikami, perhaps she had better say here—with gently sloping sides leading to a flat peak. There must be a caldera at the top.

The Great Tiger was capable of great bursts of speed, but it wasn't built for long runs. As they started up the slopes of the mountain, it began to flag.

"The gate is at the top of the Mirror Mount? Then I will

teleport to the summit," Jin decided. She no longer had Kunjee to stop her and though her lack of familiarity with the Underworld was a general barrier to teleporting, she could see where she had to go here.

"Are you coming, little ones?" she asked the Mudanren.

They hid deeper in the Great Tiger's fur and sent their peony petals shivering with vigorous headshakes.

Jin took a deep breath and moved between.

She reappeared on the edge of the Mirror Mount's caldera, snow crunching beneath her feet, an arm's length from a vermilion torii that exactly matched its counterpart on the Korikami's Tomb.

She saw neither an ice wolf nor a massive snake, but she would trust the tiger that the Achamba had not yet reached the gate. If it had already passed through... Jin's gut clenched.

*Secure the gate*, she told herself.

The mountain was made of dark gray stone and covered with snow. Besides the red gate itself, which Jin was loath to change, in case she accidentally destroyed the only door, there was nothing here for her to use. She had her own blood, but she'd kill herself trying to get enough to build a blockade.

Taking a deep breath, she summoned fire, engulfing first her, and then sending it out to ring the gate. The flames stretched until they met at the peak of a dome over the gate. Then she let the flames on her subside and drew her tessen. She spread its ribs and assumed a fighter's stance. She stared down the mountain seeking signs of the Achamba's passing.

After ten minutes, she straightened. There was nothing to see and even her magical senses returned nothing. She felt rather idiotic. She didn't even know if the snake was close.

How was she supposed to fight a giant, invisible snake anyway? And yet, she couldn't walk away. If it were just Kunjee that Achamba had stolen, perhaps she could find another way. But the souls that Jin had taken from the sea—those were irreplaceable and her responsibility.

Would the Achamba speak to her when it arrived? Or strike, unseen and deadly? Or would her wall of flames mean nothing to it?

Jin trembled as she waited. Even though they weren't warriors, she wished that she had brought the Mudanren with her—she felt terribly alone, just like when she first arrived in the Underworld. She was so close and yet so far from returning from Earth. Ridiculously, she turned toward the gate, as if she'd be able to see through it.

Was Bai waiting for her on the other side?

She didn't even know if he was in Earth or the Underworld. And yet she had to press on with her quest.

May fate smile, she hoped he was on the other side. Then— as soon as she recovered Kunjee—

Jin was buffeted by air just before two fangs pressed into her side. Her blood armor, thin, flexible, and extremely tough, bent painfully into her ribs, but it did not break.

And that saved her from the venom of the Achamba.

In her mind, Jin swung her tessen without hesitation, slicing where the Achamba's eye should be and killing it.

In reality, she squeezed the tessen's base in a moment of pure panic.

The Achamba withdrew with a pained hiss, and Jin realized it must have hurt its fangs on her impenetrable armor. That was good. That might let her negotiate.

"Wait!" she cried holding out her arms in entreaty. "You want to pass through the gate, and my fire is blocking it. But I do not want to imprison you here—I simply want my pendant back."

The snake did not reply. It moved to strike again, and Jin couldn't have said exactly how she knew where it came from—the slight shift of the air or a sound that she only half-heard—but she did know, and she leapt out of the way, leaving only the flames to guard the gate.

Jin heard a scream of pain and smelled burning fur. It must be the Only Monkey, riding behind the Achamba's head.

"Monkey," Jin said, "please talk to me. We don't need to fight."

Over and over the snake struck, and each time Jin spun away, knowing that indeed fate must be smiling on her today. But as Neela always said, *Just because fate smiles doesn't mean you should wait for it to frown.*

The Great Tiger was right; she couldn't negotiate with the Achamba. Her only options were to kill or be killed.

Resolved, Jin cut her hand with the side of her tessen and sent the blood at her attacker. Following her will, it spread along the scales of the Achamba and revealed its head. It was almost like chain-link, and Jin turned her blood into a metal net, which she ripped through the Achamba's head in the most horrifically violent act she had ever committed. Blood sprayed everywhere.

Dead, the Achamba's illusion failed, and seventy feet of dark yellow coils were revealed. A small indigo monkey ran down them, totally terrified and silent.

"Wait!" cried Jin "Where are my pendants?"

The monkey ignored her. Jin raced after it and seized it by its thick, dark mane.

"My pendants," she repeated. "Where are they?"

The monkey chittered in distress.

"I don't want to hurt you. I just need the pendants."

The small creature curled into a ball. "You are death and destruction. How can you avoid hurting me?"

"I've made friends with many immortal creatures," Jin soothed, kneeling next to the monkey.

"Tricks! Magic tricks!" it howled and struggled to free itself.

"I didn't trick anyone."

The creature struggled without replying.

Jin set her jaw, annoyed now. She didn't have time to waste comforting the monkey, so Jin pushed guilt and compassion far away.

"The pendants. Tell me where they are." She shook the creature by its ruff.

It cried, "Its grace ate them! Please, please, please let me go."

"The Achamba ate them? They are inside it?"

"Yes, yes," the monkey practically wept.

Its claim rang sweet and true, so Jin released it. It scampered away so quickly that it slipped and tumbled in the snow. Jin was troubled by its panic, but she swallowed and moved on.

The corpse of the Achamba was behind her. The idea of dissecting the snake revolted her. Knowing Kunjee and the pendant could both withstand her fire, she set the snake aflame instead.

After a few hours, its flesh burned away sufficiently for Jin to see Kunjee, bright red on its gleaming gold chain. As she bent to pick the necklace up, a painfully cold wind suddenly howled around her, whipping her hair. Jin almost ignored it, for it was like the wind on Earth, but she felt something behind her and glanced backward.

The largest creature she had yet seen was just a few feet away from her. A wolf of purest white and deepest indigo, it looked like carved ice, but its fur ruffled in the wind.

FOR the moment, the banging drums and lusty singing of festival goers in Liushi faded to the background. Bai, Cheng, and Neela were all suspended in time, and the mortals who danced and roared around them were unimportant.

Cheng's fingers were digging painfully into Bai's bicep, his broad jaw clenched and his whole body leaning forward.

Neela was stiff, her hands claws in the folds of her azure sari, her lips pressed so tight that they had all but disappeared.

Bai was frozen too. He saw the agony on Cheng's face—love that had turned to hate—and he couldn't help but remember his devastation when he found Noran dead.

It was different for Cheng, of course. The easy-going Cheng had befriended Neela, and his romantic feelings had grown slowly. But that didn't make it any less devastating for him when Neela had refused them. Bai hadn't known about their drunken encounter—if Cheng's account was accurate, then neither had Cheng or Neela, he supposed. He couldn't imagine how Cheng must have felt when Neela trapped him in stone.

In fact, maybe Bai was Neela in this situation. The betrayer.

When Noran had died, her summons ignored, had she felt the way Cheng must now?

What Neela had done was unforgivable, but watching them

stare at each other, Bai's heart ached. He wondered if there wasn't some way to mend the past.

Then Cheng was gone, and a large orange tiger was leaping for Neela.

Neela leapt into the air, and her blue sari lashed out like a serpent, winding around Cheng-the-tiger's neck.

Bai was in the air moments later, the Starlight Sword in his hand.

Bai had intended on cutting the sari that was choking Cheng, but before he could, Cheng shredded it with his claws. And then he was once again attempting to catch Neela with those powerful tiger jaws. Blue flame shot from Neela's hand, and Bai smelled scorched fur as Cheng roared in pain.

*They'll kill each other and half the mortals here,* Bai thought. He couldn't let that happen. The mortals didn't deserve to die, and Jin would be devastated. Neela had *raised* her. Half a dozen ideas flashed through his head for stopping them, but most were too lethal.

He seized Cheng and Neela's bones with his will and pulled them apart in the air. They both fought the invisible restraints, and then Cheng shifted back into a man.

Fire poured from him toward Neela, like an orange river of destruction. Bai jerked her out of the way, and she screamed in pain—he supposed being moved by one's bones wasn't exactly comfortable.

She then proceeded to make her own river of blue flame, channeled toward Cheng.

Luckily there was plenty of white all around Bai, thanks to those "Great Warrior" dancers. He seized their large paper swords, vaguely aware that he was expending more power than he'd ever had before, and created a small blizzard. It wrapped around Cheng and Neela, extinguishing their fires, and freezing both of them.

Unfortunately, Cheng had also absorbed a great deal of power recently, and his fire burned brighter, melting the snowflakes that were bombarding him.

But there was more power not far from Bai, just waiting for him.

Bai flew through the air to the White Willow, its silver leaves catching him in a gentle embrace. It was as if the tree wanted to give him the belief that had been stored in its branches. When Bai reached for it, it washed over him like a tidal wave. He gasped for breath, and then turned to the street. Every scrap of white, down to shreds of paper and loose threads, flew at Neela and Cheng, wrapping their bodies in cocoons that at last succeed in stifling that orange fire.

Bai set them both down on the ground and settled between them.

Neela met his eyes and tried to teleport. Bai stopped her though, easily winning the power battle. Her eyes widened, and she looked a little scared. "I thought you disdained Aka for becoming a god," she taunted him.

"That was before he realized people went around imprisoning others in stone!" growled Cheng. "You'll not find me such an easy target again."

Bai closed his eyes briefly, seeking calm, then met Cheng's ember eyes.

"Please," Bai begged, "can we talk about this? For a moment?"

Neela's breathing was ragged. She stopped struggling

against the cocoon and would have fallen, but for Bai catching her against his chest. She had realized that she was completely outmatched.

"She deserves death," Cheng said through his teeth.

"Maybe," agreed Bai, and he felt Neela tremble. "But like this?"

"What way would be acceptable to you?" Cheng asked sarcastically. "Or is there an immortal justice system that I don't know about?"

In fact, Bai thought there might be, but he didn't trust Salaana enough to find out. Instead, he looked at Neela and said, "I don't want Jin to return from the Underworld to learn you murdered Neela."

Neela's eyes widened, and she looked back at Bai in horror. Bai realized that she had been so distracted by Cheng last time that she had never learned Jin's whereabouts.

Bai swallowed and looked back at Cheng. "I'm not telling you to forgive Neela. But I won't let the grandmother who raised Jin be murdered while she is gone. There are already too many tragedies and secrets. So please, wait until Jin returns and can hear from both of you."

Cheng clenched his jaw. "We can't be sure that Jin will ever return." He twisted his head away from Neela, and towards the sixty odd mortals who had prostrated themselves in the dirt street. Neela once again tested her strength against Bai's, and he burned a little more of the power he'd gotten from the caves.

Finally Cheng met Bai's eyes again. "I will wait six months. If Jin has not returned by then—"

Bai nodded shortly. "Thank you."

"And what exactly are we supposed to do with her in the

meantime—seal her in carnelian?"

Bai shook his head. "She's a flower. If you seal her in rock, she'll die." Bai hesitated, sifting through the possibilities. Karana had promised Salaana's help with this matter, but after their fight on the Korikami's Tomb, that seemed unlikely. Xiao was undoubtedly still drunk at Bai's hermitage, but they could work something out. "I can trap her on my mountain. My essence trap held Jin and Xiao, so it should work for Neela."

Cheng tapped his leg impatiently. "Very well. You can release me now."

Bai changed the cocoon into a mist that dissipated slowly. Cheng said, without any heat, "Couldn't you have chosen a way that didn't leave me soaked?"

Bai looked at Neela. "I can release you as well, if you agree not to fight me."

"I'm not an idiot," she snarled, and he knew she hated that she needed him to save her from Cheng. "I know I'm no match for the Great Warrior."

Bai wished she would be a little more direct—a promise not to fight anymore—but he knew this was as much as he'd get from Neela. So he dissolved her cocoon as well. She continued to sag against him for a moment. Bai realized that she had in fact drained her power trying to teleport, but her pride was such that, when she pulled herself straight, Bai pretended that he didn't see her swaying.

"Shall we go?" Bai asked Cheng.

"Not yet," he said, and Bai was surprised to realize that Cheng's fury had left as fast as it came. Or maybe he shouldn't be surprised. He couldn't even remember seeing Cheng angry before, so perhaps his friend had simply been unable to sustain it, even given everything that Neela had done to him.

"We just put on a mighty impressive display for these mortals," he told Bai, "we should take advantage of it." He smirked without any real amusement. "Especially if you're going to make a habit of burning through power like that."

Bai nodded.

There was a large orange drum not far from them, abandoned as the mortals had tried to avoid the geysers of flame, and Cheng now stepped on it and used it to lift himself into the air. He began spouting the same nonsense that Bai had in the Sanctuary Caves.

"You really are making yourselves gods," Neela muttered to Bai. "Why?"

Bai felt a little guilty towards her, and she would probably pick the truth from his mind anyway, so he admitted, "Gang humbled me when I told him I was in love with Jin."

"So it's to impress your father-in-law?" she shook her head. "If you care so much about Jin, why aren't you in the Underworld with her?"

Bai rarely blushed, but his cheeks felt hot, and Neela cackled.

"How could you not have bothered to read the key? You deserved the humiliation that Gang dealt you."

Bai nodded tightly.

When Cheng finished his preaching, Bai summoned fog, thick and rolling, and they teleported once the street was covered. The showmanship felt ridiculous, but Bai wanted to make sure these mortals remembered and talked about them.

THE wind that battered Jin was from the Korikami. The huge ice wolf released another keening howl, and the wind grew fiercer.

Jin clutched her necklace and its dual pendants to her chest.

"I don't want to fight," she told the Korikami.

It laughed, a terrible combination of blizzards and cracking ice. "Of course you don't. You want to take that key and stroll through that gate, where you can forget about this place forever. Who died? Or is dying?" it asked.

The non-sequitur confused Jin. "Dying...?"

"Yes—why else would you come to the Underworld? Who are you trying to save?"

"My grandfather," Jin admitted.

"A grandfather? And yet you couldn't bear to let him go?" The question was rhetorical. It immediately said, "You must be the one who brought the key here. How did you get the key? Are you related to that cursed narcissist, Aka?'

Jin tried Bai's diversion technique. "I travelled to the White Mountain where it was hidden and passed through trials to get it. And I fixed it so that it could never be used to steal your power again."

"Such pureness of heart," the Korikami mocked her. "You did not deny a relation to Aka. Could he be the grandfather you mentioned?"

"You should never have been trapped here," Jin declared. "I have seen the suffering of the immortal creatures, and I know this imprisonment is wrong. Once I return to Earth, I will find a way to permanently open the gate so that you can all return to your homes."

Once again, that freezing laugh. "I don't trust you at all. If you have such an ability, why don't you open the gate here and now?"

"I don't have much time—"

"I do. And if you make for the gate, I will kill you."

Jin drew herself up. "You will try." She pointed to the ashes of the Achamba. "It also tried."

"Threats! How exciting! I haven't been threatened in millennia! Why don't you light me on fire and see how it goes?" The Korikami bared its icicle fangs in a parody of a smile.

# How Xiao Transformed

XIAO'S eyes flew open. He was breathing hard and covered in sweat, as if he'd been running, and was confused to realize he was lying down.

A strong arm slipped behind his back, lifting him slightly, and a cup was pressed against his lips. Xiao gulped the fresh water gratefully. Only after he had drained the cup did he think to look for the owner of the arm.

He was surprised by a familiar face—Dawa's dark eyes blinked once, his hair braided neatly into its familiar gray crown.

"How did you return to your natural form?" Xiao asked in surprise. "Did I—?"

Dawa was shaking his head. "Forgive me, divinity. I went to the Sanctuary Caves. "

"Forgive you?" Xiao echoed. "Don't be ridiculous, Dawa, I'm glad you are restored. Why on Earth would you ask for my forgiveness?"

Dawa's eyelids lowered, and the corners of his lips turned down. "I left you alone, and when I returned, I found you in the throes of a true dream. I'm sorry, divinity, you must have suffered."

"Just call me Xiao," he said. He lifted one hand—it felt like it was full of sand instead of blood and bone—and rubbed his eyes. "A true dream. Yes, you must be right." Xiao shuddered. "Aren't I too young for true dreams?"

He had been trying to joke, but Dawa earnestly answered, "It is not age that determines true dreams but experience."

Xiao cleared his throat. "Indeed. So how long was I out?"

"Seven days," Dawa said.

Xiao nodded. That was longer than it had taken Nanami to come to terms with her punishment. And what exactly had Xiao come to terms with?

He swung his legs over the side of the cot and would have slid into a heap on the floor if Dawa hadn't caught him.

"Divinity—" Xiao growled, and Dawa amended "—Xiao, you are physically weak. Why don't you rest on the cot while I fetch you some food? You will feel better for eating."

Xiao was impatient to be up—he felt like pacing—but he also acknowledged the wisdom of Dawa's suggestion. "Very well," he conceded. "I will wait here. Thank you, Dawa."

The older immortal nodded and laid Xiao back down. He slipped through the narrow door, and Xiao could hear him adding fuel to the fire.

Xiao sighed and mentally began reviewing his dreams.

The Infinite Jug. Every time he had disappointed himself or someone else because he had been intoxicated. Jin's utter rejection of him as a partner.

This past spring had given him a false confidence in himself. Ever since Nanami had forced sobriety on him, he had the sense that drinking was his choice. He had wanted to drink sometimes, but a sense of purpose had replaced his need for alcohol. His success at fooling the Sun Court and in protecting Nanami had filled the emptiness inside, and he had deluded himself into thinking that would last forever. He had occasionally thought about drinking those past few months, but he hadn't needed to and so had believed he wasn't addicted.

But alone in his room, with nothing to anticipate but his parents' contempt, the emptiness had been overwhelming. And so he had turned to alcohol. Every sip had made him feel emptier and, ironically, in greater need of it. A downward spiral that he hadn't noticed until it was too late.

In that cursed room, Xiao had honestly believed that it was just his circumstances. But when Bai had rescued him from the visible prison, Xiao had realized that he was still jailed by his own drinking. He had admitted that he was an alcoholic.

And so he had dreamed, retracing the path that led him to this point. He had realized that he would rather give up all substances forever than be that person again—a person who was defined by his dependencies. A person who was crippled by fear and so crippled himself further with alcohol.

But was knowing that enough? How could he stop himself from drinking again, from entering that spiral whenever life was hard?

Dawa returned with a steaming bowl that smelled of miso.

"Thank you," Xiao said and brought the soup close so that he could feel the steam on his face. It helped him feel grounded, present. The soup contained some dark mountain greens and chopped garlic. The flavors were all a little much, but Xiao was glad that they demanded his attention.

When the bowl was empty, he looked at Dawa. "Why'd you come back?"

Dawa's eyes widened. "I owe you my life. Where else would I be but at your side?"

Xiao nodded slightly. "I daresay we're equal now. You don't need to follow me for all eternity for just that."

Dawa smiled. "I'm used to following, and I won't return to New Moon Manor. If you won't accept me, then I will look for someone else."

Xiao was surprised. "Do you mean you want to be my disciple?"

Dawa nodded curtly.

Xiao rubbed his chin and was surprised to find it covered with a patchy beard. Of course, he hadn't shaved in a month— he'd have to take care of that before he went out in the world.

Was that what he was going to do? Go back into the world?

Yes. Somehow, he was.

As for Dawa—Xiao had never had a disciple before. A few immortals had wanted to pledge to him, but their interest in becoming illustrious lovers hadn't quite felt right. He suddenly understood that those who had come before had been too singular in their purpose. Dawa felt different from them, but Xiao doubted his worthiness as a teacher.

Did he, who could barely manage his own life, have anything worth teaching others?

"Why would you want to follow me?" Xiao asked. "Gratitude alone isn't enough."

Dawa cocked his head, and Xiao was reminded of his crow form.

"I was never comfortable with the way the Moon and Night deities treated you. I even challenged the Moon Goddess about it, but her response was so fierce that I silenced my worries for millennia." Dawa cleared his throat. "I'm not surprised that you have demons inside or that you turned to alcohol to drown them out. What surprised me was that you consistently treated us disciples with kindness and consideration, even when we were carrying out your parents' punishments. I thought you should resent us for never removing you from that situation. That you should yearn for revenge. But when my life was in danger, you saved me. When you changed me into a crow—I felt your love for me. The first disciple once told me that you ought to have been named the God of Love, and I agree. I want to learn from the God of Love and make this world a kinder place."

Xiao laughed in embarrassment, and then he felt ashamed that he wasn't returning Dawa's earnestness in kind.

"Very well," he finally said. "I want to be that being you see—the God of Love." He cleared his throat. "But Dawa, the God of Pleasure is an alcoholic. I want to change, but it's not easy.

"So if you sincerely want to be my disciple, I have to ask— are you willing to go with me, to support my sobriety? To help me recover if I lapse? I—"

When Xiao faltered, Dawa took his hand. It was a small hand, compared to Xiao's own, and lightly wrinkled. "I will. I understand it, as much as an outsider can anyway. I will help you avoid temptation and be with you if you falter. But Xiao—there was rumor that you did not come alone to New Moon Manor. That person...?"

Xiao shrugged. "She ignored my summons. I'm not sure of anything right now." Part of Xiao thought he should try again, seek Nanami out once more, but he also hated the idea of her seeing him like this and—what if she really refused to answer his summons?

"War is brewing among the Sun Court, and immortals will be taking sides. I think that we should go to the Wood Pavilions. Hopefully, we will find Bai—the First—there, and if not, we are sure to find news."

Dawa nodded. "But first, a bath and clean clothes."

About three hours later, Xiao smelled of mountain spring water and jasmine (for he had found a bar of soap in Bai's cave). Dawa had fetched him fine cotton robes from Maoyi. The underrobe was lavender and white; the outer was black with matching lavender embroidery on the collar. Xiao had hesitated before donning them—he had avoided those colors as a rule ever since he was old enough to choose his own clothes, but he now realized it was part of himself he was rejecting, not just Zi and Hei. And, if his memory of dissolving those black iron bars into sand was accurate, they might come in useful.

Dawa helped him brush and braid his hair so that it was clear of his face, though they let most of it hang down his back. Xiao also shaved using a silver mirror that had been next to the bar of soap (Bai must be even vainer than Xiao had thought, to own a mirror when he lived alone), and even managed to summon his dimples after.

"You can do this. You can be the best version of yourself," he murmured to his reflection. If Dawa heard, he didn't let on.

Moments later, Xiao teleported both of them to the Wood Pavilions.

WHEN Bai, Neela, and Cheng reached the White Mountain, Bai saw no sign of Dawa the crow nor Xiao. Thinking they must be inside, he asked Cheng to wait with Neela in the garden while he got everything ready.

Neela drawled, "Really, Bai, you don't have to tidy on my account. I'll disapprove of your courtship with my granddaughter regardless of how neat you are."

Bai arched one brow before he could stop himself; fate itself must find Neela provoking. He strode into his common room, but it was empty. All his dishes had been neatly stacked on the shelf and someone had swept the fireplace. Surprised, he poked his head into the bedroom. The blankets were folded in a pile on his cot, and no one was in sight.

Laying on the table was the Infinite Flask, which Xiao had considered so essential that he hadn't even understood Bai's suggestion to leave it behind.

So. Xiao hadn't spent long wallowing in his addiction after all. Bai chuckled; that young rascal was full of surprises. Given how clean everything was, he supposed that Dawa must have been returned to his natural form as well—Xiao would have cheerfully left Bai a mess.

Bai rubbed his lip. He had wanted Xiao's support in

approaching Gang, but since he had successfully harvested power from the caves and the willow, he should be fine alone.

Besides, Bai had picked up that Xiao adored Neela. Things might be simpler if Bai didn't apprise him of the feud between Cheng and her at this juncture.

He'd get Neela settled, and then he and Cheng could continue their undertaking.

Bai fetched Cheng and Neela. Neela crossed her arms and glared around the room. "This is barely better than sealing me in stone," she barked. "I need sunlight or I'll never last six months, you old fools."

Cheng rolled his eyes. "Bai can change this mountain to meet your needs—but don't make it too comfortable, Bai. It is a prison, after all."

But Bai barely heard the words; he was suddenly finding it hard to breathe. "How long exactly can you go without sunlight, Neela?" he managed.

She shrugged. "A week, I should think."

"But you've been to the Underworld before—didn't you stay there for a year once?"

"I traded with Aka for a sun charm—" she froze. "When Jin—"

Bai pressed his lips together, trying to keep his face expressionless. He obviously didn't succeed—or perhaps his thoughts gave him away—for the next moment Neela flew at him, just as she had on the Kuanbai two months ago and began to hit him.

"You always act so cursed superior, but you are just as fallible as the rest of us!" she screamed.

When his patience ran out, Bai caught her wrists. "She'll be fine," he ground out. "She's smart and resourceful."

"Is there even sunlight anywhere there?" Neela hissed through her teeth.

Bai hesitated. "Several immortal creatures emit sunlight. The Sun Bird, the Hikarisei, the Golden Phoenix... If she finds one of them—"

Neela wrenched her wrists away from Bai and collapsed on the floor, sobbing. Bai wanted to join her, but he had to believe that Jin was still alive. She would come back.

He hated himself.

He looked at Cheng, whose broad features were troubled. Seeing Bai looking at him, he tried to smile. "She brought me back from the edge of death," he reminded Bai. "I'm sure she'll be fine." Because of Cheng's innate magic, Bai couldn't tell if Cheng believed that or if he was just trying to comfort Bai.

Still, he set to work carving another room into the white stone of the mountain so that Neela could stay here for the six months that Cheng had allowed. Cheng offered to help, but there wasn't a spot of orange in sight.

The work was tiring and when he finished, Neela had stopped crying. "May fate spit in your drink, foul your food, and poison your loins," she hissed at Bai before taking a seat by the window, her expression wooden.

Bai didn't mind the abuse—he would be bitter if she had managed to trap him in her horrifically blue caravan, and he was furious with himself for letting Jin go into the Underworld unprepared.

Surely she had met the Hikarisei or other gentle creatures...

Bai closed his eyes to calm himself.

When he opened them, Cheng was looking at him

knowingly.

"I am going to collect more power," Bai declared. "Will you come with me?"

Cheng hesitated and looked at Neela before indicating that Bai should follow him outside.

Cheng went to the mountain spring and collected a handful of water that he gulped down. Bai waited patiently.

"I can't leave her," Cheng admitted slowly. "I won't attack her—unless she attacks me first—but I can't leave."

"What if I don't return for six months? Will you be able to bear her company all that time?"

Twin tears raced down his cheeks. "There was a time when six months trapped with Neela would have sounded like a dream come true." Cheng shrugged and stood. "If I grow too angry, I will leave—I swear it. But otherwise, yes, I must wait here."

Bai rubbed his forehead with one knuckle. "Very well," he said. "If—when Jin returns, I will bring her back as soon as I am able."

Cheng nodded slowly. Suddenly, he stepped forward and pulled Bai into a hug. "Thank you, my friend. Good luck."

Bai squeezed Cheng back before he pulled away. He gave him one tight smile and then teleported to the southern tip of the Jeevantian peninsula, where he had once built a beautiful fortress from white sand.

NANAMI lay with her limbs flung wide and her left foot swinging off the edge of the mattress. She didn't have a great sense of time, for the room was windowless to prevent her escape, but it had been an hour or two since a breakfast of rice and steamed greens had been brought to her; in another few hours, there would undoubtedly be more rice and perhaps fried fish. Not very much food was shoved through the slot at the bottom of the door, but Nanami didn't need more for there wasn't much to do.

She exercised by pacing the floor, and she had figured out how to accommodate her handless arm when doing upper body exercises. She wished for her shuriken and her knives, for this would have been an excellent time to master them, but Zi and Hei had, of course, confiscated all her weapons. They wisely only gave her juice or wine to drink so Nanami had been unable to make more.

Nanami had never been a great reader or scholar, but she would have given just about anything for a scroll or a book. She had realized two days ago that she would tell her captors whatever they wanted to know if they would just talk to her— she was that bored. Her biggest fear at this point was she had no secrets they cared about.

And so when the door to her prison swung open, Nanami leapt to her feet and even smiled before she remembered that these people were the enemy.

That was easier to remember when Salaana and Ichimi walked into the cell.

Salaana surveyed Nanami with her merciless red eyes, and Ichimi shut the door behind them.

"What are you doing here?" snarled Nanami.

"The Moon Goddess informed me that she had caught a thief and asked me to execute justice." Salaana's eyes drifted down, and Nanami realized she was clutching her stump with her good hand. Her fingers tightened convulsively, and Nanami forced herself to let go. Then, because she couldn't help it, she tucked both hands behind her back.

"You said you'd only take my other hand if I stole again."

"I heard you stole all the incense collectors from their temples."

"No," Nanami shook her head. "That was He Who Walks in Shadow and his band." Beads of sweat gathered along Nanami's hairline and her clothes felt damp and sticky.

"At your behest, though?"

Nanami swallowed. "I had to find a way to free Xiao from Night and Moon Deities. They had imprisoned him and were draining his power. *Stealing* his power."

Salaana glanced at Ichimi. Nanami wondered at their silent exchange, for the next moment Salaana stepped closer to her and inclined her head. "I'm listening."

Nanami swallowed. She must have been more desperate for company than she realized, for all the thoughts that had been haunting her spilled out to these most hated enemies. She even explained how she had taken the Sowon Gold, though she was careful to phrase it as recovery rather than theft.

Salaana nodded thoughtfully several times before Nanami finished.

"I notice a theme in your narrative—you are concerned about excessive power and its abuse," Salaana said.

Nanami nodded. "You know the Colors as well as I—they are too old and too powerful to properly care about others." She made a silent apology to the First, and Haraa as well, but let it stand.

"It's not just the Colors and not just age that is a risk—

power corrupts. And the most powerful being there is Jin, the Goddess of Beauty," said Salaana.

Nanami was surprised to hear Salaana echoing her own concerns. Carefully, she asked, "Has Jin done something?"

"She rebuilt a man's body," behind her back, Nanami grabbed her stump once more, remembering their failed attempt to rebuild her hand, "and has gone to the Underworld to do the same for the Sun Emperor."

"Ah, so you admit that you are glad of your father's death."

Salaana snorted. "I have never denied it. He murdered three mothers of his children; death is what he deserves, but it was only recently that I found a way to enact it."

"I heard it was the God of Wind who cast the curse, not you."

Salaana waved this away, and Nanami was sure that she was indeed the puppet master. "The point is, Jin will undo years of hard work because of sentimentality. She cannot see the Sun Emperor as he is because he was kind to her."

Salaana stepped even closer to her and bent her head so that her mouth was mere inches from Nanami's ear. "You know Jin's secret, don't you? That she was fathered by my brother Gang? That power you so abhor in the Sowon Gold, that is hers."

Nanami swallowed. "Jin didn't create the Sowon Gold, Noran did."

"Jin is young. We should stop her preemptively. If you join hands with me, I will help you convince the Moon and Night deities that their son should not marry her."

It was the wrong tack to take. Even though Nanami felt uneasy about Jin, she had no interest in cooperating with the

Moon and Night deities. She pushed her stump into Salaana's face. "How can we join hands when you burned mine away?"

Salaana stepped back, her lips pursed.

Nanami thought that would be the end of the conversation, but Ichimi stepped into the spot Salaana had vacated. "It was I who told Salaana you were a thief and so brought punishment down upon you. Do not hate Salaana for doing her duty as the Goddess of Justice."

"I do not trust her sense of duty," snarled Nanami. "It seems her justice is oddly suited to her benefit. When she had no reason to befriend me, she took my hand without hesitating. Now, she offers to spare my other if I betray my friend."

"Is Jin really your friend?" asked Ichimi. "Or is she the friend of your lover? Xiao's devotion to her is famed—but is it earned? You are right to condemn the Moon and Night deities as parents. Salaana and I agree with you—but we cannot defeat them alone. And it took you one encounter to know how wrongly they treat their child? Jin grew up with Xiao, but she has never objected to their abuse."

Nanami had been glaring at the wall, but her eyes darted back to Ichimi at that. She hesitated. "How do you know how Jin feels?"

"Everyone knows," sneered Salaana. "She calls him a drunk and useless and has always tried to maintain her distance rather than help him through his trials, despite their connection with each other. It would be unjust to force such a marriage upon Xiao."

"But you did nothing to try to stop it!"

Salaana's eyes narrowed. "I brought down the Sun Emperor."

Ichimi laid a hand on Nanami's arm. "We know this isn't the best way to go about this. We wish that we could openly accuse the Colors of their sins as well, try them before an immortal court and sentence them. But too long has power been the only law in our world. We could not act openly against the Sun Emperor, and we cannot act openly against the Moon and Night deities. But we will do our best to end this betrothal, regardless of what you decide. Please though, once you are free, won't you bring Xiao around to our side? He will not forgive Salaana for what she did to you, not without your consent. And we need Xiao to stop his parents."

"If I helped you," Nanami asked, "what would you do to Jin?"

Salaana shrugged. "Jin is currently in the Underworld. We must hope she never returns, but if she does, we will send her back."

"Send her back—you mean kill her."

Salaana shrugged. "It wouldn't necessarily mean her death—after all, she is very powerful. Too powerful. So many colors should not be in a single being. She is a threat to all of us."

"A threat to your power, maybe! She is one of the kindest, gentlest beings I have ever met. How can you call her a threat?"

"Tell me, Nanami, when you discover a clutch of baby cobras, do you leave them to grow full size? Or do you kill them before each and every one becomes a deadly enemy?"

Oh, how Nanami hated Salaana!

She was searching for a worthy retort when there came a mighty crash and a howl of agony.

Salaana and Ichimi looked at each other, then turned to the door. When they passed through it, Salaana paused and left the door open. "A token of our good will."

Nanami stared at that open door for a long moment, half-certain it was a trap, but she finally stepped through. To her left was escape, to her right was the commotion. That howling—what if Xiao had returned to get her? He would have fallen directly into his parents' trap again.

Nanami went right, following Salaana and Ichimi.

XIAO was becoming better at teleporting—it only took three-quarters of an hour to bring both Dawa and himself to the Wood Pavilions.

They arrived on the boat dock, and Xiao had the strangest sense of déjà-vu, for it was Mu Rong that greeted him.

"Xiao!" called the thickset immortal through his wild beard. "Just the man to enliven a dull day. Where's the jug?"

"Gone," said Xiao.

"What? Never say it was stolen from you!"

Xiao found himself smiling. "That is in fact exactly what happened. But I don't want it anymore." He thought briefly of the flask that he'd left at Bai's cave. Mu Rong would love it, and unlike Xiao, he never seemed to have any trouble turning his partying on and off. But Xiao let it pass—right now, he didn't even want to be in charge of passing the flask to someone else. And... Well, the very existence of the flask hurt a bit. It said that Hei liked him better drunk and passive, and Xiao didn't want to share that with others, for he hated when people stared at him with pity.

"You never needed help getting a party started anyway—at least, no more help than Kulap could provide."

Mu Rong sighed. "Kulap's in Haraa's Healing Pavilion. Every day for weeks. There was a comatose immortal, and Kulap's helping Haraa develop a treatment."

"Mmm. Sorry. Say, have you seen a white-haired guy around here? Always wears white, too, shorter than me, and arrogant as anything."

Mu Rong barked his laugh. "You mean the First. Sure, it was his friend who was in the Pavilion. But the guy woke up, oh, I don't know, a week ago, and the two of them took off at dawn."

"Oh." Xiao was almost crushed by disappointment. He hadn't realized, until this moment, how much he was looking forward to Bai seeing him and being impressed with his sobriety. "Well." Then just because he was curious, "If the guy woke up, why is Kulap still doing research?"

"That's what I said," groused Mu Rong. "They and Haraa think that it's possible to develop some sort of potion as a cure against future need." He shrugged. "I'm trying to be supportive, but it's boring."

He sidled up to Xiao and slipped an arm around his waist. "We could do something a whole lot less boring." He looked at Dawa for the first time. "Would your friend be interested?'

Xiao felt like it was a different person who disengaged from Mu Rong's arm. He couldn't remember the last time he had turned down sex. Maybe he never had. But he wasn't in the mood to sleep with anyone but Nanami, even if she had moved on.

He no longer felt the need to say yes unless he wanted to, and that was incredibly freeing.

"I'm sorry," he told Mu Rong, and because he felt the need

to defend himself against Mu Rong's gaping mouth, he added, "I committed to someone."

It was a poor choice of words—after all, Mu Rong was committed to Kulap, and they kept the sexual side of their relationship open.

Mu Rong's eyes narrowed, and his lips completely disappeared beneath his beard. "So you bought into the false promise of monogamy that your parents preach."

Xiao cursed silently. "I didn't mean—" But Mu Rong was already stomping off.

Xiao turned back to Dawa, whose face was perfectly bland. "One way of loving isn't better than any other. There are as many right ways to love as there are beings in this world."

Dawa nodded once. "I will be sure to record that in your teachings."

Xiao rubbed the back of his neck. He wasn't sure if Dawa was joking or not and decided he didn't want to know. "We might as well go to the Healing Pavilion," he decided. "Maybe Haraa or Kulap know where Bai has gone."

They had traversed about half the wooded ground to the pavilion when screaming rent the air to the left of them. Xiao turned.

It was hard to identify the cause, for the trees grew tall and thick, but he picked out a yellow-greenish blob, not unlike vomit, moving rapidly. It was so large—at least fifteen feet tall, Xiao thought, and probably eight feet wide—that Xiao rejected his initial impression of a horned lion running amok in Haraa's woods.

But as it drew closer, Xiao saw quite clearly that it *was* a lion, a monstrous lion with dark green bull horns.

Xiao was distantly aware of being afraid—this thing was so wild and fierce and unfamiliar that his gut clenched with dread—but he didn't process his fear.

The creature had come across an immortal, and it flung the unlucky being high with its horns. The immortal hit a tree, damaging the moss on its trunk.

Haraa teleported directly next to that tree, undoubtedly to check what was happening to her treasured forest. When she saw the lion, she threw up her hands and froze, clearly terrified.

Xiao began to change then, his power washing over his skin and armoring him with scales, turning his fingernails into curved swords, and stretching his limbs until he was taller than the beast.

The Night Dragon surged forward, slipping in between the dense trees as smoothly as smoke and as fast as fire. He was there even as the beast opened its maw to reveal rows of teeth for shredding. Xiao slid between it and Haraa, and those teeth bit into scales instead of Haraa's soft flesh.

# How Jin Was Reckless

THE Korikami was an autumn blizzard—all the more dangerous and destructive for coming unexpectedly. But despite its threatening words and its even more threatening aspect, Jin was reluctant to attack first. She had never killed anything before entering the Underworld, and she hated it. Even though she was eager—no, desperate—to get home, she wanted to be able to relate her adventures without shame when she got there. So as long as the Korikami was still talking, she would try to negotiate.

"I had to kill the Achamba!" protested Jin. "It wouldn't stop attacking—"

The wolf laughed again, and cold air nipped at her face. "I can do that too." It lunged forward, teeth bared, and Jin threw up a wall of fire to protect herself. The Korikami melted and immediately reformed on the other side. Its icy teeth stabbed into her leg and it whipped her through the air, just as a real wolf would treat a rabbit. Jin feared her neck would snap, so she forced herself into a ball.

She slammed into the ground. Nothing broke, but bruises bloomed all over her body, and blood welled on her thigh—the Korikami's teeth had pierced her armor.

Jin shook. There must be a way to defeat the Korikami—after all, Aka had.

She must have said something aloud, for the Korikami replied, "If Aka could have killed me, he wouldn't have tricked me through this gate. Do you have a trick up your sleeve, little girl?"

Jin cradled her grandmother and mother and unborn brother in her hands. How arrogant she had been, to take them with her! The only reason the Korikami hadn't killed her already was it wanted her to open the gate. *But I don't know how! I don't understand anything about it—what if I trap us here forever instead? If only Bai were here, to help me understand its essence...*

And then Jin looked back at the Korikami, suddenly enlightened. "You believe that as Aka's granddaughter, I can open the gate, don't you? Do you know how?"

The Korikami's lips curled back in a canine smile. "Well, that was faster than I expected. I'm disappointed—I was looking forward to fighting you longer."

It leaned its head forward until its frozen nose pushed against Kunjee.

"This is made from Aka's blood, as is the gate itself. I watched him create it. Combining them will unlock the gate, and turning them both into his blood together will remove its binding on the Underworld, letting all the doors to Earth reopen."

Jin stared at the Korikami. "But—it can't be that simple!"

"Why not? The most powerful magic almost always is. Now, are you going to do it, or should I gnaw on you a little more?"

Jin stood, but once again the Korikami blocked her path. "Swear you won't leave the Underworld until the gate is gone."

Honestly, it hadn't even occurred to her to trick the Korikami and slip through the gate, but she still regretted losing that option. It sounded so easy when the Korikami explained it, but could she really open the Underworld just like that?

"I—"

A roar came from behind her, and Jin spun to find the Great Tiger cresting the summit, the Mudanren still clinging to his ruff.

"Hello, Tiger," said the Korikami. "You look cold."

The tiger turned its glowing eyes on the ice wolf and snarled once. Then it turned its focus to Jin. "Not trying to leave without saying good-bye, are you?"

Jin shook her head. "That was not my intention, even if the Korikami would have let me." She limped closer to the Great Tiger, resting her hands on its lower shoulder. Wu Zhe and Tiao Xian leaped from the ruff at its neck onto Jin's arms. Jin gathered them both into a hug as she confessed to the tiger, "You were right. I couldn't reason with the Achamba." She looked at the ashes that had been strewn across the snow by the Korikami's wind.

"So you incinerated it?" said the tiger. "You put your life above its."

"Yes," admitted Jin, "and those of my family." She cleared her throat. "Have you decided? Whether you will try to eat me or not?"

The Korikami laughed its horrible icy laugh, and Jin understood why it was the first creature that Aka imprisoned.

"You're about as subtle as a sword," it told Jin. "'Look how I destroyed your oldest enemy. Will you still challenge me?'"

Jin's hands tightened convulsively in the Tiger's fur. She didn't want to let the Korikami return to Earth, any more than the Xuezei.

But the Golden Phoenix, the Koch-ssi, the Great Tiger and the Mudanren—and yes, the Gumiho and the Sea Serpent—they shouldn't be trapped here.

"If you will agree to my condition, then I will make the vow you ask," she told the Korikami.

"Tell me," said the Korikami.

"I'm carrying my mother's soul. The Sea Serpent told me it would last a month or two out of the sea. If I'm unable to open the gate within two weeks, you must bring my mother back to the Sea of Souls."

The Korikami tilted its head and flicked its ears. "Done."

"I swear, I will open the gates before I leave the Underworld," she vowed before the four witnesses.

And the Korikami moved aside.

THE Chattaan Kile towered over the sea on a sheer bluff. The white walls reflected the sun so intensely that sailors claimed it could be seen from twenty miles away, but Bai knew it was visible for no more than three miles, just like the horizon anywhere.

Still, it had stood for twenty millennia. Its walls remained unscarred by the sieges it had rebuffed, and prayers had sunk deep into their stones. In fact, even though it was newer than the Sanctuary Caves, Bai soon realized that it had more power stored, either because it was more accessible or because mortals at war were desperate for the aid of higher powers.

At any rate, when he finished pulling all the prayers into himself, he felt intoxicated.

Wanting to establish himself in the minds of its mortal inhabitants, he teleported before the commander of the fortress. He was aware that he was smiling madly as he offered to fight any comers.

The most difficult part for Bai was leaving his challengers alive, but since they came at him singly, it was manageable.

Bai was met with such interest and welcome by these mortals that he stayed for a few nights. He was reminded of the comradery that he had found on the battlefield, and he spent the evenings speaking with the soldiers of their dreams and the days training with them. On the third day a miracle occurred.

His opponent, the son of the fortress commander, had just knelt before him in surrender when a thousand colorful Rang Pariyon surrounded them.

Each glowing ball of light was no bigger than Bai's fist, and several of them settled on him, greeting him with a soft buzz.

For a moment, Bai stared at them, utterly bewildered, and then his heart sang with joy.

Jin must have opened the gate to the Underworld, for how else could the Rang Pariyon have returned home?

He laughed with delight. Jin would go straight to the Sun

Palace, to see Aka. Eager to meet her there, he forgot to reiterate his name to the awed soldiers and instead teleported immediately.

But when he reached the Sun Palace, it was not the scene of a triumphant return that he had imagined, but one of terror and destruction.

Golden flames towered over the red walls, and the Golden Phoenix dove overhead, screeching its fury.

IT was not obvious to Jin where Kunjee should join the gate. She circled it twice, looking for any sort of break or impression in the deep vermillion wood. Every cold gust of wind drew her attention to the Korikami's quiet chortles, and she finally snapped, "Why don't you just tell me where it goes, then?"

"I'm in no rush," replied the Korikami. The Great Tiger growled low, and the Korikami sighed. "Fine. Look at the base near your right foot."

Jin knelt. She still saw nothing, but snow was piled high at the base of the gate, so she began to scrape it free. The ice crystals there were sharp and sliced at her fingers. She touched her hands to her bloody leg and made a trowel.

Able to dig quickly now, she soon found a place where it looked like a saw had been taken to the gate. She undid the gold chain and pulled the vermillion sun pendant free.

It slid perfectly into place, even offering up a satisfying click.

At the sound, the view inside the gate changed—instead of the other side of the Mirror Mount, it was now filled with red fire.

"Dissolve it!" ordered the Korikami, blowing snow at Jin in

its eagerness. Jin took a deep breath and glanced at the Great Tiger and the Mudanren. The Tiger's eyes were glowing even brighter than usual and Wu Zhe and Tiao Xian were clutching each other's hands, their hair petals furled tight to their heads.

Still kneeling, Jin touched the gate. She closed her eyes, and let the vermillion posts remember their true nature. Suddenly the gate was gone, her fingers suspended in cold air.

Something hot and wet touched her knees. Jin looked and gasped. There was a massive puddle of blood—it looked like enough to kill a man. She was suddenly sure that Aka had built the gate in a moment of desperation, when he was losing his fight against the Korikami.

She lifted her head and gasped. Where red fire had once filled the gate, soft multicolored lights now flickered like fireflies.

"She did it," whispered the Tiger. It leapt through before Jin even rose to her feet.

Jin let out a shaky laugh and rose, turning her head to look for Wu Zhe and Tiao Xian.

But cold teeth bit into her shoulder, and Jin screamed.

"What are you doing? I freed you!"

The Korikami dragged her back from the gate and threw her against the snow-covered mountain.

"Yes," it agreed as it approached once more, "and now I'll accept your life as compensation for the thirty millennia that I have been stuck in this cursed place."

Jin was furious. "You dishonorable—"

The Korikami laughed. "What do I care for honor?"

It lunged forward and Jin barely managed to move in time.

She needed help—the gate! If Bai was indeed on the other

side...

Jin ran for it and dove into the light. She emerged in the glorious daylight of Earth and rolled several feet. She could hear the Korikami behind, but she also heard the rasp of a sword being drawn from its sheath.

She rose, a smile and greeting on her lips that quickly faded. The waiting warrior was not Bai but Gang.

BAI forced his way through the water illusion of the southern gate—there were no guards at their post—and found chaos. If the Rang Pariyon brought joy, their cruel cousins, the Nisei, brought terror. Usually they came only at night to suffocate their prey with their butterfly wings, but millennia trapped in the Underworld seemed to have driven them mad. They were everywhere, covering the faces of immortals and forcing death upon them. The victims clawed and scratched at their faces, tearing the fragile wings of the Nisei, but rarely driving them off.

Wise immortals were teleporting away, abandoning the palace to the flames and the vengeful creatures.

Bai almost teleported away too, for when he stretched out his senses, they found no unknowable pocket, and he did not think Jin had come here after all.

But he looked for a moment longer at the tragic scene. So many would die soon, all for an ancient grudge. Bai spotted a young immortal child running and tripping. A Nisei settled on the boy's face, and Bai knew the child needed help.

And then it occurred to him.

*He* could help. Just like Jin had helped the Forever Child in that little river town. Back then, he had turned his face away from the struggle, but Jin had stepped forward and helped. And he could help right here and now.

Nisei in particular had large white wings with a silver pattern like constellations across them. Reaching into that deep well he had only so recently filled, Bai pulled the Nisei away from their victims and pushed them high into the air until they formed a cloud, both beautiful and deadly. Reluctant to kill even Nisei and with power to spare, Bai left them suspended there as he turned to the immortals he had saved.

A man dressed in red leather with a golden sun was gasping for breath. A Sun Guard. Bai grabbed his shoulder and pointed at the boy. "Everyone needs to teleport out of here as soon as possible. Get the guards together and help those who can't teleport themselves."

The man's eyes widened, and he nodded. Bai released him and he started organizing the guards around him. Bai strode through the Sun Palace, some part of him noting that the number of buildings had tripled, but mostly just looking for immortals who needed help. In general, he didn't do much—he simply told the immortals that were too afraid to think rationally what to do.

Particularly shrill screams led him to a gate painted with large pink lotus blossoms. He was sure this must be Jin's residence. He pushed on the left door, and it swung forward at his touch, either because of the power that leaked from his fingertips or because Jin had already keyed it to him, even though there hadn't been any need for that.

He stepped into a flower-filled courtyard that was dominated by hissing Dalagois, serpentine beasts with oversized eagle's wings and talons. Nasty, unknowable creatures. Two women—Jin's disciples?—were clumsily fighting off the brown creatures. The only reason they were still alive was they were too few—each wanting the prey, the Dalagois kept fighting each other instead of eating the women.

"Teleport out of here," Bai shouted at the women.

The first protested, "But her divinity's—"

"Yeppeun!" screamed the other.

A moment later they had both disappeared.

Furious at losing their prey, the Dalagoi swarm turned on Bai, and two of them lunged for him at once. Bai turned them back with the Starlight Sword, and summoned clouds. One Dalagoi managed to rake his scalp and Bai wished he'd taken the time to bind the Water Shield to his left arm. Luckily the clouds came quickly this high in the Heavens. Once the creatures were engulfed, he dropped the temperature to near freezing. Just like mortal snakes, the Dalagoi went still in the cold. Those that were airborne fell to the ground, a tangled heap of scales and feathers. Bai recentered himself, and then went back into the fray.

There were a great many fires made by the Phoenix, so the air was smoky, but there weren't that many active threats. He pinned another swarm of Nisei in the air and chilled another a flock of Dalagois, but most of the work was done by the Sun Guard, who demonstrated discipline and efficiency with just a little guidance from Bai. Within an hour, the palace seemed empty. He sent forth his power, looking for anyone who needed aid.

And he was shocked to find Aka. He lay comatose, trapped by the death curse, at the top of his towering red pagoda.

Perched on the roof, licked by flames, was the Golden Phoenix. The massive bird was crowing its triumph, and its crest flared and its long tail dancing.

Bai understood the Phoenix's need for vengeance, and he certainly didn't want to fight it.

But Jin had just spent the last few months fighting her way through the Underworld to save Aka. He wouldn't let that be for naught.

Bai tested Aka's teleportation ban and had no trouble tearing through it to enter the topmost room of the pagoda. It seemed that more mortals had worshipped the Chattaan Kile over the past thirty millennia than were currently living. Or perhaps Aka's wards were weakening with his will to live.

It was agonizingly hot in the pagoda's upper room—though not hot enough to melt stone—and smoke filled his nose, so Bai stopped breathing. Bai used his magical sense to locate Aka through the thick smoke that filled the room, and he practically tumbled on top of the other immortal. Wrapping his arms around Aka's prone body in a parody of a hug, he pulled them both between.

Perhaps five minutes later, they were in his garden, surrounded by jasmine. Bai lowered Aka to the ground and resumed his breathing. He had to cough once to clear the smoke he had inhaled at the pagoda.

The sound brought Cheng and Neela at a run.

"What's this?" asked Cheng. "Why did you bring Aka here? Did his children start their war?"

Bai shook his head. "The immortal creatures are free."

Neela gasped. "Jin—she has returned?" She closed her eyes, and Bai knew she was using her blood connection to seek her granddaughter. Her lids snapped open, and she grinned triumphantly. "She's at New Moon Manor. Come, let us all go now and settle this!"

Bai looked at Cheng, who nodded.

"Very well," Bai agreed. "Let me just lay Aka inside and then we will go."

DISAPPOINTMENT and worry crashed through Jin. Had Bai passed into the Underworld with her then? Was he still there?

Thank fate she had opened the gates then—he would be able to find his way out.

And then Gang's hand settled on her shoulder, and he shoved her behind him—the Korikami had followed her. Gang raised the Sun Sword.

Following his lead, Jin assumed a fighting stance and drew her tessen. Anyone who saw them now, with their indestructible golden weapons, would know them for father and daughter. Jin shoved that thought away and flicked open the tessen's ribs.

The Korikami, that mad creature, laughed and snow swirled around them. "How delightful," it said. "I was ready to claim one of Aka's descendants as compensation, but now I shall have two!"

Gang swung his sword, and rays of sunlight slashed through the Korikami's icy body.

"It will just refreeze!" Jin warned him. "Heat does not hurt it."

And indeed, it reformed and leapt forward, grabbing Gang's sword in its teeth.

Jin spun through the air and struck it right on the nose with her tessen, just as she might tap a puppy to get it to release something. It dropped Gang's sword and howled its indignation. The falling snow changed from swirling fluff to hard balls of hail which pummeled and bruised Jin even through her armor.

*How do we fight this?* she wondered. Gang was as much a being of fire and heat as she was, and neither had any lasting effect on the Korikami.

"It craves our deaths—we must alter its purpose!" Jin called to Gang.

Gang shook his head. "Its essence is indigo. It will be immune to our influence. If we can't melt it, we must smash it!" he barked.

Indigo! Like the monkey—it had accused her of magical tricks... Was that why the other creatures had been so kind to her? Had she been unconsciously manipulating them with her yellow magic, the way Bai said she'd done to him and Xiao?

Jin didn't have time to dwell on the topic, for the Korikami lunged forward.

This time Gang spun left, and Jin spun right. The Sun Sword sliced through the Korikami's left ear, and the golden tessen through its right.

Both turned to liquid and tried to rejoin the Korikami's head. Gang sent the ear near him flying away.

"Don't let the pieces rejoin!" he yelled.

Jin had already missed the opportunity though, and the right ear reattached itself.

Determined to do better, Jin dodged the Korikami's snapping teeth and sliced her tessen through the Korikami's leg, sending a chunk flying.

Jin was terrified—it was hard work carving up the Korikami and the pieces always tried to return.

"Jin, you must isolate the pieces while I fight it!"

A puddle of now cold blood was pooled where the gate had once stood. So, as Gang shaved ice off of the Korikami, Jin enveloped it in red clay and sent the blocks hurling apart from each other.

Near the end, nothing remained of the Korikami but its fierce snapping head, which lay in the snow.

"Fate curse you!" It screamed insults until Gang smashed it into pieces and kicked them apart.

Jin and Gang both stood on the mountain for some minutes, the only sound their harsh panting. Had she freed the Korikami only to brutally kill it? Or were the pieces in those clay vessels still alive, much as Cheng had been when Neela trapped him?

That was, Jin admitted to herself, where she got the idea from. Her hands were shaking, and she found it hard to think.

She was still shivering, her eyes darting from Gang to the various clay vessels when Wu Zhe and Tiao Xian tumbled through the gate, the black peonies cradled in their arms.

That reminded Jin that there were things she must do, and she laughed, though it sounded almost like crying even to her.

"Excellent timing," she told them.

Tiao Xian sniffed. "Not everyone needs to be chewed on by wolves to feel alive."

"Speaking of seeking out trouble," said Gang, "It wasn't enough to just get the peonies? You had to open portals to the Underworld?"

Jin was trying to determine her next step, but she answered

Gang absently, "The creatures didn't belong there. They were suffering and homesick."

Gang snorted and tugged his beard. "I don't doubt it, but don't you think mortals will suffer when they return to Earth? And immortals? You and I barely stopped the Korikami together." He shook his head. "Salaana isn't going to be the only being calling for your death."

Jin thought Gang was overreacting. Most of the creatures had been rather pleasant. "I don't have time to discuss this." She glanced at the black peonies, and touched the soul pendant, but both of those could wait. "I need to go to New Moon Manor," she told Gang.

"What? Why?"

"Xiao needs me. Tiao Xian—"

Gang grabbed her arm. "Slow down. Why does Xiao need you? Before you go—"

"Zi and Hei are torturing him." Jin shook his hand off her. Should she bring the Mudanren with her to the manor? Would they even be willing to come?

"If you insist on going to New Moon Manor, I am coming with you," announced Gang.

Jin looked at him. She was grateful for his help, and she had seen her art gathered in his room at Tsuku, but...

"Why?" she asked.

"To protect you!"

Jin shook her head. He had left her alone three thousand years. Only Karana had visited her at Neela's caravan, and Aka, once. "I can protect myself," Jin said. "I need to go now—Xiao needs me."

"You're exhausted!" he protested. "I felt how much power

you used just now. You've been in the Underworld for months—"

"Yes! It's been months, and that whole time, Xiao was imprisoned in his room, and those vile beings were harvesting his power! I saw him, he's in agony! I'm going now!"

"Then let me come with you," he insisted again.

Jin stared at him. She didn't trust him. She knew he had always viewed Xiao with contempt. What if he sided with Zi and Hei against Xiao?

She took off her necklace and let the blue and orange ornament dangle in front of him.

"Do you know what this is?"

He stared at it in confusion. His expression changed slowly, becoming young and vulnerable. "My mother? How...?"

"It's not just Noran. It's Aashchary and her babe as well."

Gang's eyes jerked to her own. They were liquid gold—familiar because they were the same eyes Jin had always seen in her mirror. The same eyes that Noran had admired shortly before her death.

"I crossed the Sea of Souls, and they came to me. Aashchary still has not accepted her death. Her yearning for life made me wonder if she couldn't be resurrected."

Gang blinked. "But..."

"I was warned that she cannot survive indefinitely out of the Sea of Souls, but Noran offered her soul to protect Aashchary and the baby's."

Jin looked down. "It was impulsive to take them. And maybe wrong. I almost lost all three of them to the Achamba."

Gang reached out his hands, and Jin let the ornament settle in them.

"If you need someone to protect, protect them," she told him. She hesitated, then, to Wu Zhe and Tiao Xian, "would you care for the peonies until I can use them?"

"You freed us," said Wu Zhe. "Of course we will take care of the peonies."

"If you stay with the God of War, I'll find you soon."

Tiao Xian sniffed but didn't argue when Wu Zhe nodded.

Jin cast one more look at Gang. He knelt in the snow, the ornament pressing his hands into his lap as if its weight rivalled that of the world.

Perhaps for him, it did.

# 12

# Fury and Fire

XIAO had been at least five times bigger than Ao in dragon form, but he had little advantage over this strange horned-lion. With fur like moss and massive golden horns like those of a bull, it was almost as tall as he and all dense muscle. It looked like nothing Xiao had ever seen. Its teeth pierced Xiao's scales, a hundred points of agony, and Xiao thrashed. The creature shook its head fiercely and its teeth scored Xiao's flesh.

Xiao scratched its face with his claws, and thick red blood dripped into the creature's yellow eyes.

It let go of Xiao and roared. Xiao dove forward, grabbing the lion's neck in his mouth and slamming it into a massive evergreen. The trunk of the tree cracked, and it toppled onto Xiao. The lion screamed in pain, but it didn't seem to sustain any serious damage. All four of its paws slashed at Xiao's face.

Its claws were nasty, curved blades, and they ripped Xiao's scales out where they caught them.

The pain was terrible, and Xiao knew he had to end this quickly. He bit deeper into the creature's neck, and he tasted its grassy blood. Xiao pulled back, ripping huge chunks of the creature's fur and skin off. As soon as it was free of Xiao's teeth, it bounded to its feet and fled, more like a deer than a cat.

Xiao breathed deeply a few times. What was that thing? Should he pursue it and kill it?

While he was still deciding, Haraa appeared in front of him, her green hair writhing with a life of its own. "How dare you?" she hissed through clenched teeth.

Shocked, Xiao reverted to his natural form. "Haraa, I—"

She pointed behind her. "You. Know. The. Rules."

Xiao followed her finger to the massive tree that he had broken with the creature's back. She was upset because of her plants?

Yes, Xiao knew that it was damaging the flora was the taboo in the Wood Pavilions, but surely—

Haraa raised her hand, palm out, and Dawa stepped between them.

Dawa bowed. "Please, mistress, my lord is in shock. The Xiezhi hurt him badly just now. He deeply regrets damaging the tree, but he was eager to save your life."

Haraa's glare switched to Dawa. There was little reason in her face, just the madness of extremism, but she lowered her hand. "You have an hour," she snapped and strode away.

"Such gratitude," mocked Xiao.

Dawa sighed. "Please, my lord, do not joke about the Warden."

"You're supposed to call me Xiao." Xiao examined his chest and ran his hands down his arms. "I'm not even bleeding. Why do I feel so weak?"

Dawa crossed his arms. "It's my understanding that a dragon form is the manifestation of raw power. Damaging that form siphons away your magic." He cleared his throat. "It's considered quite risky."

"Oh," said Xiao. "I'll be more careful in the future."

"Yes, my lord. And where are we going to now?"

Xiao looked at Dawa for a moment, then at the dark ring of hair around his littlest finger. "I want to see Nanami." He closed his eyes and used the ring to search for her.

She wasn't on Earth. With a frown, Xiao looked in the Heavens. And found her at New Moon Manor. His eyes flew open.

"Dawa, the Moon and Night deities have my lover. I must free her."

Dawa grabbed his arm. "Xiao, that seems like a very bad idea."

Xiao frowned. "Do you call me 'my lord' when you're pleased with me and 'Xiao' when I'm being stupid?"

"Nothing has changed since the last time you tried to confront them."

Xiao blinked, then shook his head. "You're wrong, Dawa. Everything has changed. Even if my parents trap me again, I won't drink. I need to go, to find out what they are planning on doing to Nanami. I can't leave her there." Xiao shuddered. "I couldn't leave anyone there."

Dawa closed his eyes. "I will go with you."

Xiao snorted. "If you come with me, you might be the

shortest-lived disciple ever."

"Then that will be my fate."

Xiao groaned. "You're just trying to stop me from going."

Dawa opened his eyes and looked at Xiao hopefully.

Xiao rubbed his face and thought. "What was that thing I fought just now?"

"The Xiezhi. An immortal creature that was locked in the Underworld by the Sun Emperor more than twenty thousand years ago."

"What?" Xiao was shocked. "But then—Dawa, Jin must be back!"

"Or dead," said Dawa, and Xiao stepped back.

"No—surely not—I..." Xiao touched the little scar on his pinky and sought out his best friend.

But when he found her, she was in the same place as his lover.

JIN reappeared at the Crescent Gate of New Moon Manor. She had been tempted to go directly to the main hall, but she expected Zi and Hei to let her in, and she didn't want to waste any power breaking their teleportation ban.

She stepped forward to ring the violet bell mounted to the left of the gate, only to realize she was still holding her tessen, ribs splayed. She huffed in bemusement, then reluctantly tucked it into the sash at her waist. She was still keyed up from her recent fights.

Jin rang the bell.

Within moments, the black iron doors swung open. A violet robed disciple with silver hair ornaments came out and bowed deeply to her. Jin recognized her as Zi's first disciple. "Divinity. My lady and lord await you in the hall. If you'd follow me...?"

Jin nodded, and the woman led the way. Not that her guidance was needed—even if Jin hadn't been here a hundred times before, the wide basalt path led directly to the massive hall, with its black pillars and violet silks. It towered over the low gardens before it, demanding attention just as surely as the Moon Goddess herself.

When they entered the hall, Zi and Hei rose from their stone thrones and descended the stairs to approach Jin.

Zi stopped about four feet away from Jin, and said, "I'm always glad to greet my future daughter, but perhaps you would like to bathe and change before we speak?"

Jin crossed her arms. "I want to see Xiao."

Zi tilted her head slightly, and Jin recognized the look in her eyes—it was the exact expression Zi had worn when Jin had accidentally gotten honey on Zi's robes as a child. Jin realized that she had never spoken to Zi so bluntly before. But she didn't care.

Jin felt reckless. And angry. Maybe she did need a rest. Even now, that wasn't impossible—if she accepted that bath, Zi would probably clap her hands in delight. But Jin could see Xiao in her mind's eye, collapsed on the floor by his bed, wine soaking his shirt and his eyes filled with self-loathing.

"Why would I know where my son is?" Zi asked. "Wasn't he travelling with you on some pilgrimage for Aka's sins?"

Jin took two steps closer to Zi, her hand wrapped around her tessen's base. "I know you imprisoned him and drained his power. You think you have the right to do it just because you can—well, I'm here to stop you."

Zi laughed outright. "Can you hear yourself, child?"

Jin growled. "Either bring Xiao here or I will burn your manor down!"

Zi's eyes flashed. Hei stepped forward so that he stood by his wife's side, his own hand wrapped about the hilt of his sword. "You can try, little girl."

DAWA insisted on accompanying Xiao to New Moon Manor, and Xiao teleported them directly to Jin, for Zi and Hei had never banned him from entering the hall, only leaving it.

They reappeared in the main hall of the manor, all obsidian and glinting silver, and the tableau before them was something from a dream—or a nightmare.

Jin was shoving her face into Zi's. Both Zi and Hei were regarding her as if she were a blob of filth in their pristine shrine.

Which wasn't far from the truth.

Her hair was loose and wild, with strange leaves in improbably bright colors sticking out of it. She was wearing a strange, iridescent armor—it was the same strange metallic rainbow as that magical key she had made. Xiao hoped she hadn't made it from her own blood, but that seemed very possible, given the rusty stains crusted on both her left leg and right shoulder.

Xiao couldn't see her face, and he was a little afraid to. She was arguing about him, threatening to burn the whole place down—which did not seem like a Jin thing to do.

Xiao swallowed and called her name.

"JIN."

The call was calm, soft, but Jin whirled toward it.

Xiao stood a few feet from her dressed in black and lavender robes, his hair braided around his head, and his dimple evident in his right cheek.

Jin gasped and threw herself at him. He caught her, his arms wrapping around her shoulders as hers fastened about his waist. "Xiao, I saw…" she mumbled into his chest.

"Thanks for coming for me." Jin was humbled by the vulnerability in his voice. She squeezed him gently, enjoying the first hug she'd had in—well, it felt like years.

She pulled back slightly, to search his face. "You are alright? How—"

"Your boy-toy rescued me a week ago, silly." He tugged a loose lock of hair by her temple. "Love what you're doing with this."

"But why did you come back?" she demanded.

Xiao sighed, but before he could answer, Hei pulled him from Jin's arms, even as Zi clamped her own hand on Jin's upper arm. "We have no quarrel with you," she said, "but you must let us discipline our son."

Xiao turned toward his father, and Hei slapped him across the face. For a brief moment, Jin saw a white handprint on Xiao's cheek before blood rushed to fill it. Xiao cracked his jaw. He started to speak, but a light whip extended from each of his parents and wrapped around his wrists.

Xiao went stiff and hollered like he was being burnt alive.

Something snapped in Jin. Zi and Hei might not be called creatures, but they were demons compared to the Koch-ssi. They were far more monstrous than the Tiger—in fact, they were as unreasonable as the Achamba.

Jin spread her tessen with her free hand and slashed its razor's edge across Zi's throat.

Zi crumpled to the ground.

Hei startled when her power whip disappeared and turned to look for his wife. His own whip disappeared a moment later, and he flew toward her, his black iron blade outstretched.

Jin's focus narrowed on him, reading his every impulse and reacting.

It wasn't enough though. Jin was not his equal in martial arts. She knocked his sword to the side and wrapped her arms around him, lighting them both on fire—a pure blue flame that burned so hot that Hei didn't even scream before he turned to ash.

NANAMI almost skidded into Salaana and Ichimi, for they stopped just inside the main hall of New Moon Manor. Ichimi was even shorter than she was, so Nanami saw Xiao over her sister's head.

Breathing became difficult—it had indeed been his cry of pain that she had heard. Familiar whips encircled his wrists.

"Why did you come for me, you idiot!" For all her vehemence though, Nanami whispered the words, and tears leaked down her cheeks.

"I wouldn't be so certain he came for you," Salaana's voice was cold and precise, cutting through the fog of emotion. She stepped toward the right, and Nanami saw Jin.

But this was not the Jin she knew.

This woman was bloody and wild, and she wore strange

form-fitting armor that looked like nothing Nanami had ever seen yet was strangely familiar. Where had she...

The key. The key that unlocked anything. Jin's armor looked identical. *Surely not.*

Nanami pressed her knuckles to her mouth, horrified by the idea of armor made from blood.

Zi's hand was wrapped around Jin's upper arm, though her focus was on Xiao. *She's braver than I,* Nanami mused, *I wouldn't have the courage to hold Jin like that.*

But if Zi were braver, it seemed Nanami was wiser, for as she watched, Jin sliced Zi's throat with her golden tessen.

Nanami gasped and stepped forward, but she was restrained by Ichimi.

"You'll be killed if you get in the middle of that," Ichimi murmured. "Your power is but a spark to their fireworks."

Nanami bit her lower lip—she knew Ichimi was right, but Xiao was still imprisoned by Hei—

But Hei released his son to deal with his wife's murderer.

The Night Sword drove directly toward Jin's heart, but somehow Jin turned it aside. Sparks flew as the golden tessen hit the Night Sword, too quick for the eye to follow.

And then there was a pillar of blue light—no, of fire. Deepest cerulean, like the heart of a flame, it licked the ceiling of the hall and incinerated it, creating a window of light above them.

The fire guttered out as fast as it had come, and only Jin remained. She was covered in black soot now, in addition to the blood, and Nanami vomited as soon she realized that soot was Hei.

"Now will you approve of me stopping her?" said Salaana, and she surged forward.

Nanami could see that Jin had nothing left. Jin was crawling across the floor like a babe toward Xiao; Nanami tried to find her voice, to warn Jin that death was coming but something held her back.

She remembered seeing how Bai looked at Jin like she was the stars, and the moon, and the sun combined, just hours after they had met. That strange magic, that influence over others terrified Nanami, but she had consoled herself that Jin was gentle and innocent and kind.

But gentle, innocent, kind girls didn't murder two of the most powerful immortals in this world in a matter of moments.

Nanami hated Zi and Hei; how could she condemn Jin for feeling the same?

Salaana was close to Jin now, perhaps a foot away, flying silently over the black basalt, and Nanami still didn't find her voice.

But just as the sword arced downward, a white blur slammed into Jin, and Salaana's sword bit deep into the basalt.

Too late for it to matter, Nanami at last found her voice and screamed, "Look out!"

THE flame went out, not because Jin let go of it, but because she had drained her power. Her legs gave out and she fell on all fours to the floor. She forced herself to look at Xiao.

It was only then that the reality of what she'd done hit her. He lay on the floor, panting and staring at her as tears dripped down his cheeks.

"Xiao—I'm sorry," she mumbled, crawling toward him. "I— I just—"

A strong arm wrapped around her waist just as a sword sliced into the basalt where she had been. She followed the sword up to find Salaana, face white and eyes burning.

Jin looked behind her and found Bai.

Their eyes met, and one corner of his lips lifted infinitesimally.

WHEN Jin had whirled to face him, Xiao had been shocked.

Not by the nasty bruise forming on her cheek or the rust-red flecks that he suspected a good scrubbing would clear away, but because she was terrifyingly beautiful.

Those perfect features had gained a rawness, a desperation that made them vividly alive. More real than anything he had ever seen. He had the strange urge to kneel before her beauty—thank fate that she ran at him and pulled him into a hug before he acted on such a ridiculous impulse.

"You're alright?' she asked, and he felt hot tears dampen the front of his shirt.

Yes, this was the Jin he knew, crying more easily than a babe.

But he didn't want her to cry. He wanted her to smile. So he said, "Your boy-toy rescued me a week ago, silly." Her hair smelled strange though not unpleasant—as it would for any other being—and he pulled one of those odd leaves from a clump near her temple. "Love what you've done with this," he said dryly.

"Why'd you come back?" she demanded.

Before Xiao could answer, his parents pulled them apart.

Hei struck Xiao with his full strength, and Xiao wondered

that his head didn't separate from his neck. He cracked his jaw and tried to control his hate. This wasn't going to go the same way as it did before. Xiao turned to face his father—but he was too slow. Again.

Whips lashed him, burning into his wrists and pulling his power from him like a million tweezers plucking every one of his hairs at once. He didn't want to scream, but the agony overwhelmed him.

The world was pain.

And then it wasn't. He felt better—stronger—but also utterly askew, as if he had suddenly added twenty pounds of muscle. Trying to understand what had happened, he forced himself to look around, but it was strange to even lift his head.

He met his mother's eyes about twenty feet away. She was also lying on the floor.

No, she was dead.

Blood pooled around her head, a wound gaping in her throat like a second mouth.

Xiao was still coming to terms with that when another twenty pounds of muscle came to him.

No. Not muscle. Power. Suddenly the power that flowed within him had doubled or quadrupled. He stared at Zi and knew half of it was from her. So...

He looked away from her glassy accusing eyes and found Jin. She was covered in black ash, and as he watched, she collapsed to the floor.

She started crawling toward him, crying and mumbling something.

Xiao wanted to go to her to comfort her, but he couldn't seem to stand.

Even though he felt strong and whole, he also felt totally disorientated. His body was unfamiliar—he knew it was only the magical part of him that had changed but that didn't seem to matter. He had to relearn himself anyway.

Zi and Hei were dead. Their power had all come to him.

WHEN Bai, Cheng, and Neela arrived at New Moon Manor, Bai couldn't help but remember the last time he had gone to New Moon Manor with Cheng, to witness the invention of marriage.

"Why is there a wall?" asked Cheng, echoing Bai's surprise from half a year ago.

Bai shrugged and looked at Neela.

She was already ringing the large violet bell, but she tossed over her shoulder, "Because Zi and Hei are powerful and paranoid."

Cheng looked at Neela and said, "Perhaps I should learn from them."

Neela laughed harshly.

The gate opened and five disciples in plain black cotton bowed respectfully to Neela, before casting curious looks at Bai and Cheng. "I am sorry, Wanderer, but their divinities are busy at present—"

"My granddaughter is here, isn't she? I need to speak with her."

Neela attempted to brush past the disciples, but they drew their swords.

"Their divinities invite you to return at a later time."

Neela gestured to Bai. "This is the Great Warrior. The man

who slaughtered a hundred thousand beings. Three hundred warriors *by himself* in Cheolmun Pass. Why don't you let us in?"

The disciples slammed the doors shut.

"Well, what are you going to do now?" Neela demanded, as if he were the one who made the disciples shut the gate.

Bai looked at the height of the gate. "If I throw you over, can you manage to land on your feet?"

"Yes," said Cheng.

Neela sniffed, and Bai was sure she could as well.

So first Cheng and then Neela went over the high crescent, and then Bai jumped himself. He caught the top of the moons and hauled himself over.

The disciples had arrayed themselves on the path to Zi and Hei's hall.

Bai sighed and drew the Starlight Sword, already full size in anticipation of trouble, from its sheath on his back. "I have no desire to kill you, but if you value your lives, I strongly encourage you to retreat now."

"It's because we value our lives that we cannot run," said one, a tall man with sweat beading on his forehead.

"Ah. Well, I am sorry for you, and yet I cannot retreat either."

Bai stepped forward and the five disciples stepped back. This happened thrice more, and he laughed. "Will you retreat step by step to the hall then, and we will call it a fight?"

This spurred one woman to rush forward; the Starlight Sword sliced though hers easily, and Bai stopped his swing at her throat. Quick jabs to her vital points, she fell to the ground unconscious.

Encouraged by the lack of fatality, two disciples came at him together. Bai bent backward to avoid their swords, and they ended up striking each other's. Bai hit both of their stomachs simultaneously, and they flew backward. They both thumped the ground loudly and stayed down. Bai knew their unconsciousness was feigned.

The fourth attacker was the tall man with a sweaty forehead. He did not even complete his swing before closing his eyes. With his free hand, Bai struck where the man's neck joined his shoulder so that he melted to the ground.

The final man yelled angrily, and he fought whole-heartedly. Bai actually had to cut this one twice before managing to strike the vital points that dropped him.

Bai stood and glanced at Neela and Cheng. "Thanks for the help," he mumbled.

"You did just fine on your own," said Neela, and she strode past the fallen disciples.

Cheng followed closely—Bai knew he was suspicious that Neela would try to escape, but Bai was not worried. Her genuine determination to see Jin was clear to him.

They were less than halfway up the path when a horrible yell came from the hall. Someone was in great pain. Bai broke into a run; Neela was unable to match his speed, and Cheng stayed behind to monitor his friend-turned-nemesis.

The wooden doors that Bai had shattered in the spring had been replaced with black iron, and Bai grimaced. He tried them, but they were locked.

There wasn't anything in the door he could alter magically. He raised the Starlight Sword and heated the silver metal until it was white hot.

It cut through the iron door, but the process felt agonizingly slow. As soon as he had made an outline large enough to pass through, Bai kicked the metal free and entered the hall.

He saw Salaana first, thanks to her brilliantly red sari. He noted that she no longer wore any white whatsoever and supposed their fight had made her cautious. She was running silently across the hall, her sword ready, so Bai looked past her to find the target.

Jin was crawling across the floor, covered in blood and soot.

Never had Bai moved so fast as he did then. He was nearly twice as far from Jin as Salaana was, but he reached her first. He pulled her out of harm's way so that Salaana's blade bit into the basalt floor of the hall instead of her niece's body.

Jin turned her head. When her eyes met Bai's, his heart skipped a beat.

"Bai," she breathed, and her full lips curved into a smile.

Bai released her to push her behind him. He rose and stared at Salaana. "Did you want a rematch?" He asked her. "You seem to have recovered."

Salaana growled and pulled her sword free of the rock. She swung it at Bai—a little wildly, but with far more speed than Hei's disciples, and Bai just managed to meet it with the Starlight Sword.

"Salaana," he said, "I can see that you are still insisting on killing Jin against future crimes she might commit, but even if you manage to defeat me, the Wanderer and the Sleeper are both just outside this hall. If you insist on killing their granddaughter, there is no way this can end well for you."

"Future crimes?" Salaana challenged. "Did you not see her murder the Moon and Night deities then?"

Bai had to resist the urge to look about him, for he had seen no such thing. "Even if she did, I promise you that Cheng and Neela will claim your life if you kill her. Why don't we calm down and talk?"

"Goddess of Justice!" Neela's voice cracked through the hall. "What are you doing?"

Salaana stepped back at last, letting the tip of her sword drag to the ground. Bai tried not to care that she either feared or respected Neela more than him.

Neela hurried forward and pulled Jin into her arms. "Child, do you want fate to curse you? What have you done to yourself?"

Jin tried to pull away from Neela but failed. "You used Godsbane on me," Jin rasped.

Neela pressed her lips together. "Only because you were so foolish as to insist on going to the Underworld! And look what happened to you there. You are covered in blood. And this nasty soot."

"That's the Night God," said a somewhat strangled voice, and Bai turned to find Xiao sprawled on the floor. This prompted him to scan the hall, for he had seen no one but Salaana and Jin in his haste.

Zi was indeed lying dead in a pool of her own blood. Was Salaana's accusation true then?

And Nanami was here as well, walking slowly toward them, her arms wrapped around her body. She looked almost as stunned as Xiao.

Behind her was Ichimi; she was summoning someone. Bai suspected that if they were still here in thirty minutes, the entire Sea Clan would join them.

And by the door, almost hidden behind a pillar, was a

disciple of Hei's. Or perhaps not, for his black robes featured violet embroidery rather like Xiao's. Bai blinked once, and realized it was the crow-man in his natural form.

"If I were you, I would worry a little less about Jin and a little more about your disciples," Bai told Salaana.

Salaana's red eyes narrowed at him. "What have you done?" she asked through her teeth.

"Not I," said Bai. "It is the Golden Phoenix who is wreaking havoc on the palace."

Salaana frowned fiercely, her eyebrows slashing over her nose. "What nonsense are you spouting now?"

"I opened the gates to the Underworld," said Jin. "The immortal creatures are returning."

"You did what?" demanded Neela, and her fingers curled into claws around Jin's biceps.

Jin didn't seem to notice—that strange armor protected her—but Bai knelt and gathered Jin into his own arms.

"Well done," he told her as he stood.

She pressed her face into his neck, and Bai didn't care that he was smiling like an idiot.

"You are crazy!" said Salaana. "You are both crazy! Every immortal and mortal will be begging me for her death within a month, with those monsters ravaging the world!"

"Then why don't we meet again in a month," suggested Bai, "and see who is on the side of justice—you or Jin?"

Salaana glared first at him, then at Neela's crossed arms, then Cheng's deceptively bland expression, and finally Xiao sprawled on the floor.

"She murdered your parents. Don't you want justice for them?"

"She freed me from them," Xiao corrected her. "I can't blame her for doing what I've thought of a million times."

"Xiao," said Jin. "you forgive me then? I thought—"

The crow-man and Nanami reached Xiao at the same time and helped him to his feet. Xiao left his arms around their shoulders, as if it were difficult for him to hold himself up.

Xiao said, "There's nothing to forgive."

Bai forced himself not to react—Xiao's words weren't a lie precisely, but he was deeply upset. He was suppressing his emotion for Jin's sake.

"But you seemed so shocked—"

"I was. By their deaths, and by the power that flooded me." He breathed slowly and looked at Zi's body.

Bai couldn't help but wince. Zi looked terrible, blood soaking her robes. "I don't want the disciples to see her like this. Can you burn her body as well?"

Jin moved weakly in Bai's arms. "Of course—"

"I'll do it," Cheng interrupted. "You've exhausted yourself."

"You are...?" Xiao asked in confusion.

"Ah. I'm Cheng. I knew both your parents for many millennia. I'm sorry. Um—"

Xiao managed a lopsided shrug. Bai could see that he was barely keeping himself together.

"Then I'll get to it," and Cheng took a step toward Zi's body.

"Wait!" said Salaana. "That's it? We might need the body as evidence—"

"Oh, stop it," snapped Nanami. "Less than an hour ago, you were plotting her death! Let Cheng burn the body so that Xiao can hold a funeral for the disciples."

The word funeral drew a collective shudder from all the

immortals. It made the death real, and suddenly their own passings seemed possible.

But Cheng went to the body, and soon it was burning. It was slower than Jin's incineration of Hei, for the fire was no hotter than an ordinary blaze, and after a moment, Neela snapped, "This is ridiculous."

She reached out her hands, fueling the flames with her own power, and a blue tinge appeared at the heart of the flame.

Bai thought of Cheng's long obsession with her and thought there was a metaphor there somewhere, but it escaped him.

For five minutes, everyone stood in silence, watching Zi's body burn. Jin pressed her face against Bai's neck, unable to look, and Bai didn't need to read her essence to understand she was in turmoil. He wanted to comfort her, but he didn't want to draw attention to her struggle either, so he simply held her close.

Xiao said, "You should all go. Dawa and I can handle it from here." He cleared his throat. "Where are we meeting in a month?"

Jin lifted her head from Bai to look at him—her eyes were dry, but red-rimmed. "Won't you come with us now?" Jin asked.

Xiao shook his head. "There are things I must do—all of their worshippers transferred to me. I need to—" His eyes grew distant, and he leaned more heavily on Nanami and the crow-man. "I need to deal with that. But I will be there in a month. I will testify on Jin's behalf." He shot a glare at Salaana.

Ichimi stepped forward. "The Sea Palace—"

"No," said Nanami. "That is hardly neutral ground."

"Tsuku," said Jin. "If the Moon Deer will host us."

Ichimi's eyes widened, and she looked to Salaana. Salaana

nodded once.

"He will," Ichimi said confidently.

"Then we will see you at Tsuku in a month. Now, we also have some matters to attend to." And Bai pulled Jin, Neela, Cheng, and himself in between.

# 13

# Grief, Relief, and Belief

No one seemed to notice Nanami's cry came after the danger had passed—in truth, she wasn't sure if anyone even heard it.

As Bai fought with Salaana, Nanami hurried forward to Xiao. A stranger reached his side the same time she did.

He looked a little past middle age, with gray hair that was almost lavender. He seemed soft, with thin arms, a round face, and a slight paunch. That softness extended to his eyes, and he smiled slightly at Nanami and bobbed his head. She might not know him, but it was clear he recognized her.

Together, they each slipped an arm around Xiao's back and lifted him to his feet.

"Nanami," Xiao murmured against her temple, before doing his best to stand straight.

Nanami peered anxiously into those lavender eyes and was surprised by what she saw. She had thought it was the shock of his parents' death that had affected him, but rather than sorrow and pain, he seemed... Not drunk, but something like it.

A few moments later, she had her answer, as Xiao informed the crowd that he had inherited his parents' power. Nanami's arm tightened around his waist at that announcement.

How must she appear to others—a pathetic hanger-on? A fool who didn't know her place? A parasite?

Nanami remembered that pillar of blue flame and knew that everyone must see Jin and Xiao as a better match. Her throat felt tight, and Nanami kept her eyes on the floor as she listened to more powerful beings decide what would come next.

When Xiao announced he would not be going with Jin and Bai, Nanami felt a mortifying degree of relief. When had she become such a cringing creature?

And yet she wanted so badly to be alone with Xiao, to know what had happened to him over the past three months. To hear that nothing had changed, and he didn't regret the promises he made her at the Sea Palace.

She was also worried about him. His relationship with his parents was different than hers with Ao and Miko—it was even more antagonistic—but still, they were his parents. Could he really be okay?

And then at last it was just the three of them in the hall— Xiao, her, and the stranger.

"Dawa," said Xiao, and Nanami learned the stranger's name, "this is my partner, Nanami the Thief."

"So I gathered, my lord." Dawa spoke dryly, and Nanami was surprised to see Xiao smile.

"Nanami, Dawa was once Zi's third disciple, but he helped me escape and is now mine."

"My lord saved my life," Dawa informed Nanami, and he looked at her, his dark eyes suddenly serious. "I have watched over him his whole life, and I will serve him for the rest of mine."

Nanami bit her lip. She understood such loyalty of course, for it was common in the Sea Court, but it still felt like one more thing keeping her and Xiao apart. She never expected to have any followers—she wouldn't want them. She supposed that she had been hoping Xiao would renounce his godhood once he was free of his parents, but it seemed...

"Xiao, what are your plans?" Nanami asked. "What things do you need to take care of?"

He removed his arm from Dawa's shoulder and cupped the side of her face. He smiled at her, but the dimples didn't appear, and Nanami thought he looked sad.

"I'm going to become the God of Love, Nanami. I can feel so many mortals—they believe in me and need me. If I abandon them..."

"What? Won't they just move on to other deities?'

Xiao shook his head. "Not all of them. Many would despair, some would even kill themselves."

"But—but why? How can you be so sure?"

"My parents provided meaning in their lives. Different temples teach their followers in different ways, but the New Moon... People are taught to need their gods. They looked to my parents for guidance on everything, they pray three times a day, if not more. If they are suddenly abandoned, they will drift and fall into depression. I must organize the temples. I can change things, but only over several mortal generations. I can't turn my backs on them now."

Those lavender eyes were so earnest, searching hers for understanding, that at last Nanami nodded and leaned in for a hug. He was warm and big, and when she felt his lips against her hair, she almost forgot everything that had just happened.

"Thank you," he said.

She knew it was selfish, but she suddenly blurted, "Xiao, can the temples wait a day?"

SURPRISED by Nanami's question, Xiao paused his stroking of her back to echo, "A day?"

But he almost instantly understood what she wanted, for he wanted the same thing. They'd been apart what—two or three months? Time had been a little blurry for him while he'd been imprisoned, but his yearning for her had been a physical ache. He wanted to hold her and forget the rest of the world existed. And as soon as he realized that was what she was asking, he agreed. "Yes, they can wait a day."

His eyes caught on Zi's pyre less than twenty paces from them. He sighed. "But we have to deal with the disciples before that."

Gently he set Nanami back from him and turned to Dawa.

"Can you gather all the disciples in front of the hall? I will meet you there in half an hour with—with the ashes."

"Yes, my lord." Dawa bowed at the waist and strode to the iron doors—which now had a man-shaped hole in them. When had that happened?

Dawa twisted to try and fit his tall frame through the hole before thinking better of it and unlocking the doors.

Xiao's attention was pulled back to Nanami when she put

her hand on his cheek. "Xiao. You seem calm, and I know your parents were awful but—"

Xiao pressed his fingers against her lips, and she fell silent. "Don't call them my parents. I disowned them—I felt my vow to them break." He swallowed. "I was pretty shocked that Jin killed them. It hasn't really hit me that they are gone. I—" He shook his head before emotion could overwhelm him. "Come, I have a lot to do. We'll talk about this later."

"You don't have to protect her," Nanami said.

"What?" asked Xiao.

"Jin. You were acting like you were alright so as to not upset Jin. You don't have to do that."

Xiao paused to blink at Nanami. "Salaana was right there. She would have twisted anything I said into an attack. And why are you bringing this up?"

Nanami turned her face away from him for a moment. When she looked back, her eyes were carefully blanked. "I'm sorry. Is there anything I can do to help you?"

Xiao almost snapped at her because there was so much pushing on him, and he needed her to support him, not poke at him. But he resisted the urge because he knew that if he let any emotion out, if he stopped to process, he would falter, and there was too much at stake for that.

"Just watch the pyre for now. I need to gather Hei's ashes." He sat cross-legged with his wrists balancing on his knees, another pose Bai had recommended, and he let his awareness spread over the hall. Hei's ashes had been scattered by everyone running, but Xiao could feel each black speck. He called them to him. When he felt them coalesce, he opened his eyes to find a surprisingly small pile of ashes. Hei had been a large man, but the pile was only about eight inches high.

Xiao blinked and wiped the tears from his face. "Na—" before he even got her whole name out, Nanami was at his side, her arms wrapped around his shoulders. She pressed his head against her bosom. "It'll be okay."

He didn't reply for a long moment, just was grateful that she had let go of whatever had been bothering her.

"What should I do with them? They should be together. But I don't want anyone to worship their remains."

Nanami stroked his hair. "Let's mix the ashes together and scatter them."

Xiao nodded. "That's good. There're usually some ceramic vessels behind their thrones. Do you see anything—"

"Yes, I'll get it."

She returned moments later with a large black urn painted with violets.

"Yeah. That's perfect," Xiao realized he was crying again when Nanami swiped his cheeks with her thumb. Silently, Xiao transferred Hei's ashes into the urn.

"Is she done burning yet?"

Xiao felt Nanami twist toward the pyre, sparing him the necessity of looking. "Almost. Will the fire go out on its own?"

Xiao shrugged. "I probably shouldn't have sent them away, but I wanted to be alone."

ALONE? What was she?

Why did Xiao put Jin before himself, while Nanami was expected to do whatever he needed? Did he see her the same way he saw Dawa? So inferior that her feelings weren't worth considering?

Nanami despised herself for thinking that way. His parents had just died. She too was having trouble processing everything, and she knew he needed her right now.

But she had also spent the last few months living for this man—casing the New Moon Temples, working with He Who Walks in Shadow, stealing the Sowon Gold, being imprisoned by his parents...

When those things had overwhelmed her, she had imagined their reunion. How it would be like when they went to the Sea Palace. When she had been certain he loved her, and it had felt like they could do anything together. But she didn't feel confident and loved.

Right now, she felt tired and scared, and Salaana's suggestion—that Xiao had come here for Jin, not her—was a constant buzz at the back of her head.

But she kept her mouth shut. She would push through this.

Zi finally finished burning, and the magical flames did indeed gutter out on their own. The ashes left behind were a deep violet powder, and Nanami wondered morbidly if her own ashes would be indigo with specks of white.

Xiao gathered these into the urn and Nanami held him again while he cried.

She found tears sliding down her own cheeks; her heart ached for him. She tried to shove her resentment and insecurity far away.

IT was a relief to hold Nanami in his arms, and to have her hands stroking his hair.

Xiao could tell she wasn't relieved though. Whatever happened while they had been apart had been hard on her. He knew she needed to talk, to be reassured.

But he couldn't right now. "It should just be a few hours," he promised her. "Then we'll go somewhere just the two of us."

"It's fine," she said, though he knew she was lying, "whatever you need."

Xiao kissed her temple to thank her for the lie.

He somehow managed to clear his face and bring the urn to the waiting disciples, Nanami following close behind.

He had worried that they might revolt against him or commit suicide to follow their leaders to the Underworld, but the disciples were all subdued while listening to his speech—fate knew what he said—and after a wind carried the ashes from the gate, almost all of them pledged themselves to Xiao's service.

When it was over, he turned to Nanami.

He expected her to be focused on him and happy that they could leave at last, but instead she was watching the dispersing disciples with an intense frown.

"Nanami, are you ready to leave?"

She didn't reply, so he gently touched her arm and she jerked in surprise. He repeated his question.

"Uh—" she sighed heavily. "Well—Xiao, where are the people who aren't disciples?"

"I'm sorry?" he asked, confused by her question.

"He Who Walks in Shadow trapped me and brought me to Zi and Hei. However, they were angry about the theft of their prayer collectors, and so punished him. I need to speak to him."

Xiao was lost. "I need you to back up. Prayer collectors?

Whose He Who something-something?"

Nanami focused on him. "I knew I didn't have enough power to free you from your parents, so my hope was to reduce their power so you could free yourself. However, I couldn't steal all their prayer collectors myself, so I struck a deal with my old master, He Who Walks in Shadow. He betrayed me—which I expected, but he did it better than I anticipated. He turned me over to your parents, after stealing all their prayer collectors. Isn't that how you escaped? Didn't their power ebb?"

"Huh. Yeah—actually, I don't remember it too clearly. Bai rescued me. He must have been watching for an opportunity. Thank you, Nanami. I didn't realize—anyway, you want to help He Who Walks in Shadow?"

Nanami snorted. "Hardly. But I paid him with Sowon Gold, and I want to make sure it doesn't fall into the wrong hands. Well, any hands."

"Okay—what's Sowon Gold?"

Nanami's lips twisted. "This is quite the tangent."

Xiao collected her hand and squeezed her slim fingers. "I'm listening."

Nanami met his eyes, and Xiao's heart beat a little faster. "It's the most terrible artifact I've ever encountered," she confessed, "and two weeks ago I gave all one hundred pieces of it to He Who Walks in Shadow. I need to set that right."

There was a lump in Xiao's throat. Nanami spoke casually—nonchalantly, even—but she had gone against her principles and worked with someone she despised to save him.

"I'm sorry, Nanami, that I put you in a position like that."

She tried to shake her head, but he pulled her close. "No, I mean it. I'm sorry, and I thank you. So you want to speak with

He Who Walks in Shadow and recover the gold?"

"Yes," she said.

"Then I will help."

"You need to go to the temples," she demurred.

He squeezed her hand again. "Well, we might have to forego our day alone."

She nodded, once, quick and short, both her acceptance and her disappointment obvious. "The Night God drained He Who Walks in Shadow's power and then disciples dragged him away. Where can we find him?"

"Dawa—" Xiao called. Moments later they were brought to a room; and Xiao felt sick to his stomach. It wasn't his bedroom, but it was close enough. It was a prison of black and violet, and it was hard for Xiao to even step inside. Nanami noticed his awkwardness, for her fine brows snapped together and she said, "I could—"

Xiao cut her off with a hand gesture and stepped in. Nanami's betrayer, He Who Walks in Shadow, lay on a cot, his left arm flung over his eyes. He didn't even bother moving it when they entered, but said, in a somewhat gravelly whine, "I haven't recovered enough power for you to care. Come back tomorrow."

"We aren't here for your power," Nanami told him. "Tell me where the Sowon Gold is."

The slight man sat up with a jerk, his arm falling to reveal a plain, pockmarked face. "Nanami?" he asked incredulously. "How are you here? You allied with their divinities after all?"

"My parents are dead," Xiao informed the man, bringing those darting black eyes to him. It was unnerving to see those shifting, restless eyes, for it was a behavior that he considered a cute quirk of Nanami's. It made him realize how much time Nanami had spent with man, and Xiao felt jealous. A ridiculous feeling, given Nanami's clear dislike of He Who Walks in Shadow, but there it was. "Tell us where the Sowon Gold is."

He Who Walks in Shadow scoffed, and Xiao reached for magic. He tried to water down He Who Walks in Shadow's essential selfishness and disdain for them, but he was still unaccustomed to how readily power flowed to his will, and he ended up washing away He Who Walks in Shadow's feelings, leaving a sycophant.

He Who Walks in Shadow knelt and kowtowed. "Forgive me, divinity. The gold is in my cave. I hid it in my chamber, in the shadows under the bed. It's yours, divinity."

"You know where his cave is?" Xiao asked Nanami. Her eyes slid away from his though and her brows had furrowed again.

"I know where the cave is, but not his chamber. We'll have to bring him with us."

"Okay." Xiao wanted to ask what was wrong again, but both Dawa and He Who Walks in Shadow were there. "You'll come with us," he told He Who Walks in Shadow and the slight man slid over to Xiao's side. "Dawa, you'll stay here while Nanami and I recover the gold. Will you please deal with any other prisoners?"

"Deal with them, my lord?"

"Free them, if at all reasonable. If they are dangerous to themselves or others, transfer them to a different room, but wait until I can deal with them further."

Xiao clasped Nanami's hand on one side, and He Who Walks in Shadow's on the other. He instructed the man to bring them to his chamber, though Xiao shared some of his power reserve for the task—easy enough, for He Who Walks in Shadow's essence was black in nature.

And then they moved in between.

A METALLIC reek overwhelmed Nanami when they emerged in the Cave of Shadows. It was also dark—none of the flickering torches from her last visit were lit.

"Xiao?" she asked, rather confused. "What is—"

Something grabbed Nanami's arm and bit her neck hard, breaking the skin. She screamed in terror, for she had belatedly identified the smell as blood. Nanami grabbed her dagger and plunged it into her attacker.

Even though it should have been impossible, she wasn't surprised when her hand met coarse, sticky fur.

*Xuezei.*

Nanami was glad for the darkness, for she knew if there were light the scene would be horrific.

There was a low growl, and a moment later her attacker dropped away.

"What cursed things are these?" asked Xiao.

He didn't sound scared, just furious, and Nanami realized it had been he who growled.

Nanami pressed a hand to her neck to stem the bleeding and tried to find her voice. He Who Walks in Shadow answered Xiao's question first.

"They're Xuezei. But how are they here? The Sun Emperor locked them all in the Underworld millennia ago."

"I daresay all the immortal creatures will be coming back now that Jin has opened the gates. I thought the lion-thing that attacked the Wood Pavilions was unpleasant, but these things are vile," said Xiao, and Nanami realized that he and He Who Walks in Shadow must see the scene that the dark hid from her.

Even though she didn't want to see the source of that smell, Nanami asked, "Can we light a torch?"

Someone moved in the dark and moments later, soft, wavery light revealed about twenty Xuezei, all standing perfectly still.

Nanami instinctively jumped back from one that was frozen by her shoulder, her blood still on its mouth.

"What's wrong with them?" Nanami hissed.

"I made them stand still," Xiao said.

"Because their essence is black," Nanami whispered.

"I suppose," said Xiao.

Nanami felt a bit faint and forced herself to scan the scene. A few dozen bodies—or pieces of them anyway—littered the cavern floor. She almost regretted asking for the light. "Let's get the gold and leave," she begged.

"Divinity?" asked He Who Walks in Shadow.

"Yes, let's go," agreed Xiao.

Xiao carried the torch as he followed He Who Walks in Shadow through the labyrinthian caves. Nanami focused on his back, not wanting to see the blood streaks on the walls. Because of this, she tripped over something and found herself face-to-face with the Shadow Thief who had first brought her to the Shadow Caves a little over a month ago. His head was no longer attached to his body—the Xuezei didn't eat anything but blood, but their often tore their victims into pieces to get at their meal. Nanami gagged, and Xiao lifted her to her feet.

"Nanami—"

She shook her head fiercely, and they resumed their walk. Nanami was vaguely aware that Xiao used his magic at least twice to stop more Xuezei from attacking.

When they reached He Who Walks in Shadow's room, the thief went to the wall and twisted a mechanism that revealed a hidden shelf. He pulled out a bag and passed it to Xiao. Xiao opened it and showed Nanami the gleaming Sowon Gold.

"Yes, that's it," she agreed and wrapped her hand around his elbow. "Let's leave?"

Xiao said to He Who Walks in Shadow, "Don't stay here."

"Yes, Divinity," he agreed placidly.

Nanami knew she should be relieved that He Who Walks in Shadow was so subservient to Xiao, but it felt uncomfortably similar to Sowon Gold. As if Xiao were the Great Mother of the Bear People and He Who Walks in Shadow was an unruly hunter she was correcting.

She was relieved that they were leaving his company and this cursed cave. Soon afterward, they reappeared in the woods—not just any woods, Nanami realized after a moment. This had been her camp. The place she had confined him to a bamboo cage while waiting for his betrothal ceremony.

She shuffled her feet in embarrassment. "Aren't you using your power rather freely?" she asked. "How many teleports can you do in one day?"

He laughed. "I don't know. A hundred? You can't imagine how much power I have, Nanami."

She shrugged. She didn't want to imagine how much power he had. He was still holding the bag of gold, so Nanami plucked it from his arms. "This will probably take me a month to hide—

I don't want to leave the pieces together."

"Hide it? If it's so terrible, why wouldn't you destroy it? What does it do, anyway?"

"It changes people," Nanami said. "It controls mortals' thoughts, so that they think as the holder of the gold wills. The more pieces you have, the greater your influence. And I tried to destroy it once, but nothing worked."

Xiao stared at her a moment, and Nanami realized he was dumbfounded.

"That's—that's the terrible power? Influence?"

"Well, yes."

"Nanami—what do you think my power is?"

"You—you're the God of Love. And you shapeshift—"

He was shaking his head. "Nanami, I can influence emotion and essence. That's why people come to the New Moon Temples—for love spells and to change their spouses. Or themselves."

Nanami clutched the bag tighter to her chest, as if it were a piece of driftwood that would keep her afloat in the sea of emotions that threatened to drown her.

"No," she said.

"No?" he echoed and blinked. "Nanami, what's going through your head?" His hand settled on her shoulder, large and warm, and she focused on it.

"You aren't like Jin," she told him. "Jin changes the way people see her. She makes everyone like her—see her as harmless. That's why you protected her feelings even after she murdered your parents. But you aren't like that. You understand that people are flawed and varied, and we must let them be themselves. It is their right."

Xiao made no reply for a long moment, and then his hand suddenly dropped away.

"That's what you think of Jin?"

Nanami swallowed. "I—I know that she means well, but yes, she frightens me."

Xiao turned away from her. "Then I frighten you too."

"No—you're different."

"How so?" he demanded.

"Xiao, think about it. You were upset when your parents died. Even though they hurt you and abused you—it was hard to see them die. But you put Jin's feelings before your own because you see her as some kind of saint."

Xiao tsked. "It wasn't just about Jin's feelings. Salaana was there—if I had said anything against Jin, she would have used it. So yes, I was protecting my oldest friend! You don't need to be jealous of that—I wouldn't turn anyone over to Salaana's so-called justice. A sentiment I'd have thought you'd appreciate!"

"Oh, please!" said Nanami, suddenly angry. "From what I saw, Jin doesn't need anyone's protection!" And then, just because she had to know, "Did you come to New Moon Manor for me? Or for Jin?"

"For both of you," he said without hesitation. "I knew you were both there. I had looked for you first, but when I found you there, I looked for Jin, thinking I needed her help." Xiao sighed. "Jin is not your enemy, Nanami. And if you trust me with my power, you can trust Jin with hers. She's one of the best people I know, for she is relentless on herself and tolerant of others."

"She makes you see her that way! Think about it. Is she genuinely tolerant of your struggles? And don't you remember how quickly Bai fell in love with her? It's because she influenced him."

Xiao frowned.

"You don't do that," she said softly. "Maybe," her voice quivered, and she worked to steady it, "maybe you have that power, but I've never seen you take away someone's free will."

He jerked back as if slapped. "That's what I did with He Who Walks in Shadow. Why else do you think he led us to the gold so willingly? And those cursed creatures, to stop them from attacking us."

Shocked, Nanami took a step back. She hadn't been being fanciful then. She had been right to compare it to the Great Mother with the Sowon Gold. How could this be? Did she know Xiao at all?

"What do you mean—you changed the Xuezei? You didn't just hold them in place?"

"Sure, I made it so they won't attack anyone."

Nanami's mouth worked silently. "Ever? Then—will they starve to death?"

Xiao frowned. "I suppose. If they need blood to live."

She stared at him in horror. "You froze them—just like that—" She had made up her mind about him too quickly. She had been pulled in by his charm, his mix of vulnerability and strength, his good looks...

"They would've killed us," Xiao pointed out.

Nanami shook her head, not even sure why she was arguing. The Xuezei were monstrous. "They're terrifying yes, but it's just their nature." He could teleport a hundred times in a day. He could make He Who Walks in Shadow fawn over him. He could make it so twenty-odd Xuezei would never attack a being again, even if it meant their deaths. "You took away their freedom..."

His dramatic features, so recently handsome, suddenly seemed alien. As frightening as the Xuezei's bloodless faces.

"Nanami," he said suddenly, and it was a stranger speaking, "when we were in the hall—when Salaana tried to kill Jin—why did you call out after Bai had saved her?"

Nanami swallowed. "Did I?"

Xiao said nothing for a long time. Then he closed his eyes, too late to stop a lone tear from sliding down his cheek. "Yes, you did." He shook his head. "If you think Jin is too powerful, that her power cannot be trusted, you think I'm too powerful, and mine cannot. And..."

"If you cannot accept my power, we can't be together."

He opened his eyes and looked at her. "I have to take care of the temples and the disciples waiting for me. You obviously need to think some things through. I'll be at Tsuku in a month's time to support Jin." He hesitated then added, "You know that gold you hate so much? If you asked her, Jin would destroy it in a heartbeat."

And then he was gone.

Nanami fell to her knees, still clutching that stupid bag of gold. Her shoulders began to shake, and then sobs tore from her throat.

XIAO stood at the head of Dalbam temple. The monks came to him one after another to receive his benediction and feel his power.

Xiao felt like a fraud. These mortals thought he could teach them about love—how to find someone to love them and how to love others—but he was just as clueless as they were.

For four millennia, he had assumed he loved Jin and that she would love him. And then, when suddenly he was forced to accept that she would never return those feelings the way he needed, he had run into the first open arms he found.

He had promised Nanami forever. He had wanted to give her that. He had wanted to grow with her, to become a stronger—better—being by her side. But it seemed like she had loved only the idea of him—just like so many beings over the years, she hadn't really seen him after all.

He didn't know if she would come to Tsuku. If she did come, he didn't know if he would accept her. Would she be running to him because she wanted him or out of loneliness?

Xiao was terrified of the answer, and yet he continued to smile for the mortals before him, to shake their hands, and kiss the crowns of their heads.

But he knew that Dawa saw through his facade—he knew it when Dawa accepted the offering of wine on his behalf, and he knew it when the man stayed less than a pace behind him as they exited the main hall.

"I'm not going to break," Xiao said. "Not yet. But I appreciate your support."

"Yes, my lord," said Dawa. And they went on to the next temple.

WHEN Nanami's sobs eventually tapered off—mostly because she couldn't summon enough moisture to cry and because her head ached abominably—a Kitsune sat down before her and asked if she needed help.

Nanami honestly thought she was imagining things until it spoke again. "If you don't need help, may I eat your death?"

Nanami sat bolt upright. "No, you may not!"

*Jin opened all the gates. All the immortal creatures will return.*

"When did you come back?" Nanami asked.

The creature shrugged. "My family and I found the gate open this morning, and so we returned to Earth. I'm rather hungry, and your death seems like it would be tasty."

"I haven't hurt anyone weaker than myself," she said. "Go find some mortal bullies if you're hungry."

Nanami needed to talk through her feelings. And the creature who had always understood her had at last been freed from its prison.

Nanami teleported to Po to find the Koch-ssi.

# Faith and Failure

BAI'S mind was whirling. He thought Jin had fallen asleep in the twenty minutes they had spent between, but he wasn't sure that Cheng and Neela would be willing to accommodate her rest. He opened his mouth to deliver a speech to them as they arrived in his garden but immediately snapped it shut again.

Sitting by the small mountain spring, his shoulders hunched as if bearing weight of the world was Gang. At his side were two small Mudanren, each holding a black peony.

In the time that it took Bai to process that, Cheng and Neela started bickering.

"She knows me, so I will speak to her first—"

"What? You're the one in trouble—"

Gang's head jerked up and he turned to look at the four of them.

He took in Bai cradling Jin, and his lips pressed together,

but rather than scold Bai, he simply stood and marched over to him. "I need your help," he announced without preamble.

That sounded like a refreshing change in his attitude, but Bai shook his head. "It must wait. All of you must wait," he said, turning to encompass Cheng and Neela. "Jin is asleep, and she needs to recover."

Gang's thick brows collided, but he stepped back to let Bai pass. Bai maneuvered carefully through the doorway so as to not bump Jin's head nor feet. Aka was still comatose on Bai's cot and Jin would do better with sunlight anyway, so Bai carried her to the room he had made for Neela a few days ago.

The Mudanren followed him—Bai raised a brow at them, but they didn't seem to notice.

He laid Jin out on the bed and stretched her limbs out.

"Careful," said one of the Mudanren. "The Korikami shook her like leaf in a typhoon. She's got to be bruised under that armor."

"The Korikami?"

His eyes darted from the blood on her face to the holes in the iridescent armor that wrapped her figure. Should he check her wounds? But how presumptuous. Unbidden, he remembered the glimpse he had of Jin in the onsen before he had cloaked her body with mist.

Neela stepped in as he hesitated. She looked older than ever—her hair seemed to be thinning and the skin around her eyes seemed almost papery. "I will bathe her."

Bai no longer trusted Neela. "She said you used Godsbane on her."

"Fate save me from know-everythings!" she snapped. "I wished to stop her from her foolish mission. I swear I will only wash her and remove her armor—I will not hurt her or poison her or in any way prevent her from resting well and waking as soon as she's able."

"I will supervise," said Gang.

Bai shrugged. "Then I'll fetch you water."

Once the water was delivered, Bai returned to the garden. Cheng sat next to him.

"I shouldn't have wasted time saving Aka," Bai said to Cheng.

He couldn't help but feel that if he had reached Jin sooner, he could have arrived in time to save her from being a murderer.

He remembered how upset she had been that Guleum had cast a death curse, and her desperation to stop him from committing patricide. How would she feel when she woke and realized the enormity of what she had done?

If someone had to kill Zi and Hei—and perhaps it was the only way to truly free Xiao from them and to stop their magical assaults—he wished it had been him.

Cheng elbowed him in the ribs. "You're being ridiculous. From everything I've heard, Jin will be glad you saved Aka. Didn't she go to the Underworld for just that purpose? And weren't those black peonies I saw the Mudanren carrying?"

Bai rubbed his eyes. "Yes. You are right."

Still, he tortured himself for a moment, remembering Jin crawling across the floor, unaware of Salaana's sword pointed at her. "I was almost too late though."

"But you weren't."

Yes, he had gotten there in time. He looked toward the room that held Jin, wishing he was the one checking her wounds, but no, that wasn't his place. Yet.

It seemed like hours before Gang and Neela emerged, Gang carrying that iridescent armor. Bai rose. "I'll help clean it."

"Forget the armor," said Gang, "I need your help with something else."

"So you mentioned." He wasn't inclined to make this easier for Gang. Not after he practically threw him off the Korikami's Tomb. "Didn't I teach you that armor should be cleaned at the earliest opportunity? It makes it last longer."

Cheng snorted. Bai's lips twitched too, but he schooled his expression to earnestness.

Gang scowled, but he waded into the spring and began to clean the armor. Bai joined him, and after a few minutes of silent observation, Cheng and Neela wandered off, Neela to Bai's vegetable garden and Cheng out of the garden altogether.

Even with Gang's help (and Bai envied his ability to make the dried blood dissipate without water), evening had come by the time they finished. This night, the setting sun left the sky a rich violet, the kind of twilight from which Zi had once formed, and Bai wondered if the world was mourning her.

They brought the armor back inside his house and set it by the fireplace. Gang started a fire without Bai asking him to, so Bai set a kettle filled with water over the flames.

"Have I been taught a lesson yet?" Gang asked tartly.

Bai snorted. "With what do you need my help?"

Gang pulled a necklace from his robes—a large ornament was on it, gold set with blue and orange gemstones. He lifted the gold chain over his head and passed it to Bai.

"Tell me about this?"

Bai examined the ornament closely, but it left him

befuddled. "Jin made this."

"Yes," said Gang eagerly.

Bai snorted. "Gang, I can't read a thing about it. You know the essence of orange completely thwarts my own power of knowing. Won't Jin answer your questions when she wakes?"

Gang tsked impatiently and took the ornament back. Instead of hiding it away though, he twisted it and it separated into two pieces. He held the base out to Bai.

Looking inside, Bai went stiff. "That's Noran's soul."

"Yes," Gang agreed.

"It won't last much longer," said Bai. "And then she will be completely gone from this world."

JIN woke slowly. White cloth was the first thing she saw, and she shook her head, trying to remember the last thing that happened before she fell asleep.

New Moon Manor. Zi and Hei. Xiao. Bai.

Bai had teleported her away from the manor, along with Neela and Cheng. Had she fallen asleep in between? No wonder she was disoriented. She hadn't even realized that was possible. It reminded her of a story used to frighten children when they first learned to teleport, of an immortal who entered between while injured and never came out again.

She shivered and sat up.

A soft white blanket slid from her shoulders to her lap, and Jin blinked at the sight of the golden undergarments she'd made from Phoenix down. It was disgusting—but her arms were clean. Someone had washed her then.

She didn't recognize the room she was in, but sunshine

streamed through a window in white stone, and she felt sure Bai had brought her to his home.

She scanned the room and spotted two black peonies in a vase on a small table.

Those peonies made her feel so happy—and so hypocritical.

She had gone to such lengths to save Aka—her grandfather—saying that he deserved a chance to speak for himself, but when it came to Zi and Hei—

Fate, she had really murdered them.

Jin slid off the bed into a puddle on the floor. She was finding it suddenly hard to breath, and she pressed her hands against the fine-grained stone floor.

She breathed slowly and deeply. She didn't cry. Some part of her noted that and was surprised because usually tears came easily. She would have thought she'd cry, but she didn't.

She thought she was doing pretty well, but when a warm hand settled on her bare shoulder, she jerked in surprise—she hadn't even realized that someone else was in the room.

Jin looked up and found Bai's gray eyes on her. Usually his gaze was so intense and focused that it scorched her, but instead it was soft—like mist hiding all the sharp edges of the world.

Jin wasn't sure how long she sat frozen, her hands flexed against the stone as she searched those eyes, but she suddenly threw herself at him and he caught her.

It wasn't the first time they'd embraced, but never had she pressed so hard, so intimately against his body. One of his arms locked about her waist, the other was braced along her spine, his fingers threaded in her hair. Both of her arms were clamped around his neck, and her bosom was flattened against his chest. She belatedly remembered that she was wearing nothing but a breast cover and half-breeches.

She didn't care though.

"I'm sorry," he whispered in her ear, and his voice was a husky whisper that made her nipples pucker. "I misread Kunjee. But you came back."

She nodded and breathed in his scent. He smelled like mountain spring water and jasmine—he must have bathed recently.

Jin admitted, "I was sometimes afraid that I wouldn't. But whenever that happened, I just tried to imagine the advice you'd give me, and things worked out."

He snorted. "That is surely giving me far too much credit."

He sat on the cot and settled her next to him, holding her hands as if he couldn't bear to let go. "Tell me about your adventures?"

Jin turned so that she was leaning against him and started playing with his fingers. She was half-afraid he'd stop her, but he seemed happy to indulge her whims. She began to ramble and continued until she had reached the moment when he had pulled her out of harm's way.

"And you know what happened next better than I, for things started to go foggy after that."

"I don't wonder," he mused, "you must have been exhausted." It was the first time he had spoken since soliciting her story, and Jin twisted her neck so that she could see his expression. It was serene—almost content.

"What about you?" asked Jin. "What happened? You didn't pass through the gate?"

She had intended to let him tell his story the way she had told hers, but when he explained how he had invited mortal worship in the Sanctuary Caves, she said in surprise, "But I thought you didn't want to be a god."

He turned to look at her, and freed one of his hands from hers to cup her cheek. "I want to be your partner. And whatever I decide to do, I do to the best of my ability."

Jin felt a flush spread over her cheeks, and then, with great daring, she lifted her head and pressed her lips to his.

His lips were warm and petal-soft. He held still at first, then his hand slid to the back of her head and he deepened their kiss.

When he pulled back sometime later, Jin was breathless and her flush had spread to her whole body. Her eyes darted to the cot on which they sat, but he shook his head.

"Your grandparents and parents are all waiting impatiently for us, and this room has no lock on the inside. I've heard—"

"What!" she blurted, jumping up. She skittered about three feet back from him. Her eyes darted to the peonies again, and she at last recalled that she had left them—and the Mudanren— with Gang. She glanced at the closed door and leapt to her feet. "I need to get dressed—wait, are there clothes here? Oh, and bathe—I must smell terrible!"

A smile played on Bai's lips. "I don't think you allow others to process your scent as terrible. Even now, you smell like citrus and honey. As for clothes—" He gestured to a pile of white cloth which indeed turned out to be robes. "Let me fetch you water."

Jin waited impatiently for his return, and when he did, she asked, "How did all my elders come to be here anyway?"

Bai's lips quirked in a way that reminded her of their kiss. Her first.

Well, no, technically that hideous embarrassment at Tsuku was her first, but she would remember this one instead, since she had been led to believe a first kiss would be special.

He held up the water. "Don't you want privacy?"

Jin grabbed his wrist and pulled him into the room. "Turn your back," she ordered him. He clapped his hands over his eyes as well as turning, and even knowing who was waiting outside, Jin was hard-pressed not to tease him. "Tell me why everyone is here," she said, even as she removed her undergarments to wash.

Bai explained how he and Cheng had encountered Neela by the Great Willow.

"Jin," he said, "Cheng thinks Neela should die for what she did to him. I just convinced him to wait for your return before fighting with her."

Jin finished tying the white robes at her waist and fiddled with the belt's ends. "And then you came to find me at New Moon Manor?"

"Yes—no—I went to the Sun Palace first. It was being destroyed by immortal creatures. I brought Aka out of the chaos. He's in my bedroom."

Jin felt like she had been slapped. She had thought Aka would be safe for a few months at least. "I should have realized..." She took Bai's right hand in both of her and squeezed gently. "You've done so much for me."

And the tears that had refused to come for Zi and Hei now gathered at the corner of her eyes.

Bai's eyes widened, and he used her hands to tug her close. With his free hand he wiped her tears. "Gang is also here," he told her. "He brought the souls you collected from the Sea of

Souls."

His eyes shifted to the wall behind her. "Jin, they won't last much longer—what did you intend on doing with them?"

He was tense, his brow just slightly furrowed, and his lips pressed tightly against each other. Jin searched for the reason and realized that if he had seen the souls, he surely knew one was Noran.

His long-lost love.

"I wanted to resurrect Aashchary," she admitted. "Noran volunteered to wrap Aashchary's soul within her own."

Bai's eyes returned to her own, clearly surprised and puzzled. "That doesn't sound like Noran. You're saying she sacrificed her soul?"

Jin nodded once. "For her son's happiness. She and Aashchary found each other in the sea, and Noran wants me to resurrect Aashchary."

Something softened in Bai's eyes.

Even though they had kissed so recently, Jin suddenly felt nervous.

"Her soul is still whole. I could perhaps resurrect her as well—"

Bai's eyes widened. "Resurrect Noran? Why?' He cocked his head. "Of course, her death was a great tragedy, but Jin, I don't think you should develop a habit of resurrecting immortals. You don't even know the price yet."

"Price? What price?"

JIN looked up at him with her luminous eyes, and Bai had to force himself to focus on her question.

"When I first saw the Sea of Souls—many millennia ago

now—I saw, like you, that it would be possible to give each soul a body again. But I also saw that creating a body would cost one."

Jin's eyes widened. "But—why? When we were discussing Nanami's hand—"

Bai shrugged. "I didn't write the laws of our world; I can just see them. The why and the how often eludes me. But I suppose that restoring what still exists—thinking of Nanami's hand as part of her body rather than its own entity—is different than creating fresh. If you wish to resurrect Aashchary or Noran, you will need to destroy another body as the price."

Jin pressed her fist against her mouth. "I've made a mistake, haven't I?"

Bai wasn't sure. "If we can't resurrect the souls, we can return them to the sea. Now that you've opened the gates, it won't be so difficult."

Jin nodded, and Bai squeezed her shoulder to reassure her. He hesitated, then asked his earlier question again. "I understand why you want to resurrect Aashchary, but I am surprised about Noran. Is that also for Gang?"

Jin's shoulders hunched. "I thought you might want..."

Bai put a hand on each of her shoulders and turned her to face him. "Jin. What are you saying?"

"If you—if you still love her—I owe you."

Bai was highly annoyed with her, but he also understood that she was trying to put him above herself. He slid his hands from her shoulders to cradle her face. "Jin. I love you. I don't want anyone but you."

She bit her lower lip. "You are the greatest legend in the world. Why would you choose me?"

"Because you are kind and noble. Because your power and beauty excite me. Because you chose me."

"What? That doesn't make sense."

"No? I don't think there are many who would offer to resurrect their lover's old love. You put me before you. Not that I want you to do that, but I appreciate the sentiment." He released her and cocked his head. "A lot has happened in the past few days—and a lot needs to happen before we meet Salaana in a month's time."

Jin winced and turned her face away from his once again. "I murdered them. Salaana will demand my death."

Bai put his hands on either side of her face and turned her eyes to him. He said, "Jin, I hope you aren't contemplating letting her murder you. Yes, you killed Zi and Hei. Because it was the only way to save Xiao. Was it fair for them to harvest his power for the past five thousand years? To lock him in his room, to deprive him of company, food, and love?"

Jin's head whipped around, her eyes wider than before. "For—this wasn't new?"

Bai didn't know how to respond.

She covered her face. "I'm a terrible friend. Xiao told me the world was never the one I knew, and I thought he was being melodramatic. But he was right. Why would he keep that from me?"

Bai struggled to find the words. "Jin, I'm sorry. I suppose this is something you must ask Xiao. But before you can, we need to deal with your grandparents."

Jin wiped her face brusquely, and Bai realized she had cried more.

"We'll do this one day at a time," he promised her.

She looked at him uncertainly for a long beat, but she suddenly managed a tremulous smile. "I don't know why, but when you say that, everything seems possible. I suppose all those years give you an aura of confidence."

"Nonsense," said Bai, "I formed this way."

He was trying for humor, to lighten the air, but Jin gaped at him. "You mean that," she marveled. "Xiao is right, you are very arrogant."

"I—" Bai started, but Jin pressed her fingers to his lips.

"Don't worry," she said, "I like it."

Bai couldn't resist any longer. He pulled her close and kissed her again. She arched closer, her arms twining around his neck.

"We've been waiting hours, and you are in here kissing?" Neela barked from the doorway. "Jin, come here! Have you forgotten you are betrothed to Xiao?"

Jin went stiff in his arms and pulled back. Bai thought she was embarrassed until she said, "I'm not, though even if I were, and I chose to kiss someone else, I don't see how it would be any of your business."

"You—" Neela sputtered. She regained her fierceness to snarl, "Don't be like your mother!"

"That's a strange comment from you," Jin mused, "given you've spent my life lamenting that I'm not her." She turned to Bai. "Come, we'd better deal with them."

Bai nodded and followed her willingly. He'd spend the rest of his days following her if she let him.

JIN felt slightly mortified to have been caught kissing by Neela, but she was sick of caring what everyone thought of her all the time.

She wanted to kiss Bai—the truth was, even though she had only known him for a few months, she knew she could trust him. There was something earnest and straightforward about him compared to everyone she had ever met, even given his penchant for careful wording. And she thought he regretted not being fully forthright with her.

She knew that Neela and Karana would mock her for placing her trust in him so wholeheartedly, so quickly, but then both of them were about as trusting as a mongoose in a cobra's hole. Jin couldn't live that way—even now, in what ought to have been the most desperate, miserable moment of her life, she felt oddly confident that everything would somehow work out because Bai was on her side. Maybe his arrogance was rubbing off on her or maybe she had finally found who she'd been all along, but Jin wasn't going to let Neela dictate what came next.

She was here as their equal—she was of age, and it was time Neela acknowledged that.

Jin followed Neela from Bai's cave into the sunny garden and its familiar scent of jasmine and stopped short at the eager stares of Gang and Cheng. Her father and grandfather, yet Jin barely knew the first and the second not at all. They were strangers as well as family. Should she bow? Shake their hands? *Hug* them?

Bai caught her hand, perhaps sensing her confusion, and led her to Cheng first. "Jin, I'd like to introduce my oldest friend to you. Cheng, your savior."

Jin objected, "But you are the one who saved him," and perceived that Bai had provoked her deliberately. She tugged her hand from Bai's, and she bowed to Cheng. "I'm glad to meet you."

"You look more like Noran than anyone," Cheng mused. "That's good—she was beautiful whereas no one has ever praised my looks."

Jin raised her eyes in surprise. He had a broad face with wide features rather than a more idealized look, but his countenance was easy-going and his eyes full of approval.

"Perhaps," Jin said, "she merely made everyone think she was beautiful, just as I do. After all, beauty is in the eye of the beholder."

She glanced at Bai, wondering if he would remember saying those words to her in this garden, what felt like a lifetime ago. His mouth was quirked and when her eyes met his, he winked. Jin looked at Cheng.

"What do you want of me?"

Cheng winced. "What has Bai told you, that you should think so little of me?"

Jin flushed. "He told me that the three of you were waiting for me..."

"Yes," Cheng admitted, "but I want nothing besides to meet you. And, if after meeting, we find enjoyment in each other's company, to repeat the experience from time to time."

That offer made Jin feel better, but before she could reply, Neela did.

"Liar." Jin was surprised by the sheer vitriol in her grandmother's voice and turned to look at her.

Neela, who had never been cruel but whose careless affection and frequent neglect had cut deep over years, wore a look of hate. Her eyes were narrowed, her lip curled.

"You want to kill me," she snarled at Cheng. "And if you didn't want a child, why did you trick me in the first place?"

"I didn't trick you," he said through clenched teeth. "If you had even tried talking to me for one moment before locking me in stone for eternity, we could have figured out what happened together."

"Eternity? Hardly. I had my revenge and now you can have yours."

"I don't—I never wanted this!" and he teleported away. Jin felt dizzy. There was too much to process.

"NeeNee," she said, "why did you lock him in stone?"

Silence stretched tight and snapped suddenly. "She was supposed to be mine," Neela said. "My everything. But she was his, too."

"Beings don't belong to others," said Gang, still seated by the spring, the ornament cradled in his hands.

Neela hissed in frustration and strode into the mountain.

"You're holding her here?" Jin asked Bai.

"Yes," he admitted. "I promised Cheng that I wouldn't let her leave until—" his lips twisted. "Until they've resolved their grudge."

"So much hatred," Jin murmured, and wrapped her arms around herself.

She hesitated then walked to Gang.

"I thought to rebuild a body for her, but Bai says..."

Gang's head jerked up. "Yes?"

"He says it would cost a body. That someone would have to give up their life. So I suppose it was all a waste." She gestured to the ornament.

Gang flew to his feet and seized her upper arm, his grip

almost painful in its desperation. "I will do it. I will trade my life for hers."

Jin was aghast. "I didn't mean—"

"I know," interrupted Gang. "I am offering—no, insisting."

Jin shook her head. "You've spent my entire life ignoring me, and now—when everyone finally knows our relationship, you want to die?"

Gang hesitated. "Our relationship?"

"You are my father!" There, she'd said it.

Gang glared at Bai.

"Don't be mad at Bai," said Jin. "The secret was exposed as soon as you hired Nanami. The real miracle is that you managed to keep it as long as you did."

Gang looked down at the ground before meeting Jin's eyes again. "Yes, I'm your father. But my father always fulfilled that role for you. You don't need me—let me give my life for your mother's."

Now Jin was the one to look away. "She would be devastated that you traded your life for hers."

Gang stomped his foot, just like a petulant toddler. "We're not returning her to the Underworld. Bai said my mother's soul will shield hers for another week. You have that long to accustom yourself to the idea."

Stress seemed to nip at her from all sides, and Jin grew angry. "It's my decision, not yours. You can't force me to take your life!" She tried to snatch the ornament from his hands, but he jerked it away and turned his back on her.

Jin could see her hand shaking, still outstretched toward him. It was as if it belonged to another person. Suddenly Bai's hand was wrapped around it.

"Why don't we get you some food?"

There was a slight tremor in her voice as she said, "Food would be most welcome."

AFTER Jin ate supper, she decided she wanted to soak in a bath, so Bai filled a tub for her and went to his old bedroom. He was looking at Aka's still and empty countenance when Jin found him again. He rose when she entered, and just because he could, lifted a lock of her hair, still wet from her bath. He couldn't seem to stop touching her, reassuring himself that she was really here with him.

"How do you bear to wear this so long?" he asked her. "It must weigh several pounds."

"My hair?" she asked with a soft smile, and Bai was so glad that she could smile. "I suppose it does, but I'm accustomed to it for it has always been long."

"You like it this way?" he asked.

Her brows knit. "I'm not sure. NeeNee wanted me to grow it out—and I remember aspiring to be like Haraa when I was younger."

"What, to wear your hair like clothes?" He suddenly pictured it and felt hot.

She nodded. "Yes—though I never have."

He wanted to tell her that she could, if it was only around him, but he wasn't quite that bold. Not yet.

While he was preoccupied, she stepped around him and closer to Aka. "You can read his essence, can't you? How is he?"

"He's dying. The curse is following its natural course. If you want to save his life, we need to break it soon."

"If I want to." She turned to look at him. "Do you want to? Or do you wish him dead like—like everyone else seems to?"

Bai slid his arms around her waist and pulled her close to him. She let her head loll on his shoulder, accepting his comfort.

"I don't wish him dead. I've never particularly liked him, but I suppose I no longer wish anyone dead. But when you brought Aashchary back with you—I suppose I wondered if you'd reconsidered, since Neela was so insistent he killed her."

"He didn't," Jin said softly. "Or at least she and I don't think so. She showed me her death—Papa tried his best to save her. The concubine who stabbed her truly was mad. But Karana said he killed his mother..."

"I met Bijalee several times," Bai told her. "She hated being Sun Empress—she disliked being a goddess even, for she felt she had never been given a choice—and Aka treated her with an indifference that bordered on contempt. But in the end, she took her life, not Aka."

"I love him," she suddenly said, surprising Bai. "I know everyone talks about how selfish he is but—but he was always kind to me. He told me how wonderful I was and made time to play games with me and solicit my opinion..."

Bai hugged her tighter. "Jin, I don't think it's ever wrong to save a life."

"Does that mean it's always wrong to take one?"

He closed his eyes. He couldn't and didn't want to lie to her, but he so wanted to comfort her. "Do I think it would have been better to stop Zi and Hei from hurting Xiao without killing them? Yes. Do I think that was possible? No. Not right then."

"So if it can be wrong yet necessary to kill, that could be

applied to Papa's situation as well." She turned in Bai's arm so that he could see her face clearly, and her arms slipped around his waist. "Papa is more powerful than Zi and Hei were. Right now, we are competing with Salaana for the right to—well, to rule, I suppose, if I'm being honest. But if I break the curse—" Jin swallowed before continuing.

"It occurred to me, while I was washing, that though I wanted to break the curse to protect Gu, that I might be condemning him if I do. Papa will not easily forgive such a betrayal. He will be angry. Both Salaana and Gu—maybe even my father and Karana—will be targets of his anger. Saving him might very well mean destroying them."

She took a long shaky breath. "I still want to though. I just want to hug him one more time and hear his words and understand why all of this is happening! And what my role is. He—he always loved me."

And then she was sobbing in earnest, her thick tears soaking Bai's tunic. He stroked her wet hair. "The world is a messy place," he told her. "And the more beings in it, the messier it gets. I wish I knew the answer, but I think, in the end, it comes down to what feels right to you."

She cried for some time, and Bai wanted to punch the walls, to break the mountain itself. When she stopped, the storm inside him calmed as well.

"Do you know how to break the curse?"

Bai looked at Aka, to read the curse more closely. It was his first experience with a death curse, though Haraa had described it to him before, when a family of immortals had feuded, and the mother had brought her youngest to the Wood Pavilions for healing. "It's tied to blood. You must cut him and yourself and bind the peony between the wounds. Then let your blood call to his. If—" he faltered.

If the bond was strong enough, the curse would be broken. But—

"Jin, who cast the curse?"

"Gu, my youngest brother."

Bai hesitated. "Your youngest uncle, isn't he?"

Jin twitched. "Well. Yes."

So he would have a closer connection to Aka. Did that mean Jin wouldn't be able to break the curse?

Bai couldn't read an answer in her essence. She was powerful—almost definitely more powerful than the unknown Guleum. Would that be enough to compensate for the discrepancy in closeness?

Should he warn her? But if she doubted her ability to break the curse, she would never succeed.

"You let your blood call his. Will him to live."

"Okay. Simple enough." She swallowed and stepped out of his arms. "I'm going to do it. Do you have a knife?"

He had a penknife in this room. He offered it to Jin, and she didn't hesitate to cut her hand.

Bai surprised himself by looking away. He hadn't thought there was a violence that would make him flinch, but it turned out that his sensitivity was amplified when it came to the being he loved.

THE pain of the cut made Jin wince, even though she had been prepared for it. It seemed like it hurt worse than any wound inflicted in battle, perhaps because there was no adrenaline to make the pain fade away. She looked at Bai, seeking his approval of the method, but to her surprise he was looking away, his hands clasped, and his fingers tangled.

She was puzzled for a moment, but she realized he was worried about her. That gave her the courage to repeat the procedure with Aka. She crushed the peony between their bloody hands. And she willed him to live.

She willed it and willed it, burning through her magic in a way she had only experienced recently, but nothing seemed to change. The peony caught fire and turned to ash between their hands. But still nothing happened. She was feeling light-headed and would have fallen if Bai hadn't caught her.

"Why—why isn't it working?"

Bai collected her in his arms and lifted her up. Jin thought that she could grow accustomed to this new mode of transport—and the way Bai seemed to touch her constantly since her return.

"I'm sorry," he said, his brows hooding his eyes. "I should have warned you, but I didn't want to risk your belief." He sighed. "Your blood tie to Aka is weaker than Guleum's. I had hoped your greater power might compensate for that, but it seems only one of his children can break the curse."

Jin stared at him. "Then—then let's ask Gang."

"Now? You need rest—"

"Now. Please."

He nodded once.

He carried her once more to the garden. Gang leapt to his feet and strode to meet them. "What did she do?" he demanded of Bai.

"I tried to save your father," Jin told him, and Bai knew she was annoyed at being overlooked.

Gang sighed. "So you failed then."

Jin pressed her lips together before asking tightly, "I brought two peonies. Will you—"

Gang was already shaking his head. "It would be a waste of your other peony. I once saw a woman save her daughter from a curse—or more importantly, I felt it. I'm sorry. I told you when you started this quest—I can't mourn his death purely. Part of me wants him to die, for him to suffer for what he did to—" Gang faltered.

Jin's throat was tight. She could understand and yet— "He didn't kill Mother," she told him. "I saw her death. He tried to save her."

"I don't care." Then Gang's face brightened. "Father is dying anyway—why don't we trade his body for Aashchary's?"

Jin stepped back in horror. "How can you be so utilitarian? Is that how you were able to poison me with godsbane?"

Gang's face went white, and he knelt before her. "Jin, no, I... That was my fault. I was too vague in my instructions, for I have been fearful of anyone learning our connection for too long. I had asked my man to follow you and, if an opportunity arose, to separate you from Xiao. He knew he was not to hurt you, but he did not consider inducing a magical coma to be 'hurting.'"

"And the second time?" demanded Jin.

Gang's head jerked up. "What second time?"

Jin had initially suspected Neela, and Gang's genuine shock now convinced her that she'd been right. What was wrong with her family? Or—what was wrong with her that they'd treat her this way?

"What second time?" Gang asked again.

Jin shook her head. She returned to the original issue. "Papa cannot consent to giving his life—we should save him."

She was almost disappointed when Gang let go of the godsbane poisoning to say, "He owes her! He impregnated her against her wishes, and then, when the baby threatened his own power, he..." Gang's voice trailed off and he looked at the ground.

Jin's heart clenched. "He what?"

Still staring at the ground, he said, "He gave the child a sickness of the blood. When Karana sent his pests into the room, the baby was already ill. When the diseases combined, he died."

Gang squeezed his eyes shut. "I was so afraid she was going to kill herself after that. I found her, passed out on the floor of her room, smelling of liquor and breast milk, for both stained the front of her robes. I almost killed my father myself that day. He almost let me. I beat him bloody, and then I couldn't bring myself to finish the job, for he cried so. I exiled Karana from the court instead and hid Father's part in the death."

Tears coursed down his cheeks. "I was afraid that if she knew, she would hate me just for being his son, and I—I already loved her." He wiped his nose with the back of his hand and turned away from Jin. "I'm sorry, I just can't save him. He killed one son, so it's fitting that another is killing him."

Jin was crying too, and she was only distantly aware that Bai was carrying her back her cot.

"Maybe Karana would—"

"I don't think so," Bai said, "I got to know Karana fairly well. He blames Aka for his mother's suicide. This changes nothing for you?"

Jin shook her head. "If I forgave Karana, how could I not absolve Papa of the same crime?" She turned her head and sobbed into her pillow. Bai touched her shoulder, but she ignored the comfort he offered. It was all too much—she needed to be miserable.

As if he understood her need, Bai eventually left her alone.

# Saved and Sacrificed

ALTHOUGH Bai didn't expect Karana to save Aka, he went looking for him anyway. He tried the Wood Pavilions first, and though Karana wasn't there, two immortals said they'd heard that Salaana and Karana had both gone to the Sea Palace.

Bai couldn't foresee a warm welcome there, but when he remembered Jin crying herself to sleep, he teleported to its underwater docks. One of Ao's sons came out to greet him—either Kairoku or Kaihachi, for he could never tell them apart—and bowed.

"First, although it is always a pleasure to see you, might I suggest now is not the best time to visit?"

Bai inclined his head in acknowledgement. "I heard Karana might be here. Is that true?"

Kai-whichever hesitated, then said, "The God of Destruction is here, but…"

"Please, just let him know I wish to speak with him. I will wait here—and I promise not to instigate any fights."

A sigh, followed by a bow, and then ten minutes later Karana was strolling indolently toward Bai.

He looked much as he had at Tsuku, nearly three months ago now—his makeup dramatic and perfect, his hair casually, but deliberately arranged, and his silk robes red, black, and white. He was carrying a large peacock feather fan, and he used it now to punctuate his words.

"Hello, Bai. We must be best friends now, if you are looking me up at the home of my sister's in-laws."

"We're nearly in-laws ourselves, aren't we, Uncle Karana?"

Karana's black-painted lips formed a moue of distaste. "Don't say that. The ignorant will think I'm older than you." Then he leaned close. "How's Jin?"

"She'll be alright."

"Will be?" His eyes flickered away and back. "If you've come to ask me to intervene with my sister, it's no use. I pleaded with her, but she is resolute."

Bai felt weary. "I expected that. No, I want to know if you'll save your father."

Karana eyes widened, which combined with his thick kohl looked somewhat comical. "But the Golden Phoenix destroyed the Sun Palace. I thought... You saved him?"

Bai nodded once.

"But you never got along with Father. Even I remember how furious he was when you took his sun pendant."

"Jin wants to save him."

Karana snorted. "So noble. So loverlike. I can't stand it. I think you'd be better off asking Gang."

"Do you think I'd be here if he hadn't said no?"

Karana plied his fan slowly. Finally, "I can't. I won't support Salaana at Tsuku, but that's all I can do for Jin. I know that Salaana can be—hard—but she's my sister. I love her."

"Karana—"

He shook his head firmly, and floated back the way he came, as if nothing in the world burdened him.

His acting was so excellent that Bai had to resist the urge to clap ironically.

Bai didn't leave the docks right away. Instead he turned to face the vastness of the sea around the palace.

There had to be away. Jin had braved the Underworld and the immortal creatures to be stopped by a lack of a blood tie?

Wasn't there anyone else who shared more blood with Aka?

Suddenly, Bai knew what he had to do.

JIN woke slowly for the second time in two days. At least she remembered where she was this time. She felt warm hands clasping hers, and she opened her eyes to find Neela sitting next to her cot, her face sober.

"NeeNee."

Neela had been staring off into the distance, but now her eyes flew to Jin's face. She let out a loud sign of relief.

A half-forgotten memory came to Jin. A king cobra had bitten her as a child. It would have been fatal to a mortal, of course, and made Jin very ill, but she had survived. Probably because of her secret roots in magma and sand, she realized belatedly. While she had laid in the bed in the caravan, Neela had stayed home, holding Jin's hand more often than not. It had been one of the few times Jin had felt her grandmother's love. She felt it now, and because she had to maintain her reputation as a watering pot, big fat tears started down her cheeks.

"Oh, don't cry," groaned Neela. "I can't stand it when you cry."

"Did Noran cry much?" Jin asked, sitting up and wiping her cheeks on her arm.

Neela went stiff, then expelled a big breath. "All the time."

Jin laughed. "So I take after her the most, do I?"

Neela hesitated. "No. I wouldn't say that. She couldn't see other's perspectives. But you do. Almost too well, sometimes. I think that is from Cheng. Isn't it strange, that the one who can't feel emotions and thoughts understands others the best?"

When Neela mentioned Cheng, it wasn't with loathing. And that sounded almost like praise.

"Have you forgiven him?"

Neela cocked her head. "More like I realized I don't want to spend my last days dwelling on a grudge."

"Last days?" Jin swallowed. "Bai said that Cheng wants to kill you, but we—"

"I'm not going to let Cheng kill me. I want you to do it."

Jin jerked her hand from Neela's. "What? I'm not going to kill you."

"Gang told me about Aashchary. He said you could resurrect her if you had a sacrifice." She thumped her chest. "I've been planning on it anyway."

"I don't understand."

"I once tried to resurrect someone myself." Neela's eyes went distant, and Jin remembered the story that the Sea Serpent told her. She leaned closer, awaiting Neela's confidence, but

Neela said only, "I realized then that a sacrifice was needed. I've been planning on being one for Aashchary almost since the day she died."

Jin shook her head. Neela might as well having been chirping like a bird for all the sense Jin could make of her words.

Neela sighed. "You've never had a child, so you don't understand. I would give anything—yes, even my life—to have her well and happy. I wasn't always the best mother. I didn't realize how hard it would be nor how different she would be from me. But I always loved her more than life itself. Within hours of her death, I was trying to find a way to resurrect her—that was why I arranged the betrothal between you and Xiao."

"I don't follow..."

Neela patted Jin's arm. "I didn't realize you would be powerful enough on your own—or that the First would help. I told you, I tried to resurrect someone, and I fell short. So I know how much power is needed. I guessed that your and Xiao's children would have enough." Neela smiled and blinked rapidly. Was she holding back her own tears?

"I never dreamed this day would come so soon. I will sacrifice myself for her. I want to. And if you don't take my life, Cheng might very well waste it anyway. If not by killing me, by demanding my imprisonment."

Jin pushed off the cot. It was hard to breathe. Here she was, fighting so hard to bring everyone back to her, and it seemed like no one else cared. Gang would let Aka die, Neela was ready to commit suicide, Cheng had stormed off...

Where was Bai? He would help her process this. Whenever he spoke, in his deliberate, calm way, everything made more sense. Jin strode from the room.

Neela followed her, still going on about the resurrection.

BAI cut his finger with a dagger and then Aka's. He smeared their blood on the remaining black peony and clasped it and Aka's hand between the two of his.

He had always wondered, when Aka first came to be, if it was his will or Aka's that had brought his blood to life.

He supposed today they would find out.

He focused his will and suddenly it was like his very life was being pulled through the cut in his finger. Bai gasped. The peony turned to ash.

It was over. He slumped forward, supporting himself with his hands and panting.

"What curse of fate brought you here?"

Bai made himself stand and meet Aka's eyes with his usual confidence. "Better perhaps to ask what brought you here. It was no curse of fate but of your son. I saved you from a death curse."

Aka stared at him then glanced around the room. "Ah. So this is your home. It suits you—boring and bland."

"At least it's not pretentious nor built with another's power," Bai said baring his teeth in a smile. He wasn't sure he could have managed to save this man if he had seen him in the past eighteen millennia—Aka was even more obnoxious than he remembered.

"Are you going to lie there all day, or will you greet your granddaughter? If you won't thank me for your life, you should at least thank her."

Aka went still. "I don't have a granddaughter. Five children, but alas, not one of them wed."

"Last I knew, that wasn't a prerequisite for having children of their own. Jin. She's your granddaughter."

Aka surged up and tried to grab Bai. But he was weak from the prolonged stillness—Bai stepped aside, and Aka started to fall to the floor. Bai caught him by the neck of his robes—luckily, the cloth was strong as well as shiny—and hauled him back up.

"I'm not going to hurt Jin—or let anyone else do so, for that matter. But she still thinks you are dying, so why don't we tell her the bad news?"

Aka took a few steps supported by Bai before asking, "Did you really save me?"

"Yes."

"Huh. I wouldn't have thought you cared."

"Not about you," admitted Bai.

Aka looked at him in shock. "You fell in love with Jin?" Then he smiled. "She's even more charming than her grandmother, but I can't believe you want another fifty millennia of heartbreak. Some people never learn."

Bai just smiled back.

FINDING the common room empty, Jin strode into the garden. She had to shade her eyes against the sudden brightness, but even when they adjusted, Bai was nowhere to be seen. However, there was a new hut, made of gold. Perhaps it was garish in the simple white garden, but the sight of it was oddly soothing to Jin, and she paused to breathe.

"Yes, Gang made that monstrosity," Neela said behind her. "But did anyone fetch my caravan?"

"Where is Bai?" asked Jin.

"He left last night. I haven't seen him."

"Bai left?"

Jin turned to the voice and found Cheng. "You came back."

He shrugged sheepishly.

Jin bit her lip, then asked, "And what do you make of this new plan?"

"New plan?" he echoed. "I haven't heard it. I only came back just now."

Summoned by their voices, Gang emerged from the hut, cradling, as ever, that cursed ornament.

"Neela wants to sacrifice herself to resurrect Aashchary," he boomed. "Surely you won't object to her death being useful, Cheng?"

Cheng froze.

Jin focused on him. "You don't want her death at all, do you?"

He turned to her, stricken, but Neela scoffed. "I couldn't care less what he wants. Even if he gives up his revenge, I still want to trade my life for my daughter's."

Jin flinched. "I don't want to take anyone's life!"

"You have to," insisted Gang. "Mine or Neela's. We are both willing."

Jin glared at him. She hated him—she really did. How could he ask her to choose who to sacrifice?

She pressed her fists against her eyes, trying to hide from the three of them. Where was Bai? She needed him.

"Good," said Neela, "you're back. Talk some sense—" and

then she gasped.

Had Bai returned? Jin peered over her fingers.

Bai *was* there—and standing next to him, with a faint smile, was Aka.

IT sounded like his guests were arguing in the garden, and so Bai hurried Aka. When they emerged, it was easy to see that all three elders—if he could be allowed to call them that—were badgering Jin. Given the way Gang was still clutching the metal soul ornament, he supposed it was about Aashchary.

He cleared his throat, and Neela whirled on him. "Good, you're back. Talk some sense—" Her eyes fell on Aka, and she swallowed her words.

"Yes, don't everyone greet me at once," said Aka dryly.

Jin ran forward. "Papa!"

Aka pulled her into a hug, and Bai stepped back. Feeling awkward, he started toward the other three, but before he took two steps, Jin grabbed his wrist. "How?"

Her eyes were even more luminous than usual, and Bai felt embarrassed.

"As entertaining as it is to watch you blush, I would also like to hear your answer to that question," drawled Aka, and Bai twitched.

"Death curses are about blood. In a manner of speaking, you are my blood, so I used the rest of it to pull you back from the brink of death. Which you still haven't thanked me for, by the way."

"Indeed," muttered Aka. He still had an arm around Jin's shoulders—he needed the support. He looked past Bai to Gang.

"And what were all of you arguing about?"

Gang stepped forward. "Jin fetched Aashchary's soul from the Underworld. Neela and I want to sacrifice ourselves to resurrect her."

Aka scowled. "Neela, fine, but not you. Don't say such a thing. You are my heir. You vowed to take the Sun Throne if anything ever happened to me."

Gang shrugged. "By the looks of things, you'll live forever. Do you need an heir?"

Aka stood a little straighter and glared at Gang. "Perhaps not, but I need my son."

Bai was shocked. He had always known that Aka was proud of Gang, but this was the first time he could see that Aka loved Gang more than himself. He hadn't thought Aka capable of loving anything more than himself.

But he could see now that Jin's affection for Aka was no deeper than his affection for her. And Bai noted belatedly that Aka's usually dark red hair was streaked with gray at the temples. When had that happened? Just now?

"Jin," said Aka, "help me sit."

Bai quickly made him a wide chair from jasmine flowers—*a dutiful son-in-law?* he wondered with an internal wince.

When Aka was settled, he said, "Gang, may I see that ornament?"

Gang offered it to his father after a long pause, though Aka practically had to pry it from his fingers.

And he gasped, and that hair became even grayer—it was not Bai's imagination. "This is *Noran*."

"She is there as well," admitted Jin. "I was afraid my mother's soul wouldn't last long enough for me to resurrect it, and she volunteered to protect it."

Aka looked at her sharply. "But she is already so weak! If her soul wears out—she'll be gone forever!" His face blanched. "How long does she have?"

Jin bit her lip. "I don't know—perhaps a few days—"

Aka seized Bai's hand. *How long does she have?*

Bai looked at their joined hands—it felt like his bones were grinding together. Bai looked at the ornament. Noran's soul pulsed faintly through its lacy sides. "No more than two days."

Aka brought it close to his chest. "Then—" He straightened. "Jin, you must do the resurrection today. You will destroy my body, and I will carry Noran back to the sea when I go."

Bai had been trying to make sense of Aka—to understand the emotions he had hidden for so long—but now he looked at Jin. She took a step back, and then ran for his house. Gang made as if to follow her, but Bai barked "No!" and it seemed Gang had not totally forgotten that Bai was his teacher, for he paused.

"All of you—stay out!" commanded Bai. And he went after Jin himself.

He almost entered the common room, but he paused, and turned toward the hallway where he had once hidden Kunjee. None of his guests had gone that way—Neela, Gang, and Aka wouldn't even be able to see it, for he had tied it to Cheng's essence—but he could hear panting there.

He activated the white light on the ceiling and followed Jin. She wasn't in the first room, so Bai strode past the portraits of the Colors and into the golem's chamber. He paused a moment to look at the arch Jin made half a year ago. It was beautiful, a splash of color against the white walls, flames shifting from cerulean to crimson. Her lineage, writ for anyone to see, though Bai had missed it at the time. How hot that fire must have burned to melt the quartz!

He stepped through the arch and found Jin standing before the empty pedestal that had once held Kunjee.

He walked to her slowly and wrapped his arms around her. "Talk to me," he pleaded.

Her hands found his and clasped them. "I didn't think it through. It was an impulse, when I found mother's soul—or when it found me, I should say. She wanted to live so badly, and I—" Jin swallowed. "I missed her. No—I barely remember her, so how could I miss her? I *yearned* for her then. There's been so much sadness—so much loss—so many hurtful things my family has done to each other, I thought that if I could bring her back, it would undo some of that. But I wasn't prepared to—I thought I would do anything to bring her back, but it didn't occur to me that I would have to kill! They say they're sacrificing themselves, but they're asking me to kill them! Is it because I murdered Zi and Hei? They all think it is nothing to me, to take a life?" Her voice had grown increasingly shrill as she spoke, and she now gasped for breath.

He remembered his conversation with Neela on the Kuanbai.

*Gang loves her—she is all he has left of Aashchary.*

*I should hope he loves her for her own sake, and not just her mother's.*

And Neela had shrugged.

"It isn't that they think of you as a murderer," Bai told her, "it's that they aren't thinking of you at all." Impulsively, he scooped her into his arms and sat with her on his lap. Jin let her head drop against his neck.

"Jin, I will take the ornament to the Sea of Souls today, if it's what you want. I've been there often enough that I can manage it through a series of teleports—you don't have to choose any of them to sacrifice."

Jin calmed somewhat. She shook her head slowly. "That isn't right, is it? Then all of them—even Noran and Aashchary—will be unhappy. I will make all of them mourn just to avoid murdering one of them."

"I'm sorry that you killed Zi and Hei. I know it's a terrible burden."

She lifted her eyes to his.

"Do you remember?" she asked. "How it felt, the first time..."

A few dozen dead bandits, and a great hollowness inside. "I don't think I felt as you do, but it was its own kind of horrible," he said.

Jin placed a hand on either side of his face and stared deep into his eyes. "Has it changed how you view me?"

Bai was surprised. Was that worrying her? He almost reassured her at once, but he forced himself to reflect first.

"The first moment I saw you, I thought you were the most desirable being I had ever encountered, and I wanted to be as close to you as I could for as long as I could. That has not changed.

"When we travelled down the Kuanbai together, I saw your kindness and your open-mindedness, and I wanted to become a better being myself. That also has not changed.

"I have often felt the need to protect you. I have worried that you are vulnerable, delicate, and naive."

Jin bit her lip.

"I still want to protect you, but I also now realize that you are strong, tough, and that you see the world accurately—you simply choose to assume the best when you don't know the worst. So that has changed."

Jin laughed shakily. "You are too generous to me. I don't think I'm nearly as worthy as you say."

Bai shrugged. "I am not lying."

She smiled—more genuinely this time. "I know that. I know you believe your words. And I'm grateful. I shall strive to live up to them."

She sat for so long, her eyes focused on nothing particular, that Bai began to regret having settled her in his lap. Just as he thought his legs would fall asleep, she said, "My mother shouldn't have died. She, Gang, Neela, and Aka will all be happier if she were resurrected. And it's what Noran wanted too."

She stood. "NeeNee told me she has been planning on being the sacrifice since my mother's death. And given what she did to Cheng... It's fitting. I will follow her wishes and trade her life for Mother's." She turned to look at him. "That is, if you will help me make a body. For as I learned with Nanami's hand, I cannot make bones."

Bai held out a hand, and Jin pulled him to his feet. "I do not think there is anything I would not do if you asked it of me."

Jin's eyes widened. "Then I shall be careful not to ask you too much."

Bai caught her chin. "No. You must ask for everything so that I can delight in giving it to you."

She flushed, her cheeks peony pink. Bai enjoyed the moment. *How long,* he wondered, *will I be able to make her blush with outrageous words?*

"Forever," she answered his thought, and then very slowly—Bai knew she must still remember their first kiss—she went up on her tiptoes and kissed him.

She stepped back far sooner than he liked and led him back to the garden.

"We will make a body," Jin announced. "And NeeNee, I will accept your sacrifice."

"But Noran—" objected Aka.

"I'll bring her with me, you fool," snapped Neela.

Bai collected jasmine flowers with which to make her bones while Jin picked her image from Gang and Neela's memories. Then she knelt on one side of the petals while Bai knelt on the other. He made the skeleton first, and Jin covered it with fire.

She sagged forward when the flames went out, and Bai caught her. He wished yet again that he could read her essence. It was obvious that she expelled a great deal of power, but he couldn't tell how much she had left. While he was worrying over Jin, Neela and Gang came forward to exclaim over the body.

Bai looked down at it. Never having seen Aashchary grown, he couldn't judge the appearance for himself, but, since those closest to her seemed satisfied, he supposed it was accurate.

"No," objected Aka.

"What now?" said Neela.

"This isn't right."

"I think I remember her face better than you do," objected Gang.

"I'm not talking about her face," said Aka. He pointed at her belly. "She was in the last stage of pregnancy."

Bai looked down at the slim waist Jin had created.

"The baby!" Jin cried. "We will need to make its body too, or its soul will have to return to the Underworld."

Gang seized Jin's shoulder. "You can't let that happen! She was so devastated by your brother's death..."

"STOP shaking her," ordered Aka, coming forward to disengage Gang's hand from Jin's shoulder. Jin looked up at him and was perturbed to see an odd satisfaction on his face. "I will trade my life for the baby's, Jin. You'll take both Neela and I as sacrifices."

Jin stood up. "Why are you so determined to die? Don't you—don't you love me? Don't you want to stay for me?"

Aka's eyes widened. "Oh, sweetheart, of course I love you. But—" he glanced at the crowd. "Fate, there are too many people here. What does it matter, though, when I will be dead soon and Neela can read my thoughts and Gang my emotions and Bai everything else?" He sighed. "Jin, the being I loved the most in this world died a long time ago. And it was my fault."

"I saw Mother's death. You tried to save her—"

"Not Aashchary. Noran. We fought—we were always fighting, for I was a terrible partner to her. And because we liked fighting. But when she left me—I went too far. I answered the mortal bandits' prayers with her location. I told them a woman of gold could make them wealthy for the rest of their days. They killed her because I led them to her. Do you understand?"

His hair had gone white, and the skin of his face was crinkled and papery, like the Moon Deer's. Jin trembled, not wanting to believe his words, but they had the sweet ring of truth.

"I couldn't think of a way to undo it, so I have spent the last fifty millennia pretending it didn't happen. But when Guleum cursed me..." His face crumpled and tears ran down his cheeks. "I saw her death. Over and over again. A death curse slowly saps your will to live, and it's already too late for me. I don't want to live anymore. But—but if I do this—if I fulfill her wish after death, then maybe, in the afterlife... Maybe she will forgive me."

Jin stared at him. "She didn't leave you. Or at least, she didn't leave you forever. She was intending on coming back to the Sun Palace after a while. She just wanted you to commit to her and her alone. She told me so. But she loved you until the end." Jin closed her eyes. "You have done so many terrible things—you have made so many beings deeply unhappy. And not just our family—the immortal creatures..."

"Yes," Aka agreed. "But I had you as a granddaughter. So you can spend your life fixing all the wrongs of mine."

Jin stared at him. She wanted to hate him. She wanted to be angry. But she just felt sad and tired. And, despite everything, she still remembered him as the man who taught her to play Jieqi, who praised her paintings on the wall of her residence, and who made her feel beautiful and loved every day after she moved back to the Sun Palace. "Fine," she said. "You too can make your sacrifice."

She knelt again, stared at the beautiful yet alien body of her mother and then its too flat abdomen.

"I don't know how to make the baby," she confessed. "How will we get it inside?"

Bai rubbed his lower lip, and Jin wondered how it was possible for him to be so perfectly collected and capable and *hers*. "We'll grow it. Just the way babies grow. Sped up, of course, since we don't have a thousand years." Bai took her hand in his and pressed them both against her mother's womb. "I know the process," he explained. "Follow my thoughts and use your power."

Jin focused on him and he focused on her, and just as she had when she built Aashchary's body, Jin felt like she was falling in a world of white. But she wasn't alone—a warm hand held hers, she added her own power to the world, red and yellow, orange and blue, and the colors swirled together, making purple and green and brown and then mixing with the white to create peach and lavender and all the colors of the world.

And then the colors exploded, and Jin knew no more.

BAI saw Jin once again start to collapse onto the now swollen belly of Aashchary's body, but he was too slow to catch her this time, having expended a great deal of power himself. However, Gang was ready and pulled her up into her arms, carrying her like a baby.

"What happened?" he asked. "Did something go wrong?"

"No," sighed Bai, as exhausted from this so-called family as he was from helping build two bodies. "I don't think so. It just takes quite a lot of magic. I don't think she can do more until tomorrow."

"I'll be fine," Jin said, stirring as her eyes fluttered open. "But Bai is right. I can't..."

"That's alright," Gang said, and he propped her against the

white chair Bai had made earlier for Aka. Cheng, who had stayed well back, a passive observer, came forward now to sit near her—and catch her if she fell. "You don't need to do more."

"But—"

"I can finish it," Gang announced. "It's just the transfer of souls now."

Bai paused. "Are you sure—"

"Don't forget, I'm more powerful than you," said Gang.

Bai tilted his head. Gang's innate well of power was not as deep as his—not anymore, since he shared yellow with Jin and red with her as well as his father and siblings—but he certainly had a lot of mortal worshippers. Was war so popular with them?

"Besides," added Gang, "this way I will be responsible for their deaths."

And to that Bai had no objection. He hesitated, then moved to Jin's other side. She collected his hand and looked at him nervously. He tried for a reassuring smile, but he felt rather nervous himself.

Gang shook the souls free from the ornament. Aashchary's and her baby's flew into the waiting bodies, but Noran's bobbed in confusion until Aka caught it in his hands.

Gang glanced at Neela and Aka, then to Bai. "What now?"

Bai focused hard, reading their essences. He could see their lives in their fingertips, Neela and Aka trying to will their lives to Aashchary and the baby—but their lives couldn't escape their bodies.

"You have to destroy their bodies," he told Gang.

And Gang set them on fire.

Cheng cried out at this and jerked, and Jin took his hand as well. The two of them were crying, and, for the first time, Bai could see the similarity in their features. Feeling like an intruder, he looked back at the fire.

The flames felt like they took forever to die, but eventually Bai saw Aka's soul—strong and vibrant—and Noran's—pale and faint—disappear together.

"She forgave him then."

Jin shrugged. "She never blamed him—she blamed herself for using her magic foolishly. If she hadn't squandered it, the bandits couldn't have killed her."

Bai turned to look at Jin in shock. Did that mean he could also absolve himself of guilt in Noran's death?

No, he would still regret not coming to her aid as soon as she asked. If he had—would Noran and Aka have reunited? And Gang been free to marry Aashchary and Jin raised by her true parents—

He stopped the litany of what-ifs. For maybe if he had saved Noran, Jin would never have existed at all. He squeezed her hand, and she squeezed his back.

Aka and Noran's souls winked out—gone to the sea. Neela's lingered for a moment, as if reluctant to leave Aashchary, but then it disappeared as well.

"Does it bother you to see them together?" Jin whispered to Bai.

He knew she meant Aka and Noran. "No," he said, and it was the truth. "I am happy for them."

And then Aashchary sat up.

And Bai realized she was mortal.

JIN'S breath caught as the woman opened her eyes.

Aashchary. Her mother.

Jin knew she was crying, as always, but she didn't care. She tugged her hands free of Bai and Cheng, and ran to her mother's side, suddenly full of energy again. She felt like she could take on the whole world—she could do anything.

Aashchary was staring at Gang. And before Jin's eyes, his hair deepened to red-gold and the wrinkles about his eyes disappeared. He now looked like the man that Aashchary had shown Jin in her memories.

Aashchary laughed and leaned forward. Mindful of her bump, Gang caught her in a hug.

Jin sat down next to them, and Aashchary turned her head to look at her. At first she was confused, but then her eyes widened in understanding. "Jin," she breathed. She let go of Gang to catch Jin's hands. "Oh, my beautiful baby. You lived up to your title."

Jin winced, and Aashchary laughed. "And how you hate being seen as beautiful before anything else!"

Jin smiled eagerly. "Can you read my thoughts then?"

"Certainly," said Aashchary. "Reading a daughter is a mother's special power."

Jin tilted her head. That wasn't quite the answer she expected. "I mean—because you are blue. Like NeeNee and I."

Aashchary kept smiling but didn't say anything.

Something was wrong. Jin didn't know what it was, but something was wrong.

Instinctively, she looked at Bai for the answer.

"She's mortal," he said. "She gained Neela's life, but not her immortality."

Jin shook her head, wanting to deny Bai's words. She looked back at Aashchary, still smiling steadily at her.

"But—NeeNee gave up her life so that—and Papa—" Jin glanced at her mother's rounded stomach. "The baby."

"He's mortal as well," said Bai.

"No," said Jin, grasping a sudden hope. "You can't read them because they are orange! You don't know—"

"Jin," said Bai, "I can read them. Both of them. They have no magic."

Gang took a deep breath and squeezed Jin's hand. "Can't you feel it? Father's power flooded to me. Didn't Neela's come to you?"

Jin had felt it, but she had dismissed the euphoria as excitement over Aashchary. She remembered Xiao after his parents' death. The way he had seemed almost intoxicated. The way she felt now. Both Aka and Neela's power was at her disposal.

"But—they traded millennia for a handful of decades!"

"They traded their sorrow for my joy," said Aashchary. "So that I could live with the man I love and raise a family. Just like we always wanted."

Gang was smiling too. And he said, "I will never be Sun Emperor."

This time Jin knew what she was feeling. All the yellow power she had shared with Gang was hers alone, for he had broken his vow to Aka.

But instead of elation, she felt fury. "You—tricked me! Get out of here!" she screamed at them. And she was vaguely aware that pillars of flame appeared at her sides.

❀ ❀ ❀

BAI knew as angry as Jin was right now—as betrayed as she felt—she would be devastated if Aashchary and Gang died. So he pulled them between and away from Jin's fire.

He had chosen to bring them to Jeevanti, not far from the Dataa River, the spot where Neela had mentioned leaving her caravan a dozen times as she tried to bully him into fetching it for her.

"Oh, dear," said Aashchary. "She's very emotional, isn't she?"

"Yes," said Gang. "Perhaps I should have given her time to grow accustomed to your mortality before I joined you."

"You think?" Bai bit off in exasperation. He stared at the two of them. "You couldn't have at least waited and faced Salaana at her side? After all she did for you?" He realized his hands were both clenched, and he forced himself to relax them. He remembered how Gang had accused him of loving Jin only for Noran's sake. At the time, he had been offended, but he now saw that Gang had been revealing his own feelings. His love for his daughter had been shaped and warped by his mourning for her mother. Bai wanted to attack Gang, to hurt him. Instead, he gestured at the caravan. "Well, I guess that's yours. I need to get back."

But Gang grabbed his arm. "I'm sorry I drove you away from the gate. I was wrong. I could do this because I know you'll be at Jin's side."

Bai closed his eyes briefly. Then, looking directly into Gang's—which had become a light brown— "Yes, I will be. But you should have been there anyway."

Aashchary gasped, and Bai looked at her.

She was ringed by Rang Pariyon, the gentle fairies that had appeared at the Chattaan Kile just a few days ago.

"I had almost forgotten the immortal creatures, amongst everything else," Gang mused, and his hand tightened on Bai's forearm. "Tell Jin to use the Sun Guard to manage the creatures."

"You no longer have a right to worry about that," said Bai, even though he knew it was a stupid thing to say.

Gang nodded. "Yes, I'm sure you would have thought of it yourself." He released Bai, and said, "Good luck."

Bai hesitated before he teleported, wondering if Neela had left any food in her caravan. Mortals needed to eat almost constantly. Gang and Aashchary were surprised when he returned a half hour later with bundles of steamed buns and dried meat. Bai nodded brusquely at their thanks, and then returned to Jin.

JIN had not intended to start a fire. Her emotions had erupted, along with more power than she had ever known. In fact, as flames danced and flickered around her, she thought someone else had made them for they felt uncomfortably hot.

So she stood there, the outside world hidden by flames, wondering when they would end.

And then she realized she had created this wall.

Like a child throwing a tantrum because they didn't get enough presents.

Jin was mortified—but that made it harder to stop the flames instead of easier. What would they all think of her?

But, she slowly realized, wouldn't it be better to stop the flames now, of her own accord than to let them die because she had exhausted her power? How long would that take, anyway?

Days? Would she never run out of power but sustain this fire for the rest of eternity—or when she fainted from dehydration?

And like that, the flames were gone.

She braced herself for disappointment and recriminations, but Gang and Aashchary weren't there. Neither was Bai. Only Cheng was, watching her from a safe distance, and his broad face was open and calm.

"Hi," he said when their eyes met. "You must be pretty hungry—Bai told me you need to eat and drink. I think you've had what—a few bowls of soup over the past few days?"

Jin nodded and pressed a hand to a sudden rumbling tummy. "Food would be good."

"Why don't we go out to get something? Bai showed me Liushi—you must know a good place to eat."

Jin swallowed. "Maoyi. The best restaurants are in Maoyi."

Usually Jin loved Maoyi, with its vibrant colors and the smell of spice that seemed to permeate the city, but today she barely noticed it. She and Cheng sat across from each other at a bamboo table set with stir-fried noodles, roasted duck, grilled eggplant, and steaming rice wine.

Cheng opened the meal by filling her small earthenware cup with wine from the pot.

Jin tended toward moderation in her drinking ever since one youthful indulgence with Xiao, but she drained the cup at once. Maybe it was purely psychological, but the sweet burn of the wine steadied her, and she began to help herself to the food. She was ravenous, she realized with the first mouthful, and she ate with intensity, ignoring Cheng. She was relieved when he made no demands on her attention. After a while, the plates before them held nothing but sauce and a few stray scallions.

"I wasn't ready for this," she told Cheng, resuming a conversation that had happened only in her head.

"I wasn't ready to be a grandfather," he mused, "but here I am."

Jin snorted, then refilled his wine cup.

Cheng lifted it and studied the liquid. It was both like and totally unlike having tea with Aka.

"What is 'this'?" he asked. "The death of Neela and Aka? Or inheriting their power? Or Gang and Aashchary...?"

"All of it," she admitted, setting an elbow on the table and her chin on her fist.

He nodded. "Each could be overwhelming on its own, so I can't imagine what it's like altogether. Let's address them one by one, shall we?"

"Okay," Jin said. She was bemused by his practicality but also relieved. She could easily see why he and Bai were good friends.

"I think Gang and Aashchary must be the simplest. You feel like they have died because they will only live fifty years at the most while you have eternity. But Aashchary had no choice in the matter—and now that Gang is mortal, he gets to spend the rest of his life with her, rather than feeling as you do."

Jin nodded once. She understood that, but she still felt abandoned.

"Of course you could join them—you could give up your immortality."

Jin reared back. "No."

Cheng laughed. "I didn't think you'd want to; I was just pointing out that you had options." He grew serious again. "And even if you stay immortal, it doesn't mean you've lost the chance to know them. In fact, I think you would be wise to at least keep tabs on them. Other immortals probably will."

Jin nodded slowly and sipped wine. "There are lot of aspects of this that haven't even occurred to me yet, I was so caught up with my own angst." Her cheeks grew hot, and she looked at Cheng. "I'm sorry I lost my temper."

He grinned, then ruffled her hair. "I think it would have bothered me more if you hadn't! Are you ready to talk about Aka and Neela?"

She shrugged. "As ready as I ever will be, I suppose."

"This was what they wanted."

"Yes—and I thought I had made peace with that, but would they have still wanted it if they knew..."

"Yes," said Cheng.

"Why are you so sure?"

"Neela was once in love with a mortal man. He died from an accident when he was still young. So far as I know, it was the only time she committed romantically to another being. She told me, after, that it would be better to live a short life as a mortal with the one you loved than an eternity alone. So I think she would be glad that Gang and Aashchary are together."

Jin bit her lip, as if to hold back the words that wanted to tumble out, but they burst free anyway. "Why wasn't I enough? She always held herself back from me. I think because she was planning this all along. But why—why couldn't I have been enough?"

Cheng moved around the table and hugged her. It should have felt strange, for he was a virtual stranger, but instead it felt oddly familiar and comforting.

"I asked myself that more times than I can count," he

confessed. "Neela and I were good friends, and I fell in love with her, but she never fell in love with me. I was never able to budge her heart." Cheng shrugged. "Even magical beings such as us can never truly know another—I'm not sure we ever even truly know ourselves. Our feelings are strong, and sometimes no amount of logic or rationality can change them. Sometimes the best we can do is accept them."

Jin nodded and took a few deep breaths.

"Okay. Then the worshippers and the power..."

Cheng released her and sat back on his heels. He grinned once again, his broad mouth splitting his face. "You're on your own there. I don't even understand how worship works."

He gulped down the rest of his wine. "Are you ready to go back? Bai will want to make plans with us."

Jin nodded. "Yes. I am. Thank you."

# Nanami's Decision

NANAMI arrived at the Koch-ssi's shrine—well, it used to be her shrine, but none of the structure had survived the last eighteen millennia.

Thick green vines hung like ropes from trees that stretched far above Nanami's head. The leaves created such a dense canopy that the light here seemed to be passing through a green filter.

There wasn't a flower in sight.

*Fool!*

Even if the Koch-ssi had returned to Earth, she wouldn't necessarily come here. Still, not ready to give up, Nanami fought her way through the thick vines toward the ocean that she could hear though she couldn't see it.

And she was rewarded, for standing upon the sand, its arms spread as if the embrace the sun, was the Koch-ssi.

Breaking free of the thick foliage, Nanami ran toward the Koch-ssi. The creature turned at the sound of her footfalls and smiled.

*Flower. I hoped you would come.*

The Koch-ssi held out her hands and Nanami seized those thick cattail fingers. The Koch-ssi pulled her close, and Nanami was enveloped by a half-forgotten hydrangea bosom.

"You're back!" Nanami exclaimed and was a little nonplussed to find her voice thick with emotion.

*Yes.*

"I'm sorry," Nanami confessed. "I wanted to help you—I tried to steal the key, but I never even got close."

The Koch-ssi laid its hand on Nanami's head. *Oh, flower, of course you couldn't have. You mustn't feel bad about the things you can't do.*

Nanami had to force a smile. The Koch-ssi's words were too similar to her mother's and Ichimi's, but of course the Koch-ssi had no way of knowing about Xiao. "You must be planning on restoring your gardens. Can I help?"

And so Nanami became the Koch-ssi's assistant in the days that followed, transplanting and trimming the almost strangled vegetation. It was physically challenging work, and she slept well each night even though she spent the days worrying about Xiao.

She soon realized that she didn't want to part ways with him, but she didn't know how to make amends. And she didn't regret everything she said, even if she knew her timing had been wrong. His ability—and Jin's—to influence other beings unsettled her. Independence and free will had always felt essential to Nanami, and she couldn't be with someone who did not agree.

She thought she'd been hiding her feelings well, but on the third day, the Koch-ssi surprised Nanami while they were removing rocks from the soil.

*What has you so sad?*

Nanami froze. "What do you mean?"

*Flower, I can always tell when something is weighing on you. In the past, you were always eager to share your burdens with me. Has it been too long? Can you no longer confide in me?*

Nanami rubbed her dirty palms together, focusing on the gritty sensation so that she should keep her voice light. "I fell in love. But I'm not sure if it will work out."

The Koch-ssi asked her question after question and soon Nanami had told her all about her expulsion from the Sea Dragon's family, her years as a thief, and how she fell head over heels the first time she ever saw Xiao.

*He must be very handsome,* mused the Koch-ssi.

"Yes, but it's not just that," Nanami tried to explain. "He's— he's *warm.*" Nanami glanced at the Koch-ssi to see if her words made any sense, and she found its berry mouth smiling.

*That's good,* the Koch-ssi said. *You have always needed warmth. Why do you doubt the relationship?*

"Well. For one, we're not on the same level. He's now one of the most powerful immortals in the world."

*You are far from powerless.*

"Most immortals are a spark," Nanami said. "I'm a candle. But Xiao is an inferno. I'm closer to the spark than the inferno."

*And of course an inferno can destroy a candle.*

"Yes." Nanami blinked. "I mean, no. Xiao wouldn't hurt me. I'm not afraid of Xiao."

*Aren't you, though? You are afraid of something.*

Was she? Well, yes, she knew she was. That power scared her. But she wasn't afraid of Xiao. How could both be true?

She had been unwilling to acknowledge his power as a part of him. In their time together, he had rarely used any power at all. And the times he had, it had been for her—when he broke Salaana's wards and when he became the Night Dragon.

And so she had let herself believe that was all there was to it—and that was what he had meant, when he left. He had said if she couldn't accept his power then they couldn't be together. She couldn't just pick and choose the easy parts—she knew that. But that was what she had done.

"I don't need to be afraid of Xiao. I know that. I suppose— what frightens me is to love Xiao is to involve myself in power struggles where I'm irrelevant." She swallowed. "Koch-ssi, yesterday the Moon Goddess and the Night God were killed. I watched it happen, and it terrified me because until I saw it, it was inconceivable. And I thought—well, you said it when I first came—I can't compete with power like that."

*I don't think that is exactly what I said, but I believe that is what you heard.* The Koch-ssi sat down on the ground and looked up at the sky. *Do you know what the hardest part of living in the Underworld was?*

Nanami shook her head, confused by the non sequitur.

*Being dependent. There is no sunlight in the Underworld—the only way for me to live was through the benevolence of the Golden Phoenix. I wasn't the only one in such an uncomfortable situation of course—the Mudanren and the Habito also depended on sunlight from other creatures—and the Phoenix was ever gracious but...*

*It's a scary thing, to depend on another being. To trust them with your life.*

*I enjoyed living with the Phoenix and we became good friends, but I never forgot that I needed it while it didn't need me. And now that I am home and free, I breathe easier.*

*But.*

*I am a solitary creature. I always have been. You—you are not. Despite your choices for the past several millennia, I know you enjoy the company of others. You prefer it to solitude. You have always yearned for love. So I do not think my decision is necessarily the right one for you.*

"But—to make the choice to be dependent on someone else!"

*Mortals do it every day,* the Koch-ssi told her. *They marry and have children because they need others. Marriages for them are a pooling of resources—and children are needed to carry on their legacies and care for them in their old age. Their lives are cycles of dependence.*

Nanami rubbed her face. She thought suddenly of the farmer who had given her a ride to the Wood Pavilions, carrying her to a crossroads she could never have anticipated.

He had been so happy—and yes, he must have been dependent on his wife. She managed the house and raised their children and worked the fields with him. He needed her.

Just like Nanami needed Xiao.

*Need.*

Sometime during those endless days in the fishing dinghy which carried her to exile, Nanami had decided to never need anyone again. Half the reason she chose He Who Walks in Shadow as her master was his personality made it impossible for her to care too deeply about him. He was the only being she had allowed herself to associate with because there was no risk of him ever becoming necessary.

She had pushed Xiao away when he needed her most because she was scared. Scared that he wouldn't choose her over everyone else, scared that she wasn't as necessary to him as he was to her.

She had given him a test he couldn't pass because she wanted him to put her above everything and everyone else. That hadn't been fair—he was barely holding himself together, and millions of responsibilities in the form of mortal faith had just fallen to him—and she had acted from fear. To protect herself; to push him away before he pushed her.

The Koch-ssi seemed to sense that it had said enough, and they resumed digging for rocks in silence.

Nanami thought for two days. On the third day, she told the Koch-ssi, "Xiao didn't leave me. I pushed him away. But even so, I'm not sure I can accept his power."

*So what will you do?*

"What I do best—observe and make a plan. I'm leaving for Dalbam Temple."

*May fate smile on you, flower.*

"And you, Koch-ssi."

XIAO had always enjoyed O'o. It was a liberal, open-minded city where people of all forms and inclinations were welcomed with fervor. The citizens were fiercely independent, given to vigilantism and dramatic gestures.

But all which had charmed him now chafed at him, for those traits reminded him of Nanami.

And for all the times he had come to O'o, he had always avoided entering the central building of Shingetsu Temple. But to claim it as his, he would enter it today. He glanced at the small shrine to the left of central building that had been designated for him. Would it be taken down? Or perhaps he could dedicate it to Dawa?

Something small and green skittered down the side of the shrine as Xiao watched.

"What was that?" he asked.

"Habito," Dawa said. "Don't worry, they are benevolent. It's a good sign they live within the temple."

Xiao sighed. Immortal creatures seemed to be popping up everywhere these days. Plenty seemed fine—good even—but he'd seen enough destruction from the antics of others that he was worried what would be said at Tsuku in a few weeks. Ah, well, that was a problem for another day.

Dawa stood patiently at Xiao's back, a silent supporter. That support was just as weighty as any judgement—Xiao did not want to disappoint Dawa. He had been quite wise in avoiding disciples up until now—alas, times change.

Xiao strode forward—he knew Dawa was following for he could hear the older immortal's quick steps behind him. They mounted the tall and deep steps far more easily than any of the mortals around them—this was not due to their powers but simply a result of their height. Perhaps Hei had specified the size of these steps to some unfortunate priest thousands of years ago so that they would suit his long legs. At any rate, they were quite appropriate for Xiao and the nearly as tall Dawa, though an elderly mortal practically had to sit on her butt and scoot to descend them.

Xiao paused in surprise as soon as he passed through the massive doorway—it was quite colorful compared to most New Moon temples. The pillars were stained black and painted with clusters of violets, which in addition to the mandatory purple had green leaves and white, blue, and even hints of yellow in the petals. But even more shocking than the paint were the statues of Zi and Hei located at the head of the temple.

"Were those carved by a mortal?" he wondered aloud.

"Indeed, my lord."

Zi and Hei's statues were usually made by them, of amethyst and obsidian or similar materials. But these were wood.

Furthermore, instead of being seated on thrones and staring out upon their petitioners with solemn expressions, they were looking at each other, locked in an embrace. Movement was suggested by the way their robes had been carved and Xiao belatedly realized they were dancing.

"They tried to capture the moment they met. When Hei fell in love with Zi as she danced and so became an immortal."

"Yes," agreed Dawa.

At the other temples, Xiao had reshaped the statues to form one of himself. But the idea of removing this statue made it hard to breath.

"This is why you suggested we do the Zhongtuese temples first," said Xiao after a moment. He didn't wait for Dawa's acknowledgement, instead saying, "We'll leave it."

Dawa hesitated. "But—"

"I'll build another statue in front. But let us leave this one."

"Xiao—"

"No, I insist."

Dawa shrugged.

Xiao gathered the shadows in the temple for his statue, a feat which made the surrounding mortals gasp in awe and prostrate themselves before him.

He then accepted the vows of the monks attached to the temple.

When it was all done, it was quite late, and Xiao wanted a drink.

But he didn't need Dawa to stop him; he wanted a drink, but he also wanted to be whoever he was becoming. So instead he settled for salty and greasy street food that was served on sticks and lots of water.

That night he dreamed of Nanami and dancing with her. When he woke in the morning, he was clutching his pillow too tightly.

WHEN Nanami entered Dalbam Temple, she was shocked to see Xiao.

Not the real Xiao, of course, but a massive statue of him. It was disorienting to see his head twice the size it ought to be, but his smile was still winsome and maybe just a tinge bit sheepish.

She walked close to the statue and had an odd sense of déjà vu. Looking at his statue brought a sense of voyeurism, just like when she had spied on him at the Wood Pavilions.

It was also a little overwhelming. Over a hundred mortals were gathered in the room, making it close and hot, praying to their new god. Two monks were monitoring the crowd with dazed expressions; when a group of worshippers left, new ones were allowed in.

"Why is it so busy today?" Nanami asked them. "It's no festival."

"Didn't you hear?" said the shorter monk. "The son of the Moon and Night deities himself came here just three days ago. The God of Love. I saw him reshape the statues in his image myself."

That surprised Nanami—given Xiao's repeated failures in altering so much as a petal in Jin's garden, she wouldn't have expected him to be able to reshape the stone statues. But of course, if he hadn't, who could have?

Nanami mimicked their heart-shaped hands raised to the statue and bowed. Then she shifted among the crowd, listening to the few prayers that were made aloud. Most of them were what she expected, pleas for love and romance, but one was a father demanding that his daughter find a more appropriate lover. He burned thirteen sticks of incense to be sure that his prayer would reach the god's ears, and Nanami was thoroughly annoyed with him.

But wouldn't Xiao ignore a prayer like that? Or—he couldn't possibly attend to each of these prayers himself, could he? Did his disciples answer them using his power?

Despite having twenty-six millennia to her name, Nanami knew little about worship and deification.

When the man left, Nanami followed him. He was carried by sedan to his house, a two-storied affair in the merchant district of Daedo, and it seemed the sedan chair carriers were in fact household servants. Nanami wasn't surprised that he was wealthy—indeed, it often seemed that those who had the most were the ones who were never satisfied, creating a never-ending cycle of unhappiness and work.

She wasn't sure what she wanted to do—perhaps nothing—but finding out if the man's prayer would be answered was an itch she had to scratch.

It wasn't too hard to keep tabs on the house—between the family and servants, there were twenty people living there, and the doors were frequently opened for deliveries and excursions. That very afternoon, the eldest daughter of the house—the target of the prayer—left the house to meet her lover by the reflecting pool in the public square.

Nanami wasn't impressed by the young man—he had a pretty face but a lazy manner and a way of fussing that grated on Nanami. He and the daughter flirted cloyingly, with obvious metaphors and hyperbolic compliments that caused the daughter's maid to roll her eyes repeatedly. Their meeting ended with him placing sloppy kisses on his lady's hand to her obvious delight.

Two days later though he came to the house and knocked on the door only to be rebuffed by the same maid.

"What's this? I wish to speak to Tae-rim. She missed our meeting yesterday."

The maid continued to refuse him entrance but agreed to tell her mistress that he would wait until he had an explanation.

It came shortly, in the form of a note. The young man read it twice and then crumpled it, his face crumpling in a similar manner. He threw away the note and Nanami collected it.

In the writing of Daedo, it said, "You are a fop. I am tired of you. Do not call again."

Nanami was not convinced the young woman had written this herself, so that night she crept over the wall of the house and listened to the lady talk to her maid as she got ready for bed.

"I'm glad you came to your senses, milady. Your father is pleased."

The young woman yawned. "I don't know why I ever thought him handsome. He is tiresome in the extreme." Then she giggled. "Did you see Hae-on last night? Now there is a man a woman can admire! He has already started managing his family business."

She sounded fully sincere, and Nanami decided that her father's prayer must have indeed been answered.

Frustrated, she bought three sticks of fried chicken skin on the way back to her room and ate them all so quickly that they burned her tongue.

The girl's change was not exactly alarming—indeed, given more time, she might have changed her opinion on her own. And yet, it was so like the Sowon Gold that it made Nanami shiver.

XIAO sat in the garden of New Moon Manor with Dawa listening to his second and third disciples list their current plans for converting the smaller temples scattered throughout the mountains. He gave his blessing when they finished and sighed after they left.

"I hope Nanami is doing alright," he said to Dawa. "She must be lonely."

Dawa, who had been reviewing the written plans of his juniors, rolled them up and set them aside. "My lord, I do not understand why you worry about her when she drove you away."

"Love asks nothing but gives everything," Xiao told him, and had to laugh when Dawa began recording it.

"What are you doing?" Xiao asked.

"It's my first duty to record and share your teachings," Dawa said seriously.

"How do you know if I'm teaching or just being flippant?" asked Xiao.

"Can't you be both?"

Xiao groaned. He rubbed his face. When he spoke again, he was in earnest. "I had to deal with this now, but yes, I still care about Nanami, and yes, I will seek her out when this is finished so that we can resolve what's between us."

"But it might disappoint you."

"It might," agreed Xiao.

NANAMI travelled to several other large New Moon Temples—Shingetsu and YeYue and XinYue and Nayachaand—but although there was always evidence of Xiao's visit, he was never there. She followed three more mortals after their prayers, to see if Xiao—or perhaps his disciples—really used magic to change them, and each time it seemed they had. She was forced to admit that the result always seemed beneficial, but it still sat ill with her.

Another thing that weighed on her was the Sowon Gold, for it was cursed heavy, literally and emotionally.

She hadn't hidden it yet because she had realized Xiao was right.

She should ask Jin to destroy it. But when she remembered the way Jin had cut Zi's throat, Nanami felt scared.

However, it seemed that facing Jin—who she knew could be monstrous—was easier than seeing Xiao's beloved face through a haze of unease. So Nanami went to the White Mountain.

When she arrived near the mountain spring that she, Xiao, and Jin had sought so long ago, Nanami was surprised to see it once again looked frozen. Of course, this time she was sure that it was some trick of Bai's, so she walked toward it.

Only to be turned around.

Curse it, was she not welcome here?

Nanami was tapping her foot in irritation when a cheerful voice said, "Do you need any help? Nanami, isn't it? I think I remember your coming-of-age celebration."

Nanami turned and found herself facing the Color Orange.

"Sir," she said.

"Ha!" His mouth split his face with a grin, and he said, "Call me Cheng."

Nanami had met Cheng before—he had indeed come to her coming-of-age ceremony, and she had seen him at her grandfather's with some regularity—but she had always been a little wary of the Colors and was far from familiar with him.

Aware that she sounded stiff, Nanami said, "I've come to see Jin."

"Oh, good! We tried to tell her she needed to see her friends, but she keeps using her responsibilities as an excuse. Ever since the deaths..." Cheng paused, his big smile fading.

"You mean the Night and Moon deities?" she prompted, when the silence stretched too long.

Cheng blinked slowly, shuttering and unshuttering his ember eyes. "No. I'd better explain before you go in." He didn't though. Instead, he chewed on his lip and Nanami's foot began to tap again.

"Jin found her mother's soul in the Underworld. And her unborn brother's. She brought them back, but she didn't know the price of resurrection was a life. Aka and Neela both insisted on sacrificing themselves to bring Aashchary and the babe to life." He heaved a sigh.

"So the Sun Emperor and the Wanderer are gone?" Nanami asked, simply because she was so shocked.

"Yes, but that's not all. Jin did bring Aashchary back to life, but she was a mortal. Powerless. So Gang broke his vow to Aka and became mortal too."

Nanami wrapped her arms around herself. So Jin had been abandoned by her family, just like Nanami.

Nanami's harsh words on the Yanou came back to her now—she had mocked Jin for being too eager to please her family. Nanami had always been a rebel, and her abandonment had cut deep. How would it be for Jin, who had lived to impress her elders?

Nanami coughed. Earlier Cheng had called her a friend. She wasn't sure that was accurate, but...

She was something. "Please, I'd like to see her."

The confrontation that Nanami had imagined of course didn't happen. Instead, Jin, bearing only a passing resemblance to the wild warrior of New Moon Manor, flung her arms around Nanami. Smelling in Jin's sweet citrusy scent, Nanami realized Jin was also eager to please her. Feeling tender despite her doubts, she hugged Jin back tightly.

As for the destruction of the Sowon Gold, it was no sooner asked than done because Jin trusted Nanami's judgement.

Nanami felt guilty for not returning that trust. She expected

Jin, the mind and emotion reader, to call her out for her suspicions, but Jin didn't. Probably out of politeness.

But Jin did ask about the sorest subject of all.

"Why isn't Xiao with you? Is he still busy with the temples?"

Nanami shrugged. "We had a fight. He told me not to come back until I could accept all of him."

"Oh," said Jin. "I thought you had. The drinking—"

"His addiction isn't all of him," Nanami said. "I thought less of you for accepting only his good parts, but it seems I only accepted his bad. When I was looking at his weakness, he didn't seem so far from me. But now, as the God of Love, as both Black and Violet..."

Jin hugged her shoulders. "You are Nanami the Thief, who makes her own rules and challenges everything she disagrees with. Even the most powerful being in the world."

Jin smiled at the last, and Nanami had to suddenly laugh, for indeed, she did challenge Jin, didn't she?

"Well, then, most powerful being, don't you think you should give me back a hand?"

"Oh, of course!" said Jin, and she ran off to fetch Bai.

As Nanami watched Jin's pink skirts flap, she ruminated on that "of course." Some people would ask if Nanami deserved her hand back—she had after all, stolen. Jin probably thought Nanami's thefts were justified, but Nanami herself knew better.

Less than five minutes later, Jin came scurrying back, pulling Bai by the wrist. Bai was not scurrying, but he was walking quickly, allowing Jin to pull him along.

He was also grinning.

Nanami couldn't help but smile at the sight.

Could it possibly not matter how and why Bai had fallen in

love with Jin, just that he had and was happy?

Bai used jasmine blossoms to assemble her bones, and then Jin enveloped them in fire. Nanami bit her lip so hard that it bled—the pain was terrible.

But when the fire faded, there was her hand.

Jin and Bai immediately started a technical discussion, comparing it to the resurrection of Aashchary. They seemed to have forgotten Nanami existed.

She rose and walked away.

"It's lonely, isn't it?"

Nanami turned to find Cheng once again.

She said dryly, "What, you mean the two lovebirds who bring new meaning to the phrase, 'eyes only for each other'?"

He laughed. "Yes. But you have your own lover, so perhaps it's not as bad for you?"

Nanami sighed. She had been thinking it was worse—because she was stupidly staying away from that lover when all she wanted to do was run into his arms.

"I've got to go," she told Cheng.

His eyes widened in surprise, but Nanami didn't wait for his reply.

Twenty minutes later, she found herself once again standing before the massive crescent gates of New Moon Manor. *If I partner Xiao, will I have to live here?* she wondered.

The idea of a stable home, which she had lacked since the justice disciples destroyed her house six millennia ago, was appealing, but New Moon Manor? Nanami shuddered.

Taking a deep breath, she rang the large violet bell.

The black iron gate opened, and a disciple looked at her with wide eyes—she had been recognized. He bowed and begged the "lady" to follow him.

Nanami did so and was led to a back garden where Xiao was practicing his swordsmanship by himself.

He was bare chested with a faint sheen of sweat on his dark tan, and Nanami squeezed her hands together.

Xiao's eyes widened in surprise, and he sheathed his double swords. He approached her quickly, his hands outstretched, but he let them drop before touching her.

"Nanami," he said. "You wish to talk?"

Nanami tried twice to speak before she nodded instead. Wishing and doing were separate things, after all.

XIAO waited for Nanami to say something, anything. But it soon grew obvious that she wouldn't—or couldn't—speak.

"Nanami, can you accept my power or not?"

"I don't know."

Xiao stared at her in disbelief, and then he felt angry. Three weeks, and she had sought *him* out, but her mind was no more settled than it was when they'd parted?

"Then why are you here?"

Nanami hesitated, and Xiao wanted to comfort her, but he held back. "Because I want to. Accept your power, I mean. I've spent the last few weeks observing your worshippers and seeing how their prayers were answered. Sometimes, I understood why they were. One woman prayed for greater patience so that she would not fight so much with her family, and you helped her achieve that. But other times, I couldn't understand. One man asked for his wife to stop flirting with others, and you changed her."

Xiao rubbed his head, trying to follow her objection. "You don't think I should have stopped her flirting? When it was upsetting her husband?"

Nanami shook her head. "Her choice to flirt or not flirt is more important than her husband's feelings."

Xiao knew exactly whom she was talking about. They were a young couple, passionately in love, and for the most part they got along well. But the husband had asked his wife to stop flirting, and she kept protesting that flirting was not the same as infidelity. Xiao knew that, if left unchecked, it would drive a bigger and bigger wedge between them until their happiness turned to misery.

"Why does changing someone bother you so much? People change each other all the time—if people want someone's love, they court them. Mortals dress to please each other, paint their faces, give up their vices or even their families. Why should it matter if the change comes from me or them?"

"Because of choice! If that woman chose to stop flirting to please her husband, that would be one thing. But she didn't! The husband only has a right to change himself, not his wife. You shouldn't change someone who doesn't want it!"

Xiao was shocked. And then ashamed.

"You—you're right. My parents—that is, Zi and Hei—"

He sat down suddenly. Zi and Hei had always changed people to be the best version of themselves—according to Zi and Hei. Xiao had abhorred the way they had controlled and manipulated others, including himself, and yet, in taking over their roles, he had started down the exact same path. He had felt overwhelmed of course, but how could he have made such an obvious mistake?

"I'm sorry, Nanami, I—" He swallowed. "You're right. It's one thing to change someone who asks to be changed, but it's quite another to change someone on someone else's request. Even if it would be to their benefit."

She hugged herself. "Yes. Well, I wasn't expecting you to agree so quickly. You see, the more mortals I observed, the more I felt that sometimes your—well, cheating—to help them be who they wanted wasn't wrong after all. But I cannot accept it when you change someone who doesn't want it—"

Xiao smiled. She was babbling.

He was now sure that she loved him after all. And this was no mountain they had to overcome, just a molehill. He pulled her close and stopped her rambling explanation with a kiss.

A few minutes later they separated.

"You've made me all sweaty," Nanami complained, but she was smirking.

"I wonder what I should do with all the prayers that are for others," Xiao said, not bothering with her complaint. "New procedures—"

Nanami held up a hand. A hand that had been missing that last time he saw her. "I'll take care of them," she said, but that was no longer important.

Xiao seized her hand. "Nanami—your hand."

"Yes. Well. I made up with Jin. She is after all your best friend."

He tried to kiss her again, but she tugged her hand free and tapped him on the nose.

"Don't distract me. For each of your prayer collectors, I want a small one of my own attached. And I will steal prayers that shouldn't reach you. If you'll trust me to steal the right ones, of course."

Xiao started laughing. His thief—some things never changed. "Nanami, I will trust you with everything."

She grinned and this time she didn't stop him when he leaned in for another kiss.

NANAMI stretched out in the silken sheets next to Xiao, then turned to look at him. He was gazing at the ceiling wearing a smirk—there was no other word for such a self-assured smile. She had been braced for a fight, but Xiao was—as trite as it may sound—a lover, not a fighter. And speaking of fights...

"Xiao," she said.

"Mmm."

"I don't want to live in this house. What do you think of making a new one? Maybe near the sea?"

His eyes slanted toward her. "Already asking for bed favors?"

"Well—"

He flipped so that she was pinned beneath him. "Near the sea? A tower on the horizon? I think that could arranged... if you arrange something for me first..."

She inhaled sharply as his hand slid down her body, then did her best to make her eyes sultry. "As my lord wishes," she purred.

He laughed, and then they arranged themselves very favorably indeed.

# TSUKU

## HOME OF THE MOON DEER AND HIS FAMILY

Tsuku was built thirty millenia ago in the shadow of Taitou, the largest mountain in Crescent Moon. It is always full of visitors, who come to share their darkest secrets and stay for the private onsens.

# How Everyone Came Together

NANAMI was almost regretful when Xiao declared he had done enough managing of the temples for now and that he was ready to go to Tsuku. She held her tongue until they arrived outside its wooden gates. Then, even though three of Xiao's disciples were standing behind them, she tugged on Xiao's sleeve. He turned to look at her in surprise.

"Xiao," she confessed, "I haven't been to Tsuku since I was banished from the Sea Palace. They might..."

"They won't," he said confidently. "I'm far more intimidating now than I was three months ago. Besides, you're a goddess now."

Nanami poked him. "We agreed not to use the term

'goddess'."

"Ah, right, an-immortal-with-prayer-collectors." He turned to face her, and his hands settled on her arms. Very quietly, he said, "I know you aren't afraid of what they might do and say so much as how it will make you feel. I can go alone if you would prefer."

And there it was. The offer she had been wanting, and yet now that it had been made, she would despise herself for accepting it. "No," she said. "It's just—did we have to come so early?"

"I've never been here. I want to understand the dynamics before the confrontation."

"But I have been here," she protested. He tilted his head in challenge.

"Ten millennia ago," she acknowledged. She leaned forward. "Xiao—it was Aunt Atsuko's hair stick that I stole before I was disowned. Aunt Atsuko is grandfather's hostess. She runs Tsuku."

He said nothing, and finally Nanami stuck her tongue out at him. She said, "Fine, let's go."

Xiao knocked on the door.

Atsuko herself opened it.

She bowed and Xiao, Nanami, and the three love disciples mirrored her.

"Welcome to Tsuku, divinity. I am Atsuko, the eldest daughter of the Moon Deer."

"Lady Atsuko," said Nanami, worrying that Xiao might offend her aunt with his casual manners, "might I introduce Xiao, the God of Love?"

She was certain that Atsuko knew exactly who Xiao was,

but Atsuko liked things to be stated properly.

"A pleasure, divinity." And she turned to Nanami and held out her arms. "And niece, is not a hug more appropriate between family members?"

Nanami froze in surprise. Family?

She might have stayed there, ignoring Atsuko's outstretched arms if Xiao hadn't pushed her into them.

Atsuko released her from the hug after a few moments but kept a grip on her forearms. "You've stayed away too long," she scolded Nanami. "We have missed you. Father will be particularly pleased to see you—it is too hard for him to leave the house nowadays, so visitors must come here."

Her grandfather, the Moon Deer, had gone into a decline after his second daughter and her son died. To hear that he no longer travelled at all though—

"Yes, please, I would love to see him." She blinked twice, refusing to cry, and glanced at Xiao over her shoulder.

He was smiling, and Nanami realized her aunt really had hugged her. Called her family.

A warmth filled her chest, and their party entered Tsuku.

Atsuko invited them to take tea with the family, and that warmth from earlier began to spread, even when her cousins threw her jealous looks after learning she was partnered with Xiao. Nanami couldn't help but smile smugly. Yes, she, Nanami, the plain one, the embarrassment, the *Thief*, had stolen the heart of the God of Love, the most powerful being in the world. Well, the second or maybe third most powerful. He was a big deal at any rate, and he had chosen her.

Xiao was obviously aware of her pride and amused by it. He kept making excuses to touch her—he tucked her hair behind her ear, his fingers grazed her knuckles, and when her cousins sighed longingly, he winked at Nanami. Her grandfather wasn't there, but when tea finished, Atsuko invited them to come see him.

"Xiao," she whispered as they followed her aunt down the outer walkway that encircled Tsuku, "My grandfather collects secrets. Many of them bring him sorrow, but if you can tell him a happy one, he will consider it a great gift."

Xiao's face became thoughtful.

When they entered the room, Nanami was a bit overwhelmed by the smell of camphor. The windows had been opened to let the autumn breeze freshen the air, but it was obvious to her that the source of the scent was her grandfather.

He was swaddled almost like a baby, and his skin glistened with the oil. His face was dominated by his wet brown eyes, and his head bobbed on a too thin neck.

"Nanami," he said in a whistling voice that was not the one she remembered, "come close, child, and introduce me to your friend."

Nanami wasn't quite sure what she said, but it must have been appropriate because Aunt Atsuko nodded in approval, and the Moon Deer took Xiao's hand in greeting.

Xiao leaned forward and whispered at length in the Moon Deer's ear. The old man's eyes grew even rounder, and he shook—Nanami was alarmed until she realized he was laughing.

"What did you tell him?" she whispered to Xiao when he returned to her side.

Xiao placed a hand over his heart in dismay. "My love, you aren't asking for me to break confidence and share the secret with you?"

"I—" she looked at the Moon Deer and then back to Xiao. "No—" and she felt heat wash up her neck and over her cheeks.

The Moon Deer laughed harder. "You chose well, Nanami. I always told Ao that you were the cleverest of his children."

Nanami flushed. "Grandfather—do you not know? I have been disowned."

"Pshaw! As if I need my son-in-law to tell me who my grandchildren are! I don't care what that stubborn dragon says, I listen to my heart." And he clapped his chest. Even though she blinked hard and fast, this time a few tears escaped.

The next two hours—constrained by the fact that the Moon Deer needed to rest again—were full of healing and joy and family. And Nanami was certain that Xiao liked the Moon Deer as well as the Moon Deer liked him. Not that she doubted he would, for Xiao liked almost everyone.

When they left, Nanami found she was practically bouncing with excitement. "Xiao, I'm so glad you brought me here."

"Don't forget this isn't a reunion," said a stern voice ahead of them.

Surprised, Nanami turned to find Salaana and Ichimi standing in the rock garden.

Some of her happiness dimmed. She had, for a moment, forgotten they were here to witness the confrontation between Jin and Salaana.

"Though anyone can see you aren't in mourning," Salaana went on, glaring at Xiao.

Ichimi wrapped a hand around her wife's arm, and Nanami fancied she could see Salaana's hackles settle.

"Divinity, welcome to Tsuku," chimed in Atsuko, stepping

out from behind Nanami and Xiao. "Please, might I remind everyone that we encourage peaceful discussion and that we will wait to have it until all interested parties arrive?"

"My apologies, Lady Atsuko," said Salaana with an inclination of her head, "I spoke thoughtlessly."

Lady Atsuko bowed, accepting Salaana's apology, and offered to show them to their rooms.

BY the time evening fell over Tsuku, Xiao was feeling rather nervous. It turned out that Salaana had brought all one hundred and forty of her disciples—they camped outside of Tsuku's gates. Guleum and his mother had also come and barely acknowledged Xiao at all. Within an hour after that, Ao and Miko arrived. Xiao supposed he had to be grateful that they didn't bring their eleven other children along with them to make Nanami miserable. They were coldly polite to Xiao and Nanami, treating them like strangers, and Lady Atsuko diplomatically arranged things so that they were as far apart at dinner as possible. Karana arrived halfway through the meal and greeted everyone as if they were gathered for an ordinary dinner, ignoring Salaana's glares when he stopped by Xiao.

"Xiao," he muttered, "have you seen Jin? Do—"

Xiao shook his head to the first question, and Karana abruptly muttered, "Never mind," and moved on.

Nanami squeezed his hand under the table, and Xiao realized his three disciples were all watching him expectantly. He wished Dawa were among them, but it had seemed wise for Dawa to manage everything at home.

He gave them a reassuring smile, but that night, Xiao

cuddled Nanami close and woke her twice with his restlessness.

"Shh," she told him, and rubbed his arm though she was still half asleep. "It will work out."

Xiao kissed the top of her head.

He must have eventually drifted off, for a dawn summoning woke him. He sat up carefully, so as not to disturb Nanami.

Of course, millennia of living riskily had made her a light sleeper, and she immediately opened her eyes. Those indigo depths sharpened with awareness.

"Everything alright?" she asked.

"Yes," Xiao said and kissed her forehead. "Go back to sleep. I should be back when you wake again."

Nanami had stayed up late talking to her cousins; Xiao knew she would sleep until noon if nothing disturbed her. She nodded and curled back into a ball. Unlike him, she wasn't worried about Jin's confrontation. She had told Xiao over and over that there was nothing Jin couldn't do.

Before following Jin's summons, Xiao slipped from his room and left Tsuku's grounds—he could have broken the Moon Deer's teleportation ban, but he saw no reason to be rude. He didn't think about where he would end up until he came out of between ten minutes later.

Angry and bitter, the ruins of the Sun Pagoda stabbed at the sky. Since the palace drifted somewhere above Zhongtu, dawn had yet to reach it, and the only light came from a bonfire. The dark didn't impede Xiao's vision though, and besides the ruined pagoda, he could see nothing but charred debris within the once red walls of Aka's inner sanctum. The most ornate garden that Xiao had ever seen, two large halls, and a towering pagoda, all reduced to ash. This was the destruction of the immortal creatures—mainly the Golden Phoenix, Xiao had heard. He shuddered, and turned to Jin.

She stood before the bonfire, her hands clasped demurely, and her face set with sorrow. Now that he acknowledged her, she stepped forward. She was no longer the wild woman that Xiao had found in his parent's home, though she was once again wearing her iridescent armor, which shimmered like oil in the wavering firelight. Nor was she the girl to whom he had been betrothed, though her hair once again fell from the crown of her head in a thick braid. She was a stranger who had murdered his parents, who had collected the lives of her grandparents to perform the first resurrection, and yet—she was also his best friend. The person who burned her fingers by trying to eat sweet potatoes before they cooled, who had blown on his when he did the same.

She visibly hesitated a moment before catching Xiao's hands.

"Thank you for coming," she said. "I wanted to talk, just the two of us."

Xiao had intended to greet her, but instead he blurted, "Is NeeNee really gone?"

Jin's lashes lowered to her cheeks, and she gave a jerky nod. "Yes. I'm sorry, Xiao." She cleared her throat. "I have a lot to apologize for. Your parents—"

Xiao pulled her into a hug, and her forehead bumped his chest. "Jin, don't apologize for that. They—"

"I know," she murmured. "I saw you, when I was in the Underworld."

He pulled back just enough to peer into her face. "What do you mean?"

Her lashes swept up, so that their eyes met, and Xiao saw hers had changed. Oh, they were still gold, but...actually, they reminded him of Bai's. A bit intimidating, even though she was looking at him gently.

Jin said, "You summoned me, right?"

He nodded.

"I couldn't teleport to you, but I had waking dreams of you. I saw what they were doing to you. That was why I came here as soon as I could. And then—" Big tears leaked  out of the corners of her eyes, and Xiao guffawed.

"Always a crybaby."

She wrenched herself free from his hands and stuck out her tongue, and Xiao felt even more confident that she was still his Jin at heart.

"It's worth crying over! Why does everyone give me a hard time for crying?"

Xiao held up his hands. "Okay, okay, it's fine, you can always cry with me."

She snorted and wiped at her eyes with the back of her hand. "I was a bad friend. I didn't even know—I thought you were just whining, all the times you hinted at... I'm so sorry about that. But I also know that I shouldn't have murdered Zi and Hei. I—I wanted to stop them, to punish them, and I was too tired to think..." She shook her head. "I don't mean to make excuses. I just want to make it up to you, if that's possible. Otherwise... Otherwise, I don't think I'll have the courage to face Salaana today."

Xiao felt like he'd been punched in the gut. "What's that supposed to mean?"

"She says that I'm dangerous. That I cannot be trusted. She

wants to execute me, for the crime of killing your parents."

"And you think that she has a point."

"Doesn't she?"

Xiao shook her shoulders. "Doesn't Bai have something to say about this idiocy?"

Jin crossed her arms. "I'm not suicidal. It's just, I should be punished in some way."

"And so you want me to punish you. To set you some penance that will bring you absolution." Xiao shook his head. "I can't do that." His feelings about Zi and Hei's death were complicated, but mostly he wanted to forget about it. And he certainly wasn't mad at Jin. He was grateful to her—grateful that she had done the thing he would never have been able to bring himself to do, grateful that she carried the burden of their deaths.

Jin's pale face turned deathly white. "But you must!" she wailed. "Now that Papa and NeeNee are dead—" She swallowed. "Who can—judge me? Tell me if I was right or wrong? Bai is too biased—I know that. He would forgive me anything. But you—they were your parents..."

Again Xiao shook his head, more fiercely this time. Once he would have denied Jin nothing, but no more. This weight was too much for his heart, and he would no longer take on whatever others asked of him. He was still shaking his head, when a new voice spoke, soft and gentle and wholly terrifying.

"My dear child, if it is judgment you seek, why not come to me, the arbiter of justice?"

BAI slid his arm across the bed, but when no warm body met

his hand, he opened his eyes. The room was dark, vague shadows and rough shapes and nothing obviously Jin-shaped. He sat up and collected starlight in his hand so that it glowed softly.

The room was empty except for him. Probably Jin couldn't sleep as tomorrow was the scheduled meeting with Salaana. Bai knew that Jin was perfectly capable of facing down her aunt, of course—she could probably face down *him*, if she were so inclined—but he also knew that she still felt guilty about killing Zi and Hei.

There was a part of her that, despite all of Bai and Cheng's reassurances, wanted to submit to Salaana's justice. He slipped out of bed to look for her, but he soon realized she was gone.

Bai touched his new bracelet around his wrist, braided of Jin's hair. He could follow it to her.

He wanted to do just that, yet he held back. She must be seeking solitude, something Bai could hardly begrudge anyone. As the moments passed though, the temptation to follow grew. Bai hesitated, then went to wake up Cheng. Either he would help Bai find the patience to wait or insist they go immediately and Bai wouldn't be the only one ignoring Jin's wishes.

JIN had never seen Salaana like this. Instead of her hair towering on her head, it hung loose down her back, a tendril cupping Salaana's cheek and softening it. Her usual red and white sari had been replaced by an indigo kimono, tied loosely around her waist, as if Salaana had been sleeping naked and had just slipped on the robe.

She must have set a ward or something that Jin had

triggered by entering the ruins of the Sun Palace. How long had she been here, listening to Xiao and Jin's conversation?

Salaana took two steps forward, and she brought her hands to Jin's cheeks, cradling them with all the tenderness of a mother. Uncomfortably, Jin remembered the last time Salaana had touched her cheek—it had been a slap because Jin had dared to ask for an extra cookie.

Salaana was a like a different person now though, and some part of Jin realized that she was seeing Karana's sister rather than Aka's daughter, the Goddess of Justice. Karana had always told Jin that Salaana was very kind to him, and Jin saw Salaana's capacity for love for the first time.

*But why?* Jin wondered, a little afraid. *Why would Salaana give me kindness? She has never liked me. That's why she was so ready to lock me in the Underworld. It wasn't an impulse, but a long awaited desire.*

If Bai were here, he would surely encourage Jin to follow through with their plan. After all, he had pointed out that if Salaana struck Jin with lightning even once, it might be fatal, for Jin was a quarter flower. He and Cheng had told her to act quickly, decisively, to demonstrate her sheer power to everyone at Tsuku so that no one would dare challenge her.

But they weren't at Tsuku, and Salaana wasn't offering a challenge. Instead, she was offering... Forgiveness? A path to redemption that Xiao had denied her?

Jin had never heard of Salaana doing such before. Her justice was known to be swift and merciless. But—perhaps Karana had softened her? Perhaps Salaana had felt the death of Aka and regretted his passing? Perhaps she wanted to help Jin, to be a sister—or an aunt—at last?

Maybe Jin was not so abandoned by her family as she thought.

More tears welled  at this thought, and Salaana wiped them from Jin's cheeks with a tenderness Jin had only ever felt in Aashchary's memories.

"Jin?" said Xiao, his voice wavering. He had always been frightened of Salaana, and he clearly didn't trust her now. But even with all that she had learned in the past year, with all that she had seen and done, Jin still believed in kindness and second chances and love.

Maybe Salaana really could absolve her of this guilt.

When Jin ignored him, Xiao grabbed her hand and tried to teleport, but it was nothing to stay exactly where she was. Xiao might have the power of two Colors, but Jin had more. And she had as many worshippers, having inherited all of Gang's and most of Aka's.

This past month, she had followed Bai and Cheng's directions, travelling to the war temples, speaking with Gang's monks. And today, after imprisoning Salaana, she would go to the sun temples and claim them as well.

Or so she had told Bai and Cheng.

But this morning she had slipped out of the mountain and come here, to the home she had ruined by freeing the immortal creatures, to seek the right to live from Xiao.

He had been unable to give it to her, and now Salaana was here. Maybe Jin didn't need to imprison her after all. Maybe there was a better way.

Jin didn't want to forget her mistakes. She had always lived her life as honestly and directly as possible. If Salaana set a price for Jin's sins, then she would pay it.

"Tell me about the past few months, Jin," Salaana's voice was chai tea. Warm and sweet and soothing. "Tell me everything that has happened since Papa collapsed."

And then Jin was talking. She explained how Haraa had diagnosed the death curse, and she had set off to fetch the black peony. How she soon learned that Gang cuckolded Aka, and that Neela had trapped Cheng in solid stone for crime of being Aashchary's father. How the immortal creatures had terrified her, and yet their suffering led her to free them. How she had met Aashchary and Noran in the Underworld, and how Aka had caused so much suffering through his selfishness. Salaana listened intently, kindly, eventually holding Jin against her bosom, and Jin almost forgot that Xiao was still there.

Jin described how she and Gang had sliced up the Korikami, inflicting a fate far worse than millennia in the Underworld. How she had to do it, because she had to get to Xiao.

How Zi and Hei had been torturing him. How she had failed him.

And then that awful moment when she realized that she had killed Zi, had ended her life in seconds. Followed by Hei's challenge, before she could stop and think, and she had to kill him as well. Or die.

She didn't want to die. She wanted to marry Bai.

"But Jin," said Salaana, her voice still so soft, so gentle and loving, "Do you deserve that? Should you be allowed to live when you have caused so much destruction?"

Salaana gestured to the ashes around them, now clearly visible, for the sun had reached them while Jin poured her heart out to Salaana.

"You had to stop the Korikami," she told Jin, "but who was

here to stop the Phoenix? The Nisei and the Dalagois? Do you know, twenty immortals were killed when the palace was attacked."

"That's not Jin's fault!" objected Xiao.

"Whose fault is it, then?" asked Salaana.

She tipped Jin's face toward hers, their eyes meeting. And Jin was shocked to see death in those eyes.

Oh, not imminently. Jin had thought Salaana didn't intend to kill her because she hadn't attacked, because she had shown patience, but Jin now read Salaana's thoughts.

Salaana didn't want to murder Jin. She wanted to execute her publicly. She wanted Jin to kneel before her at Tsuku and beg for release. If she killed Jin, she would establish her dominion over all immortals. She was reading Jin's emotions, feeding in to them, to gain power over Jin.

"You don't care about me," Jin said in shock. "You care about yourself. Your justice is twisted and ugly because it is self-serving."

And that's when Jin realized that there was only one person who could absolve her. One person who could judge her actions and decide on an appropriate penance.

And that person was Jin.

All the beings that she'd spent her life trying to please had abandoned her, and Jin had spent the last several months fixing problems created by their poor judgment. So now it was time to trust her own.

She pulled away from Salaana and declared, "You must choose, Salaana. You may vow your fealty to me and swear not to threaten my life again, or I will lock you away until you are ready to do so."

XIAO wasn't sure who was more shocked, Salaana or himself. Salaana recovered first though, and her patently false compassion transformed to cold fury before Xiao's eyes. And just as when Nanami lost her hand, Xiao knew what was coming next, but he couldn't move fast enough.

Lightning arced from Salaana's fingertips.

But it did not go toward Jin—instead, it bent backward, harmlessly discharging in the ground behind Salaana.

Bai stepped forward, standing at Jin's side.

"When did you...?" Xiao asked.

"We got here an hour ago," muttered a voice at Xiao's shoulder—Bai didn't even seem to register Xiao's question. Xiao twisted his neck and found Jin's newly-discovered grandfather—Cheng, he was pretty sure. The orange-haired man went on, "I don't think the three of you would have noticed if a tornado had passed through here."

Xiao nodded, a bit awkwardly, before turning back to the unfolding drama.

Salaana's face was bloodless—she was more scared of Bai than of Jin.

Probably because, despite her power, Jin did stupid things like crying on the shoulder of someone who wanted her dead.

But Salaana was also proud, and she said now, "How dare you imprison *me*?"

"I dare because I can. Now, will you vow your fealty?"

"I would never swear to such as you," snarled Salaana. "You are already worse than Aka ever was. You think power alone gives you the right to rule?"

"Power alone gives me the responsibility of ruling," Jin

corrected her. Jin glanced at Bai, and her expression softened minutely. "Gives us the responsibility. Because of our power, we had to take over the Sun Guard after Gang's—" she hesitated briefly, before saying, "death. Bai has organized sweeps to control the creatures, just as it was he who helped the immortals trapped at the Sun Palace. You never instructed the Light Hands to help."

Salaana hissed. "It wasn't my responsibility—I didn't free the creatures!"

Jin shrugged. "If you wanted to rule, you should have done something about it. Instead, you fixated on me and your own petty desires. That's why it's now my responsibility to imprison you."

Salaana was engulfed in fire, but mere moments later, the flames turned to the iridescent metal that Xiao now considered Jin's trademark. She was caged. She attempted lightning again—pointlessly, with Bai here, but, to Xiao's surprise, Bai didn't seem to intervene. Instead, the lightning fizzled at the bars themselves.

"Your essence is trapped inside the cage," Bai told her. "Neither you nor your power can escape it now."

Jin turned to Bai, setting a hand on his arm. "To Tsuku?" she asked.

Bai nodded.

Xiao was prepared to teleport with them, but Jin pulled him between, will-he-nill-he, her power seemingly infinite.

They appeared moments—no, it couldn't have been that fast, could it have?—later at the gate of Tsuku. Xiao was momentarily confused—he couldn't see Salaana or the massive cage Jin had made. Had Jin left her in the ruins?

Cheng elbowed Xiao's side and pointed up. Following his finger, Xiao found Salaana's cage twenty feet above their heads, slowly rotating.

JIN was not as calm as she was pretending. She had practiced for this, yes. Bai and Cheng had drilled her all week, teaching her to move objects with her will alone, to split her magic in many directions at once. There was enough of it to split it a million different ways, if only she could manage her own will.

But despite her power, despite the fact that she was following through with the plan that the three of them had made, Jin was scared.

That was her *aunt* up there in that cage. When everyone saw, would they accept Jin's dictates? Or would they view her as crazy? The villain who had unleashed the immortal creatures on them?

And so, even though they had agreed that this was Jin's task, to prove herself to the other immortals, Jin was glad that Bai was at her side.

She turned to him now and murmured, "Thanks for taking care of the lightning. I forgot to watch for it."

Bai looked quite fierce. "You should have summoned me."

Jin smiled slightly. "But you were already there, anyway!"

He huffed, but then grinned. "And I always will be."

NANAMI'S sleep was once again disturbed, this time by cries of shock. She stretched on the futon, a bit befuddled, as she remembered Xiao leaving in the early twilight. He'd said that he'd be back before she woke—it seemed like a bad sign that he wasn't.

Nanami flew out of bed and quickly checked her clothes, before tearing out of her room. In general, people walked around Tsuku with deliberation, but whatever was upsetting everybody meant no one cared about her lack of decorum.

And Nanami saw the cause of the hubbub soon enough—floating high above the gate of Tsuku was a cage. First Nanami recognized the metal—*please tell me that Jin didn't bleed for this one!*—and then she recognized Salaana, inside. Had the confrontation already happened then, and Nanami had slept through it? Well, how embarrassing. She hurried out the gate, just as everyone else was doing, and for one tense moment, she realized that the shoulders bumping hers belonged to the Sea Dragon.

He refused to look at her, even though six other bodies were pushing them together, and the next moment, they popped out the other side. Nanami saw Jin and Bai, holding hands and looking as cloyingly in love as when she had seen them at the White Mountain. Behind them were Cheng and Xiao. To either side of them were two armies—one in indigo and one in red. The Light Hands and the Sea Dragon's entourage. Cheng, Bai, and Jin were all ignoring these minor immortals, but Xiao was eying them uneasily. Indeed, he looked a little out of place. Nanami hurried to his side, leaving the crowd lined up just outside Tsuku's gate.

She caught Xiao's hand, and he smiled at her. Their side might be the few, but it was definitely the one that would take the day.

Nanami flinched at the thought. Was this it then? The

immortal war that had been brewing? Nanami glanced up at that cage once again. Wasn't the war already over?

And then Jin claimed everyone's attention, declaring, "One month ago, I destroyed the gate that kept the Underworld separate from Earth and killed the Moon Goddess and the Night God. A week later, I resurrected my mother through the voluntary sacrifice of the Wanderer and the Sun God."

The crowd began to murmur, and Nanami knew that even this crowd, which was accustomed to miraculous workings, was having trouble believing Jin's claims. Jin spoke again, and the crowd quieted, unwilling to miss her words. "My aunt believes I should be punished for these acts. Anyone who wishes to may now try."

XIAO was grateful for Nanami at his side, but he could tell that even she was mildly horrified by Jin's declaration. He scanned the crowd and saw that Jin had set herself apart from them. Like Bai always had—this was probably his idea, fate mock him. Bai was shockingly stupid when it came to people.

Ao stepped forward from the crowd, and his soldiers all tensed. They were ready to throw their lives away for their master, and Ao was furious.

So Xiao stepped forward and gave Ao his best smirk, the one with both dimples. As Xiao intended, Ao remembered their fight. He fell back into the crowd. "Jin, love, why does your family make everything about them? Yeah, I get it, people want to know that the Sun Emperor has stepped down, but come on, do you have to make it sound so dramatic? You're managing the temples, Bai's got the guard dealing with the creatures—I heard the Bandoans have already welcomed the Phoenix home. Seems to me that everything is finally settling down. Isn't that right, Karana?"

That was a gamble. Karana was standing at the back of the crowd looking like he'd eat dirt before getting involved. But fate smiled, and so did Karana.

He stepped forward, and everyone made space for him. Remembering the burning of Xiling, no doubt.

"You were always a good judge of character, Xiao. I'm afraid my family is addicted to drama. Just look at me." And he plied a massive black fan made of crow feathers beneath his kohl-lined eyes. He then asked Jin, "So where are you putting this rather large cage?"

"In the Heavens," she said. "I'm going to build a house for her, but she won't be able to leave it. You'll be able to visit her—in fifty years or so." Jin blushed and snapped her mouth shut.

But Xiao was glad she babbled. It had reminded everyone that she was a person, and one that had only had her adulthood ceremony a thousand years earlier. She didn't look like a big, bad goddess anymore, but a young woman who was trying very hard to make the best of an unfortunate situation.

Karana sighed languorously. "Seems like the best option. Given that she wanted to kill you and all. Carry on."

Jin nodded, clearly a little in shock.

"Wait!" cried a voice. Ichimi. Xiao scowled at her, wondering if she were about to destroy the atmosphere he'd contrived.

But Ichimi said only, "May I go with her?"

Oh-ho! Bet Salaana didn't like that tone of voice. Xiao

looked up to see Salaana seethe silently—well, but she'd been seething—as Jin said, "Oh, yes, of course. I'm sorry I didn't offer earlier."

She turned to the Light Hands. "And any of you as well, if you wish."

Xiao saw Karana's lips twitch. He looked at Nanami, who was also now more amused than anything. Seeing him looking at her, his thief winked.

Of course, Jin's cuteness was tempered by the fact that she engulfed the volunteers in more fire to make cages for them before flying said cages up to Salaana's and merging them all. Well, no one had ever accused Jin of guile, and Xiao doubted they ever would.

A few hours later, Xiao was still doing damage control. Jin had sent Salaana's cage off to the Heavens and had probably already changed it into a gorgeous manor, given her abstraction during dinner. Xiao meanwhile was working the crowd to Nanami's obvious bemusement.

"Don't think you'll get credit with me for pleasing my family," she told him dryly. "I know this is on Jin's behalf."

"Can't it be both?" Xiao had protested, with a quick kiss to the ear.

She had smiled.

In the end, it was Karana who did them the most good, by asking Bai, very publicly, "So what are your intentions toward my niece?"

"It would be better to ask her intentions toward me," said Bai. "As I will follow the Threefold Goddess's wishes."

"I'm going to marry him, of course." Jin blushed. Xiao was sure that three of the Moon Deer's granddaughters would have killed her, if it hadn't been already been established to be a dreadful idea.

"We could make it a double wedding," Xiao suggested, thinking everyone would laugh.

Jin took him seriously though. "Only if you let me plan it. I have a lot of ideas, and I want it to be just so."

Xiao smirked. "I've never had any ambition to plan a wedding. What about you?" he asked Nanami.

Nanami arched a brow.

"Now you're in trouble," muttered one of the Moon Deer's granddaughters. "You can't ask a question like that in public."

Nanami threw a glare at the cousin, then said, "I suppose, since you rebuilt my hand, I'll let you plan the wedding as a reward."

Jin laughed, "A fair trade."

# The Colors of Joy



JIN was grateful for Bai's hand in hers. It felt as strong and capable as always, a source of warmth and support. She turned to look at him and saw compassion and worry in his eyes.

"It doesn't have to be today," he said.

"I'm okay," she told him. "I'm ready."

Over the past year, the two of them had converted all the sun temples to threefold temples, they had established refuges across Earth from immortal creatures, and they had established laws for immortal beings. There was more to do of course—Bai was talking about an academy for immortals and organized immortal patrols of Earth—but that could wait until tomorrow.

Because today Jin had at last come to visit her mother, father, and baby brother.

The three of them had settled along the Kuanbai, in the foothills of the Great Ladies, so close to Jin and Bai's own home on the White Mountain and yet so far away in terms of power. The house was a small one, not much bigger than the blue caravan that sat in the yard. There were two horses in a paddock with a small barn. They must have been for the caravan, since Gang and Aashchary couldn't move it with their wills as Neela had. There were chickens in the paddock, looking for insects to eat, and this was clearly a common occurrence, for the horses ignored them.

It looked simple to Jin, but she knew they must be fairly wealthy by mortal standards.

There was singing coming from behind the house. Jin followed the sound, tugging Bai along beside her, and found Aashchary stirring a large iron pot over a stone stove. The baby was cooing on her back, trying to sing along with his mother.

Jin waited patiently for Aashchary to notice her.

When she did, she curtseyed, "Oh, hello! Can I help you, my lady and my lord?"

Jin was shocked. She looked at Bai; there was a faint frown on his brow, and he was studying Aashchary as if she were a fascinating puzzle.

Jin turned back to her mother.

"We were passing through and smelled whatever you're cooking."

Aashchary looked doubtful and perhaps even nervous. Jin took a step closer to the pot and realized her mistake. Aashchary wasn't cooking food but dying clothes. Its scent wasn't unpleasant, but it wasn't exactly appetizing either.

She floundered for a way to salvage the situation, and ended up blurting, "You don't recognize me, do you?"

Aashchary bit her lip nervously. "I'm sorry, my lady. Did my husband work for you? He won't be home for a day, for he is escorting an official to the next town over. The Dushtbandar have been increasingly bold of late—you're lucky if they didn't bother you."

"Ah, is that so." Jin swallowed. Bai would surely explain in detail later, but Jin could tell what had happened. A year of mortality had taken Aashchary's memories of her former life. Was Gang the same? "Well," she said with false brightness, "I'm sorry to have bothered you."

"Do you want to leave a message for my husband?"

"No, no, that's alright."

*It's better they forgot,* Jin decided. *They must be happier this way.*

Aashchary bobbed her head awkwardly.

"Have a good day," Jin mumbled and led Bai away.

At the yard's edge, she checked the teleportation ban that she had placed around the house when Gang and Aashchary had first settled here. It was fine; no one immortal could break it.

The two of them stepped past it, into the woods. When Jin was sure they were out of sight of the house, she said to Bai, "Let's go."

"Jin—"

She leaned forward and kissed him on the cheek. "Let's talk at home."

WHEN Bai woke the next morning, Jin was not lying beside

him. He felt briefly worried, but he heard her moving around the common room.

When he entered though, she wasn't alone. She must have summoned Cheng. The two of them were using a long string to measure the room, and Jin kept calling numbers.

"What's going on?" he asked, a little bewildered.

"You said I could paint the walls," Jin reminded him.

"Yes." He looked out the window he had added at Jin's request and saw that it was barely past dawn. "Now?"

"Mmm. There's a few weeks before any mortal festivals, so this is a good time."

Bai looked at Cheng. He was grinning.

Bai said, "A good time indeed. I'll make some breakfast."

"That would be wonderful!" agreed Jin, and she continued to take measurements.

*9 years later*

WHEN Nanami had agreed to let Jin plan her wedding, she hadn't expected it to take ten years, but she had to admit that these glorious wedding robes were worth the wait. The outer robe just reached her ankles, and its skirts were split, making it as easy to move in as her breeches and tunics, yet it was luxurious silver silk. Every inch of it held twining vines of indigo, black, and violet thread, and Nanami knew that Jin had sewn these stitches herself without the use of magic.

There was something rather special about receiving a gift from the most powerful being in the world that had taken that amount of time to make. In some ways, it felt like a better present than the hand with which she adjusted it.

"Well? Do you like it?" Nanami looked up at those shining gold eyes. If it were Xiao, she would have teased him by acting blasé, but Jin was too earnest for that.

"Yes. It's perfect."

Jin smiled and hugged her.

She pulled back after a moment, though she kept a grip on Nanami's hands. "Nanami, I did want to see you in the robes, but there was another reason I called on you today."

Nanami arched a brow.

"You don't trust me. Not fully."

Nanami stiffened. "I—"

"No, don't deny it. I feel it. I know it would upset Xiao, which is why I wanted to talk with you alone."

Nanami felt nervous. Was this the moment that she found whether or not her tidal pool of magic could withstand the influence of Jin's oceans?

"I'm not going to magic you. I want to say, it's okay. I'm grateful."

Well, that was unexpected. "You are grateful that I don't trust you?"

"I don't trust myself fully sometimes. Do you know, I took the lives of three murderers yesterday to resurrect the family they killed? I didn't even hesitate when the prayer came. There was a time that taking a life was devastating to me, but now..." She shrugged. "Sometimes I worry about Salaana's predictions, that I can't be trusted simply because of the amount of power I have. That I shouldn't be in this world. And so I'm glad there is someone close to me who remains just a little suspicious of my judgment.

"Nanami, I want you to tell me if you ever disagree with what I do."

*And if you don't like hearing it?*

Jin smiled sadly, and Nanami knew she had heard her thought. Jin raised her hand. "I vow to never retaliate or punish Nanami the Thief for any criticism she makes of me, my magic, or my deeds. I vow to grant her immunity from me and my disciples."

"Well," said Nanami. "I'll keep that in mind."

And then Jin took out her wedding robes to show Nanami.

"Fate laughs, Jin, are you determined to have every color in the world at this ceremony?"

XIAO stood about a hundred paces to the left side of the Great Hall, the central feature of the immortal meeting ground that he and Jin had built in the Heavens. Jin had been unwilling to rebuild the Sun Palace, even though she continued to suspend its ruins in the Heavens. She said they served as a warning to those who would imprison others for power. Of course, most beings misunderstood, thinking them a monument to *her* power, but Xiao knew her intentions were pure.

He also knew some of her reluctance to rebuild was because of how deeply her family had hurt her. Xiao tried to say as much, but Jin had waved him off, saying she had no right to complain, since they had been kinder to her than his had been to him.

Xiao knew that wasn't quite true. His parents had obviously abused him, but the more subtle neglect Jin had experienced her whole life, culminating in the way they had abandoned her in her hour of greatest need had been damaging. He was glad that Bai seemed to not only tolerate Jin's clinginess but actually like it. Xiao still couldn't understand Bai as well as most beings, but he trusted him wholeheartedly. Bai and Jin seemed to understand each other better than anyone else he had ever met. Xiao thought it all seemed a bit boring—there must never be a surprise in their relationship—but he could tell it was right for them. Nanami had been surprised by the two of them living in Bai's mountain home instead of a new magical site, but Xiao hadn't been.

In fact, when Xiao told Jin that they needed to build this divine hall five years ago, she had been reluctant, asking, "Isn't it unnecessarily pretentious?"

Xiao had wondered if she was quoting Bai consciously or if they were merging their thoughts after five years as constant companions. "The immortals need a place to meet, Jin. A new Godsmarket, maybe a theatre, a petition hall. Don't tell me you enjoy that mile long line up the White Mountain."

It was the line that convinced Jin to agree, and they had built this place from the most glorious sunset that Xiao could remember.

Despite her initial reluctance, it was gorgeous. Wider than the Sun Palace, it was mostly gardens. In fact, between the ponds and the wisteria, it reminded Xiao of Jin's old residence, though Bai had made all the buildings. Jin had said the white was a perfect canvas and filled the walls with paintings of immortal beings and creatures getting along. Blatant propaganda, of course, but pretty all the same.

And today they would be holding their wedding ceremonies here.

"I always thought you were a being who understood the benefits of polyamory," came a voice at his side, "but I hear you won't accept a lover besides Nanami."

"Not unless she accepts them too," Xiao said, turning to greet Karana. "Is Gu coming?"

Karana shook his head. "I don't think Jin should let him visit Salaana."

"You're not alone there, but Jin gets oddly stubborn about certain things." Jin had originally said she wouldn't let anyone visit Salaana for a few decades, but she had relented within a year. Between the manor she had built and the constant stream of people in and out, Xiao thought it was hardly a prison.

Except that Salaana couldn't leave of course, and neither could her power. Xiao still didn't understand exactly how they accomplished that last, but he knew it was something that Bai had bent his will around.

"Gu always said all he wanted was to free his mother," Xiao went on, "but that can't be true given how angry he is."

"He's prone to anger these days, and Salaana feeds it." Karana shook his head. "Enough of that. It's your wedding day. You're disgustingly happy."

Xiao smiled. "You might try falling in love, you know—a little happiness would do wonders for your complexion."

"Brat. Where's Jin?"

"Each of us is waiting in a different cardinal direction." Xiao spread his arms. "She made this. What do you think?"

Karana stepped back and swept his eyes critically over him. "How come it's not purple and black?"

"The same reason you wear black—because I like blue better."

"Do you miss Neela?"

Xiao flinched. He looked up at the sky. "What are you trying to do, make me late to my wedding? You're supposed to be seated already."

Karana patted him on the shoulder and strode toward the hall, the same path that Xiao would follow in a moment. Xiao took a steadying breath, pushing aside the past and looking toward the future.

Just a few minutes later, the music of a guzheng signaled Bai's entrance. It sounded good to Xiao; he hoped for the musician's sake it pleased the far more particular Bai.

BAI entered the hall slowly. It was very full, possibly a thousand immortals. And of course, a great deal of space was taken up by the Great Tiger who looked like he was contemplating a snack in the form of the other guests. And since Cheng was the only immortal willing to sit within ten feet of the tiger, there was a lot of wasted room as well.

The last time he had seen such a big crowd was for Zi and Hei's wedding. He supposed Aka's weddings had been just as big, but he hadn't been invited to them.

He knew his mind was jumping around, so he focused on the moment. One of the Moon Deer's granddaughters was playing the koto for his entrance—she was skilled. His robes whispered as he walked at an unnaturally slow rate to the center of the hall. When he reached it, he couldn't help but look to the west, where Jin would come from, even though he knew she would enter last.

The koto player briefly paused, then began a new song, this

time accompanied by a pan flute.

NANAMI strode quickly up the steps when she heard her cousin blow the first notes. She faltered on the steps when she saw the size of the crowd, all staring at her. Well, except Bai. He was placidly looking toward the west, and Nanami sure he was waiting for Jin.

Why had this seemed like a good idea? She and Xiao could have had a private ceremony at Tsuku, with just the Koch-ssi, his disciples, and her mother's family.

She met the Koch-ssi's gaze now, and its berry lips curved in an encouraging smile.

For its sake, Nanami managed a smile herself.

She squared her shoulders and marched to a dais next to Bai's. Okay. Xiao would be next.

ANOTHER guzheng joined the first two instruments—Dawa. Xiao grinned and started walking.

Nanami's eyes met his as soon as he entered. He could practically see the sweat beading on her forehead, so he winked. She broke into a grin, and his heart skipped a beat. He went to the dais and pulled her into a fierce kiss—the crowd murmured in shock and probably disapproval, but Xiao didn't care.

He set her back, smoothed the front of his robe, and looked at the musicians expectantly. Luye, Jin's disciple, was seething at his display and had missed her cue, so Xiao mimed flute playing to her.

She jerked in surprise, and he rather thought her first note sounded a bit too forceful before blending harmoniously with the others. But maybe it was supposed to sound like that—he was far from a music expert.

JIN paused on the threshold of the Great Hall, letting everyone see her face before she started crying, as she knew she would. There was an impromptu chorus of cheers from the Mudanren, led by Wu Zhe. Tiao Xian was at its partner's side, shaking its head in mortification.

Jin smiled and looked past them and the rest of the crowd to the musicians, where Luye met her eyes. Jin's smile transformed into a grin. Still playing the flute, Luye beamed back.

And then Jin turned her focus to the daises in the center of the hall.

Bai looked utterly perfect in all white; Xiao dashing in blue; Nanami dramatic in silver. And Jin could tell from the crowd's approval that she was beautiful in her flaming silks. She mounted the dais. Bai took her hand, and tears of happiness began welling in her eyes.

1000 *years later*

IT was a little past midnight when Nanami appeared in Dalbam temple. The monks who were on night duty were both leaning against the door frame, possibly asleep.

That was just how Nanami liked it. She ran up a pillar and pulled herself onto the high beams from which the prayer collectors hung.

Instead of the alternating amethyst and obsidian ornaments from Zi and Hei's day, Xiao's ornaments combined both stones, and each featured a tiny indigo drop on a silver string. It was these that Nanami had come to check, for they let her steal prayers that were meant to alter others. It took her about two hours, creeping along the beams, to check them all. Xiao had pointed out that if she accepted a disciple or two, they could do this task for her, but the truth was she liked sneaking about the temples in the darkest part of the night and checking them herself.

When she was content that all were working as they should, she jumped to the floor.

She winked at the oversized Xiao sitting at the front of the temple and then frowned. What was on his shoulder?

She climbed the statue for a closer look and was shocked to find a miniature version of herself holding onto Xiao's braid and seemingly whispering into his ear.

She leapt down and shook the monks by the door. It turned out they weren't sleeping for they immediately came to attention.

"Sorry, we didn't hear you come in," said the older one. "Did you need more incense?"

"No," said Nanami, "but what's that?" She pointed to the tiny statue of herself.

The monks looked at each other as if they doubted her sanity.

"That is the image of the Love God," said one very slowly. "This is his temple."

"No, not the big statue! The little thing on his shoulder."

The other monk smiled. "That is the Love God's Heart. His little lover. He fell in love with her when she snuck into his room. Her pendants hang on his prayer collectors, guiding him in selecting the right prayers."

Nanami blinked. Who spread this tale? Dawa? No, probably that new disciple who was always making up long stories.

"You called her his little lover. She's not truly tiny, is she?"

"Not always," said the first monk, "but she can shrink herself at will. That's how she snuck into his room."

Nanami opened her mouth to correct them—it was Xiao who was shrunk, but then she remembered that gods sometimes gained abilities based on their mortal worshippers' beliefs. If this story grew more popular, would she be able to change her size at will, regardless of whether or not she had Nishikai powder?

Now, that had some appeal.

"How delightful," she told the monks. "The Love God's Heart. I hope you will share this story—it's so beautiful."

"Yes, isn't it?"

When Nanami returned home to the Tower on the Horizon, she was humming absently. Xiao stirred as she crawled into bed.

"Did you have a good time, my heart?"

*My heart, indeed.* "Oh, yes," she told him. "It was quite productive."

BAI'S hands were full of packages of cheese from the best paneer maker in Shahar, but he felt a desperate prayer and decided to stop in at the Tiguna Temple.

At the front of the temple were two statues. The woman bore only a superficial resemblance to Jin. She held a flower in one hand and a stylized flame in the other. Next to her was a man in white robes (his hair was dark and far too long) holding a brush and a sword. A young woman, dressed in white, knelt in supplication before the man.

*A scholar wanting to enter service in a noble house.*

There was a large exam next week that could determine the path of a Jeevantian scholar's life. This young woman was from a poor family; success on the exam could lift her family out of poverty. Impulsively, he set down the cheeses, removed the illusion ring that Jin had made him, and ripped a strip of white cloth from his sleeve. He changed it into a fine paintbrush, the kind that could be used for writing.

He tapped the woman on the shoulder.

He hadn't managed Jin's trick of making herself practically glow, but his white hair, gray eyes, and white robes still tended to impress mortals.

This woman—a girl really, she hadn't reached her majority—gaped. "Divinity!"

Bai held the brush out to her. "This won't give you answers," he told her sternly. "It will keep your mind clear and calm, and make sure what you write matches your intentions. No small errors."

She accepted the brush with both hands and fell to the floor, thanking him profusely.

Bai humphed. When he picked up his cheeses and teleported, she was still shouting praises to the empty air.

When he reached home, he looked in on Jin and found her napping. That was good—she had been having trouble sleeping, for she was starting to get too large to sleep on her back, and she didn't like sleeping on her side. Bai had made her a pillow for support, and that seemed to help, but he couldn't imagine another two hundred years of this. He resisted the urge to push her hair out of her face lest he wake her and instead began cooking. He had never been particularly fond of dairy, but Jin constantly wanted it. He knew it reminded her of childhood, and the mortal who sold him yogurt claimed it was good for pregnant women. Bai didn't know if that extended to immortals, and he couldn't read Jin's essence to check, but it certainly seemed to make her happy.

While the rice boiled, he diced the paneer, then put some spices in hot ghee.

"That smells wonderful." Jin stood in the doorway, smiling sleepily at him. Bai grinned back. "It will be done in ten more minutes."

Jin slipped her arms around his waist and kissed his back. "Thank you. What happened to your sleeve?"

"Oh—" He remembered the mortal at Tiguna Temple.

She laughed. "And you always say I'm a soft touch! How happy you must have made that girl." Bai stopped his preparations and turned so that he could hug her back.

"I'm fine. The baby's fine." She reached a hand up and laid it along his cheek. "How could it be otherwise when you take care of us so well?"

He frowned. He was nervous about being a father. He'd given plenty of criticism out to parents over the years—could he possibly live up to all his advice?

"Probably not," Jin said, "but you'll do well enough. We'll make sure our baby is loved. The rest will fall into place. And maybe you'll even learn a little humility."

"Oh, surely it won't go that far."

She laughed, her eyes glowing.

Bai leaned down and tasted those laughing lips. As always, they brought color to his white world. The colors of joy. He loved those colors just as he loved Jin.

Best of all, she loved him too.

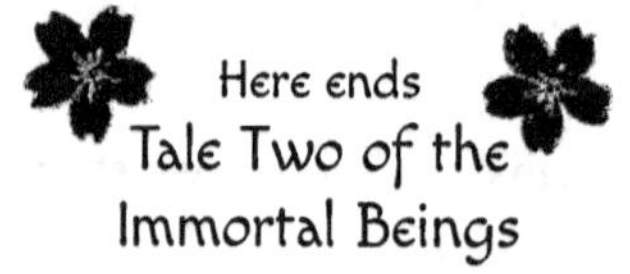

# Glossary

**Aashchary** – Born to Neela 82,000 years after creation, Aashchary became the Goddess of Thought through her own efforts. She was noticed by Aka, who wished to marry her. She took him as a lover but only accepted his proposal when she discovered she was pregnant. During her marriage, she held the title Sun Empress. She was murdered under mysterious circumstances while pregnant, leaving behind one living daughter, Jin. A blue and orange immortal.

**Achamba** – An immortal creatures that resembles a massive snake, it is native to Jeevanti.

**Ah** – a large island south of the Crescent Moon.

**Aka** – Once a drop of blood, Aka became the first red immortal 26,000 years after creation. Aka became the first God shortly after mortals appeared in the world, and eventually the Sun Emperor, ruler of all, after he confined the immortal creatures to the Underworld. He has been married three times (see Goddess of Lightning, Aashchary, and Goddess of Flight) and has had six acknowledged children (see Gang, Salaana, Karana, God of Belief, Jin, and Guleum). His first lover (though they never married) was Noran, and she is the mother of his eldest son.

**Ankhbayar** – a Bear People apprentice.

**Ao** – Once part of the midnight ocean, Ao became the first indigo immortal 31,000 years after creation. Ao is famous for turning into a dragon and is called the Sea Dragon. He is worshipped by mortal sailors though he denies being a god. He is married to Miko and has thirteen children and more than twenty grandchildren. He disowned Nanami 86,000 years after creation.

**Atsuko** – daughter of the Moon Deer, sister of Miko, lady Atsuko has run her father's household since her mother's death. A white immortal.

**Bai** – Once a piece of white quartz, Bai became the first white immortal 25,000 years after creation. He is known as the First because he was the first being to appear in the world. He invented writing, art, music, and mathematics and is so known as the Scholar. He became obsessed with martial arts after the death of his love, Noran, and was also called the Great Warrior. After he retreated from the world, many immortals believed he had died. Bai has pure white hair and gray eyes; he is slightly above average height and is extremely fit.

**Bando** – the peninsula separated from the Zhongtu region by the Byeong Mountains. Bando is a mortal nation as well as an immortal region and claims an unbroken line of rulers for 40,000 years.

**Batu** – a young Bear People hunter.

**Bear People** – a mortal tribe in Ehkoron.

**between** – how immortals refer to the time lost during teleportation; between is remembered only by the sense of time passing.

**Bijalee** – see Goddess of Lightning.

**black** – the ninth color, black magic changes the essence of things. See Hei.

**blue** – the sixth color, blue magic reads thoughts. See Neela.

**Bulgae** – immortal creatures that resemble dogs made of fire.

**Byeong Mountains** – mountain range that forms the border between Zhongtu and Bando.

**Cave of Shadows** – the name of He Who Walks in Shadow's hideout. Although the hideout must sometimes be moved, to avoid Salaana's disciples, it is always a cave.

**Chattaan Kile** – a fortress made by Bai that sits on cliffs in southern Jeevanti.

**Cheng** – Once magma, Cheng became the first orange immortal 27,000 years after creation. He was not seen for a period of 18,000 years, having been sealed in turquoise, and is called the Sleeper.

**Cheolmun Pass** – a narrow pass in the Byeong Mountains, which form the border between Zhongtu and Bando; Bai famously killed 300 mortal soldiers here.

**Cold Peaks** – a mountain range forming the border between Zhongtu and Ehkoron.

**Colors** – how the first nine immortals are known collectively. Also, the way the essential natures of immortals are categorized. All immortals can identify their natures by a set color, though it is only obvious in the appearances of the Nine Colors and their offspring.

**Crescent Moon** – a long island east of Bando; the Moon Deer lives here.

**Dalagois** – Immortal creatures that a resemble a fusion of serpents and eagles, they are native to Ehkoron.

**Dawa** – Zi's third disciple.

**deity** – an immortal who has mortal worshippers. The beliefs of those worshippers amplify the power of the deity but can also limit their abilities if the mortals specifically believe a deity cannot do something. Disciples of a deity thus spend much time ensuring the worshippers' beliefs align with their deity's goals. Deities are properly addressed as "divinity."

**disciple** – immortals who follow and learn from another immortal are called disciples; most deities have disciples.

**Dushtbandar** – Immortal creatures that resemble monkeys and hoard both valuables and bones, they are native to Jeevanti.

**Earth** – one of the three realms in the world, the others being the Heavens and the Underworld.

**Ehkoron** – the northernmost region of Earth, north of the Cold Peaks.

**Forever Child** – a mortal whose cognitive ability does not surpass that of a child around age five or six; they usually are quite short with facial features that remain childlike as well.

**Ganbold** – a Bear People hunter.

**Gang** – Full name Sunlight Glints on Steel, Gang is the son of Noran and Aka and the first born-immortal. He was declared God of War at his birth 57,000 years after creation. He was trained in martial arts by Bai between 4,000 and 15,000 years of age. A red and yellow immortal.

**Gate to the Underworld** – a red gate made by Aka to control passage between the Underworld and Earth; to open it, one must have the key Kunjee.

**god/goddess** – see deity.

**God of Belief** – the son of Aashchary and Aka born 92,000 years after creation, he died as an infant; his full name was Mind Brighter than Sunlight. A red, orange, and blue immortal.

**God of Destruction** – see Karana.

**God of Pleasure** – see Xiao.

**God of War** – see Gang.

**God of Wind** – see Guleum.

**Goddess of Beauty** – see Jin.

**Goddess of Flight** – mother of Guleum, she is the current wife of Aka and the current Sun Empress; she is an orange immortal who was once a bird.

**Goddess of Justice** – see Salaana.

**Goddess of Lightning** – Bijalee, the first wife of Aka, and the first Sun Empress, she was a white immortal who was once lightning. She committed suicide. Her children are Salaana and Karana.

**Goddess of Thought** – see Aashchary.

**godsbane** – an herb that grows in the valley where Noran was killed that can poison immortals in five ways.

**Godsmarket** – a marketplace in the Sun Palace where immortals sell and trade goods.

**Golden Phoenix** – an immortal creature that was once the patron of Bando.

**golem** – a magical construct that has a singular purpose.

**great-mother** – title of the Bear People's leader.

**Great Ladies** – a mountain range that forms the border between Zhongtu and Jeevanti.

**Great Willow** – A magical willow made by Bai 29,000 years after creation. It amplifies power. and is worshipped by mortals in Liushi. Tea made from its leaves grants clarity and insight; it is particularly popular with scholars and magistrates.

**Great Warrior** – see Bai.

**green** – the fifth color, green magic heals. See Haraa.

**Guleum** – The youngest son of Aka and the Goddess of Flight, Guleum was named the God of Wind at his birth 97,000 years after creation, but he does not yet have any mortal worshippers as he has not yet reached his majority. His full name is Sunlight through the Clouds. A mostly red with some orange immortal.

**Gumiho** – Immortal creatures that resemble beings with fox-ears and nine fox tails, they are one of the few creatures that breed. Their native land is unknown, but they distinguish themselves into clans, and are also called Kitsune and Huli Jing.

**Habito** – Tiny immortal creatures that look like leaves, they are native to Crescent Moon.

**Haraa** – Once a leaf, Haraa became the first green immortal 29,000 years after creation. Haraa is known as the Warden and is the ultimate doctor for all immortals. She is the mistress of the Wood Pavilions, which has only one rule for its many guests: Do not damage the plants.

**Heaven** – one of the three realms in the world, the others being

Earth and the Underworld.

**Hei** – Once a shadow, Hei became the first black immortal 33,000 years after creation. Hei is now known as the Night God and invented marriage with his wife, Zi, 46,000 years after creation. He has one child, Xiao. He is the master of New Moon Manor along with his wife.

**He Who Walks in Shadow** – the best thief in the world and Nanami's onetime master.

**Huli Jing** – see Gumiho.

**Hyeon-ju** – a young Gumiho (or debatably, a Kitsune/Huli Jing).

**Ichimi** – the eldest daughter of Ao and Miko, Ichimi is also Salaana's lover. She is skilled with a tessen and considered both beautiful and tactful. She was once married, but her husband left her when she suffered a miscarriage. A mostly indigo immortal with a little white.

**immortal being** – a being that will not (it is believed) die of old age; the oldest immortal being is Bai, who is 75,000 years old as of this tale. Immortals can be formed spontaneously, from anything, when they persevere in existing. The oldest nine immortals (the Colors) each formed 1000 years apart; after that, an immortal appeared spontaneously each year. It is commonly believed that this change accounts for the dramatic decrease in power between the first nine and all subsequent immortals. All power an immortal has can be categorized as one or more colors. Immortals can also be born if at least one of their parents is an immortal. In this case, the born immortal gains access to their parent's power pool. If the family members compete for their pool of power, it comes down to will and need. Immortal pregnancies last 1000 years and born immortals reach adulthood after 4-6,000 years. As adults, Immortals age due to trauma, stress, or grief.

**immortal creature** – (almost) all immortal creatures were locked in the Underworld through Aka's efforts; the first to be locked up was the Korikami 75,000 years after creation and the last was the Golden Phoenix 82,000 years after creation.

**indigo** – the seventh color, indigo magic nullifies yellow (influence thoughts), violet (influence emotion), and black (influence essence).

**Infinite Jug** – an artifact made by Hei which dispenses limitless alcohol.

**Jeevanti** – The westernmost region of the world, it is known for a colorful aesthetic and rich, spicy food. Neela, Haraa, and the Goddess of Lightning all came to be in Jeevanti.

**Jin** – Full name Sunlight turns Petals Gold, Jin was declared Goddess of Beauty at her birth. She was born 95,000 years after creation and has been worshipped since becoming an adult at four thousand years old. After the murder of her mother, Aashchary, the second Sun Empress, Jin was raised by her grandmother Neela. When she came of age, her Aka insisted that she return to the Sun Palace to live. Of average height with an idealized figure, gold eyes and brown hair, Jin is considered extraordinarily beautiful. A red, orange, yellow, and indigo immortal.

**Kaihachi** – the eighth child (or seventh, excluding Nanami) of Ao and Miko; Kaihachi is married with children. A mostly indigo immortal with a little white.

**Kairoku** – the sixth child of Ao and Miko; Kairoku is married with children. A mostly indigo immortal with a little white.

**Karana** – Full name Sundered by Sunlight, Karana is the younger child of the Goddess of Lightning and Aka. He was declared the God of Destruction at his birth 78,000 years after creation. Except for the Cult of Karana in Jeevanti, Karana is not worshipped by mortals. Instead, statues of him are made with closed eyes, so that his attention will not fall where they are placed. A mostly red immortal with some white.

**Kitsune** – see Gumiho.

**Koch-ssi** – an immortal creature with an affinity for plants.

**Korikami** – the first immortal creature that Aka locked in the Underworld.

**Korikami's Tomb** – once the home to the Korikami, this large volcanic mountain now holds the Gate to the Underworld.

**Kuanbai River** – "The wide, white river," the Kuanbai starts in the Great Ladies and ends at the Double Bay. Bai's spring is a tributary of the river.

**Kulap** – an immortal who spends a lot of time at the Wood Pavilions and is partnered to Mu Rong.

**Kunjee** – Kunjee is the key that allows one to pass through the Gate to the Underworld. It is a vermillion sun pendant.

**Land of Winter** – a large island north of Crescent Moon, it is dominated by the Korikami's Tomb.

**Laughter in the Shadows** – full name of Xiao.

**Light Hands** – the name for disciples sworn to Salaana.

**Liushi** – coastal city in Southern Zhongtu on the Kuanbai River; contains the Great Willow.

**Luye** – the second beauty disciple, Luye was a born immortal whose parents tried to win favor with the Sun Emperor by sending her as a concubine to the Sun Court. Color unknown.

**magic** – the word immortals use for their associated powers. All magic is categorized by the color over which it has dominion and comes with an associated ability. The first nine immortals—originally known as the Colors—have significantly more magic than all other immortal beings, but all immortals have some magic.

**Maoyi** – city on the southern tip of Zhongtu region famous for its street food.

**Miko** – the third daughter of the Moon Deer; according to legend she was seen by Ao while swimming in the sea, and the two immediately fell in love; she married to Ao 70,000 years after creation and is called the Sea Queen by mortals. She has thirteen children and over twenty grandchildren. A white immortal.

**Moon Deer** – a white immortal (many believe the second, after Bai) who will remember and keep all secrets told to him; his home is Tsuku. His wife died long ago; he has three daughters, notably Atsuko, who runs his household, and Miko, who married Ao, and many grandchildren. A white immortal.

**Mount Korikami** – see the Korikami's Tomb.

**Mudanren** – immortals creatures that look like peonies, they are native to Zhongtu.

**Mu Rong** – an immortal who spends a lot of time at the Wood

Pavilions and is partnered to Kulap.

**Nanami** – also known as Nanami the Thief. Once the seventh child of Ao and Miko, born 74,000 years after creation. Nanami was disowned after she was caught stealing her aunt Atsuko's magical hair stick 86,000 years after creation. She was the first disciple of He Who Walks in Shadow until they had a falling out 94,000 years after creation. Short and slight, Nanami has navy hair and eyes, a round face, and favors plain trousers and tunics. A mostly indigo immortal with a little white.

**Neela** – Once a dayflower, Neela became the first blue immortal 30,000 after creation. She had one daughter, Aashchary, and has one surviving grandchild, Jin. Neela travels Earth as she wishes in a caravan and is called the Wanderer.

**New Moon Manor** – the residence of Zi and Hei, New Moon Manor floats in the Heavens; it was made of shadow and twilight 40,000 years after creation.

**Nine Colors** – see Color.

**Nisei** – immortal creatures with butterfly wings that suffocate beings in their sleep.

**Nishikai powder** – A magical powder made from Nishikai shells. Nishikai are immortal creatures that escaped Aka's attention for they exist only in the deep ocean. They are harvested by the Sea Dragon and the powder of their shells can make anything grow or shrink in size.

**Noran** – Once a grain of yellow sand, Noran became the first yellow immortal 28,000 after creation. She was Aka's lover, the mother of Gang, and Bai's unrequited love. She was killed by mortal bandits 58,000 years after creation.

**North Sea** – sea off the coast of Ehkoron.

**O'o** – the largest city in Crescent Moon.

**Only Monkey** – an immortal creature that serves the Achamba and resembles a monkey, it is native to Jeevanti.

**orange** – the third color, it nullifies the powers of white (knowing the essence), red (feeling emotion), and blue (reading thoughts). See Cheng.

**Po** – a large island south of Ni.

**red** – the second color, red magic feels emotion. See Aka.

**Rang Pariyon** – Immortals that look like tiny beings with butterfly wings, they are native to Jeevanti.

**Salaana** – Full name Sunlight's Allure, Salaana is the oldest child of the Goddess of Lightning and Aka. She was declared Goddess of Justice at her birth 76,000 years after creation. She is a fierce deity who is known to be harsh and decisive, making her equally revered and feared among mortals.

**Sanctuary Caves** – originally made by Cheng and then supplemented by Bai, this caves are worshipped by mortals for restoring things to their natural state, including curing most diseases as long as the ill remain inside.

**Scholar** – see Bai.

**Sea Dragon** – see Ao.

**Sea Palace** – the underwater residence of Ao, the Sea Palace is contained within a magical dome of air.

**Sea Serpent** – an immortal creature that Bai rode.

**Sleeper** – see Cheng.

**Sowon Gold** – an artifact made by Noran; mortals will do their best to fulfill the wishes of anyone holding Sowon Gold.

**Sun Emperor** – see Aka.

**Sun Empress** – the title of Aka's wife. There have been three, the Goddess of Lightning, Aashchary, and the Goddess of Flight (current).

**Sun God** – see Aka.

**Sun Court** – the immortals who live in the Sun Palace.

**Sun Palace** – the city in the Heavens that contains Aka's residence and those of his children; it was made of light from the setting sun 46,000 years after creation.

**Sundered by Sunlight** – full name of Karana.

**Sunlight Glints on Steel** – full name of Gang.

**Sunlight Turns Petals Gold** – full name of Jin.

**Sunlight through the Clouds** – full name of Guleum.

**Sunlight's Allure** – full name of Salaana.

**teleport** – the word immortals use when they magically move from one place in the world to another. Teleporting takes a great deal of power; the average immortal can only teleport once a day and it takes them about an hour. Bai is famous for being the best at teleporting—he can teleport in five minutes and has teleported as many as thirty times in a single day.

**Tiao Xian** – a crotchety Mudanren.

**true dream** – an immortal dream that revisits actual memories that an immortal rejects as their history. It is accompanied by a high fever, can last indefinitely and can be deadly, particularly to immortals who need to eat or drink.

**Tsuku** – in Crescent Moon, Tsuku is the home of the Moon Deer and his family.

**Underworld** – one of the three realms in the world, the others being the Heavens and Earth.

**violet** – the eighth color, violet magic influences emotion. See Zi.

**Wanderer** – see Neela.

**white** – the first color, white magic knows the essences of things. See Bai.

**White Mountain** – Bai's origin and home, the White Mountain is the tallest mountain on Earth and is perpetually snow-capped. It is on the border of Ehkoron and Zhongtu.

**Wood Pavilions** – The home of Haraa, the Wood Pavilions are a section of forest with twenty-odd copper-roofed buildings. They are known for wild parties and hedonistic living but are also the best place to go for healing.

**Wu Zhe** – a cheerful Mudanren.

**Xiao** – Full name Laughter in the Shadows, Xiao was declared God of Pleasure at his birth. He was born 95,000 years after creation and has been worshipped since he came of age. He has no disciples but is popular with mortals. Most of his parents' temples have a small shrine to him. Tall and lightly muscled, Xiao has long black hair and lavender eyes. He is usually smiling, and his dimples are famous. Xiao, along with Jin, is called a useless god in the Sun Court.

**Xiezhi** – An immortal creature that resembles a cross between a bull and a lion, it is native to Zhongtu.

**Xiling** – Once the capital of the largest mortal country within the Zhongtu region, Xiling was burned to ash by Karana for reasons known only to him.

**Xuezei** – immortal creatures that drink blood.

**yellow** – the fourth color, yellow magic influences thoughts. See Noran.

**Yeppeun** – the first beauty disciple, Yeppeun was a mortal courtesan who ascended to immortality after dying of a fatal disease at the age of twenty. Color unknown.

**Zhongtu** – the largest region on Earth, to the east of the Great Ladies and the south of the Cold Peaks; the Wood Pavilions are here.

**Zi** – Once twilight, Zi became the first violet immortal 32,000 after creation. Zi is now known as the Moon Goddess and invented marriage with her husband, Hei, 46,000 years after creation. She has one child, Xiao. She is the mistress of New Moon Manor along with her husband.

# A Note About Language

The immortals speak a divine language and understand all mortal languages spoken to them. There are as many mortal languages in this world as in our own; because I am more interested in studying existing languages than creating my own, I drew names from the real-world languages whose cultures and myths inspired elements of this world. The cultures in the book are very loosely derived from ones in our world. Zhongtu is derived from China, Tibet, and Thailand; Ehkoron from Mongolia; Jeevanti from India; Bando, Po, Ah, and Ni from Korea; the Crescent Moon and the Land of Winter from Japan.

Just like in our languages, the words of Immortal Beings shift and change. When I write a name in English—such as the White Mountain—the characters know what it means (just like the name Joy has a clear meaning in English). When I use a different language—such as the Kuanbai River—it represents a meaning that has shifted or is no longer used, and the characters may or may not be aware of its roots (just as only linguists and history buffs will know a town called Chester was probably once a fort). Some names I took wholly from a language (Bai means white in Chinese), while others are variations I created (Salaana, whose full name is Sunlight's Allure is derived from "phusalaana" or allure in Hindi). Others have ambiguous etymologies—Gang means steel in Chinese and his children have pseudo-Chinese names, but being named by Noran, I think Gang is really a shortening of "gangchoel" which is steel in Korean. I wanted to convey different characters' self-identification with different cultures or regions of their world—which is why Ao and his family, who feel tied to the Crescent Moon, all have pseudo-Japanese names while Zi and Hei associate with Zhongtu. Some characters have transplanted themselves—Haraa is from Jeevanti (Haraa means "green" in Hindi) but lives in Zhongtu. And a few names I created without regard to their meaning—the city Xiling could have a few meanings in Chinese, but I choose it for its sound rather than its possible definitions.

If I have made a mistake in my use of various languages, please forgive me and know my intent to celebrate and reference the influences on this book.

# Acknowledgments

Just as I have grown as a writer, my beta readers have grown too, and I am ever more grateful for their support and suggestions. Joshua Pawlicki—I could write four pages describing everything you did for this book and still not convey how much it meant to me. Helen Luk—I frequently worried that I wouldn't finish the first draft, and your determination that I do so helped me so much. James Hanson—I appreciate just how critical you are willing to be. Cheryl Chudyk and Faith Enuol—you both said almost the same things, so I knew you were right about Nanami and friendship! James Zola—wow, I think Bai's arc would have been left hanging in the air without your insights. Margaret Ball, error-finding queen, I hope Chapter 17 meets with your approval now! And thank you to Gail Hanson for catching errors and telling me how good I was doing.

## About the Author

Edith Pawlicki lives in Connecticut with her husband, twin sons, dog, and rabbit. She fell in love with words in fourth grade and finds writing necessary to free the worlds and characters in her head. When she isn't busy being a mom and author, she enjoys cooking and crafts. In addition to the Immortal Beings series, she has also written a YA science fiction novel, Minerva. Find her and her books at edithpawlicki.com or an Instagram @edithpawlicki.

# Book Design

This book features two open-source fonts: Macondo Swash Caps by John Vargas Beltran for chapter titles and Amiri by Khaled Hosny and Sebastian Kosch. The images by each chapter number and at each scene break are scanned cherry blossom impressions from a Japanese ink stick. Behind the maps and diagrams is handmade origami paper. Interior formatting was done by Edith Pawlicki.

www.ingramcontent.com/pod-product-compliance
Lightning Source LLC
Chambersburg PA
CBHW070231200726
48293CB00005B/1578